Year 2000...ish

CHAPTER ONE

Mick jumped off the bus with a remarkably light spring in his step considering it was such a cold, wet dismal April afternoon and he'd been working since six that morning.

For the first time in over three months he actually felt like laughing out loud.

He had had a lot on his mind lately, what with the wedding and things but now all the worries seemed a million miles away. The reason for his sudden change of heart was simple. He had just picked up the tickets for his stag holiday in Benidorm and the holiday fever was on him. He knew there was still seven days to go until they were off but he couldn't wait.

The pressures of arranging a wedding can fall heavily at the best of times but they can really build up when you're not even sure that you want to go through with it.

It's not that he didn't love Sue, of course he did. He always had. Him and Sue had been childhood sweethearts and neither of them had ever had another partner. They hadn't even considered it. Honest!

Mick and Sue had lived together for the last two years. In fact he couldn't imagine living without her. So much so that three months ago he had asked her to marry him. Jesus, how could he have been so stupid. Up until then everything had been great and he had never had a worry in his life. They shared a nice terraced house, an old house, cosy and full of warmth. It was just up the road from the pub and the betting shop. Brilliant. Alright there was the odd blot on the landscape, no life is perfect, Sue's mum living next door reaching four blots on the old landscape scale. "Just popped in….." she'd say and then stay two hours talking inane drivel to anyone even pretending to listen. Mick had once told Sue "She talks the biggest load of bollocks I've ever heard"

"Don't talk about mum like that" she had snapped. "Even if it is true"

Anyway apart from the odd blot life was pretty idyllic.

Which was why he had asked Sue to marry him. He hadn't given it that much thought before hand, it just sort of came out. They had been cuddled up on the settee, on a cold January night, watching Michelle Collins in a play about going to start a new life on a Scottish Island and conning this bloke, who loved her, into going with her. They had been discussing the morals of the story, inasmuch as Mick thought Michelle Collins was a devious conniving bitch who

should be in prison anyway for what she had done to Ian Beale, and Sue thought she was lovely, a good actress and she thought it was really nice that she wanted to take her kids and give them a better life in a new place.

"Why doesn't she just marry him then?" he had asked, not unreasonably. "If she's so bloody nice"

"She doesn't love him in that way. He's more of a friend. And what's marriage got to do with it. That doesn't mean she doesn't love him in her own way" Sue insisted.

"No. If it was proper love, she'd marry him. Stands to reason. That's what people do in real life. Get married"

"We're not married, are you saying you don't love me enough?" she asked, sitting up so she could see his face when he answered.

"What... That's different... That's... Well... I don't believe... Well" he stuttered in the vain hope that this would be enough to convince her that he loved her more than anything in the world and that they didn't need to get married to prove their love to anyone else. Of course it would have been better to use those words instead of blundering on like a man with something to hide.

"Thanks" she said huffily and got up to put the kettle on. "That sounded really convincing"

"Sue" he called after her, but it was too late, she was gone. He sat back on the settee and wondered how he had managed to get himself into the bad books. "It was that bloody Michelle Collins" he decided. She had caused trouble wherever she had gone. He got up and followed Sue in the kitchen, where she was busy washing a few pots while she waited for the kettle to boil. He sidled up behind her and put his arm round her waist and held her tight. "Sue" he said, nuzzling up to her ear until he could feel her shiver delightfully as she always did when he did that.

"Don't you try and get round me like that Michael Mathews" she laughed, while squirming away from him.

"Ah come on Sue. You know I didn't mean it. You know I love you, always have" He smiled and grabbed her again and stroked her bum as he held her tightly. "Ever since that first day at Infant School" he said to her and she blushed slightly, knowing what was coming next. "When you showed me your knickers". She playfully pushed him away but he caught her and pulled her back to him. "For my dinner money" he added and she laughed out loud and slapped him on the arm when she managed to free her hand.

"You fib" she laughed as she chased him across the kitchen. He allowed himself to be caught as he circled the table and turned into her arms. "You know very well it was because they were all frilly and I was proud enough to burst. I showed them everybody as I remember" she told him.

"Yeah but you kept coming back to me. I think I owed you two weeks dinner money by the time your mum fetched you."

They laughed easily together and then came together for a long, passionate kiss. As they eventually pulled apart Mick had looked her, dreamily in the eyes and, without thinking, said "Marry me Sue". She laughed at first, then when she realised he was serious she sat down on the table and thought about it.

4

She was about to tell him that she wasn't sure, as she thought they were quite happy as they were when he suddenly dropped to one knee and took her hand in his "Please Sue" he asked sincerely "Will you marry me?".

Of course she couldn't say no, now. After all, here was a man who she had loved since she was five, who she had grown up with and lived with for the last two years. In all that time though, they had never discussed marriage. They always took it for granted that they would always be together and never seemed to need to confirm it for anyone else's sake. Now, however he was on one knee proposing. How could she turn him down when it obviously meant so much to him. "Yes" she said simply and he jumped up and kissed her, happy and giddy at the thought of marriage. Sue watched him and joined in to a point but she had a nagging feeling that they had set something in motion that would end in tears. Their idyllic little lives were never going to be the same again.

Mick wondered if he had done the right thing. He wanted to say "Ha. Got you"

and make a joke of it, but he could see the unadulterated pleasure on Sue's face and he knew he couldn't do anything to spoil her happiness, so he laughed and giggled and, later on, made plans with her, all the time with a nagging doubt at the back of his head that was saying "You daft twat, you've done it now". He didn't know what he was expecting to go wrong but go wrong he knew it would. Relationships, eh.

Anyway, as Mick pulled his collar up against the cold, it was the first time in ages he had actually felt excited about the future. Next Monday to be exact.

That was when they where off. The lads. Spain. Benidorm. One week of sun, sand, sea and sex. No not sex. He had promised himself, not to mention Sue, that he would be good. Just to be on the safe side he made himself promise again. Could he do it?

Course he could. It was only a week. "Fuck me I'm not an animal" he said to himself.

As he turned the corner the drizzle became a bit faster so he ran the last fifty yards or so to the pub where he was meeting the lads. Rushing in, he shook himself like a wet dog and looked round the room. There were only a dozen or so patrons in the Maggies taproom so he spotted them straight away over by the dart board. The Maggies had never been a dinner -time pub but came to life most nights and was generally a young person's pub. It wasn't really Mick's local, the Queens was nearer, but that was definitely a fogey's pub. Rumour had it that after ten at night they only served Ovaltine.

The lads had their name down for a game of "arrers" and where patiently waiting their turn. He turned to the barmaid and ordered a pint. "Alright Tom"

he greeted the old man sat in the corner nursing a half pint. "Half for Tom" he said to the barmaid. "Thanks very much lad" smiled Tom through broken stained teeth. At his feet sat Jack, an old, beat up Jack Russell cross that looked as though he had been in a thousand fights in his younger days. And lost them all.

Mick put Tom's drink down on the table and walked on, smiling, to the dartboard. He put one hand in his jacket pocket and pulled out an orange

envelope. "Oh this year I'm off to sunny Spain" he sang happily but tunelessly.

"Y viva Espania" two of his mates finished off. "Fuck off" said the third.

"Aw come on Danny don't be like that. It's only for a week. We'll soon be back" answered Mick in a placatory fashion.

"We'll fetch you some rock"

Danny was upset because he wasn't going. Danny was unemployed and married whereas the other three were all working and single. They had all grown up together and had been best friends since meeting up at Brinsmarsh Manor Infants. When they had left school Danny had gone down the pits as an apprentice electrician while the other three had done their apprenticeships at British Steel. Now the pits had all gone and Danny was struggling to find full time work. They had offered to lend him the money for the trip but he had his pride and refused.

"Besides which" offered Jeff, the tall dark haired, self titled, sex machine of the foursome "Since you put on all that weight we don't want you going all suicidal when you have to lay on the beach, like a tub of lard, watching yours truly pulling every decent bird in Benidorm."

"Decent?" asked Ron, the fourth member of the gang, "Your standards must have raised. You'll usually shag 'owt wi' a fanny. In fact, not only does that include every pug ugly bird in Rotherham, but I've heard female dogs won't come out after dark 'cos of you."

Ron wasn't really having a go at Jeff, he was just attempting to deflect the humour away from Danny, who he knew was upset at missing out on the trip besides being sensitive about the extra weight he had slapped on since he had been laid off.

Ron was the father figure to the others. They all looked up to him and respected him. He never let them down, was fiercely protective, never said a bad word about anybody, and was amazingly and devastatingly hard. Many times they had talked their way into trouble and where more than relieved to see Ron wade in and sort it out.

"And you can fuck off too" answered Jeff

Sue was busy typing a letter for her boss, Mr Ahmed, the Asian third partner of Smith, Brown & Ahmed Solicitors, when Ros rushed in.

"They're in" she gushed "We can pick them up at tea time on the way home"

"Good" answered Sue without looking up from her work "I'll phone Claire and Linda later and let them know"

"No need" Ros said "All taken care of. Linda wanted to see them so I said we'll all go back to mine tonight to celebrate"

Sue looked up for the first time "Celebrate the arrival of our flight tickets? If I didn't know you better my girl I'd think you were letting your hair down."

Ros blushed slightly. She knew she wasn't the best looking of the foursome that was going away but she wasn't ugly and had had boyfriends in the past.

Nothing serious as yet and she certainly wasn't in the same league as Claire, who incidentally Ros thought was much too free and easy with her favours.

"Anyway my place, eight o clock" she said as she turned to leave.

"To be perfectly honest Ros" Sue said, turning away from the VDU that she was working on "I'm really looking forward to this holiday too. I've been so wrapped up in the wedding and everything that if I don't have a break soon I'll crack up."

"Your mum been keeping you hard at it again?" asked Ros, coming back into the room and sitting on the edge of the desk.

"Oh no more than usual" laughed Sue "You know my mum. Everything was booked, organised, reorganised, arranged, rearranged, rebooked, checked and double checked about a month ago. No it's not that. It's, well I'm not sure really, I suppose I've just been so happy with Mick I just don't want to get married and spoil it, that's all"

"Cold feet love, that's all it is. Stop whittling. Everything'll come out in the wash. A holiday'll do you the world of good. Get your mind off things, just soak up the sun and relax"

"Yeah you're right. And to be honest I've already started soaking up the sun, in a fashion"

"What do you mean?" asked Ros

"Well you know I always go to the gym on Tuesdays, down Wellgate, in town?." Ros nodded.

"Well the last two weeks I've been having half an hour on the sunbed after my aerobics."

"You sneaky cow. Why didn't you tell me, I'd have come with you?"

"You don't need 'em" answered Sue, defending herself. "You're dark skinned anyway. The sun only has to peep through a cloud and you turn into Whoopi Goldberg. I'm much more fair skinned" she said stroking her cheek with the back of her hand and talking all posh.

"Yeah maybe so but you could still have told me. I love sunbeds. They always make me feel all tingly"

"Me too. In fact I've hired one for the week. It's being delivered tonight. And I know someone else who likes 'em"

"Mick?" asked Ros

"Yeah. Just the thought turns him on. I think it's the ultra violet rays"

"Or the goggles" offered Ros and they both laughed.

"Come on girls there is much work to be done" said Mr Ahmed, entering the room. He crossed over to Sue's desk and deposited a bundle of papers for her to type up. "I have said many times…" he began and both girls couldn't resist smiling at each other as it was a habit of Mr Ahmed, when regaling them for whatever reason, to always begin with `I have said many times`. " I have said many times that there is a time and place for everything, and work is not the place for gossip and idle chit chat". " No Mr Ahmed" they chorused. Mr Ahmed could be a stickler for office procedure when he wanted but he had a heart of gold and was by far the nicest of the three partners. He lived in nearby Rawsthorpe with his wife and son who where both doctors. He was Sue's boss.

Ros was secretary to Mr Smith who had the hots for Sue. In truth he liked most women, indeed most of his clients were woman and he wasn't averse to a spot of after hours if he felt it in the client's best interest. Old Mr Brown was the

other partner and his secretary was Mrs Tomkins, who didn't like the girls. She was an old spinster and didn't have a nice word to say about anybody. When Mick met her he said she looked as though she had been born at the age of fifty. He reckoned she knew the secret of eternal old age as opposed to youth and was actually hundreds of years old.

"See ya' later" mouthed Ros and went back to her own office.

Danny walked down Atlas Road with all the enthusiasm of a one legged man at an arse kicking contest.

He had left the lads in the pub making transport arrangements for the following week. He had had enough. He wasn't going so why should he worry whether they could all fit in one fucking minibus? He was happy for them, of course, just jealous. Jealous they were off to the sun, jealous they had good jobs, jealous they had a future to look forward to but most of all jealous they were single. As he did every day he approached his house, he wished fervently that

Sheila wouldn't be in. On really bad days he wished she had left him a note on the kitchen table saying she had left him for good. Sometimes his little daydreams became even more fanciful and she had added a P.S to the note saying she knew she had to leave him as he was too much of a man for her and she was too tired and worn out to cope any longer. It was his own fault, he knew. There was really nothing stopping him from walking out of his marriage.

It had been something of a farce from the start. Pride as much as anything kept him there. Or a lack of it. He didn't want to admit, to himself and to others, that they were right from the start and Sheila was a crap choice of a wife. He hadn't had to get married either, as the old joke goes, he could have waited another week. Ha ha. Only in Dannys case it was actually one day. One more day and he wouldn't have married her, even though at the time he had convinced himself that he really wanted to. Sheila had a reputation, to say the least, and this was one of the things that attracted him to her. It was certainly an experience when they first started going out. He had never known anyone like her. She wanted it at any and every opportunity. And he was only too willing to oblige. This heavenly state of affairs continued for about three months and then to be perfectly honest Danny had had enough. To put it bluntly, he was knackered. One Friday night he decided to tell her straight and end the whole thing. Unfortunately she got in first and informed him that she had missed her period and was pretty sure she was in the club. Danny agonised over what to do for the next couple of days. In the words of the Clash "should I stay or should I go, If I stay there will be trouble, If I go it will be double". He mulled it over alone, not wanting to tell the lads, and in the end came to the conclusion that not only did he and Sheila have nothing in common, but they were totally unsuited to each other. On the other hand he quite fancied the idea of being a dad and then of course there was the sex. He reasoned that if he could slow her down a bit, and limit her to, say, twice a day, seven days a week, he might live to see forty. In the end he decided to become a daddy and do the honourable thing.

Also a guiding hand arrived at this time to assist him in his decision making.

Now guiding hands can take many forms from the spiritual to the spirit bottle but whatever form it takes it is still a guiding hand. Danny's guiding hand arrived in the form of Sheila's younger brothers, two vicious thugs who turned up on his doorstep one night wielding a baseball bat and a pair of garden shears. Danny immediately realised the clubbing potential of the bat but looked bemusedly at the shears. Only when his wedding tackle was placed between the blades did the full extent of their possible horrific use hit him. Cringing inwardly he fought for control, valiantly, as he listened to their description of his fate if he didn't do the right thing by their sister. With sweat pouring from his brow he informed them that he had every intention of honouring his commitment and wouldn't shirk his responsibilities. They told him to get a ring on her finger within a month so she wouldn't bring shame on the family. "Ha"

he thought, "that's rich coming from someone whose dad was in prison for assault (again), whose mother had been done for shoplifting three times and whose sister was the biggest slag in Brinsmarsh." "No problem" he said instead.

Within one month Danny had arranged a wedding (St. Bernard's in town) and a reception at the Queens (the catering and the décor isn't much to write home about but you get a very high class of fighting at the end of the night). He also borrowed a caravan for the week at Ingoldmells, Skegness, from a distant aunt (she would remain distant too, the van was crap). He already had a house, which his mum had left him when she died the previous year. It was a trim little terraced on the same road as Mick and Sue's and Danny had lived there all his life.

Eventually Danny had to tell the lads, of course, if for no other reason than he needed a best man, and they took it quite well really although they felt really sorry for him getting mixed up with Sheila's family.

"You don't have to marry her you know" ventured Jeff.

"No I know that. I could always just forget all about it until one night I was reminded by Babe Ruth and Edward fucking Scissorhands" Danny answered sarcastically.

"Don't worry about them" joined in Ron "I'll take care of them"

Danny thought a while then shook his head "No I'm a big boy now, I've made my bed so I'll lie in it."

"Yeah but you'll not get much sleep with Sheila in it" added Dave and they all laughed but Danny's sounded a little forced.

"Anyway" he continued "I'm quite looking forward to being a dad".

Mick raised his glass "To the groom and future daddy" he toasted.

"And let's hope it has it's mothers looks, not it's dad's." added Ron

"And gets more sleep at night than his mum will allow his dad to get." added Jeff and they all raised their glasses and happily downed their drink in one.

The day of the wedding came and went in a bit of a blur for Danny. The worry that he was doing the wrong thing and would regret it outweighed any happiness he felt. Sheila looked stunning in a magnificent white (bit of a

liberty that but she more or less got away with it) lacey thing she had bought from town and great chunks of it were hugely enjoyable. Everyone seemed to have a good time and even the attitude of her mad brothers seemed to soften against him. They were simple men who would fight first and asked questions later, and that's only if they could be arsed. At the end of the night three young lads tried to gatecrash, to get some extra drink, and were promptly beaten to a pulp so Danny knew for a fact that at least the brothers had had a good time.

Everyone congratulated them, although some seemed a little forced, and they got in their cab late that night, quite drunk, to be taken on the two hour journey to their honeymoon haven. They arrived in the early hours of the morning and Danny carried her over the threshold. They then made love until the sun came up when they promptly fell into a deep sleep.

Danny had a lovely dream where he was in the park with Sheila. They were laughing and clapping their hands at something just out of view. They were obviously happy and by the way they constantly touched or hugged each other they were obviously very much in love. As the camera in his mind panned out he could see what the object of their rapt attention was. A little boy with golden locks and a cherubic grin was happily to-ing and fro-ing on the swing. "Daddy"

the boy called happily "look at me Daddy"

"I see you son, I see you." Dream Danny called back.

"Look Mummy, look. I'm swinging" he chirped happily.

"I can see you my little man." She laughed back at him.

They hugged each other and laughed at the little boy trying his hardest to get higher and higher.

"Fuckin' hell!" the voice said softly in his ear and he stirred slightly in his sleep. "Fuck me!" it continued a little louder and he opened his eyes reluctantly. The dream was so powerful to him he was loath to release it but as he heard the voice mutter softly "Fuck!" he came back to life.

"What's up love" he called when he realised Sheila was no longer in bed with him.

"I've come on" she answered flatly.

"Come on what?" he asked and smiled to himself.

"Just come on" she replied after a few seconds.

Slowly the picture of marital bliss disappeared from view and another altogether different picture hove up. This one had an old witch called Sheila telling him through broken yellow teeth that he wasn't having a child anymore so he might as well just fuck off so there.

Danny jumped out of bed and ran, naked, to the door. Crashing through it he was oblivious of the open outer door. His eyes searched out Sheila and he found her through the door on his right, sat on the lav.

"You've done what?" he asked incredulously.

Sheila sat with her head hung down, her hair falling spectacularly over her face. In her hand was a folded tissue with a dark red smear across it. She stared at it blankly.

"You can't come on you daft cow, you're pregnant!". For some reason Danny thought he could talk her out of it.

"Oh no I'm not" she mumbled.

Slowly, the realisation that his dreams were not going to come true, overwhelmed him. He kicked out at the door jarm, instantly breaking his unprotected toe. As he screamed out in pain, he danced round the room trying to lift his injured digit up in the air, surprising two passersby out walking the dog. They stopped short, staring in through the open door. It's not everyday you see a naked man dancing in his caravan sucking his toe and singing, albeit badly. Not even in Skeggy.

"Shit, shit, bastard, shit" he muttered as he regained control of himself, and the searing pain became a dull throb. The old couple walked on, tutting to themselves, about the morals of the younger generation, and Danny eased himself onto the old, almost threadbare, settee and stroked his toe. His mind was spinning, a thousand thoughts jostled for control, but one kept rising to the surface ahead of all the others so his subconscious fetched that one out and gave it to the mouth to use.

"You never were pregnant, were you, you lying cow?" he shouted.

Sheila's head snapped up. She had been lost in her own thoughts for some time, and although she was aware that Danny had hurt himself, she hadn't taken that much notice. She was bitterly disappointed that she wasn't pregnant. She loved Danny, had loved him more each and every day they had been together so she had desperately wanted this to work out. She had even found herself daydreaming of what it would be like to be a proper family. Not like her own family life, which she knew was pretty dysfunctional, but a real, happy, do things together, family. She thought that with Danny that she could have this, but here he was accusing her of tricking him into marriage. "What did you say?" she asked leaning forward to better hear his reply.

Now most logical minded men, who didn't have a death wish, would at this point mumble "nothing" and let it drop but Danny would never be known as

"Mr Logical". "You fuckin' tricked me" he shouted even louder than before.

Like a lioness attacking a startled gazelle she threw herself out of the small bathroom. Taking in the whole room in one quick blink of an eye she saw her pray sat, naked, on the settee rubbing his foot. To aid her speedy flight she had kicked away her knickers from around her ankles but still held on to the small fold of tissue. Looking up, startled by the lightning attack, Danny didn't have any time to formulate his own strategy, or any escape plan. Instead he did what any self respecting man would do in those circumstances,. He screamed loudly and tried to curl into a ball. Fully clothed this would have been a sad sight to behold but butt naked with his arse showing and all his dangly bits exposed it was truly shocking. Sheila, who was now only wearing her short see-through black baby doll also showed everything she had got as she dived on top of him, raining down blows with all her might.

The old couple were actually circling the caravan as part of their daily routine and they stopped in their tracks as they spotted the wildly thrashing couple through the window. They could see the mans arms flailing helplessly around as the semi- naked woman jumped up and down on him, hitting him all the time. Every now and again the naked bodies would disappear under the

window sill and the old couple, still with disgusted looks on their faces, craned their necks for a better view. They couldn't hear the voices, of course, the never ending curses and oaths, the name calling and the vile promises of retribution.

"Fuck off"

"Fuck you"

"Bitch"

"Twat"

"Lying whore"

"Useless tosser with a doormouses dick"

"Slag"

"Puff"

And on and on. At one point Sheila rubbed the tissue in his face and he could see her blood streaked across his nose. Danny screamed and tried desperately to get away. Suddenly his naked arse appeared at the window with his tackle hung down like the last turkey in the shop, and the old woman gasped and clung on to her husbands arm. The old man looked horrified and for a split second he thought his wife would have a seizure. They clung to each other as the hypnotic vision in front of them changed, firstly from a male naked arse then to a female one, next to flailing arms then back to two naked torsos locked in a Greek wrestling hold.

"Come on "panted the old lady as if pulling herself out of a spell

"Are we going for the police dear?" her husband asked, knowing her as well as he knew himself after all these years.

"No. Let's go home to bed" she answered huskily. He stared at her, not fully comprehending her reply, then a lurid smile broke onto his craggy old face

"She's only gone and got turned on by it" he smirked to himself.

"Alright love I just hope I can remember what to do. It's been a long time you know" he breathed.

"Don't worry love, if you get stuck just ask. I've always had a better memory than you" she giggled and they hurried off to their caravan further down the field.

Danny had managed to extricate himself from Sheila's all enveloping body and was trying to make a dash for the bedroom. His broken toe hampered him a little at first, then even more so as he caught it on the table leg. He screamed and doubled up to soothe his toe and Sheila pounced on him, clawing and scratching. At one point, as he bent further forward, she tumbled over him and landed on her back, the wind knocked out of her for a second, he realised he had a golden opportunity to end it there and then. He had a free shot to her exposed jaw and he knew full well that if he hit her now it would knock her out. Danny mused over this for a full two seconds and, just as he made the decision that no matter what he could never hit a woman, she reached up and poked him full in the eye. He screamed even louder now and both his hands shot to his face. He tried opening his eye but the pain was unbelievable so he gave that up and concentrated on covering up his nuts because he could feel her hands trying to find them. Her left hand scrabbled around for a while as he

kicked his knees up in a vain attempt to hide his tackle. Then her right hand came into play and slipped past his thrashing legs and squeezed as hard as she could. He ought to have been grateful, in a way, because all of a sudden he could open his eyes again. He couldn't see yet, but that may have been the tears, and when he tried he found that he couldn't close them. In fact, he realised they were getting bigger. The more she squeezed the more wide open they became. Sheila, without letting go of the spoils, rose to her feet, taking Danny with her. They now stood, face to face, hot and sweaty, breathing heavily. Sheila's breath was now becoming more even as she had taken control of events but Danny's was short and rasping, as if he was afraid that a deep breath would part him completely from his balls.

"How dare you say that I tricked you, you little fuckin' worm" she whispered in his ear and squeezed a little harder for effect.

"I...I.." he began and she cut him off by digging her nails into the soft skin under his sac.

"Shut up" she ordered and he nodded vigorously to show her he understood.

She composed herself, making sure she got this just right.

"I loved you. I want you to know that. I would have done anything for you. I would have mended my ways, become a one man woman, stayed in nights, played with the kid, been a doting mother. Why? Because I thought you loved me. I honestly thought that you would never ever do anything to hurt me. I felt totally safe with you. Well I was wrong wasn't I. The first little crisis that comes along and you fuck everything up. Do you really think anyone would want to trick you into marriage. You must think a hell of a lot of yourself. What did I marry you for eh, your money. Well I haven't seen much evidence of that yet." And she tossed her head indicating the cramped little caravan. "Or maybe it was your prowess as a lover I was desperate for. Well I've got bad news for you there sunshine. You're not that good. I've had loads better than that.

Loads. So come on tell me, you little scumbag, what is it that I'm so desperate to get hold of. Come on what is it.?"

Danny shook his head, to show that he didn't have an answer, then stopped as it just served to cause him more pain down below.

19

"Don't know" he breathed and then winced as she squeezed him again. Tears were now running down his cheeks, as he fought desperately to find an answer. Not just any answer though, the right one. The one that made her release him from her grip. "I'm sorry" he said simply. He held his breath waiting for her response. She stared into his face for ages then squeezed as hard as she could. Danny honestly thought he would faint when she suddenly released him and he collapsed to the floor. In agony he curled up into a ball and sobbed. She simply stood over him, with disgust written in large letters across her face, enjoying his pain and humiliation.

"I will make you pay for this you bastard. I'll make you pay" she breathed then tossed her hair to one side and looked at the tissue still clamped in her hand.

Smiling she dropped it onto his wracked body. "Something to remember me by" she smiled as she stepped over him to get changed to go down to the beach.

She had a marvellous time over the next couple of days, on the beach, in the nearby pool, and at night, down at Fantasy Island, where one night she pulled a rugby player from Leicester who was all over her like a rash, and who broke into fits of laughter, when she told him she was actually here on her honeymoon and her husband was in the local hospital with a broken toe, a detached retina and a hernia.

CHAPTER TWO

In their little terraced house, on Atlas Road, in Brinsmarsh, Mick and Sue were having their tea. "Are you going out tonight love, only Ros has arranged for the girls to go round hers to sort out the holiday arrangements" she asked between mouthfulls.

"Yeah alright love I might have a walk down the road later on then" he answered, meaning he would call in the Maggies for a pint.

"You, er, won't be going out till after eight though will you?" she asked coyly

"No it'll be late on. Why?" he asked, cutting into his Pork Steak.

"Oh nothing really. It's just that the delivery man said he would be here for eight"

"What delivery man?" he asked then put down his knife and fork. "Sue what have you been ordering. You know we said we were on a budget for a while, just till the holidays and the wedding were over"

"Oh it's nothing much" she whispered, tilting her head slightly, and looking more demure than Greer Garson in Mrs Miniver "It's just a sunbed".

"Yeah" he muttered excitedly

"Mmmm" and she flicked back her hair coquetishly.

"I love sunbeds, they turn me on. I think it's the goggles." He smirked. Sue grinned.

"I thought we could have a session every morning and evening right up to the holidays." She said.

Mick looked thoughtful. "OK" he eventually replied, "but it won't leave much time for getting a tan" and she giggled lovingly at him.

"Only me" shrilled a voice from the kitchen.

"Shit" whispered Mick.

"Come in mum" called Sue while giving Mick a dirty look.

"Just popped in for a minute dear" she announced as she appeared round the kitchen door carrying a cup and saucer. "tea made is it?"

"It's in the pot mum" Sue answered, nodding towards the old teapot in the middle of the table." Yeah help yourself Nellie" nodded Mick, wanting to add

"You usually do" but not daring. Sue gave him a withering look because she knew what he was thinking.

"Ta love" Nellie said as she sat down and pulled the pot towards her.

"What you been doing all day mum?" Sue asked when she was satisfied her mum was settled.

"Oh the usual. Get up, clean up, wedding shopping, come home, cook, oh I've done you a nice lasagne for the freezer, I'll pop it round later" she answered.

"Mum you don't have to keep cooking for us. We can manage you know." Sue interjected.

"I know love, but it gives me something to do, cooking for one's no good so it makes me feel, ya' know, needed." She looked down at the tablecloth and stirred her tea, slightly embarrassed.

"You are needed, and wanted. You're welcome round here anytime, you know that." Sue said and she got out of her chair and went round the table to her mum and gave her a hug. She looked at Mick imploringly. "Isn't she Mick?"

she asked, in a voice that left him no options.

"Course she is." He said quickly. She wasn't a bad old girl, really, she just got lonely, being on her own, so she called round to see them a lot. Sometimes it got on his nerves but, he didn't mind too much as he actually felt a bit sorry for her. Of course it also kept Sue happy. "Especially if she keeps bringing some snap round" he added, patting his belly. "I haven't had a custard for a while"

"I'll do you one tomorrow" she answered happily and picked up her cup. Sue smiled at him lovingly.

The "Bronze God" sunbed man arrived at eight o clock and put the double canopy, sixteen tube, fast tan bed in the spare bedroom then Mick got showered and changed and went for a "walk down the road" to the Maggies. Ron and Jeff were in and Mick gave them a "do you want one" sign across the semi crowded room. They both nodded so he ordered three pints which he carried over to them.

"All right lad" called Old Tom from his usual place in the corner. Mick glanced across. "All right Tom, you still here? called back Mick. It was close to nine now and old Tom always liked to be away for nine.

"Just finishing this then I'm off" Tom said and nodded to the inch of beer left in his glass.

"'night then Tom" Mick said and carried the drinks over to his mates.

"Cheers" he said as he placed the three pints down on the table.

"Cheers" they chorused and they all took a long draught and placed the half empty glasses in front of them.

"Not long now !" offered Ron

"Holiday or wedding?" asked Mick as he wiped the froth from his upper lip.

"Holiday of course" smiled Ron

"Who gives a toss about the wedding?" asked Jeff and Ron shook his head.

"What wedding?" he asked.

"Piss off" Mick said and had another drink.

"Where's Sue going?" asked Jeff, lifting his own glass.

"Lloret de mar" answered Mick.

"Been there" Jeff said with a broad grin developing on his handsome face.

"Great night life. Had a different bird every night" He leant forward, conspiratorially, "I had two birds this one night. Sisters they were. I picked the younger one up at a club and after a few drinks and a bit of the old boyish charm…."

"You got her drunk" butted in Ron.

"No I didn't….well a bit tipsy maybe, but anyway, after a few drinks we go back to her hotel. "we'll have to be quiet" she says , 'cos her sister's asleep in the room. Anyway, after a couple of hours of "the biz" she falls fast asleep.

Knackered I suppose. It must be hard for any woman to keep up with a stud muffin like me."

Ron and Mick smiled to each other. The sad thing was, Jeff believed it. Really.

"Anyway, after a bit I gets up to go for a piss and a wash, you know, clean up the old man and that, when I realise someone is behind me. I look in the mirror and this bird is stood watching me.

At first I thought it was this one I'd just shagged but then it dawns
on me it's not, it's the sister, and she's only stark bollock naked.
She's about ten years older than the other one and I found out later
she was married with a couple of kids. Her husband had a fear of
flying, so he had paid for her and her sister to come on holiday
together, said he trusted her. Mad bastard. Anyway she's stood
there wi' nowt on and I'm stood there wi' nowt on and I've got my
old man in the sink and a nice lather going on and she says "I'll do
that for you if you want". Being the gentleman that I am I says "If
you want to I don't mind" and she walks across and washes the old
feller. "I could hear you in there" she says, " and now I think it's
my turn".

Well, what can you do, so we have it away twice in the bathroom.
Anyway it's getting light outside when I finally get into bed with
the first sister and I'm well fucked, I could sleep for England, but
the younger one turns over and climbs on top of me, and I'm off
again. I look over and the older sister is watching me and she's
only playing with herself."

Jeff stopped here and took a well deserved drink. The other two
watched him, smiling to themselves.

"Jeff" Ron said eventually "You were sixteen when you went to
Lloret, and you went with your mum and dad"

Jeff took another swig, emptying his glass, oblivious to their
disbelief. "Yeah I know. My mum nearly killed me when I got
back that morning."

Mick looked at Ron to see if he believed the story but Ron just
shrugged his shoulders. It could be true or it could just be Jeff's
fertile imagination, you never knew with Jeff.

"Who's she going with anyway?" Jeff asked

"Ros from work, she lives in the village, in them new flats. She's
Sue's best friend and her matron of honour. Claire from work,
she's a right goer, you'd like her Jeff, and Linda McCarthy from
across our road."

26

Ron nodded, he knew Linda of course, they had all grown up together, and he had met Ros in passing, it was only a small village and eventually everybody met everybody else.

Mick looked up as Danny walked in the room. Danny shook his hand in the air in front of his mouth asking them if they wanted a drink. Jeff was just lifting his empty glass up to show he was ready, when Ron caught his arm and returned it to the table.

Mick smiled across at Danny and shook his head, indicating they weren't ready for another one yet.

"I'm empty" protested Jeff

"He's skint" commented Ron

"Don't drink so fast, it's bad for your digestion" added Mick.

"Hiya. What's up" asked Danny as he sat down. He couldn't help but notice the atmosphere, and he looked around at his mates for a clue as to what had gone on.

He noticed Jeff's empty glass.

"I thought you weren't ready for one. I'd have got them in if you'd said."

Jeff looked from one to the other. He was pissed off that they had had a go at him, but he knew they were right and he had no desire to hurt Danny's feelings.

"It's alright Danny, I'm trying to slow down a bit, it's, er, the old digestion y'know, it's been playing me up a bit"

Danny nodded. Mick smiled and Ron grabbed hold of Jeff's head and pulled it towards him and dug his knuckles into his skull, which brought a scream of pain from his victim.

"Right I think you've rested long enough between pints, so I'll get them in" announced Ron as he picked his glass up, drained it and walked off to the bar.

When he returned, with four pints of best, Mick was telling them something.

"So I want you lot to be on your best behaviour with the ladies" he was saying.

"It's a big day for Sue, and me of course, so I want it all to go well. That means.." and he turned to face Jeff directly, "…no shagging the Bridesmaid's till after the reception"

Jeff smiled and held up his hands in mock surrender.

"They are ladies and are to be treated as such. Oh, by the way, Sue want's us all to go out Sunday night, a sort of farewell to us all, sorry Danny." Danny shrugged. "it'll also give us a chance for us all to get to know each other better before the wedding. Down Jeff." Jeff looked taken aback, but he knew what Mick meant so he gave the boy scout sign and announced "Dib dib dib I'll behave Arkala. I promise."

"Speaking of the fairer sex, how's Sheila, Danny, I haven't seen her around for ages."

Ron didn't notice the effect his words had upon his friends. They all did statue impressions. Mick even stopped still with his pint to his lips.

"Used to see her every Friday, down the Grab a Grannie, but she hasn't been in the last few weeks. You put your foot down or what." He blindly carried on.

At last he looked around him and noticed, for the first time, that they were all staring at him, willing him to shut his gob.

"What?" he asked.

It was common knowledge in Brinsmarsh, that Sheila was having a torrid affair with her supervisor at the PK nut factory where she worked. Tactfully, no one

was mentioning it to Danny, although he knew, but Ron was renowned for not listening to gossip of any kind so nobody had bothered to tell him.

"Leave it" advised Mick.

"Leave what?" asked Ron who was being particularly slow on the uptake tonight. Danny rose from the table and tactfully lost two quid in the bandit while Mick explained the situation to Ron. When he returned, although there was still an atmosphere, the subject had changed to football in general, and Sheffield United in particular. They all supported Rotherham United but also Sheffield United from a distance and the way they had been playing lately that was definitely the best way.

"Nuts anybody?" asked Jeff, holding up a packet of PK Salted Peanuts and they all looked at each other, the atmosphere now lifted, and laughed out loud, even Danny.

Sue was pouring the wine when Claire and Linda arrived.

Claire, as ever, looked beautiful and immaculately groomed, Linda looked frumpy. Claire was possibly the best looking girl in Rotherham and had had a string of boyfriends over the last few years. She had a fondness for each one, to a varying degree, but for reasons she had never fathomed, none had ever lasted more than a couple of months.

To be honest Claire was getting a little worried about it, and was more than a little envious of Sue's upcoming marriage. She had tried everything she could think of to keep a man but in the end they had all walked away. What she hadn't worked out was that although she had been blessed with a body to die for, sensual lips, the sexiest eyes, and legs that went all the way up, there was something missing that was needed to sustain a lasting relationship. There was nothing upstairs. She was a bungalow. She wasn't retarded or anything, she just wasn't very bright, and to be honest, she was a little shallow. Actually she was so shallow you couldn't drown in her.

When God was handing out tits she was at the front of the queue. When the big man announced it was time to dish out the bodies she was right there but when He shouted out "Brain time" she must have buggered off to do some shopping or something, arriving back around the same time as Bennie from Crossroads and most, if not all, of the Spice Girls. Anyway, after a few weeks of going out with her, even the shallowest of men, wanted to have some form of conversation, and this had caused the aforementioned problems. She just had very little to say. If it wasn't for Sue's wonderful nature, Claire wouldn't have many female friends either, but Sue tended to see the good in people first and had befriended her immediately.

Linda, on the other hand, was best described as plain. She was overweight, and undersized. It was difficult to tell whether she was too fat or too short. Her hair wanted cutting and colouring and she needed someone to go through her wardrobe and sort her out a new look. She was shy and recalcitrant too so it would be fair to say she didn't have a lot going for her in the old "catching yourself a man" game. However she was a brilliant friend, loyal to the last, and would never dream of letting anyone down. Sue loved her to bits and they had

been friends for years. In turn Linda worshipped Sue and wished with all her heart that she could be like her and have the things that she had. Particularly Mick. Linda always went weak at the knees whenever Mick was around. She would give anything to have a hunk like Mick in bed with her. Lately she had lowered her sights somewhat and had now settled on any man, as long as he had a pulse. Linda was a virgin.

"Come on girls, we almost started without you" shouted Sue from the kitchen, as Ros took their coats and hung them up. Claire's was a little leather designer number, Linda's a beige duffel coat that her mum had bought for her. Ros ushered them into the room.

"Bottoms up" Sue said as she entered the living room with the tray and four glasses of wine.

"Up *and* down soon eh" giggled Claire. Ros and Sue smiled indulgently and Linda coloured up.

"Tickets are on the table, shall we split them or keep them all together?" asked Sue.

"Keep them together eh" offered Claire "Let Ros look after them She's in charge. She's our Darth Vador."

"Darth Vador. What's he got to do with it?" asked Sue.

"Not Darth Vador. Him the Scouts have. Or is it Girl Guides? You know"

answered Claire. They all looked at each other. Obviously they didn't know who the scouts or the girl guides had.

"Arkala" Claire suddenly shouted in triumph. And they all nodded. Of course.

How silly of them. "Anyway Ros' the oldest so she should have the responsibility" she continued.

"I'm the eldest by about six months" argued Ros aghast at the thought of being the eldest and designated responsible adult.

"Yeah but you're the most grown up of the four of us Ros." pressed on Claire, regardless. "In fact you're the most grown up of anybody I know"

Ros looked distinctly hurt.

"I mean that in the nicest possible way" Claire added. Although Claire and Ros had known each other for years they weren't particularly close friends. Claire thought Ros was too prissy and Ros thought Claire a tart. They were both right of course but like beauty, prissy and tart are only skin deep and no one should just be taken on face value.

"Ding Ding, end of round one" called Sue and both Ros and Claire visibly softened.

"OK I'll look after the tickets" Ros volunteered, then "Right. As requested, we should all have our passports with us tonight." All the girls reached into their bags and fished out their passports. "OK let's have a look at those photo's" and they all leant in and giggled.

Next day Mick was on twelve hours. Normally he didn't mind the overtime as the extra money always came in handy, but today was really dragging and he had had enough. It was about three o clock and he had finished his jobs for the day so he was now sat in the cabin having a cuppa. The reason he was so keen

to get home was a simple one. He was horny. He had worked out that Sue would finish work about four thirty and would be home about five. She would put something in the oven, so he reckoned she would then go on the sunbed at about five fifteen. If he stayed for the full twelve hours he wouldn't get home until half six at the earliest. Too late to catch her unawares on the bed. That was it then. He made up his mind to finish at half four, have a shower, and be home for quarter past five. Perfect.

Sue glanced up at the clock as the phone rang. It was three o clock, she noticed, as she answered it. "Smith, Brown and Ahmed, how may I help you?"

"Can I speak to Sue please?" said the voice on the other end.

"It's me mum, what's up?"

"Nothing love. I'm in town, wedding shopping, and I wondered if there was anything you wanted. You said yesterday you were going shopping after work"

"Thanks mum, but it's OK. I'm just calling in for a bikini so I'll need to try it on. I've seen the one I want at Topshop so I shouldn't be long"

"Alright love, see you later. I'll pop round tonight to have a go on that sunbed if it's alright"

"Oh no" thought Sue who had every intention of a very sexy night based around that sunbed. Besides Mick would go barmy if he knew Nellie was going to spoil his fun. Thinking quickly she said "Tell you what mum. I won't be home till about half five and Mick's working while six so he won't be home till half past. Why don't you use it this afternoon when there's nobody there. It'll save us having to queue up for the thing tonight."

"Alright love. I've a bit more shopping to do yet, but I'll go on it as soon as I get back. I'll be all done for half five so I'll put you the kettle on"

The pips went.

"OK mum. See you later"

"Bye Bye love. See you later."

At four thirty Mick clocked out and hurried over to the shower block with one thought on his mind. He had a quick shower and dressed and was on his way in no time. Mick always went the same way home so he crossed the car park and went back through the mill and out of the back gate. He jogged up the spare field but had to wait a couple of minutes to get past the big gates of Curly's Distribution Centre as a queue of lorries was blocking the path. Eventually a gap appeared so he impatiently ran through it and over the top of the hill and round the golf course. Mick was a member of the golf club, as were most workers at the steel mills, so he knew most of the players out on the course. He waved to a fourball walking up the fourteenth and commented on a crap shot one of them had just made and they shouted something back to him that contained quite a few swear words. "The club secretary would have a ducky fit if he heard that" he thought to himself, and without slowing his pace, he went up the slope and came out onto the main road next to "The Greens" , Brinsmarsh's poshest pub and restaurant.

Now Mick was on the top of the hill and it was literally downhill all the way home. He couldn't get a picture of Sue laid on the sunbed out of his mind so he put on a bit of an extra spurt.

Nellie turned the key in Sue's back door and let herself in. She had done it many times before, usually to put them a pie in the oven or click the heating on if it was a particularly cold day. She stretched her back, which had been giving her a bit of gip lately and walked through the kitchen into the front room. She opened the living room door and went into the small hallway where she hung up her coat. She couldn't wait to get on the sunbed as she knew the deep heat would make her back pain disappear almost immediately. She climbed the stairs, feeling a little twinge, as she went and across the corridor to the spare room at the back of the house. Halfway along the corridor was the old chest of drawers that Nellie had given them when they first moved in together and on top of it were two pairs of small red goggles. Next to them were two beautifully wrapped presents. Nellie looked at the cards on them. One was from Mick's Aunt Ada, who had never married, and never went to weddings but always sent a gift. The other, which was wrapped in a shiny foil, had a big red ribbon stuck to it. This was from Nellies older sister, Eilleen, and her husband Jim who ran a guest house in Cleethorpes. They had phoned to say they were too busy to come to the wedding, but they had sent a gift anyway. Nellie sniffed, as she knew neither present was likely to be expensive and looked much nicer while still in their pretty wrapping. "Mutton dressed as lamb" she thought to herself and picked up one of the goggles and went into the spare bedroom, closing the door behind her. Nellie closed the curtains and turned the light on. She pulled out the sunbed, which was beside the window and set it up. Stripping off, she noticed her reflection in the wardrobe mirror, and turned slightly to get a better view of herself. "Not bad" she thought "for a woman of... my age" and she smiled to herself, in the mirror, as she lifted up her ample bosom and pirouetted, gently humming to herself. Her belly was getting much rounder than it had been, and now seemed to have the consistency of dough, and her thighs were now much heavier and thicker than before but overall she was pretty satisfied with her lot. Her boobs were still holding up and her arse hadn't reached the floor yet so there was still life in the old dog. Not that she had anyone to show it to. Still it was nice to think that even if no one else ever saw it, she still had a decent body. She let her boobs drop back down to her belly, and turned to the sunbed and set the timer for thirty minutes. Then she put her goggles on and lay down under the shiny tubes. When she was comfy she reached over and flicked the switch and with a little crackle the tubes burst into life and flooded her whole body with warmth. Within minutes Nellie was snoring softly like a new born baby.

Mick came round the corner at full speed, his mind on the delights he had now convinced himself were sure to follow. He hurdled the small gate and ran up the path that led to his and his neighbours front doors. His hands were almost shaking as he fished out his keys and he quivered with anticipation as he

attempted to open the door. To his utter disgust the key wouldn't fit and a mad panic almost engulfed him that he might be too late and Sue would have finished and got dressed. It suddenly dawned on him that the key wouldn't fit because there was a key in the lock on the inside. He smiled mischievously as he realised that by entering through the back door he would be able to sneak up on Sue without her hearing him, scaring her as he walked in the bedroom door, then rushing over and comforting her etc etc etc.

His lip curled at the prospect and he smiled like a young Terry Thomas who had just pulled a lovely bit of

"totty". It was a wonder, really, that he didn't twirl an imaginary moustache and purr "well hello".

He ran through the little gennel that led to the back gardens and vaulted the fence, finding the back door key on the way. Carefully he inserted it and let himself in, shutting the door behind him. He set off stealthily across the kitchen then stopped in his tracks as a thought struck him. "Lock the door in case of unwanted visitors" and he nodded to himself. He reached over and locked the back door and whispered in a mock high pitched voice "It's only me..". He looked in the direction of Nellie's house and laughed. Turning he made his way through the kitchen and into the living room. Quietly he eased round the furniture and opened the door into the hall. Up the stairs he went, even avoiding the third step as it creaked, smiling all the while. As he reached the top step he heard the soft whirring that he knew was the sunbed and his smile became even more manic. He inched his way across the landing and noticed the blue light coming from under the door. So intent on his quest was he that he bumped into the chest of drawers on the landing. Startled, he stared at it as though he had never seen the thing before in his life, then gradually his expression changed as he took in the items on top of it. It was the goggles that first caught his eye and an idea struck him immediately. Then he noticed the presents and in particular the wrapping and his idea blossomed. Giggling like a demented schoolgirl, he threw his clothes off and picked up the goggles and put them on. Suddenly his world became a dismal dark red and he realised he couldn't see a thing. He pulled the goggles onto the top of his head and reached over to the presents. The second part of his plan was simple. To put the big red bow on his old man. He pulled at the bow and the sticky back easily came away from the foil wrapping. Still giggling to himself he gently stuck the bow to his shaft. Looking at this new gift proudly, he wondered if it would fall off as soon as he started walking. He jumped in the air, his todger following suit and the bow stayed in place. He walked to the end of the corridor, watching his shiny red bow swinging, with pride. Then a bad thought struck him. What if it hurt when Sue pulled it off to "open" her pressie. So he carefully peeled the sticky hard card away from his tender skin. Not too bad. So he stuck it back in place. He set off again to the bedroom when another thought struck him. What if, in the heat of passion, Sue didn't gently peel it off him and instead ripped it away in a mad lust filled frenzy. So he tried it. He braced himself then ripped the bow away from his expectant member. Tears welled up in his eyes as the pain shot from member to brain, registered, then went back downstairs again.

He bit into the back of his hand to stop from crying out loud then hastily looked

to see if there was any damage. With great relief he saw just a slight chaffing.

"I can live with that" he thought and stuck the bow back into place. He faced the bedroom door and muttered under his breath "And now the piss de resistance" and placed the goggles over his eyes. He inched his arm forward and felt for the door handle, finding it after a bit of fumbling and gently opened the door. Immediately, the blue ultra violet light gave him sight, so he edged round the door and stood there in all his glory, naked, save for the bow and goggles. Proudly he announced "Special Delivery for Miss Thomson" and gave a little wiggle so his "pressie" did a little dance.

Mick knew something was wrong, but he couldn't quite work out what it was exactly. As he looked directly at the sunbed he squinted a little at the bright light, even with the goggles on. He could see Sue, naked, on the bed but there was something different about her. She had put on weight for a start. Her boobs were much bigger as well and were sort of lolling to the sides and resting on her arms, instead of sitting there, pert and pretty, like two overgrown fried eggs. Mick definitely didn't recall her belly being that big either. Mick took a couple of steps forward and could clearly see stretch marks on what must be the biggest arse he had ever seen close up. Then, as his eyes continued their sweep, he almost cried out in shock as he saw her bush. Not the beautiful mount of venus he was used to, covered in a soft nuzzly down, but a huge black hairy beast of a thing that seemed to follow him around like those paintings with the eyes.

At the same time as Mick was having these disturbing revelations, Nellie was being awakened from her slumbers by a voice, which she thought, for some strange reason, had said "Special Delivery for Miss Thomson". She had opened her eyes and slowly tilted her head to see, much to her surprise, a naked man with a red bow stuck to his willy. Now, if Nellie had looked up from the bow (and the willy) she would have clearly seen Micks face with a very puzzled expression. But she didn't. Her eyes were transfixed to this strange sight. After all, it was a few years since she had seen a willy at all, and this seemed a particularly good specimen, if her memory served her correctly, and it was gift wrapped.

She watched, still half asleep, as the gift wrapped willy did a little dance and then after what seemed an eternity, she saw it moving towards her. With a thundering crash the real world returned to Nellie so she did what any self respecting Yorkshire lass would do under the same circumstances. She screamed.

The scream cut through the testosterone fuelled fog that seemed to have gripped Mick's mind and he instantly knew what was wrong and why Sue appeared to have aged thirty years and put on sixty pounds. It was Sue's mum.

Nellie, on the other hand, still hadn't taken her eyes from the dancing dick, so she hadn't recognised her future son in law yet. Halfway through her scream, she started to rise. Silhouetted against the ultra violet tubes she was a fearsome sight so Mick did what any self respecting Yorkshireman would do when confronted by a naked mother in law. He screamed.

At exactly the moment that Mick's bloodcurdling scream broke the air, the timer on the sunbed clicked to nought and the room was plunged into darkness.

Mick stepped backwards, then turned, in an effort to escape. Somewhere in the back of his mind was the knowledge that he must, whatever else happened, get out of that room and get dressed. In the newly blacked out room he lost his bearings for a second and stubbed his knee on the side of the bed. Screaming in agony he hopped around the little space that was available, holding his injured knee up into his body as deep as it would go.

Nellie pulled down her goggles and peered into the gloom. Her eyes hadn't adjusted to the new lighter shade of darkness she now enjoyed but she could still make out the unmistakable shape of a naked man dancing on one leg and shouting a war cry. Mick's back was turned to her so she still hadn't recognised the intruder. She looked around the room until her eyes rested on a set of golf clubs in the corner and she grabbed one. For the record it was a Lynx four iron and Mick's favourite club and Nellie waved it in an arc around her. Her assailant now appeared to be singing to his knee, or even trying to put it in his mouth. What sort of deranged pervert was he. Smack. She caught him on the side of the head with a blow that could ordinarily have knocked him out, but fortunately for him he was just bending down to attempt to put his foot to the floor to make his escape easier. The glancing blow sent him sideways, however, and resulted in the goggles being knocked from his face. At last he had an idea of where the door was so he risked his injured limb and made a run for it.

Nellie was still swinging and her motion on the next arc sent her flying forward as she completely missed her mark. She managed to stop herself from falling by grabbing the bed but lost her grip on the club for a second. She shot her hand out, blindly, to find it and came into contact with Mick's bum, almost sticking her fingers up his hole as crouching, with the pain of his knee he tried to find the door handle. Mick screamed out again. "What the hell is she doing?"

he thought as he found the handle and opened the door. In the relative safety of the landing he turned and shouted "Nellie. Stop" just as she found the golf club and jabbed it forward into his groin. The dull pain almost overwhelmed him and he collapsed to his knees. Through tear filled eyes he could just make out Nellie raising the club above her head and for an awful second he thought he was going to die. He would die here in his own house, naked, with a red shiny bow stuck on his todge, seemingly attacking his future mother in law. The shame of it. He was almost glad he would be dead because everyone would make his life hell after this.

"Please Nellie. It's me" he groaned as he waited for the killer blow.

It was the voice that got through to Nellie. She recognised it, and what's more she recognised who it belonged to. She stopped mid swing and asked "Mick?."

"Yes" he almost cried with relief that at last she wasn't hitting him. Nellie lowered the club and stared at him in disbelief. What the hell was he playing at, attacking her like that. Was he mad. Did he think he could molest her and Sue would never find out. She knew she still had a lovely body, she had been admiring it not half an hour ago, but it had never occurred to her that Mick had

been fancying her. At first she was quite flattered that she could still arouse such passion in a young man, but then she became angry when she realised that he had been willing to cheat on her daughter with her, her mother. Anger exploded into control of her mind and she raised the club again.

Mick was trying to work out how the last few minutes had happened. Alright it was embarrassing enough to creep up on your mother in law whilst naked, with a bow on your cock but what the fuck made her attack him like that. Was she mental or something. He reasoned that she would be angry with him or embarrassed but that was no reason to attack him with a golf club surely. At least she had calmed down now. Just then he saw her raise the club above her hand so he dove to his left and rolled away out of view. "Nellie" he shouted

"What are you doing?" but as he came to his feet he saw the naked Boadicea charging into view so he thought "fuck it" and ran for the stairs

"You pervert" she screamed after him as he disappeared down the stairwell.

She charged after him. "You cheat" she called as she made the stairs and chased down them. She could see him now, at the bottom, trying to open the front door and thought she had him. "Are you mad" she shouted. "Did you think I wouldn't tell Sue?."

Mick vaguely wondered what she meant but tried to concentrate on getting the door open and was greatly relieved, when, with a click, it opened and he was out like a shot. "Come here you bastard" she yelled as she followed him out into the bright sunshine. He was already down the path and was just hurdling the gate when she appeared outside, but she carried on gamely in her assault.

Mick landed on the causeway and bumped straight into old Tom who was out walking his dog. He caught hold of him before Tom fell to the floor and steadied him on his feet. The dog yapped at this sudden attack on his master but made no attempt to defend his master's honour. Those days had long gone.

"Sorry Tom" Mick said as he let go of him and for the first time Tom noticed he was naked. He gasped in amazement. He had never touched a naked man before and he couldn't honestly say that he liked it. He hadn't touched that many naked women either, come to think of it. Still he could always live in hope. Something caught his eye so he turned and to his utter amazement a naked woman wielding a golf club was bouncing towards him. Both he and Mick stared at Nellie in a state of shock. Even the dog stopped yapping and just gawped at her. As she reached the gate Mick tried to win back some control and raised his hand like a traffic cop. "Nellie stop. There's been a terrible mistake. I'm sorry alright, but this has to stop."

Nellie did stop. She thought about it for a few seconds, during which Tom took in every inch of her body. And that's a lot of inches.

She made a decision. "Michael. Get back in the house now before you catch your death o' cold" she said, haughtily, as if talking to a small child, caught playing out without his jumper on.

Mick hesitated for the merest second then opened the gate and walked past her with his head hung down like a naughty schoolboy. Well, like a naked naughty schoolboy with a bow stuck to his willy. He made sure that as he passed her

they didn't come into contact, that would have been too horrible, and she for her part turned her head so as not to see his nudity.

As he disappeared up the drive she surveyed Tom, who, along with his dog, was still staring at her nakedness. "What's the matter Tom?" she asked as she turned to go back in the house "never seen a naked woman before" and she crossed her arms under her enormous bosom and strode magnificently back inside.

Five o clock is a funny time in most places and Brinsmarsh was no exception.

It's the time of day when no one, absolutely no one, is walking about on the small side streets. Oh, the main roads are all busy. Full of weary workers on their way home but the side streets are a no go area. The kids are all in the houses waiting for their tea and watching the telly. It's basically the same programmes they watch as well. It's either one of the ten episodes, repeated ad infinitum, about a laughter free zone in which an American teenager, whose daddy happens to own the network, explains, in her own inimitable way, all about life, badly, or if you're a boy you watch that slitty eyed bird on CITV.

Most of the mums are in the kitchen, rushing to get the tea on, so they can settle down to watch neighbours and most of the dads are the ones flying round on the main roads, or in the pub. Or watching that slitty eyed bird on CITV.

Anyway, fortunately for Nellie, absolutely nobody, except for old Tom and his dog saw what had occurred that afternoon and Tom was in a bit of a state. It had been half a lifetime since he had seen a naked woman and, although he had thought about it a lot during that time, the real thing seemed a lot better than the memory. And there was more of it. He had of course seen women on the telly and in magazines but they were almost without exception thin little things with no meat on them but this had been a real women, an Amazon, who had been chasing herself that young lad from the pub. There was a woman who knew what she wanted, and apparently she wanted it gift wrapped with a big bow on it. He ran the picture again in his mind and felt a little faint.

Mick ran up the stairs and collected his clothes. He was just pulling on his trousers when Nellie brushed past. Tactfully he looked away as she imperiously marched into the bedroom and closed the door behind her. Tucking himself in he decided his best bet was to go downstairs and put the kettle on and two minutes later Nellie joined him in the kitchen. She rattled a few cups round in the sink and avoided eye contact with him. Mick sat at the kitchen table pretending to read a paper. In the background they heard an ambulance siren wailing. Mick risked a glance at her and she sniffed loudly so he quickly looked back down at the paper.

"Whatever where you thinking Michael?" she asked as she wiped three cups dry and put them on the work surface.

"Sorry Nellie. It was a mistake" he answered flatly, without looking up.

"I'll say." She sniffed again and flicked the switch off on the kettle. "Did you seriously think I'd do anything behind Sue's back"

Mick slowly raised his head. "What the fuck is she talking about?" he thought.

"What do you mean?" he asked.

43

"She's my daughter Mick. My only daughter. As flattered as I am I would rather die than do anything that could hurt my daughter."

Mick stared at her. Was she mad? What was she going on about? Then slowly a little light bulb flickered into action and it dawned on him what she meant.

"No Nellie you've got it wrong.." he began

"No Michael you've got it wrong. You should have realised we couldn't have an affair. It's much too complicated."

"An affair. An affair. Was she fucking mental." He thought "I'd rather have an affair with old Tom." A picture of her, naked on the sunbed appeared from nowhere into his brain and he shuddered involuntarily. Then in the picture he was climbing on top of her and he almost cried out loud.

"We must pretend this never happened" she ordered

"Yes please" he said and the picture began to fade

"We must never let Sue know of today's little escapades. In fact we will never mention it again. Do you understand?"

"Oh yes I understand. We will never, ever, ever mention it again"

At that moment the back door burst open, Sue rushed in.

"Guess what?" she blurted out full of excitement.

Mick, thinking there was something wrong, coupled with a feeling of guilt, raced over to her and took her shopping bags and led her to a chair. "What's up love?" he asked concernedly, but he didn't look her in the eye. She stroked his hair lovingly, touched by his concern. "Not me love. Didn't you hear the ambulance?" They shook their heads. "Old Tom's had a funny turn right outside our gate. Collapsed. Somebody phoned the ambulance, thought he'd had a heart attack. Linda's dad was out there, he said that the paramedic said he's OK, just had some sort of a shock. They're keeping him in for the night, just to keep an eye on him"

Nellie and Mick stared at each other, both losing a little colour from their faces, which Sue missed completely. "The funny thing was" she said "his dog has collapsed too and the paramedics have had to take him. They're going to drop him off at the vet's on the way to the hospital. Apparently he's in a worse state than Tom"

Nellie and Mick continued to stare at each other then Mick's lip quivered a bit, then he snorted a little, then tears welled up in his eyes as he fought the urge to laugh. Then, all of a sudden, he gave into it and let all his pent up emotions out and roared with unconcealed joy.

Sue stared, uncomprehending, at him, as though he had gone completely mad.

She turned to her mum for confirmation that she was witness to her future husbands complete mental breakdown and was amazed to see tears running down her face as well and her shoulders rising and falling as she battled to hold back her mirth, without much success. Sue looked from one to the other then shrugged her shoulders and picked up her shopping bags and turned to go upstairs. "There's nowt so queer as folks" she muttered to herself as she shut the kitchen door behind her.

CHAPTER THREE

Ros was packing her suitcase for the second time. Ros was bored.
There was nothing wrong with the packing the first time but for
want of something better to do, she had neatly unpacked, put
everything away, then started all over again. Less than one hour
later she was staring into the case and wondering whether she had
remembered everything and was debating whether or not to start
again. God she had to get a life. She sat down on her bed and
looked around. The bedroom was immaculate, and very tastefully
decorated. It seemed to have taken her forever to get it right. She
looked round her and wondered whether to redecorate. Maybe
after the hols, she decided. She walked out of the bedroom and
into the living room and looked around her. Again the room was
tastefully decorated but she knew, no matter how bored she was,
she wasn't going to redecorate in here. It had taken her two weeks
to strip this room and she was in no hurry to repeat it. The whole
flat seemed to be lacking something, and she had been looking for
that something for a while now. Not urgently looking, with a
passion, but certainly on the look out. Her body clock was ticking
away and she wanted to acquire these finishing touches before she
was too old. Ros was twenty nine and what she needed was a man.

Ron was flopped across the settee watching the telly with his
mum. His mum was knitting and watching the telly (how they do
that I'll never know, I only have to look away from the screen and
I miss the only interesting bit). Ron was bored and found it
difficult to concentrate on the programme. He idly wondered
whether he ought to pack his case but decided it was much too
early and he would probably be best doing it right at the last
minute. He let his mind wander. He had been thinking about his
holiday and was quite looking forward to that but then he found he
had drifted off at several tangents. He had moved

onto work, got bored with that and gone back to the holiday, then off at a tangent to aeroplanes, then air hostesses, pilots, bus conductors (you don't see them now but when Ron was little he had wanted to be a bus conductor), hats, hair, baldness, men, young men. Then he stopped. Quite suddenly as it happens, and with a bit of a shock. He had caught himself thinking of men again. He had been doing this quite a bit recently and it worried him. He reasoned that he wasn't queer or anything because he didn't get aroused when he thought about these men. And they were usually young, virile men with sweaty, oily bodies. He couldn't be queer because he didn't get a hard on.

Trouble was he hardly ever got a hard on these days. He had been out with quite a few girls. Not in the same league as Jeff, admittedly, but he had done alright and he had always gone through the same routine of trying to get into their pants. Well it's expected. But his heart was never in it and it had nearly always ended in disaster. He had been lucky that up to now all the girls had been very nice about it and word had not got out but he lived in mortal fear that someone would open their mouth that he couldn't manage it and that his whole life would be in ruins. Of course, the more he worried, the worse the situation became. In the end he had decided to leave girls alone completely and that's when he noticed his mind kept drifting to boys. He sat, blindly staring at the screen, silently praying that he wasn't queer. He didn't want to be queer. He thought about his mum and knew she would be devastated. He was glad his dad wasn't around anymore to witness his shame and he felt a little tear form at the memory of his old man.

He then wondered how the lads would take it. Mick would probably be alright, but he would be disappointed. Jeff would just take the piss constantly and Danny, well Danny had enough problems of his own so he would probably take it in his stride. Work would be difficult though. A lot of the blokes there were knocking on a bit and didn't take kindly to stuff like that. They would all be watching how he behaved to them as well, wondering if he was fancying them.

What if he got aroused in the shower? What if somebody dropped the soap and he got all excited? Thank God he had been having trouble getting an erection.

What if everyone just said "fuck off queer" and ostracised him. Could he handle that? He would have to live in a shadowy world of gay friends furtively meeting in gay bars and dancing in gay clubs full of leather clad men with Freddie Mercury moustaches and pierced nipples. He could feel sweat forming across his brow and running down his back. His palms were all sticky and he was breathing funny. With an effort he pulled himself together and stopped panicking. After all he hadn't actually done anything so maybe he wasn't queer. Maybe everyone felt this way at some stage. If he asked Jeff he would probably say he had fancied men for years, it was just one of those things.

Maybe. Maybe not.

Climbing off the settee he went into the kitchen to put the kettle on and made a decision. There was only one way he was going to find out if he was queer or not and that was to actually try it. He didn't want to try it here though, in Rotherham. He would try it on holiday. He would get away from the lads for a bit and give it a go. There was bound to be some kind of gay bar there. He

would try it once, then he would know one way or another. Right, decision made. Shit.

As the bright lights flashed and the music boomed around her, Claire was having the time of her life. Dancing was her second favourite thing in the whole wide world. She was a beautiful girl and always dressed to show herself off. She knew the other girls in the club thought her a tart but she didn't care.

She was young, free and single so why shouldn't she enjoy herself. Sometimes, when she was out, she just wanted to dance, but on other occasions, and tonight was one of them, she wanted a man. A lot of men would come on to her during the night, so she could afford to be fussy. Tonight she had picked out her man, a blond Adonis, who she hadn't seen before. Up till now he hadn't paid her much attention but as Ricky Martin began to belt out "Shake your bon bon" she gyrated sexily in the middle of the dance floor. Her mini skirt showed off her long slim legs and the silver micro boob tube showed off everything else.

Hardly a male eye in the room wasn't fixed on her during that dance and every woman in the place turned green and called her a slag.

As the music came to a stop, many of the blokes there wanted to clap but knew if they did they were in big trouble and weren't getting anything that night. As the DJ mumbled something incoherent he cued up a soft ballad and Claire spotted, out of the corner of her eye, the blond Adonis moving towards her.

Accompanied by Robbie Williams telling the world of his Angel, the blond Adonis held out his hand and with a coy smile Claire took it and smooched closer to him. "Easy" she thought.

In the soft candlelight Jeff raised his glass and toasted the girl in front of him.

"Salut" he smiled and she reciprocated shyly. This wasn't really Jeff's thing.

He much preferred dancing the night away but this girl was a bit different. He had pulled her the week before and had sussed she was the quiet type straight away and if he was going to get into her knickers he would have to work at it and take his time. He didn't mind. It was all part of the game. Some required a greater effort than others and that was fine by him. It would all be pretty boring if they were all just the same. He had actually met her at the bus station, which I must admit sounds a pretty naff place to pick up birds, but Jeff had done it a few times there. To a lot of people, Southerners in particular, an evening out may well start with a mini cab ride, but to most Northerners it starts on a bus.

Which means, if you think about it, that at some point there will be people waiting to meet other people in the bus station. Girls!

Jeff always travelled into Rotherham on the bus and found it incredibly easy to strike up a conversation with any waiting girl and had on many occasions arranged a night out on the strength of that first casual meeting. On a couple of occasions, he had actually talked the girl into not waiting any longer for her friend and scooped them off into the night.

This evening had been going quite well and Jeff was considering whether to take the relationship onto the next level, sex, or to bide his time and play the gentleman for a little longer. He had started off well, meeting her at the

restaurant bar, buying her a drink, and hitting her with a few well chosen (and well rehearsed) ad libs. They chatted easily all through the evening and at the end of the meal neither of them was in a rush to leave. Jeff appeared the perfect attentive dinner partner, listening to what she had to say and responding favourably when required. The girl was perfectly at ease now and was telling Jeff her entire history and Jeff was all ears. Or so it seemed. Jeff was actually suffering inner turmoil. His head was telling him that this girl was not ready yet so he shouldn't rush things or he would just frighten her away. His heart was telling him that this was a nice girl. The kind that would only go to bed when there was genuine feeling there. His loins were saying "Go on son. Get in there"

LOINS 1- HEART AND HEAD 0.

To be honest Heart and Head hadn't won a game for years. Even in very close games where the decision could have gone either way Loins had always nicked it right at the death. It had always been this way with Jeff. It didn't matter how slow he had promised himself he would take things, at the end of the night he couldn't help it. He wanted the lot. He didn't always get his own way of course, more often than not he got a slap in the face for his troubles.

51

Relationships were not his strong point. In fact he had never had a serious relationship with anyone. Still you're only young once.

In the darkness of her bedroom, Linda lay, still as a rock, hardly breathing.

Although it was night time, strictly speaking she was day dreaming. It was Linda's abiding ambition in life to be swept off her feet and most of her free time in the day was spent dreaming about it. Most of her night time hours were also spent in much the same way. For the past few months her dream man had taken the form of a large Nordic type, full of long blond hair and rippling muscles. He seemed to spend a large proportion of the dream ripping his shirt off to reveal his perfectly honed body glistening with oil. Lately Linda had been having reservations about her Nordic God. It had actually occurred to her that it must cost him a fortune in shirts, what with all those baby oil stains and all that ripping off and what have you. Reality did tend to crowd in on Linda's dreams and spoil them. Much like her life really.

In her dreams she was also much thinner than in real life. While not exactly being Roseanne Barr she was no Kate Moss either but in the comfort of her own dreams she was whatever she wanted to be and that was slim and sexy.

The location for the dream was important. She had settled on a Norwegian castle on a hill overlooking the fjords and snow swirling over the open country side. At the open windows the wind blew the long silk curtains causing them to billow and swoosh into the candlelit room. Surprisingly, with all that wind blowing around, the candles never blew out and the two perfectly formed figures on the bed never felt the cold. The warmth of their love kept them cocooned. Passions spent, they lay entwined in each others arms.

This week however she had totally revised the dream. Due to the nearness of the holiday she had changed her partner from Nordic God to Latin Lover.

Much leaner and swarthier than his predecessor, this Lothario didn't just sweep

her off her feet and throw her on the bed, no, he went for the full seduction scene. Still as slim and beautiful as ever she was in a hillside villa looking out over the clear blue Mediterranean Sea. She could smell the bouganvilla and she tasted the wine in her hand. In the distance a guitar softly played, it's eerie tune wafting in on the warm breeze. Her lover stepped up behind her touching the softness of her neck and whispered sweetly into her ear. His breath was light, yet manly and although his language was alien to her, she understood every word he said. They made love, softer and gentler than with the Nordic God but no less passionately, and lay entwined on the large bed. Curiously the part she liked most and the part she dwelt on the longest was, in fact, this post coital embrace. She didn't seem to spend too long on the actual sex part because, and she had been brutally honest with herself here, she didn't know an awful lot about it. Was it that important, she asked herself many times, surely it was the closeness and the love two people felt for each other that were the most important things. Linda was a virgin.

Danny reached down and knocked over his can of lager. He quickly retrieved it and wiped up the little patch of froth on the carpet with the back of his hand.

He was alone because, as it was Saturday night, Sheila had gone clubbing down town. Of course she may not have actually gone down town, she may have gone off somewhere with the supervisor from work that she was shagging. He didn't really care one way or the other. He watched the telly blindly, which actually is the best way to watch Saturday night telly as there is almost always absolutely fuck all worth watching. It's a tradition.

He had earlier flicked between Cilla's Blind Date and an ex Arsenal footballer getting a lad and a lass to see who was the fastest to thread some needles. The winner then went on an all expenses paid holiday to somewhere far away. Well as long as they don't waste the license fee eh. He had missed the lottery show when he had gone into the kitchen to make himself a sandwich and open another can. He was now torn between watching the third repeat of a "classic"

Casualty episode or a riveting re run of an Inspector Morse episode where apparently he would reveal his middle name. Danny hoped it would be Elvis but knew it would be something more intellectual. He sighed and ate his cheese sarnie.

He would normally have gone out on a Saturday, just to the Maggies or the club, if there was a decent turn on, but tonight he didn't feel like it. Truth was he was a bit pissed off that the lads were going away on Monday without him.

He hadn't minded before when they had mentioned it, but now, as it got nearer, he was feeling very left out. They had all been friends as long as he could remember but they were gradually splitting up and he hated it. He had been the first to get married, and what a nightmare that had turned out to be, but he had still gone out with the lads more or less as before. Now Mick was tying the knot and he figured they'd be the kind of couple to have a big family. That would rule Mick out. Jeff was always with a bird, and although it was usually a different one every week, eventually one would pin him down. That just left Ron. Ron didn't go out with many women but he wasn't getting any younger

and as he saw the others settling down was bound to start thinking in that direction. Danny was terrified of being left behind. It wasn't that he had a fear of growing up or moving forward or anything, it was just that he was shit scared he would be left with Sheila. He flicked the channel again and noticed that Casualty had finished. The announcer was saying that after the news, Match of the Day was on. Oh well, he'd watch the football then. He half watched as the newsman told of atrocities in Kosova, murders in

South Africa, earthquakes in Asia and various other disasters to have hit mankind since the six o clock news. "This has been a fun night" he thought as he went to the kitchen for another can. As he shut the fridge he heard the man say something about the lottery results so he grabbed his ticket off the fridge door and stuck his head back into the living room. Two lucky dips, he had, one for him, one for Sheila. They did the same every Saturday. She left him a pound on the kitchen table, he put the money on when he went to football.

"Six" the man said

"fuck it" Danny answered.

"Eight"

"Got that"

"Eleven"

"Got that"

"Twenty seven"

"Got that. That's a tenner"

"Twenty nine"

"Fuck me that's four"

"And thirty seven"

"Yeeeeeessssss"

"And the bonus ball is…"

"Come on you bastard, come on"

"Twenty five"

"Bollocks"

But he was smiling broadly. Five numbers would give him a grand more or less. Not millionaire class but in his financial state anything at all was like, well it was like winning the lottery.

"And early reports suggest there are no jackpot winners" went on the newsreader and Danny punched the air because he knew that would mean his payout would be more. All the divies went up when there wasn't a jackpot payout. He turned and looked in the mirror. He brushed his hair into place with his fingers and winked at himself.

"You are going on holiday pal" he said to the grinning face in the mirror.

Mick and Sue walked past Danny's house on the way to the Maggies. Looking in they could see a light on and assumed he would be out later. They had been a bit quiet with each other all evening. They were both looking forward to the holiday but were a little apprehensive about being apart. They walked slowly, holding hands, each lost in their own thoughts.

"I love you" Mick suddenly said out of the blue. Sue looked slightly taken aback at this sudden declaration of devotion.

"I love you too" she assured him and squeezed his hand.

Mick stopped in his tracks and turned her to face him. "No I really mean it. I really love you" he insisted.

"Mick what's the matter?" she asked concernedly "I know how much you love me and I hope you know how much I love you." She looked deep into his eyes.

"Oh I know that" he laughed "I'm sorry, I'm just being stupid. I…" He paused unsure whether to go on. "… I was thinking about the holiday and how I didn't want anything to happen to spoil what we have."

"What do you mean, spoil anything. How? In what way"

He looked sheepishly at the ground. Despite the dim light she could see he was blushing. "Ya' know" he said "If, like, one of us, ya' know, did something while we were away."

"You big daft soft bleeder" she chided, but she was smiling inside. "I promise, cross my heart, that I won't be going off with any men while I'm away."

He smiled, still blushing.

"There's only one man I've ever fancied and I'll always fancy him till the day I die" and she nuzzled up close and kissed him.

"Me?" he asked innocently.

"You" she said simply and pulled him closer "and if you even think about going with anybody else…" she paused dramatically and kissed him again. Her hands roamed down his shirt and to the front of his jeans. She cradled him and he held his breath as she lovingly whispered "….I'll chop your fucking balls off."

Sunday was a busy day for them all. The girls were all up bright and early and went shopping in Meadowhall, the giant shopping mall only a mile or so from Brinsmarsh. They were after last minute necessities such as lipstick, suntan oil, after sun lotion, chocolate (Linda had insisted as she had heard that it was crap over there) and Tampax. This latter item, although obviously useful for four girls travelling abroad had become a necessity for Claire who, much to her regret, had started her period the night before. The discovery of which had sent the blond Adonis doing a runner. He had offered to see her again when things were a bit better for her but she was feeling a bit pissed off so she told him to

"stick it up his arse" and went home.

The lads did what they did every Sunday morning. They played football.

They played for their local team, Athletico Brinsmarsh, and had done so since they were eighteen. It was a decent side playing in a decent level of Sunday football and, although they had never won anything, they had always been there or there abouts. Their closest shot at the big time had come when they were knocked out in the semi finals of the Montague Cup by the Whiston Warriors. These two were now mortal enemies and their games together were usually blood curdling affairs.

When I say, they all play, I am slightly exaggerating. Danny, as mentioned before, has put on a lot of weight lately, and has now been relegated to the

substitutes bench. He kidded on that it didn't bother him, and the lads teased him over it, but deep down it hurt like hell that he had become a fringe player.

Mick was the regular number nine, playing as an old fashioned centre forward, Jeff was a nippy midfielder with a cultured left foot and Ron was probably the best, and certainly the hardest, centre half in the League. Danny had been the teams flying right back, getting up on the flanks to support and feed the forwards. He could still get up there but it took him a week to get back. His place had been taken in the team by young Duggie Stone, an eighteen year old, who possessed all the speed that Danny used to have. Danny hated him.

Back in Meadowhall, the girls were gathering pace. Try as they might though they couldn't cheer Claire up. She had waited for this holiday for ages and was really looking forward to meeting lots of new men. She had never had a Spaniard and wanted to put that right. Coming on at this late stage was sure to put the dampener on everything.

"Could be worse" tried Ros in an effort to brighten her up a bit.

"Oh yeah, how?" Claire asked sulkily.

"Could be me" finished off Ros, and Sue and Linda laughed lightly along with her.

"Yeah but nobody would ever know, if you know what I mean" Claire cattily answered back. Ros visibly coloured. Sue jumped in before things got out of control "Anyway, there's more to life than just sex." Claire looked up sharply as if to give a dirty answer but Sue jumped in again "and you know that's true so stop pretending, and showing off. If push comes to shove you'll just have to have a few girly nights out with us, won't you, eh." Claire scuffed her foot on the floor and sighed "yeah I suppose so. If all else fails" but she was grinning now. She hooked her arm round Ros' and announced "come on then. I need some shopping therapy. I've only got three bikini's so let's go get some more"

and they all headed off to the nearest shop, with the mood much more convivial.

"What the fuck's up with Danny?" Ron asked Mick as they were getting changed for the match. Mick shook his head. He had noticed it when Danny had called for him earlier. He was very hyper and whistled all the way to the ground. He had even asked Mick about the holiday and that was the first time he had ever actually brought it up. He had asked Mick the name of the hotel they were staying in. Mick had been so taken aback by the sudden interest that he had completely forgotten and for the life of him he couldn't think of it.

"Dun't matter. Jeff'll know" Danny had said and sure enough as soon as they met up with Jeff he had asked him.

"Fuck knows" Mick answered Ron. "Could be drugs" he continued lightly.

"Should have taken some ages ago then" murmured Ron who hadn't seen Danny this happy for a long time. Danny walked past them. He was already changed and had his track suit over his kit. "What's up boys?" he asked.

"Nowt's up with us. What about you. I haven't seen you this chipper for yonks." answered Mick.

"I'm alright. Why?" Danny said, still with the smile on his face. It would take a lot to knock that smile off today.

"Well you're doing my head in with all that fucking whistling for a start" Mick said and Danny laughed at him.

"Nowt wrong wi' being happy is there?" he asked.

"No. But you've been such a miserable twat lately it's a bit worrying"

retaliated Mick. Danny smiled. It was a smug smile that said "Ah but if you knew what I know you'd be smiling too."

"Right you useless set of fucking wankers listen up." Boomed a voice from the doorway and all conversation stopped and everyone moved quickly to their place and sat down quietly. Framed in the door was an enormous giant of a man.

Big Ron Marsden was their manager. He was also the founder of the club.

Twenty odd years ago he had been on a touring holiday in Spain and had found himself in Madrid. He fell in love with the place especially the football ground.

He had come home raving about it and had taken the Brinsmarsh Working Men's Club team and renamed it Athletico Brinsmarsh and entered it into a better league. His one mistake was in the name. Nobody realised at first until the new kits arrived and then some bright spark spotted that as they were now playing in all white perhaps it was Real Madrid that Ron had seen that day not Athletico. Everyone in the changing room that day had laughed and Ron, who wasn't noted for his sense of humour, was not amused. He had hit the clever bastard that had been ridiculing him and broken his jaw. Funnily enough no one had ever mentioned the colour of the kit again. Ron had also elected to spell the name Athletico with an "H" in it reasoning that the Spaniards had probably got it wrong and were just too pig headed to change it. Again nobody argued with him so the name had stayed with them since that day.

Ron had lately taken to wearing sunglasses at all times since he overheard someone comparing him to Big Ron Atkinson. He hadn't heard the full conversation which had actually been "Old Ron, he knows less about football than Big Ron Atkinson" "Ah but he loves his sen about as much as Big Ron".

It was enough for Ron to be compared with the great man and ever since had worn the shades and insisted everybody call him Big Ron. A few weeks earlier he had turned up on the Sunday morning wearing a wig. Ron had been bald most of his adult life and none of the players under him had ever seen him with hair. This didn't prevent him from wearing a rug that he thought made him look the spitting image of his hero. That day he had given his customary pre match talk to the sound of complete silence as every person there stared at what could only be described as a dead rat on his head. Mick had almost mentioned it when he first spotted it as he thought somebody must have slipped it on without Ron knowing but fortunately for him he hadn't and eventually he had realised it was meant to be there. Tears of laughter had gradually run down cheeks as they all battled to hold it back. Tubby Turner, the keeper, had bitten his lip so hard he had drawn blood and had to have two butterfly stitches before the game and Paul Smith (midfield) had literally pissed himself and had to send home for clean shorts and pants.

Now however they were getting used to it a bit although last week it had been particularly windy and Ron had been wearing a wooly hat. At the end he had come into the changing room and removed his hat. Unfortunately he lifted his wig with it and had recited his full aftermatch speech bald. At the end he had walked outside and put his hat back on. Backwards. Later they had all gone to the club for a drink, as usual, and Big Ron had carefully removed his hat, smoothing his hair into place. He had then spent a full lunchtime sitting in the club with his wig on back to front. And not one person told him.

Big Ron barked his orders out as his team sat, to a man, taking in every word. It wasn't that Big Ron gave great team talks, it was just that he always gave the same one, almost word for word. "Get stuck into the bastards. Be first into every tackle and don't come out of it without the ball. If you can't get the ball, get the man. Don't forget, these Bastards think they're better than you so it's up to you to put them right. Now get out there and kick arse."

It wasn't a brilliant speech but the lads all looked forward to hearing it. It was tradition. Everyone smiled, except Danny who, although he looked to be paying attention, was actually going over his plans for the next day.

"Danny, are you listening, you fat bastard?" shouted Big Ron and Danny jumped guiltily "Yes Ron" he spluttered.

"Big Ron" corrected Big Ron.

"Sorry. Big Ron"

"What did I say then?" asked Big Ron

"When?" asked Danny, playing for time.

"Just now"

"You said 'what did I say'"

"Before that"

"You said 'Big Ron'"

"Before that" said Big Ron who was going a shade of purple. Everyone in the small room held their breath. Danny was taking Big Ron close to the edge and with a man with so fragile a temper that was a dangerous thing to do. Ron, who was sat between Danny and where Big Ron stood in the doorway, tensed, ready to spring up and stop Big Ron if his temper suddenly snapped. He was the only one in the room who was capable of doing it too.

"You said" began Danny, taking a deep breath " 'Get stuck into the Bastards.

Be first into every tackle and don't come out of it without the ball. If you can't get the ball, get the man. Don't forget, these bastards think they're better than you, so it's up to you to put them right. Now get out there and kick arse.'"

Danny looked round to see smiling faces and then turned back to Big Ron "or something like that."

Big Ron stared at him angrily. He couldn't make up his mind whether Danny was taking the piss. Not realising that he actually gave the same speech every week, he was impressed with Danny's recall, but that went against his gut instinct that he hadn't been listening at all and was somehow making a fool of him. He decided to let it go. This time.

"Right then. Let's play football" he finished lamely and turned to leave.

"OK Ron" piped up Danny, who was pushing his luck a bit

"Big Ron" shouted back Big Ron without breaking step and he was gone.

Mick grabbed Danny round the head and wrestled him a bit. When they came back up for air Mick said "you're going to push your luck too far one of these days."

Laughing, Danny said "You worry too much Mick. Besides Ron wouldn't let him kick my arse too hard would he."

Ron looked over "Don't you fucking believe it. I wouldn't have stopped him if he'd come steaming over then. I wouldn't have even tried" he lied.

"Yeah sure" countered Danny, who stood up and stretched "Come on then " he suddenly shouted "let's kick arse."

To much cheering and shouts of "Come on Brinsmarsh" and "Up the Brinny"

the players filed out into the sunlight in a waft of liniment. As Jeff came up beside Danny he suddenly grabbed him in a headlock, and Ron, who was now stood behind them, reached over and pulled Danny's tracksuit and shorts to his knees. Whilst Danny screamed, Ron gave a push forward, sending them tumbling out onto the grass, surprising the opposition keeper's wife and two young daughters who were patiently waiting outside. To cheers, Jeff and Ron, ran off to the pitch leaving the half naked Danny to hastily dress himself and apologise to the highly offended trio. It didn't help that at exactly the same moment as Ron and Jeff ran off, the opposition ran out of their changing room.

The first man out, was in fact, the goalkeeper who seeing Danny pulling up his trousers and his wife attempting to cover the little girls eyes, called out to him and chased him round the pitch. Fortunately for Danny, Brinsmarsh won the game easily and, claiming a slight groin strain, Danny wasn't called off the subs bench so the keeper or his mates weren't able to exact any revenge. At the end of the game Danny hastily changed and made his getaway to the club, where he felt safer.

Ten minutes later the rest of the lads trooped in and ordered drinks. Some went to the snooker table but most congregated round the dart board. Danny was in the middle of them when Big Ron came in looking perplexed. "What's up Ron?" asked Mick when he saw him. "Big Ron" corrected Big Ron. "Sorry"

smiled Mick. "What's up Big Ron?" Big Ron scratched his head, which moved his wig to one side, causing furious nudging between the watching players as they all tried not to laugh. "There's a couple of coppers in the foyer asking if anyone saw the flasher up on the pitches earlier. I didn't see anything but they're coming in here to see you lot." Danny's face went white." Fuck me"

Ron said "they must mean you" looking at Danny. Danny went even whiter.

"It's your fault, you bastard" he accused Ron. "Sorry" was Ron's only offer.

"They've got a description. Short, fat with a small nob, but that might be down to the cold eh" Big Ron was telling Mick and Danny almost argued back, ready to defend himself on the last item if not the first two. "You ought to just leave"

Ron was saying to Danny. "We'll cover for you" Danny thought about it and nodded "Yeah. I think you're right" and he quickly downed his pint and made for the door. "Not that way" shouted Ron "they'll see you." Danny searched the room and spotted the emergency exit. Gratefully he pushed it open and Ron, who was right behind him called "Straight home. No flashing" as he

closed the doors behind him. He turned to the laughing faces of his mates.

"He's getting easier" he laughed and they all cheered and then went about their normal Sunday lunchtime business of having a few pints and a game. "When will you tell him we were having him on" asked Big Ron. "Tonight probably,"

Mick answered "we're all going to the Maggies tonight. Sort of a leaving do before our holidays."

"I wouldn't have thought Danny would be bothered with that. He's not going with you is he?" Big Ron asked between sips.

"No, he's not. Funny that. I thought he'd have the dolls on but he insisted on coming tonight." It seemed strange to Mick and he had been trying to work it out all day. Danny hadn't mentioned the holiday for ages and now he didn't shut up about it. Maybe he was up to something, but for the life of him he couldn't think what.

CHAPTER FOUR

Sunday night was always a good night in Brinsmarsh. The club usually had a good turn on and The Maggies had a disco, which for years had been hosted by Derek Dodd of Derek Dodds Disco fame. Derek had the monopoly on all the local disco's due to a bewildering lack of competition, which was fortunate for Derek because he was crap.

For as long as they could remember the four lads had gone to the Maggies on a Sunday night. Occasionally they had preceded their visit with a trip to the club but they always ended up back at the Maggies. Over the years they had met girls there, taken girls with them, fallen out with girls and avoided girls.

Sunday night at the Maggies was always full of girls. Tonight, however, they had all been ordered to be on their best behaviour as Sue was fetching her friends for a night out before their trip early next morning.

Around eight o clock Mick walked in accompanied by Sue and Linda. Linda had been many times before of course, as she lived in Brinsmarsh, and she waved happily to some girls she knew as they filed through into the tap room,

which is where they usually started as it was a bit quieter in there and they could all have a chat. Jeff was already there and he waved them over to a table he had been saving under the window in the corner. The girls went straight to him and Mick went to the bar.

"Hello Jeff" said Sue, kissing him on the cheek. "You know Linda don't you?".

"Only from school" he answered and reached across and shook her hand "You were in the year below me I think" he smiled to her. Linda blushed furiously.

She knew Jeff, of course, by reputation but although they lived in the same village their lives were totally different, and their paths had been unlikely to cross. She was now very flattered that he remembered her from school and she didn't know what to say back. She giggled.

"Yeah" he continued easily "you had a gorgeous mate you used to knock about with. All the lads used to fancy her. Oh what was her name?" Linda felt crushed and coloured up even more to highlight her embarrassment. "I think it must have been Sue" she said meekly and Jeff turned to Sue, smiling. "So it was" he said softly and looked deep into her eyes.

"I hope you're not flirting with my missus" warned Mick as he sat down, placing four bottles of Bud on the table.

"I was" smiled Jeff lightly "and I was doing alright too." Sue smiled easily and looked across to Mick who winked at her. They were both used to Jeff and his non stop flirting. He couldn't help it, and he meant no harm and in any case Sue rather enjoyed it.

Mick took a swig from his bottle and looked round the room. "Full tonight" he commented. "What time are the others coming.?"

"Eight o clock" answered Sue and Ros and Claire entered as she spoke. Sue waved to them and they waved back and stopped off at the bar before joining them. Ros had a Bacardi Breezer and Claire a glass of wine. As they sat down Mick did the introductions. "Ros, Claire, this is Jeff" he turned, to indicate Jeff who was staring at Claire with his mouth open.

"Hello" Ros and Claire said in unison.

"Huh" grunted Jeff.

"Nice one Mister Smooth" laughed Mick and Jeff quickly pulled himself together. "Sorry" he said "miles away there. Hello I'm Jeff" and he offered his hand. Claire shook it warmly, used to men's attentions. "Claire" she reciprocated. Jeff held her hand and looked into her eyes.

"Ros" offered Ros, holding out her hand.

"Hello Ros" answered Jeff without releasing Claire's hand or taking his eyes off hers. Ros sighed and put her hand back down.

"Do you fancy a dance Claire.?" Jeff asked and Claire nodded so they both got up and went into the other room just as Danny entered with Sheila.

"I didn't know Sheila was coming tonight" Sue said to Mick.

"Nor me" he answered, shrugging his shoulders.

Danny got their drinks and they wandered over. After introductions Sue said

"What brings you here then Sheila, we don't usually see you here on a Sunday"

"No" she replied, taking out her chewing gum and dropping it into the ash tray.

She took a drink from her Vodka Source and continued, all the time looking

around her in a bored fashion. "I don't usually bother as a rule but to be honest I'm skint so it's a toss up between staying in and watching telly or going out with fat boy here. Telly lost". Sue nodded and for the life of her couldn't think of anything else to say. Danny smiled uneasily, praying that Sheila wouldn't show him up too much. He was gobsmacked when she had told him she was coming with him. It was the first time they had been out together for months.

Danny suddenly remembered something and spun round to Mick "Yes you Bastard. Don't think I don't know about this afternoon. I knew all along that there wasn't a copper outside."

Mick laughed out loud. "You lying Bastard. Why'd you run off then, through the fire exit."

Danny coloured up "I was late for me dinner"

Sheila snorted. "Yeah, like I'm gonna sit at home making your dinner"

Danny coloured up even more. He didn't want the lads to think that he didn't have a normal home life where the little lady served up Sunday Roasts. It had never occurred to Mick that Sheila would sit at home and cook Sunday Roasts but Danny had a very distorted view of what his friends thought of his circumstances. They all actually saw it for what it was, a sham of a marriage where they pretty much lived their own lives, but they would never say anything to Danny about it. As long as he kept up the pretence then so would they. Danny, for his part, thought that they all believed he had a good marriage so kept up the charade so as to avoid the shame of admitting it all to them. He decided to change the subject so he asked Linda if she was looking forward to the holiday. Linda nodded and was about to answer when Sheila butted in "I'm sick of hearing about this fucking holiday. He's not even going and he hasn't shut up about it all afternoon." Mick looked at Danny curiously and saw him blush slightly. He was definitely up to something.

Ron came in then and walked over carrying a Bud. After the obligatory introductions Ron looked at Mick and moved his eyes slightly towards Sheila as if to say "What's she doing here?" Mick shrugged his shoulders slightly answering "I haven't got a fucking clue".

"Where's Jeff?" asked Ron, looking round the packed room.

"Dancing with Claire" Sue answered and they smiled at each other.

Over the next half hour or so everything went along in the same sort of vein, with pleasantry meeting pleasantry and, apart from Sheila's acerbic put downs to Danny, they all got along pretty well. Jeff and Claire rejoined them after a while and Jeff fetched her a fresh drink and stroked her hair and was generally very attentive. Conversations varied and often several topics were ongoing at the same time. The girls had just started gossiping about George Clooney and some news that had been in the paper that day about him and the lads had moved on, as ever, to football. They had watched the match that afternoon on Sky and were discussing the merits of player rotation at Manchester United who had thrashed their lowly opposition that day without really stepping up a gear. Ron held the opinion that Roy Keane was the key to United's superiority whereas Jeff held the view that it was the balance of the side that made them invincible. "You watch" he was saying "whenever Ryan Giggs is out, they look

lopsided and teams get in amongst them too fast." "Yeah" opined Ron "but it's the engine room where all the hard work is done. That's where Keane gets it.

He never stops for the full ninety minutes." They all nodded. They couldn't argue with that although Jeff still preferred his assertion that Giggsy was the key man. "Listen" offered Ron, obviously warming to his theme "I had Sky interactive on, and for fifteen minutes they had the player cam on Roy Keane and, straight up, at the end I was knackered. The man never stopped. He was everywhere"

Claire, who had been nudging up close to Jeff for a while now, had tired of listening to the girls idle chit chat had turned her attention to the boys. Not that she was interested in football, it was just to get a bit nearer to Jeff. "How do they do that?" she asked, and the lads turned to her, surprised at her joining in.

"Do what?" asked Jeff, keen to get in her good books. Claire looked beautiful tonight and Jeff was already making plans for later. And now it seemed she had an interest in football. He could love this girl if she played her cards right.

"How do they get the player cam on the player. Do they wear it on their head" she asked sweetly "or do they carry it round with them." She thought for a moment. "It would put them off wouldn't it" and then she brightened as a thought struck her. "If I was playing, I'd just wait until it was the other teams goalie's turn to carry it, then I'd shove everyone forward. It's bound to be easier when he's carrying a camera round with him." She stopped then, pleased with herself for sorting out the boys and showing them how easy it would be to win at their silly little game. The lads looked at each other and then at Claire, to see if she was joking. Then Mick tactfully asked Sue if she wanted to dance and Jeff and Ron asked Claire and Ros. Danny turned to Sheila who stopped him in his tracks with "Don't be so fucking stupid. Just go and get the drinks in. Better get Linda one seeing as she's been left on her own again." She leant across to Linda "Still can't get a bloke eh love, try dressing up a bit more.

Ditch the duffel coat. Lose a bit of weight and put some lippy on. There's bound to be some daft bastard out there who would take you on." Sheila was a firm believer in the motto "You have to be cruel to be kind." She also firmly believed that sometimes you just had to be cruel.

Ron, much to his amazement, was enjoying himself dancing with Ros. They weren't throwing themselves around or anything, just nice and steady, and they talked together non stop. After a couple of numbers, he moved in closer and they held each other, talking all the while. Later, Mick fetched Linda in from the other side and he and Ron took it in turns to have a dance with her. Danny and Sheila eventually wandered through and did manage one dance but they had a bit of a barney after that and Sheila stormed off in a huff. Danny didn't say anything to the others but he had caught her giving the eye to some lad and had asked her not to embarrass him in front of his friends. She had leant close to him and whispered into his ear that "he could stick his precious friends up his arse" and gone off to the ladies. Danny walked over to his friends and picked his drink up. He studiously avoided making eye contact, which was easy because, as they had all seen Sheila storm off, they were all doing the same.

Ros seemed to make a decision and picked up her handbag and excused herself.

The recently decorated washroom was almost empty, there was just one girl looking in the mirror, adjusting her make up. Ros smiled an acknowledgement and joined her at the mirror. Ros finished applying her lipstick and returned it to her bag. She walked to the first stall and pushed gently at the door. It swayed open easily. She repeated this with the next stall, but the third was locked. She tapped gently on the door.

"What" said a snuffly voice from behind the door. "This one's taken." Ros recognised the voice and answered it. "Are you alright Sheila? It's me, Ros."

"As if you care" the voice snuffled back. Ros thought a moment. "Well I don't really. But we all saw you storm off the dance floor and no one else was going to come and see if you were alright so I thought I had better do it" she said with brutal honesty. She heard more snuffling noises from behind the door and that noise that people make when they try to laugh while still crying and snot and tears shoot out together and they try to snuffle them up again. Snotgozzling I think it's called. Eventually Sheila found her voice "Thanks for the tact. I feel a lot better now." "Look" said Ros "let's go get a drink in the tap room. We can talk. I don't think they'll bother fetching us for a while." After a few moments there was the sound of peeing and then the rustle of clothes and then with a flush of the toilet, Sheila appeared, looking a bit smudged round the eyes. Ros smiled at her and Sheila stared back.

"Why?" asked Sheila.

"Why not" answered Ros which shut Sheila up. She adjusted her make up in the mirror and they went out together to the tap room and ordered drinks. Most people had gone in the best side so it was much quieter now and they found a table easily. They sat down, uncomfortable in each others company and were unsure what to say next. Sheila broke the ice in her own blunt way. "I've known you since we were at school and this is the first time you've ever wanted to talk to me." she said. Ros took a sip from her drink. "We never hung around with the same crowd of people" she said simply and Sheila jumped in.

"That's because you all looked down your noses at me and my kind." Ros took another drink and thought about it for a while. "True" she said and then

"Sorry".

"Oh don't bother apologising now. I'm a big girl, I can take care of myself" she responded angrily and loudly. Drinkers at a nearby table stopped talking and listened. "It was back then you should have apologised. God I wanted to be like you lot so much it hurt" She was letting it all out now and the release of pent up emotion felt good. "But you set of snobby bitches wouldn't lower yourselves to bother with the likes of me, would you, eh" she challenged and Ros flushed visibly and looked around her at the other drinkers. The eavesdropping neighbours all pretended to be doing something else until she turned away from them and they immediately stopped and continued their earwigging. "No we wouldn't I guess. However I do recall speaking to you on the end of your street and you bit my head off." She said and Sheila thought back. She did remember it. She had been hanging out with her friends, smoking, on the street corner.

Most of them had either left school and were unemployed or were still in

school but never bothered to go. She remembered being embarrassed when this

"posh bird" as her friends had called her, had spoken to her in a friendly manner and because of peer pressure had snapped out something which she had thought witty but which was just cruel. The tall elegant young lady in the immaculate school uniform had legged it, afraid and hurt by this sudden display of anger. Sheila visibly softened and even smiled to Ros "Yeah I'm sorry as well." She offered "It's a kind of defence mechanism, only I like to get my revenge in first." Ros smiled back at her and the animosity between them seemed to disappear a bit.

"You and Danny" ventured Ros, feeling more at ease now "I know this might sound nosey, but is everything alright."

"You're right it does sound nosey, but seeing as you asked, no everything is not alright. Well spotted"

"Is it just tonight or are you always like this" Ros persisted.

"Bleedin' hell. Are you always like this. I'm glad we didn't become friends at school now. I'd have had to give you a right good hiding"

Ros blushed furiously. "I'm terribly sorry. I didn't mean to be so nosey. I can't help it sometimes, I just seem to get involved in other peoples troubles. I'm sorry" and she picked up her bag and made to leave.

"No. Sit down" ordered Sheila and Ros stopped halfway out of her chair. The people at the next table leant forward to get a better view of things and Ros coloured up even more. "I'm sorry" said Sheila "and if I've coloured up like you, we're going to look like a set of Christmas tree lights" and they both laughed, the tension gone. Sheila continued, loudly, "And if these earwigging twats don't stop noseying into my conversation I'm going to shove one of these bottles right up their arse" and she toyed with a bottle that was on the table.

The group at the next table immediately became locked in conversation with each other as if the thought of listening to other people was an alien concept to them. Sheila smiled at Ros and Ros smiled back. Feeling better, Sheila then proceeded to tell Ros why she was so pissed off with Danny.

In the best side Mick returned from the bar and sidled up closely to Sue.

"Looks like Ros and Sheila are having a nice heart to heart" he said, nodding towards the tap room.

"Really" exclaimed Sue "Ros and Sheila. Now that's a combination you don't see every day. At school Ros was terrified of Sheila and her gang"

"Maybe she's going to glass her now she's got her on her own" he laughed

"Maybe" said Sue thoughtfully. They looked across the dancefloor at Claire and Jeff.

"What do you make of those two?" asked Mick

"Well, knowing Claire, they'll be in bed together in an hour or two, even though she's supposed to be staying at Ros'. If she takes him back to Ros', she'll go do lally."

"Why's she staying with Ros" he asked.

"Well, in case you've forgotten my love, we're off on holiday in the morning and Claire staying at Ros' saves her an extra journey then"

"Oh yeah" he smiled "A holiday. I'd forgotten all about that." He looked back to Jeff and Claire, who seemed to be sharing the same skin, they were dancing so close. "He's definitely getting it tonight" he said and Sue nodded in agreement "If he gets any closer" she said "he'll be getting it now."

Ron and Danny came up to them. Danny had a concerned look on his face.

"They're a long time in the bog" shouted Danny. "Do you think you ought to go in and have a look at them?." he asked Sue.

"No need" she said "they're in the tap room having a drink".

"What" he screamed, a terrified look replacing the concerned one. "What do you think they're talking about?"

"Perhaps they're swapping knitting patterns" suggested Ron

"Or perhaps Ros is giving Sheila tips on how to keep a man happy in the bedroom" smiled Mick. Sue frowned at him and then at Ron.

"Or perhaps" she began, and picked up her bag and drink "they're talking about what a set of Bastards men can be when they want" and she marched off to the tap room.

"I suppose I do love him still, in my own way," Sheila was saying, almost wistfully "But I'll never forgive him for that morning after our wedding. Never.

He hurt me and I've been hurting him back ever since, the Bastard". She pulled heavily on a cigarette. They were quiet for a while as Ros collected her thoughts. "But" she began and then stopped. It was alright having a little one to one chat with Sheila but Ros was well aware that her temper could snap at any moment. She looked round and decided she was near enough to the door to make a run for it if she started.

"But" repeated Sheila, through a haze of smoke which made Ros cough. They had talked for about ten minutes during which time Sheila had told Ros the full story of her and Danny's wedding and its terrible conclusion the next morning and how Sheila had decided to make him pay for his cruelty.

"But he hurt you unintentionally" she blurted out and subconsciously she grabbed her handbag in readiness for a quick escape. "His was just a knee jerk reaction to what, for him, must have seemed a terrible betrayal. Whereas you.."

77

she paused then decided to go on "..have set about to systematically hurt him emotionally and physically ever since. You have never given him a chance to explain or to make amends or to justify or defend himself. You have belittled him behind his back and embarrassed him to his face. You have humiliated him in every way you could think of and all the time you have been having the time of your life and now you have the gall to sit there and say you love him in your own way. To be honest I don't know how you've got the nerve." Ros stopped now, fully aware that she had gone too far. The people on the next table picked up their drinks and hurried to the other room, rushing past Sue who had just come through the door.

"Hello you two" she said breezily "What are you chatting away about eh. Boys I bet eh" and she sat down with a forced grin on her face. They both stared at her.

Sheila suddenly snatched at her cigs and lighter and put them in her bag. She stood up to go. "Listen Snow White and Cinderfuckin'rella. This is the real world. You" and she pointed at Sue. "might think you've found Prince Charming but he'll shit on you just the same. And you" and she turned to Ros who leant back despite herself, "Want to mind your own fucking business and get a fucking life. Get a man, you sad old spinster and stop being so jealous of those that can get one whenever we want" Tears ran down her face and there was a catch in her throat as she picked up her drink and flounced out of the room.

Ros and Sue stared at each other for a while, not sure what to do or say.

Eventually Sue said "I only said hello".

Ros took a big drink and was going to stand up but her legs felt weak so she sat back down. "It must have been the way you said it" she said and smiled weakly.

At the end of the night they all marched off together, except for Danny and Sheila who had left when Sheila suddenly stormed into the best side and ordered Danny to take her home. Danny thought about putting up a fight in an attempt to regain a little self respect, but thought better of it, as he knew she would just get some other poor sod to take her.

As they reached the end of Atlas Road, Ron offered to walk with Ros, as Jeff and Claire had gone on in front never giving her a second thought. Mick, Sue and Linda waved them goodnight and went up the hill.

They walked in silence for a while until Ros broke the ice. "So you're Mick's best man then?"

"Yes" he answered.

"What about the other two, don't they mind?"

Ron thought for a while. "No" he replied.

"And is your speech full of these witty one liners?." She asked.

Ron turned and looked at her. He coloured up and hoped she couldn't see it in the dark.

"I'm sorry" she said. "I've embarrassed you, you've gone all red. Take no notice of me. I seem to be always saying the wrong thing lately."

Ron stopped walking and she turned to face him. "No" he said "It's me who should apologise. You were just making conversation. I er I didn't mean to be rude it's just that I sometimes, well I get a bit tongue tied talking to girls". He examined his shoes in the light of the street light and avoided her gaze. He was wondering why he had just told her that. He had never said that before to a girl, or anyone else for that matter. They stayed like that for a while until Ros put her arm through his and said "Come on then, loves great young things will be worrying about us"

"They won't even notice we're missing" he laughed easily.

"They will in a minute, Claire hasn't got a key" and Ron smiled broadly and walked on proudly with her on his arm. It had dawned on him that he enjoyed Ros' company and, and this surprised him, he found her very attractive.

"If only I wasn't gay" he thought.

The next morning was spent in a blur of activity for everyone. Mick and Sue were up, showered and fed early doors and were sat having a cup of tea with Sue's mum until Mick suddenly realised he hadn't packed any shorts or trunks so they all ran around trying to find them. When that was cleared up and they resumed their cup of tea until he, red faced, admitted he had forgotten underwear as well. Nellie tut tutted and Sue shouted at him as she opened his case to discover he had also forgotten toiletries, which were in a nice new bag in the bathroom, and two new shirts which were still in the bag he had bought them in, in their bedroom.

Ron was up early too, as he hadn't started his packing yet. However it was all done and dusted in less than ten minutes, mainly because his mum had laid everything out for him in neat piles. He didn't even check it, just folded it up neatly into his case and zipped it up.

Jeff was late getting up, but then he had been late getting to bed. He had spent a very good night with Claire and although he hadn't had sex, because she had

"got the painters in" as she had so delicately put it, they had come pretty close and he knew it was only a matter of time before they went all the way.

Ros was up really early as she had loads of last minute checks to do. She also cooked two full breakfasts for her and Claire, who just stared at hers and drank her tea. Claire herself was up late despite Ros shouting her every five minutes.

She had enjoyed her night out with Jeff and although they hadn't had full sex because, as he had said, "hey up Rotherhams at home" she knew it would only be a matter of time.

Linda's mum woke her up early with a cup of tea in bed. She had only just got to sleep, what with all the excitement, and couldn't wait for the off. When she got downstairs, the house was nice and cosy. The fire was on full, and a full breakfast on the table. As she sat at the table, wrapped in a big furry dressing gown, covering her flannelette pyjama's and fluffy slippers on her feet, her Dad sat in his favourite chair, by the fire, smoking his pipe and reading his paper.

As usual he didn't say much, just watched her with great affection as she tucked heartily into her bacon, sausage, egg, beans and tomatoes, and not for the first time, found himself wondering where she got her appetite from. Both himself and his wife were of smaller build than Linda. "Costs me a bloody fortune" he muttered lightly as he shook his head and returned to the paper.

Danny had been laid awake for ages but had pretended to be asleep each time Sheila came into the bedroom. He waited, impatiently, until he heard her close the door behind her as she left for work, then jumped out of bed. He danced all the way to the bathroom, where he washed and shaved, then all the way back to the bedroom where he dressed. He pulled a small football kit bag from the cubby hole, which was supposed to be a walk in wardrobe but was in fact filled with all the junk they had accumulated over the years. He pulled out his football boots and shinpads and peered inside to make sure it was empty. He spotted an evil smelling jockstrap in the corner and wondered idly how long it

had been there as he tossed it on the bed. He moved across to the wardrobe and looked inside for something "summery" to wear. He

81

picked out one decent shirt and a pair of lightweight trousers. "That's the evening wear" he thought

"Better get something for the day". One T shirt and a pair of football shorts later he was ready. Downstairs he found a pair of trainers, which he put on and the loafers he had worn the previous evening, which he stuffed into his bag. As he shut the cupboard door he spotted, hiding at the back, a pair of flip flops.

"Perfect" he said out loud "evening, daywear and the beach. I'm just a lean mean holiday machine" and he spun round and moonwalked in a crap Michael Jackson impression. "Passport" he suddenly shouted and went back upstairs in search of it. He found it, half an hour later, in a carrier bag stuffed full of old photos which, despite himself, he couldn't resist skimming through. Eventually he put the past away and stood at the end of the bed. "Something else" he thought, then cracked into a big smile. "Money". He walked over to the big vanity unit that had been his mums pride and joy when she was alive and reached behind the swinging mirror on the top. He had very cleverly taped the lottery ticket to the back of the mirror, very cleverly reasoning that, as Sheila didn't clean up much anyway, there was no reason for her to swing the mirror round revealing the back. He turned the mirror over and gave a little girly scream when he saw the ticket was gone. He turned the mirror the right way and stared at it then turned it back again in the faint hope that in the last few seconds he had turned into Paul Daniels and could make it reappear. Bastard.

He moved nearer to the mirror and peered over the back. "Please God Please"

he repeated under his breath and his eyes lit up as he saw the lost ticket leant up against the skirting board. Reaching over he found his arms weren't long enough so he pulled the dresser out and crawled round it. He quickly examined the ticket and was satisfied everything was in order so he slipped it into his back pocket. One of the few advantages of being overweight was that as your jeans are so tight nothing ever falls out of the pockets. Danny patted his concealed ticket like an off duty Asda worker and decided he had better get a move on. He went back downstairs and picked up the phone. He dialled the operator and asked for the B A desk at Manchester Airport. Once he was through to them he asked about flights out to Alicante that day and was told there were seats available on a late afternoon flight. The lady agreed to hold him a seat until he could reach a travel agent that morning and pay for it. Now all he had to do was get to Rotherham and cash in his ticket at the post office.

Later that morning, on a crowded minibus winging it's way over the Stocksbridge bypass Mick turned to Sue and over the awful row of several terrible voices singing along to The Verve on the radio, said "I still feel rotten about Danny. I mean where was he this morning." "I don't know love. Perhaps he'd gone out." she suggested.

"Nah. Too early. Nobody goes out at that time of morning unless they have to.

And Danny doesn't." he moped.

"Wasn't Sheila in?" asked Ron behind him.

"No she's on days" he turned and answered.

"Perhaps he was still in bed then."

"No. I banged on the door. He would have heard me."

"Well perhaps he didn't want to" offered Ros who was sat next to Ron.

"That's what worries me. He might have been in bed, pissed off that everybody's left him." He turned to Ron and with a worried look on his face asked "You don't think he'd do owt stupid do you.?"

Ron thought a minute then shook his head "No. He's daft but not that daft.

He'll be sulking somewhere but no, he'll not do owt stupid."

Danny stretched his legs and rubbed them vigorously. He was in a toilet cubicle in McDonalds in Rotherham. He had been there thirty minutes now except for two occasions when he had peeped through the door to see if they had gone yet.

He looked at his watch anxiously and stamped his foot a little. "Come on you Bastards" he thought, and not for the first time. If they didn't leave soon, he was going to have to make a move. He glanced at his watch again and raised his eyes to heaven.

When he had arrived in town earlier, he had discovered he had an hour to kill before the post office opened. He had worked out that he was cutting it fine to cash the ticket, buy his airline ticket and get the train, but if nothing went wrong he could just about make it. He had decided to call in at McDonalds and have some breakfast while he waited as he had a gippy tummy, which he put down to the excitement of his little adventure. He had ordered his breakfast and coffee and devoured them. Ten minutes later he had ordered another coffee and then another. He was debating having a fourth or opting for a milk shake when nature called and the rumbling in his guts told him it was now or never, so he had sloped off to the toilet leaving his bag on his seat. It was as he was leaving the lavs that his problems started. He had turned the corner, looking at his watch, and deciding it was time to go when he had spotted, coming through the door, Sheila's two brothers. He had quickly retraced his steps and had been in the cubicle ever since. He had thought about just going out and facing them but he knew from bitter experience what a pair of Bastards these two were. He was sure that they would balls his plans up if they could, maybe even follow him to the post office and see him get his cash. He was sure that would be an end to it.

They would either just take the money from him and give it to Sheila or march him round to the nut factory and make him explain why he hadn't told her about it straight away. Of course

Danny knew that if he got away with this and went to Spain it was only for the week and then he would have to come back and face the music, which would undoubtedly include a good hiding from his wife's siblings but he had shoved that to the back of his mind. He had convinced himself it was worth it. Besides he genuinely believed that after all the shit he had taken from her and her family he deserved this. Fuck 'em. He looked at his watch again and made up his mind. He had to go now or his timings were all thrown to cock and he might miss the plane. Taking a deep breath he opened the cubicle door and crept to the outer one. He hesitated and then thought "sod it" and opened the door to reveal her brothers reaching for the door handle to enter. He emitted a little squeak and stepped back. Although no smile or, in fact any visible expression showed itself in their expression,

Danny did see a light of recognition in their eyes as, without even breaking stride, they bundled him backwards into the washroom.

"Ah Edward" he muttered to the eldest brother who already had him by the throat and was forcing him backwards over the sink. "Edward?" he asked in a growly sort of voice. Danny cursed himself under his breath. Ever since their intervention into his life, when they turned up with Garden Shears and Baseball Bat he had thought of them as Edward Scissorhands and Babe Ruth for a while now but he had never said the names to their faces. Until now. "Bill" he said uneasily as the strangle hold tightened. He tried to look over his attackers'

shoulder and could just see his other brother in law scowling at him. "Ben" he offered as if introductions all round were de rigeur in McDonalds washrooms when you are being strangled by nutty in laws.

Bill and Ben. What were their mum and dad thinking of eh. Didn't they have any sort of idea what sort of a life they were offering someone by naming two brothers Bill and Ben. They must have been ribbed mercilessly at school.

Maybe that's why they were such Bastards now. Maybe the ritual humiliation they received had turned them into the psychopathic scum they were today.

Maybe that's why their Dad did it. Like Johnny Cash's Boy named Sue, maybe the father did it to make them stronger as he knew that he was likely to spend a lot of time in jail, him being a thief, mugger and all round twat and all that, so he had given them these names to make them learn at an early age how to stand on their own two feet. The truth, of course, was slightly different. Bill and Ben's mum and dad had no imagination whatsoever and had simply given them names that were easy to remember, and spell. It was only at the Christening of Ben, the youngest, that someone had remarked on the high comic potential of naming your two boys after the most famous Flower Pot Men in history that they had realised what they had done. This resulted in the unfortunate sight of the silly young man who had first noticed the link being stretchered off to hospital where he spent the next two months in recuperation and the boys father being dragged off to jail where he spent the next six months in solitary.

Family parties eh. Tchh.

Bill (or Edward) held him tightly over the sink and pressed down hard on the collar of his denim jacket choking off any complaints. Danny could smell his breath and it was horrible. He wondered what McDonalds sold that could make anyone's breath that fetid. A Big Mac FishDogshitGarlicNoFuckin'toothpaste Burger perhaps.

"What the fuck are you doing 'ere" Bill growled in a threatening manner that for him could pass as polite interest. Danny opened his mouth but nothing came out. He tapped his throat, indicating he couldn't speak. Bill (Edward) loosened his grip a millimetre and Danny found himself able to converse. Danny rightly assumed that Bill had done this sort of thing before. Always better to deal with professionals.

"Shopping" he wheezed through the small gap he had been allowed. Bill thought a moment, his brain slowly ticking over. "Early!" he exclaimed but his grip loosened a little more. Danny, feeling a little more confident, smiled what he thought was an easy all mates together smile. Bill visibly backed off at this

terrifying grimace. He immediately released the jacket from his steely grip, thinking he had gone too far and Danny was dying. Sheila would kill him if he accidentally murdered her husband. Danny felt the blood rush to his head and he stood up and straightened his clothing. He felt fully vindicated in the use of his friendly smile. "It's much better to be nice to people than to be violent. It always works" he thought.

Now he was released and able to look them straight in the eye, Danny didn't feel too bad. His confidence and cockyness that he had felt earlier returned and he felt able to handle the Brothers Dim. "What brings you two lads down here then?" he asked chirpily and was truly amazed when Bill grabbed him by the collar again. Bill had realised of course that Danny wasn't dying so had decided to revert back to terror tactics. It didn't always get results but it was much more fun. "I asked first" he stated and Danny couldn't argue with that.

Not if he knew what was good for him. "Birthday present" he blurted out without really thinking it through. "Whose?" demanded his assailant.

"Sheila's" he squeaked. The response was immediate. Bill released his grip and stared into Danny's eyes as if he had just heard that the world was ending.

Terror. No, Sheer Terror gripped him. He turned to his brother who Danny could see was in much the same state. "Have you bought her something?" he asked needlessly and was rewarded with a glum shake of the head. "Shit" he said simply. Thoughts were whirring around his head but he didn't have any control of them. Danny watched, fascinated at the torture on the faces of his two adversaries. "Boots" announced Bill and the younger brother

87

beamed from ear to ear at this piece of brilliant thinking from his much revered elder. Boots the chemist was perfect. They could get her some of those nice smellys, in the big boxes. Ben liked shopping in Boots, the smells were all so nice and ladylike. Sheila always smelled nice, not like his mum who stank of fag ash and chips. They had once bought her smellys for Christmas but she had thrown them in the bin and made them go out and rob a tobacconist's for some fags.

On Christmas day. Mums eh. Anyway it would be nice to go into Boots and get warm and enjoy the nice smells. "Come on" ordered Bill who was turning to leave. "Let's find a shoe shop" "Why?" asked Ben, genuinely puzzled.

"For the Boots" answered Bill, irritated that his younger brother never seemed to pay attention. "What' ya think I meant. Boots the fuckin' chemist" he said sarcastically and roared with laughter. Embarrassed Ben looked at his feet and then at Danny who tactfully looked away. "No" he wittily retorted. "Come on then" Big brother ordered and they both rushed out of the lavs and out of sight.

Danny turned to the mirror and straightened himself up. "Don't rush lads" he said to his reflection. "It's not for another eight months" His reflection smiled back but looked over his shoulder just in case they returned. He felt his stomach churning so he went back in the cubicle and had a good clear out and walked out with a smile on his face. Which was very different to the expression of the next person in there.

He crossed over Corporation Street and onto Millgate and as he turned the corner he could see people entering the post office. As casual as he could he ran into the post office and was disgusted to see there was a queue already

forming. He stood behind an old man carrying a bag. A bag. Shit, he had left his bag in McDonalds. He turned round and ran back up the road. He entered the shop and spotted his bag where he had left it. As he retrieved it he heard an old man complaining loudly about the drains in the toilet. "It's seeping through the door now." He moaned. The assistant Manager, a bright spotty youth aged about ten, went in to take a look but returned a few seconds later with tears streaming from his eyes. "Better phone DynaRod" he coughed "It's terrible in there" Danny decided now was a good time to beat a hasty retreat so he picked up his bag and left, holding his nose and tut tutting at the terrible stench. "Sorry Sir" called the Assistant Manager. Danny waved back as if to say "It's alright.

It's not your fault" which , of course, it wasn't. "Have a nice day" the spotty youth shouted as he opened the big glass door. "I will pal, I will" he muttered as he went out into the sunshine.

Ten minutes later, after queuing for the wrong window, he had been directed to the correct spot. To his utter disgust he discovered that he needn't have queued at all as the lottery window was separate from the rest of the post office. He looked around him and realised that his only exit was back through the maze of ropes that are standard requirements in all post offices. "It's like Hampden Fuckin' Park" he muttered to himself as he climbed over the ropes instead of walking through them. I think he actually meant to say Hampton Court but he was close. "Pardon" old woman barked nearby. "Nothing" he muttered and rushed to the lottery desk.

"Can I help you Sir" said an attractive young assistant.

"I want to cash this winning ticket please" he announced grandly then immediately thought better of it and looked round sheepishly. The three or four old fogeys that were there to cash their pensions just carried on as if they hadn't heard, which they probably hadn't as they were all deaf. He turned back to the pretty assistant and smiled winningly. The girl took the proffered ticket and ran it through the machine. Danny held his breath.

"Two Thousand Five Hundred and Eight Pounds and Eighty pence. It's a good payout this week isn't it. How would you like it" Danny swallowed. This was more than he had dared hope for.

Even Sheila wouldn't begrudge him having part of this would she. Eh.

"How can I have it" he asked through dry lips.

"You can have a cheque for the full amount or One Thousand Pounds in cash and the rest in a cheque." She smiled sweetly.

"Cash and cheque please" he smiled back. He collected and recounted the cash and pocketed it then put the cheque in an envelope along with a post office compliment slip upon which he wrote "See you next week- Love Danny". He wrote Sheila's name and their address on the envelope, put a first class stamp on it and posted it in the little post box outside. Next he ran round the corner to the travel agents and, apologising for being late, he paid for his ticket and was back on the street in less than three minutes. He slipped the ticket into his bag and headed off to the station. Bus to Sheffield. Train to Manchester. Plane to Spain. Life is good.

CHAPTER FIVE

At the airport Mick and the others checked in then, having an hour to kill before their flights, decided to split up and explore. It was Jeff's idea actually.

He was determined to get Claire on her own before they went their separate ways. He had been something of a gentleman last night but this morning he was feeling particularly horny and he wanted desperately to do something about it. Sue and Linda decided to look for a present for their mums so they dragged Mick off to the gift shops. Playfully he slow timed them declaring shopping was out for the duration of the holiday but as they shoved he graciously allowed himself to be cajoled into it.

Ros asked Ron if he fancied a drink and even though it was a bit early he agreed so they went off to find the nearest bar.

Jeff and Claire made themselves comfortable at the back of the coffee shop and he tried his best to get to know her better, much to the embarrassment of a teenage lad who was drinking there with his middle aged mum and dad. As they played tonsil tennis he stroked her thin cotton t- shirt until her nipples became erect. Then he whispered sweetly but urgently in her ear. Claire shook her head and apologised, reminding him of last night when she had explained her predicament to him. She was a bit miffed that he had brought it up again so soon but was loath to tell him and create an atmosphere at the start of their holiday. "Listen Tiger" she said "keep your old man in your trousers till we get back and I promise you a night you won't forget in a hurry". He almost blew it by trying his luck one more time but for once thought better of it and gave in graciously. "OK Love, I'll hold you to that" he smiled. She reached across and squeezed his balls gently. "No you can hold me to these " she whispered and the teenage lad legged it to the gents while he still had time.

Ron sat on the high bar stool and fiddled with his glass making marks on the condensation with his thumb. He was being pretty non committal at the moment as Ros had just asked him about past girlfriends.

"How about you?" he asked "any skeletons in your cupboard?"

"Not really" she said, toying with her own glass. "There's been a few. Nothing to write home about." She smiled. "I'm like you I suppose. I'm too picky"

"Yeah and you're not getting any younger" he said seriously then laughed to show he was teasing. She smiled back easily "And you had better get a move on before that bald patch gets any bigger" and she nodded towards the top of his head. Before he could stop himself he instinctively reached for the back of his head but half way there stopped and laughed. "Touche" he said and raised his glass in salute. Ros raised hers and they clinked glasses. Ron was starting to regret turning gay.

Mick held the delicate swan high and read the price tag underneath. "Look at the fu.." but he stopped just in time. "..prices" he finished lamely.

"It's beautiful" Sue answered, herself admiring a little glass lady.

"It's half the price in Rotherham market" he insisted.

"You pay for the quality love" said Sue, exasperation creeping into her voice.

"Yeah but if you put one of these and one from the market in your mum's house, who would know the difference eh?" he went on, logically.

Sue stared at him then turned to Linda who was shaking her head sadly. "Men have no idea, have they" she sighed.

"None whatsoever" Sue answered and they both looked at him with sympathy in their eyes.

The girl's flight was the first to be called so they all made their way to Box 10.

Mick gave Sue a long lingering kiss until Ros dragged them apart for decency's sake then he kissed Linda which won him extra brownie points from Sue.

Jeff kissed Claire but not with the same intensity as earlier. She was pleased he had understood earlier and hadn't caused a fuss like a lot of men would. Jeff felt totally pissed off but was determined not to show it. Of course he didn't'

understand. He was a man. She could have said she had a migraine, athlete''

foot, beri beri and said one of her parents had died and he still wouldn't have understood. She winked at him and said "See you when I get back" and he smiled without any real warmth. She turned and followed Sue and Linda through the gate.

Ros looked at Ron, unsure what to do. She had felt something there, a spark or whatever but he hadn't made any move so she was unsure of his feelings and didn't want to spoil anything by grabbing him.

Ron stood there, utterly miserable. He was totally unsure of his next move. He hadn't a clue whether he should kiss her on the lips, kiss her on the cheek, shake her hand, punch her on the arm in a matey way or just wave and walk away. He decided kissing her was a bit much as they were only friends but walking away was bad manners so he ought to shake her hand as a compromise. Unfortunately he decided at exactly the same time as Ros decided to take the bull by the horns and make the first move. She would kiss him. Not passionately of course, just tenderly on the lips. Demure, but leaving him with no doubt as to her feelings. As she leant forward and upwards, he reached out with his hand and hit her in the stomach. It wasn't so much the force as the shock that made her double up and roll on the floor. She let out a gasp of air which caused Mick and Jeff, who were waving to the girls, to turn round.

"What the fu…" Mick said as he reached down to pick Ros up. Jeff helped him and between them they got her to her feet.

Ron was beside himself. "I'm sorry. I didn't mean to. Fuck me."

"What was that for?" asked Jeff as he held Ros who was staggering a bit.

"It was an accident. I didn't mean it. I was just saying goodbye" he groaned.

"What do you do for "hello", nut 'em" asked Jeff unsympathetically.

"I'm alright. Really" wheezed Ros as she got her breath back. The girls came running over. "What's up" asked Sue, looking at her friends purple face.

"Ron hit her" offered Jeff and the girls swung round to face him.

"I didn't" he exclaimed. "Well I did but it was an accident. I was just saying goodbye"

"Well. Say goodbye to someone your own size next time" said Claire and the girls took Ros by the arm and led her away. Jeff and Mick stared at Ron then put an arm round him and took him back to the bar.

Distraught, Ron decided it was probably just as well he was gay.

Thirty minutes later the girls were raising a glass or two in celebration of the start of their holiday. Sue clinked Ros' glass, "Here's to us" she toasted.

"To us" the others chorused. Sue was in the aisle seat next to Ros with Linda, who had never flown before, taking the window seat.

"And the best holiday we've ever had" said Ros clinking glasses with Sue then turning round and doing the same with Linda. "The best holiday we've ever had" the others repeated. "And lots of girly fun together" laughed Linda and raised her glass again. "And lots of girly fun together" they giggled. Claire, who was in the opposite aisle seat, raised her glass and clinked Sue's. "And as many horny blokes as we can pull" she cheered. The other three stared at her.

Claire shrugged her shoulders. "Just kidding" she said, then added "To us".

"To us" they echoed.

Mick knocked over one of the miniatures that adorned his tray. It was empty, just like the six others that sat alongside it. He stood it upright and raised his glass. "To a good holiday" he said and they all took a swig.

"With a good time being had by all" offered Ron, who had recovered from his earlier trauma with the help of a few stiff drinks.

"And without Ron beating up every bird we meet" said Jeff and the other two stared at him. "Sorry" he smiled apologetically "Couldn't resist it" He raised his glass. "To absent friends" he offered and they all silently toasted Danny. "I hope he's alright" thought Mick as he finished off his drink.

"Smoking or Non smoking" asked the pretty young lady behind the BA desk.

"Smoking" he said and watched her print up the ticket. He whipped out a wad of money and counted out the exact fare. It was a lovely feeling to have so much cash on the hip and he savoured every minute. He looked at the ticket then checked his watch. He had over two hours to kill so he went to look for a café to get something to eat in the hope that it might settle his stomach.

Danny's guts had played him up all the way here and beside the crap he had done in McDonalds he had been forced to go twice on the train.

After he had eaten he paid another visit to the lav then went into the bar where he had a couple of pints. He lit up a Benson and savoured it. He had been on roll ups since he had lost his job so this was luxury and he was determined to make the most of it. As he blew smoke rings he thought of Sheila and smiled wryly at the thought of what she would do when she realised he had gone. He reckoned she wouldn't miss him tonight. She would think he was just sulking because his precious friends had gone away without him. If the letter arrived the next day she would see it on Tuesday lunchtime after her shift, but it may actually not arrive until Wednesday, in which case she would be spitting feathers at his continued absence. Whenever she read the note of course she would do her fucking nut in and he would pay for this for a long time, but as he sat there with a real fag and a good pint, waiting for a plane to the sunshine, he decided that whatever the price, it was worth it. Or it would be if his stomach would stop churning.

As the doors opened, the mid afternoon heat hit them. One hour later the bus from the airport had deposited everyone who wasn't going to Lloret off and was completing the last part of the journey. As they left Fanals and headed over the small mountain the girls had they first sight of Lloret De Mar. Big, bold and brash it stood like a testament to good living, yet over the rolling hills they could

see farm lands and small white villages. "It's beautiful" gasped
Linda and the others smiled. As they drove down the steep hillside
they passed hotels and bars, shops and *bodegas* all bustling and
busy. Two minutes later they were down on the promenade where
on one side young lively people were wending their way between
bars and on the other young beautiful people were sunning
themselves on the magnificent golden beach. They rubbernecked
their way to the other end of the resort till they reached the foot of
the small cliff that juts out over the sea where the small castle
stands forever guarding the locals from invading foreigners.
Judging by the number of English and Germans sunbathing below
it, I would suggest it tries a bit harder.

The Hotel Rosemary Park hove into view and their faces lit up at
it's beautifully manicured gardens which tastefully hid the free
form pool and the long elegant balconies which adorned the front
covered as they were in Bouganvilla.

Twenty minutes later the girls were safely ensconced in their
rooms. Claire and Linda good naturedly argued over the beds
while Sue and Ros immediately unpacked and tidied in theirs.
They then met up on their adjoining balconies where they enjoyed
the sea view.

"OK what shall we do first?" asked Sue.

"I could do with a nice swim and a sunbathe" Ros said.

"I'm hungry" said Linda.

"I could murder a drink" offered Claire.

Sue leant over the balcony and peered down. "Alright then. May I
suggest we adjourn to the pool where, unless I am very much
mistaken, there appears to be

waiter service providing food and liquid refreshment. That should
keep us going until" and she looked at her watch "the evening
meal is served in around three to four hours"

With girly giggles the four of them went back into their rooms and changed into their cossys .

At around the same time the lads were checking into their hotel, El Maritimo, a couple of blocks from the Poniente beach. Mick and Ron went to their room and threw their bags on the bed and went back into the corridor to meet Jeff who had done likewise in his. Mick had said that they could get a room with three beds in but Jeff insisted he would prefer his own space as he had every intention of filling it with a different girl every night and he didn't want the

"oldies" putting him off his stroke.

"Everything put away?" asked Mick as Jeff shut his door behind him.

"More or less" answered Jeff who had thrown his bags on the chair, glanced out of the window and turned round to meet his mates.

Two minutes later they were in the bar with three foaming beers in front of them. "Scholl" Mick said as he raised his glass to his lips.

"No I think it's Estrella" answered Jeff, leaning over the bar to get a better look at the beer pumps.

"I was making a toast you tosser" said Mick in mock disgust.

"Ah right. Scholl." Jeff raised his glass "And to his wonderful shoes"

Mick looked at him in bemusement and then at Ron who was smiling. "Cheers"

they said and downed their drinks in one.

They ordered three more and settled down. "Any plans?" Mick asked.

"Nah. Let's stay here" Ron said, feeling quite at home in the friendly atmosphere.

"Well let's at least sit in the fuckin' sunshine" countered Mick "I'm all for drinking all week but I'm fucked if I'm doing it inside. I'm getting married in a month and Sue'll kill me if I turn up all pasty faced."

"Yeah and if you dangle your feet in the pool every now and again you can tell her you've been doing your exercises" offered Jeff helpfully.

"Jeffrey you are a genius and are herewith promoted to fitness consultant and chief excuse maker for the duration of this holiday" and he stood up and saluted him. Jeff stood also and sloppily saluted back. "Thank you Sir" he said formally "You won't regret this" and they then retired to the pool area. There they rolled up their jeans and kicked their feet in the cool water.

"This is the life eh" said Ron after a while.

"Yeah" answered Mick as he looked up at the clear blue sky. "Tell you what though. If it stays like this I might take my shirt off tomorrow"

They all looked down at their white chests. Three Englishmen abroad, sat by the pool in their rolled up jeans and polo shirts.

Linda snored softly as Sue flicked away a fly and watched her friend fondly.

She had just been thinking how strange it was that with just her cossy on Linda didn't look fat at all. She looked round and curvaceous and quite shapely. She

99

had bigger breasts than Sue had realised and she realised that it must be the way that Linda dressed that made her look fat and frumpy. She made a mental note to have a word with Claire and get her to sort Linda's wardrobe out while they were here and to do her make up. She looked round and saw that Claire was dozing lightly and Ros didn't look too far from it either. They had enjoyed their light lunch of grilled sardines washed down with a few lagers and were relaxing for a couple of hours prior to getting ready for tonight.

Ros was daydreaming about Ron. Subconsciously she touched her belly and decided that when they got back she would go and see him and explain to him that it was her fault he had accidentally punched her in the stomach. He couldn't possibly have known that she was going to kiss him at that exact moment. She hoped he wouldn't be fretting about it too much and a smile played on her lips as she thought that he probably would. Not a bad thing really, she had decided. He would probably spend the whole of his holiday thinking of her. She couldn't wait to get back.

Sue saw the smile appear on her friends mouth and wondered who she could be thinking of. She racked her brain but couldn't come up with anybody.

"*Buenos tardes*" a voice cut in beside her and she spun round to see a tall swarthy looking young man. She noticed Claire and Ros raise themselves to their elbows.

"*Scusi.* You are English yes." The young man went on. Sue nodded.

"I can always tell. The English girls are so, er, how you say, beautiful, yes" and Sue saw that he had blushed slightly as he said it.

"What do you want?" demanded Ros who was immediately on the defensive.

"I am sorry" he said, standing up straight "I have not introduced myself. I am Giorgio your waiter and if there is anything I can get you please ask"

His eyes took in all four girls one at a time, and Sue fancied that he had spent a little longer perusing Linda's body than theirs.

Ros felt uncomfortable. It was all very well relaxing in your bikini with the girls but when there is a strange man ogling you it's a different story.

Sue, on the other hand, had taken an immediate liking to the young man. She felt relaxed and although she could see him eyeing them up, she didn't feel threatened. He was harmless she had decided and felt at ease with him.

Claire sat up slowly and reached behind her unhooking her bikini at the back.

She then dipped her shoulders forward and allowed it to fall down her arms and away from her body. She caught the top and dropped it on top of the bag at her side. When her hand returned it held a bottle of sun tan oil (factor thirty) from which she poured out a blob and rubbed it on her pert erect breasts. Giorgio's eyes were almost on stalks and try as he might he couldn't get them to move from these visions of loveliness.

"Giorgio" she purred softly to him.

"*Si*" he said with a distinct catch in his throat.

"I would like something long…" and she stopped and slowly licked her lips.

Giorgio's heart beat so fast he was sure they could all hear it.

"….and cool. Any suggestions"

Giorgio's mind raced. He fought desperately for something witty to say. This English girl was coming on to him, wasn't she. He had

101

been a waiter for two weeks now and all his cousins and friends, most of whom were also waiters, had told him that if he played it cool, the girls, especially the English girls, would be all over him. Up until now he hadn't had much luck at all. Last week he thought he had pulled a nice Scottish lass but when he made an approach her soft Scottish burr that had so attracted him (along with her 38 DD tits) suddenly turned into a thick Glaswegian See You Jimmy dialect most of which he couldn't understand. He had however got the gist of it and had retreated round the pool, watched by all the holidaymakers, and had been found an hour later, still shaking, by the manager who gave him a right bollocking for upsetting the guests.

As about a minute had gone by and he still hadn't come up with anything remotely witty Claire put him out of his misery and said "I'll have a lager then"

and laid back down, bored with him. He wasn't her type, she had decided. Too slow and definitely not sophisticated enough.

He realised he had taken too long and had blown his chance to impress with a witty throw away remark. With a blinding flash of inspiration he suddenly realised that in answer to the question "Can you suggest something long and cool?" he should have immediately replied "How about my nob"

"Too late now" he thought, disgusted at himself. He was hopeless at this. Even when the English girls threw themselves at him he managed to miss them.

He stood up and, without thinking, adjusted his trousers around the crotch area and went off back to the bar to fetch the drink.

"Claire you are nothing but a tart" scolded Ros as soon as he was out of earshot.

"Just having a bit of fun Ros" she answered, placing her sunglasses delicately back in place. "I'll explain it to you one day"

"He's just a waiter" went on Ros, a little louder now, as she hated being called a prude and she was sure that's what Claire was doing. "And you were just flaunting yourself". Secretly Ros quite envied Claire her lack of inhibitions.

Sometimes.

"I suppose you're right" Ros conceded and sat up straight as she made a conscious decision. She reached behind her and undid her top and caught it as it fell away revealing her creamy white breasts.

"Way to go girl" clapped Claire and she swung round to Sue who was watching amazed at Ros suddenly clothing off. "Come on Sue, let's have a look at what Mick plays with through the cold winter nights."

Sue blushed. She wasn't sure. She had never sunbathed topless before, except on the sunbed but if Ros could do it she was buggered if she wouldn't. She pulled the string at the front of her bikini and it opened to reveal pert milky sit up and beg breasts which she showed off proudly, if not self consciously.

While not being as big and round as Ros' hers were about the same as Claires.

She giggled nervously and placed her top on the bed beside her in case of emergency.

With one of those snot gozzling inhalations of air that people sometimes perform when coming out of a deep sleep too fast, Linda woke up. She rubbed her eyes and propped herself up on one elbow. "What's up" she asked, still half asleep and looked round her. Her eyes slowly took in the three of them and as she focused on each one individually they each in turn breathed in and forced their chests out. They all smiled at her and Ros and Sue giggled.

"Ah" she said. "I wondered if we were gonna, you know, do that"

"We're on holiday Linda" responded Claire "We can do what we want. We're young, free and single and we're getting our tits out for the lads" Sue and Ros giggled again.

"It's up to you Linda. Just 'cos we have doesn't mean you have to" said Ros soothingly.

"Seems a shame to cover 'em up though. Yours are bigger than ours put together." laughed Claire and the others laughed too.

Linda thought a moment and came to a decision. She swung her legs over the bed and reached behind her. She twiddled for a moment then suddenly free of the pressure they had previously been under, her blue lycra cups shot forward, instead of dropping sexily down like the others had. Suddenly they were on the floor and Linda bent down and retrieved her errant top. Her massive mammarys shot forward and took a few seconds to stop. Suddenly freed from their lycra prison they seemed to want to explore the outside world before settling down on their natural home, the belly.

Subconsciously Sue and Ros, who were the nearest, shied away so as not to lose an eye to a nipple. Linda placed her arms protectively round them then thought about it and showed them off "Sod it, we're on holiday" she explained and then thought again. "No pictures though and don't tell me mam, she wouldn't understand. She'd have a ducky fit"

"OK Linda. No sweat. No photos, no telling tales. It's our secret" she stopped and thought for a second "I suppose that goes for anything"

"That's right love" butted in Claire. "Anything that happens on this holiday stays with us". The others nodded. Linda breathed in, in an attempt to hide her rolls of excess fat. "I'd better put some cream on" she announced "Don't want to go home with burnt boobies"

Linda was sat facing them and they all watched fascinated as she rubbed cream over her enormous orbs. She didn't see Ros look over her shoulder and spin round on her bed and lay on her stomach. She also didn't notice a surprised Sue do the same. As she squirted a large blob into her left hand she rubbed it on the right half of her 42 FF's . The coldness of the cream immediately made her long nipple stand to attention, which was the first thing that Giorgio saw as he placed Claire's lager on the floor between the sunloungers. At first he didn't notice Linda or her nakedness, such was his attention on Claire. He had been thinking of something witty to say while he had got the drink but hadn't come up with anything yet. As he released the glass his head was inches from Linda's chest. With nothing clever or funny springing to the front of his mind, he miserably decided he should just ask for the money, enjoy the view and piss

off. "That will be two hundred peseta titties" he announced as his eye fell on the two inch nipple covered in the white cream.

"Pardon" asked Claire, fishing in her handbag.

"You're nipple" he said, unable to move his eyes.

"My what?" asked Claire, looking up confused.

"Breasts please" he muttered.

"Breasts?" asked Claire who hadn't the foggiest what he was on about.

"Hmm." He offered but was lost in a dream of his own making which included him rubbing cream in those magnificent mountains which had grown so dear to him. With an effort he tore his eyes away and looked at the owner of this perfect pair. Linda was staring into brown pools, so deep she felt she could reach in. In his eyes she saw immediately his inner kindness and innate decency. There was also something else there. Lust. This would normally have terrified Linda, to see that in someone's eyes but there was something about this man that made her feel at ease. She trusted him implicitly Giorgio, who had wrestled with his brain for control of his eyes and won, just, stared into the bluest, clearest, most innocent eyes he had ever seen. He was lost in their depth and

105

beauty and swept away in their humanity. A moment ago he had been unable to resist her boobs and now he could not look away from her eyes. It seemed that everything about this girl, no this woman, this *Madonna* captivated him. He gave up trying to resist and swam in the warm waters of her gaze.

Claire was feeling a bit pissed off watching this mutual admiration society.

Before they had set off she had thought about any competition she may have had from the others. She had decided that Sue wouldn't do anything anyway, had dismissed Linda entirely and decided that some men out there may go more for the schoolmarm type so Ros would be their ideal. If they were into the more masculine type of woman then, she had thought, they weren't the type of men for her. She liked a man who liked a womanly woman. She looked more like a woman than Ros and she expected to be treated more like a woman.

It had been something of a shock when Ros had taken her top off so easily. She never would have thought it. She was a bit surprised too when she realised what a magnificent body Ros had. There wasn't a spare ounce of fat on her and semi naked she looked lean and beautiful. Sue too had surprised her. She knew Sue had a decent body because she did dress quite well, but again with just a bikini bottom on she had looked better than Claire had imagined. When Linda had taken her top off Claire had just seen the couple of spare tyres and the enormous jugs. She knew men liked something to get hold of but surely that was too much. She was now a bit peeved to see this "Don Quixote" (She actually meant Don Juan but for Claire this was a very good stab into what for her must be a very dark dark.

She didn't fancy Giorgio, to be honest she thought him something of a plank, but when she took her clothes off she expected men to sit up and take notice.

"Alright children" she tutted "Staring game is over. It's a draw"

Giorgio looked at her, confused then stood up sharply. He kicked the lager over and clumsily tried to mop it up with his cloth. Linda leant forward and held his hand. "It's OK" she whispered "I'll do it"

He stared again into her eyes and wanted more than anything to hold her and kiss her but fearing a repetition of the Scottish incident of last week he bottled it and instead smiled weakly

Sue and Ros were still on their bellies but hadn't missed a thing. Sue was mesmerised and overjoyed by the obvious mutual attraction between the two.

Ros too thought it more than sweet and willed Linda or Giorgio to take it further and kiss the other.

Giorgio took a deep breath and stood up. "I must go" he said sadly. Linda nodded. "OK" said Claire for her. He looked round at Claire as if seeing her for the first time. "There is no charge for the drink *Senora,* it is on me.

Claire looked down at the spilt lager, which was seeping into her handbag and wetting her wrap. "Not quite" she sniffed "but it was almost on me"

Giorgio ignored her and smiled again at Linda. He bowed slightly and turned and left. Linda watched him go and sighed deeply as he disappeared behind the bar. She smiled disarmingly as Sue and Ros jumped up and sat beside her chattering about her swarthy Spanish Waiter.

"That'll be Jeff" Mick shouted through to the bathroom as he climbed off the bed. He was ready to go out and had been reading a mag as he waited for Ron to finish in the bathroom. He put his bottle of San Miguel on the bedside table and noticed the condensation running down the neck. Like all good Brits abroad they had bought a crate of beer and put it in the bidet to keep cool. He flung the door open and walked back in the room without looking to see who was there. "Ron's nearly ready" he said "grab a beer, they're in the bog thing"

As he neared the bed he realised no one was behind him so he turned and went back to the door. There was no one there so he went out into the corridor where he was suddenly engulfed in two big hairy arms. He tried to wriggle free but the arms had him tight. He almost kicked out aiming for the shins when suddenly he was pushed away. He bumped into the wall and spun round, fists raised.

"We're on holiday-ay, we're on holiday-ay, for one whole week, for one whole week" sang a voice which he recognised immediately. "Danny" he shouted in amazement at the dancing figure before him. Danny stopped and smiled broadly "Too right cobbler" he drawled in a mock Australian accent for some reason. Mick stared at him, wondering how the fuck he had got there then a big smile filled his face. He was genuinely pleased to see his friend. He rushed forward and grabbed him. "What the fuck. I mean how did you get here." he blurted out.

"I'm on my hols" Danny grinned "and I thought while I was in these parts I'd look up a few mates who were staying round here."

"Yeah but, well you know, where did you get the money" he asked, a bit embarrassed.

"Something came up" Danny grinned. He looked over Micks shoulder into the room "Well are you going to invite me in or are we spending the whole fucking week in this corridor" he asked bluntly. Mick laughed and picked up his kit bag. "Where's the rest of your stuff?" he asked.

"At home" Danny laughed and followed him into the room.

Mick threw Danny's bag on to the bed and picked up his bottle. He reached across the bed and got the bottle that was meant for Ron when he came out of the bathroom. Danny knocked the cap off and raised it to his lips. "Cheers" he said as he downed it in one. "I needed that" he said "I've been on the go since early doors." He sat on the bed, then laid back and farted making himself at home. Mick smiled and took a drink from his bottle. "Alright Danny, let's have it. How have you got here and how did you pay for it. If you've done something stupid you know Sheila's going to kill you, don't you"

"Fuck Sheila" he said and almost added "everybody else has" but didn't. "I told you, something came up. Actually five somethings came up. Let me see, there was an eight, yeah, an eleven, a twenty seven, a twenty nine and a thirty seven." He stopped and thought for a second, running the numbers through his mind. He smiled and announced "Yeah that's them. Five somethings" Mick looked puzzled and shrugged his shoulders. "Oh and they paid out two thousand five hundred and eight pounds and eighty pee" added Danny.

Mick thought a second and shot his arm forward at Danny, throwing beer on him "You won the lottery" he shouted. "That's funny, so did I" said Danny as he wiped himself off.

"Fuck me" said Mick and he sat down on the bed. Danny sat down next to him.

"So I thought , what better way to spend this loverly money than going to see my old muckers in Spain." Mick smiled "Glad you did pal"

They sat there quietly for a while then Mick asked "What did Sheila say, I mean she must be happy about the big win and that but what did she say about you pissing off over here"

"Nothing" he answered truthfully.

"She didn't mind?"

"She didn't know"

"She didn't know?"

"No"

"Danny, she's going to rip your balls off when she catches you" Mick told him concernedly.

"She'll have to sew 'em back on first" he smiled through gritted teeth and then anger took him over "I don't give a flying fuck what she says. I'm having a holiday with my mates and she can bollocks, her and the fuckin' Kray twins. In one weeks time I'll shit myself when I go home but for now I'm, having a good time with my mates so the rest can fuck off."

"Steady on boy" Mick advised and then considered it for a moment. Maybe Danny was right, he had been having a time of it lately so maybe he did deserve something like this. Whatever, it wasn't really his business so why should he spoil everybody's holiday by harping on about it. "Alright pal, it's your funeral so we'll drop it, yeah"

"Top man" Danny said and looked up smiling as Ron came into the room. He had on his trousers and shoes but was searching for his shirt.

"Sha'nt be long" he said absently as he found it on the door handle of the bathroom. He flicked it to look for creases and went back in to finish dressing.

"Take your time. I've got all fuckin' night" Danny laughed.

Slowly Ron backed out of the bathroom and into the main room. His shirt was on now and he was fastening his buttons. His head spun round to see Danny and Mick grinning at him.

"What the fuck are you doing here?" he asked.

"Come to see my muckers. Somebody's got to show you lot how to have a good time haven't they." laughed Danny.

Bemused Ron asked the obvious question "Yeah but how did you afford it, you know?"

"We've done all that. Look let's go and get Jeff and I'll explain it all to you over a drink or two. I need to see him anyway. I had a word with the manager before I came up. I gave him some bullshit about travelling round Europe and meeting up with you lot and anyway he says for a nominal fee, payable in cash of course, I can stay in Jeff's room for the week. If it's Ok with Jeff of course."

Danny said while looking in the mirror and brushing his hair with his fingers.

"That would do" he thought, "ready to hit the town"

"Jeff'll not mind" said Mick "but I think you'll be as well shifting your bed in here, 'cos he has every intention of being a shagging machine this week, and he'll not want you disturbing him"

"We'll see how it goes" said Danny "But for now, come on let's party" and he led the other two out of the room and they went to meet Jeff, go out and get pissed.

CHAPTER SIX

The girls were almost dressed to kill. Linda was the first ready partly because she couldn't wait to get downstairs as she was hoping Giorgio would be there and partly because, after Sue had had a word with Claire, Claire had helped her with her hair and make up before she herself had got ready. Linda now stood in front of the full length mirror and pirouetted and hummed softly to herself.

Claire came out of the bathroom, wearing just a small towel, and rubbing her hair with another. She watched for a moment then commented "What's up with you, you seem in a bloody good mood"

"I'm, on holiday. I'm allowed to be in a good mood" she retorted.

"We're all on holiday" Claire said "but we don't have to dance round like some demented Dawn French all night".

Linda stopped dancing and humming and thought about it, then started dancing and humming again and obviously thought "bollocks" to it.

Claire shrugged and carried on drying her hair.

"I'm going down to the bar for a bit" ventured Linda "I'll meet you all down there."

"Anybody interesting going to be there" teased Claire. Linda coloured up.

"No" she said "It's just that I'm thirsty and…"

"Leave it" ordered Claire "I'll fetch the others and we'll meet you downstairs"

Linda smiled at her and, picking up her bag, rushed out of the door. She rushed down the corridor and decided that the steps would be faster than the lift. They were, because she took them two at a time. She rushed into the foyer and just stopped herself running across it. She gathered herself and straightened her dress. She looked around the crowded foyer, full of families going out into the night and stiffened her back. At home she wouldn't dream of going into a pub on her own, but she felt she had no choice. If she was going to get Giorgio talking to her, she knew she had to do it when the others weren't around. Self-consciously she went into the bar and looked around. It was pretty quiet as most of the guests were either still dining or had gone out. Later the place would be heaving but early evening, it had a light airy feel to it. Linda couldn't see any staff at all at first then she noticed one of the waiters, who she had seen earlier at the pool, serving behind the bar. There was no sign of Giorgio however and although she waited a good five minutes she couldn't see him.

Down hearted she sat down at an empty table to wait for the others. Then, from a room at the back of the bar carrying a big bag of ice, Giorgio appeared and her eyes lit up immediately and her heart beat quickened. She watched as he poured the ice into a cooler and chatted amiably with his friend. She couldn't help but admire his dark swarthy good looks and lean frame and began to have doubts as to her ability to hook this handsome man. She looked down at herself and saw a fat frumpy spinster and thought it might be better to wait in the foyer for the girls. She looked up at him again and thought how impossibly handsome he was and sighed. He glanced across as he wiped the bar with a cloth and her heart leaped as she saw his face immediately light up. Hurriedly he discarded the cloth and said something to his friend who looked up at her and said something back. The friend was laughing but Giorgio said something to him that shut him up and then he rushed over to her table. He tucked in his shirt front as he walked and combed his hair with his fingers and she smiled at his loveliness.

"Senora" he said, with a little catch in his throat.

"Linda, please" she corrected and he smiled revealing beautiful big white teeth.

114

"Linda. Thank you, yes" he said and then just stood there, as if unsure what to do next. A thought suddenly came to him and his eyes lit up "Would you like a drink, yes, on the house"

"No thank you" she answered and she saw the disappointment in his face and hurriedly went on "I'm waiting for my friends. They will be here any second, but you can buy me one later. If you like"

His eyes said that he would like, and his smile said that he couldn't wait. He seemed to relax a bit now and he sat down beside her. He looked at her and she could feel herself colouring up.

"The sun, it suits you Linda, it gives you a nice glow"

Going even redder, now that he had noticed her redness she touched her face and neck, which felt hot. "Thank you" she spluttered "but I think I will just go red and not golden brown like the others."

He looked over her body again and his eyes rested on her fine orbs, straining at the thin linen of her dress. "You are fair skinned" he said to her boobs "the soft rosy glow suits you. It looks very beautiful. You look very beautiful"

"How romantic" she thought. "What a nice, sexy, handsome young man, and what a nice thing to say. She couldn't imagine an Englishman saying something as romantic as that. An Englishman would be too crude. If he kept this up he could have her tonight." She giggled at the thought and coloured even more "Pack it in" she thought as she watched him "He'll think I'm gonna explode"

He suddenly raised his arm and she realised he wanted to shake hands, so she thrust hers forward.

"Giorgio Eduardo Phillipe Dos Nascimento" he said formally.

"Linda McCarthy" she answered, embarrassed by her ordinariness.

"That is a beautiful name *senora*" he smiled and she felt better. He took her hand, turned it and kissed it gently. She would normally have been totally embarrassed by this sudden showing of old fashioned affection and respect but, much to her surprise, she felt at ease and happy with the way the evening was going.

"Linda" he said moving a little closer "Tomorrow is my day off and I thought, perhaps. I mean, would you. If you are not busy that is,…"

"Spend the day with you" she finished off for him. He nodded.

"I would love to"

He beamed a big, genuinely happy, smile. "I will show you all the best places around Lloret" he said happily. "Not the tourist places you understand, the genuine Spanish areas. If you like I will take you into the mountains and we can dine at a real Spanish farm in a beautiful walled garden covered in Bougainvilla. The scent from the flowers and the food, aah, it is enough to make you feint" His eyes were closed at the thought and she too closed hers and she could swear she could smell the deep pungent aroma. It was almost like a heavy perfume. In fact it was like Claire's perfume.

"Falling asleep" Claire said as the three girls came up beside Linda. "You want to practise your technique love" she said to an embarrassed Giorgio "get 'em to fall asleep after you've had your wicked way, not before. It's much more fun"

Giorgio quickly got to his feet and seemed to hop around on each foot, so unsure of himself was he. Linda felt herself colour up and determined to stop doing it. "Claire" she ordered in a bossy voice "give over. Leave him alone"

and she stood up and moved closer to him, as if protecting him. Claire smiled, unconcerned at any discomfort she may have caused. Sue and Ros looked on in bemusement at this sudden showing of protectiveness from their friend. They had never seen Linda this way and, it had to be said, it suited her. She looked suddenly like a grown woman who had something worthwhile to fight for.

From nowhere the other waiter suddenly appeared. He was smiling broadly, and while on the surface there was nothing wrong with him, there was something about him that inspired distrust and dislike.

"Senoras" he breathed in a deep husky voice which he imagined sounded sexy and alluring but didn't. The innocence and naivety that Giorgio seemed to transmit was in sharp contrast to the aura of caddishness and lack of trust given off by him. He was over confident and overbearing and all the girls took an instant dislike to him.

"May I get you a table. The best table in the house for the most beautiful ladies, yes"

"Fuck off" thought Claire

"No thank you" said Sue

Claire reached round him and grabbed Linda's arm. "We have to go now" she informed him.

He brushed his chest against the firmness of her breast and he could feel her erect nipple through the thinness of her silver crop top.

She straightened visibly and almost took a swing at him. If she had been in Rotherham she would have, certainly, and given him a gob full too. She had second thoughts here though and decided to let it go, just this once. If he did that again though, he would be picking his balls up in a bag from reception.

She pulled Linda towards her and looked him in the eye, quite clearly warning him off. Maybe it was the difference in the language or something but all he saw was a challenge.

"Perhaps you would like to stay for a drink alone while your friends continue on their way, eh. I, Manuel, will take care of you" he offered in his lofty manner.

Claire edged closer to him and said in a sweet voice, just loud enough for the others to hear "How's fuck off sound".

He thought about it a while then answered innocently "It sounds not very nice"

"That's like you then" and she turned and flounced out pulling Linda with her.

After a few yards, a sprinting Giorgio caught up with them. "Tomorrow Linda?" he asked breathlessly.

"Room 247. Nine o clock" she whispered back and with that they were off, Claire pulling Linda along as she craned to get a last view of the man of her dreams and Ros and Sue bringing up the rear.

Giorgio and Manuel watched them go.

"I will have her before the week is out" Manuel opined.

"I think not" Giorgio said, turning to his friend.

"She wanted me. I could tell. She plays hard to get, that is all"

"No I think she thought you a low life" Giorgio replied with unerring accuracy.

Manuel took immediate offence at this slur on his manhood and turned to his friend with a madness on his face that Giorgio had not seen before.

"Listen my friend. You stick with the fat girls. I will handle the beauties, yes. I know when they play hard to get, I have seen it before but believe me I always get my way. If I say I will have her before the week is out then you can believe me. It will happen" He was virtually spitting out the words by the end and Giorgio wondered why he had taken all this so personally. They had only known each other for a few weeks and they had got on well. He hadn't seen him lose his temper before and he didn't like it. He knew that his trusting open nature meant he tended to get on with most people but he felt that Manuel was someone who should perhaps be kept at arms length from now on. Besides, he had called his new girlfriend fat and he couldn't forgive him for that. Fat. She was nothing of the sort. She was round and cuddly and very, very sexy and Giorgio couldn't wait to see her again in the morning. He took one last look in the direction she had left and turned back to the bar to do some work. Manuel followed his gaze and promised himself again that he would have the mouthy English girl before the week was out. "One way or another" he said under his breath.

Curled up on the large chair in Mick and Ron's room Danny tried again to fall asleep. He concentrated hard on it then wondered if that was the problem.

Maybe he should stop concentrating and just relax. He turned in the chair, trying to get comfy and felt his stomach gripe. He held his guts and prayed that it would go away. He had been to the lav twice already that morning and he knew he would get a bollocking off the lads when they went into the bathroom later. The stench was awful.

He had planned to be sleeping in Jeff's room of course, but around one o clock that morning Jeff had pulled a scouse bird and gone off with her before Danny had got a key from him. The others had said that he could doss down in their room but they had forgotten to tell him that it would have to be on the floor or in this chair. He felt another twinge and let a small fart go. The stink nearly knocked him over and he tried desperately to cover his face with the thin linen sheet. After a few seconds he gave up and in the half light went over to the sliding balcony door. He shivered in the sudden coldness of the early morning and scratched his balls. He wondered idly whether his upset guts were from yesterday when he first noticed that his shit stunk or as a direct result of the shish kebab he had had when they left the last bar last night. He closed the door and was returning to his chair when he felt his stomach lurch. It stopped him in his tracks and he doubled up in agony. He heard a gurgling sound, not unlike water going down a partially blocked plug hole. His hand shot to his arse in an effort to stem the tide and apart from the odd dribble it worked. He made the toilet in three seconds and two seconds later a huge smelly wet explosion ripped through the air. His stomach had obviously decided that it could no longer tolerate the disgusting stuff it was harbouring and had sent strict

instructions to the arse to get rid. Like a well oiled machine the arse did exactly that and in quite a magnificent fashion. Apart from a streak across his boxers the stuff never touched the sides shooting like a powerful water pistol directly into the pan. Danny's face went from the picture of agony to one of absolute serenity in the space of a few seconds. As the smell hit him however it screwed up like a dog chewing a toffee. This cycle was repeated over and over again for five minutes until Danny was convinced that he couldn't possibly have anything left inside him. He looked between his legs and was surprised it hadn't bubbled over the seat but quickly whipped his head back.

"Jesus Christ" said a muffled voice from the doorway. Danny looked up to see Mick with both hands covering his mouth and nose.

"Sorry" he offered to his rapidly retreating friend.

Ten minutes later Danny emerged shamefaced from the bathroom. He looked round the dimly lit room but no one was there. Through the balcony window he could make out two shivering figures huddled in white sheets.

"Sorry" he said. They saw his lips move but couldn't hear him although they could tell what he said.

"Fuck off" they chimed and likewise although he couldn't hear them the meaning was clear.

He picked up his sheet, which had fallen to the floor during his run to the bathroom, and wrapped it round himself. Gingerly he stepped to the window and opened it. Gently he lowered himself into the remaining plastic chair. His arse was red hot and the coldness of the chair felt fantastic against it. "Sorry"

he repeated as he got himself comfy.

"That was disgusting" said Mick, who was pulling his sheet up round his nose as the open door allowed the smell to escape onto the balcony and away into the fresh morning air.

"There's no wonder you and Sheila don't get on if you drop one of those out every morning" joined in Ron, who was also covering his face having just received a whiff.

"I don't, you pillock. I've got the shits" Danny defended himself.

"Nah" said Mick in mock surprise "I thought that fuckin' smell was your aftershave"

"It must have been that kebab last night"

"Well you couldn't just have a donner like us could you. Oh no. I'm on holiday." Mick mimicked "I'm having a shish. I'm a big boy. I'm a right clever bastard me. I'm going to shit mysen' in the morning and stink the whole fuckin' room out I am."

"Well you just had a shish in there pal and if they all smell like that I don't ever want one" offered Ron.

"Fuck off. I'm in agony you twat" groaned Danny as he pulled his legs up to his chest. "I need to lie down" and he tenderly raised his red bum off the cool plastic chair and headed back to the bedroom. He reached behind him and pulled his pants away from his arse where they were sticking because of the little damp patch that he had left earlier when he had drawn mud.

Ron and Mick watched him go and both laughed out loud when they saw the damp patch.

"Fuck off" Danny called over his shoulder as he tried to get comfy on the chair.

His mates immediately felt sorry for him and ashamed that they hadn't been more understanding.

"You can't sleep there" Mick said "You need a bed"

"I haven't got a bed" Danny answered rather obviously.

"I know but you can't sleep there, It's not fair. Take Ron's"

"You're fuckin' joking" jumped in Ron "Didn't you see his arse?"

"Yes. That's why I said he could take yours" grinned Mick.

"Well I can't go back to Jeff's room. He's not in. I've been up most of the night and he hasn't come back. He must have gone back to that Scouse bird's place" Danny groaned. He felt another attack coming on and farted loudly. Ron and Mick dived for the balcony and desperately shut the door behind them.

"That does it" said Mick taking big gulps of fresh air "He can sleep in the fuckin' corridor for all I care, but he's not staying in there."

Ron shivered and held his sheet tightly around him. He glanced idly across at the next door balcony and smiled broadly. "The windows open" he told Mick in a triumphant voice. Mick looked at him quizzically then followed his eyes to the open window and smiled back. He stepped back into the room and tried to speak without breathing. "Danny, come on, we've got you a bed" he whispered through clenched teeth. Danny rose from his chair and blindly followed, taking his sheet with him. When he arrived on the balcony Ron pointed to the one next door. "The windows open" he explained. "You can climb in and go to bed".

Danny looked at the gap between the two balconies and decided to go for it.

"Anything for a bed" he groaned as he climbed onto the chair and raised one leg up and over the railings. He farted loudly and stopped for a second, panic in his eyes until he was sure it was safe to move again.

"Better hurry up" offered Mick unhelpfully.

Ron held his nose and wondered aloud about the state of Danny's pants.

"Bollocks" Danny countered as he safely landed on the other side.

"I'm only asking" smiled Ron.

Danny looked back at them, now grinning as they were free of their smelly burden.

"I hope you both get piles and shit hedgehogs for a week" he said and turning, opened the sliding door and disappeared from view.

In the semi darkness he passed Jeff's bed and felt for his own. He edged round it and came across his kit bag. He quickly dropped it to the floor and gratefully sank into the bed. The cold crisp sheets felt like heaven to him and within minutes, curled up into a ball with his hands hugging his belly, he was sound asleep.

Fifteen minutes later the key turned in the door and in walked a smug looking Jeff pulling along the giggling Scouse girl he had met earlier. He had in fact, as the lads had guessed, gone back to her hotel after a long walk on the beach full of kissing and cuddling, only to find her roommate already entertaining two

geordie lads. Jeff was quite willing to stay and join in but his new friend had said no and they had adjourned back to Jeff's.

As his eyes became accustomed to the dark he swore softly under his breath as he made out the unmistakable shape of Danny tucked up in bed. He had known Danny hadn't got a key and had assumed that he would have crashed next door.

He didn't mind that Danny was there but he was worried that this bird might.

He didn't want her doing a runner now just because his fat mate was watching from the next bed. Girls eh.

"Gissa kiss" she purred and he happily obliged as his mind raced with ideas and possibilities. He stroked her pert bum through her thin blue dress and couldn't feel the tiny G string that he knew was nestling there. His face lit up as an idea struck him and he whispered softly in her ear. She smiled wickedly and nuzzled up to him and then he led her by the hand into the bathroom.

He didn't turn on the light in the bathroom, just leant across the bath and pushed the shower button. Then he pulled back the curtain as hot water gushed out and almost immediately filled the small room with steam. Gently he pulled the girl towards him and softly caressed her hair. Tenderly he kissed her neck and his right arm snaked its way round her back and undid the fastening on her dress. As it fell to the floor he looked appreciatively at her round firm breasts and kneaded them lovingly with both hands

He tried desperately to remember her name but didn't manage it so he didn't bother with any small talk and instead tugged his own clothes aside.

Like a scene from a movie she silently pulled down her white knickers and revealed a beautiful golden triangle, which brought a tingle to his spine and things. Gallantly he held out his hand which she took in hers and he held her gently as she raised her leg and climbed into the bath. Following her closely, he pulled the shower curtain into place and held her to him under the full force of the refreshing warm jets of water. From somewhere she produced the bar of soap and proceeded to rub along his chest until she had a lather. He took the soap from her and reciprocated. They then massaged each other, gently discovering each others body for the first time. After a while he turned her and gently worked his hands down her back and onto her bottom. Provocatively she arched her back thrusting her bottom against him. He kneaded the soft firm mounds with soapy hands and then turned her again to face him. As she turned they heard a noise. It was a cross between a man blowing a raspberry and a chair being pulled on a shiny floor. The girl (shit, what was her name) looked inquisitively at him. "It must have been your foot sliding on the enamel bath"

he guessed and shrugged his shoulders. She giggled again and moved closer, cupping his face in her hands and kissing him passionately on the mouth. Then she slowly moved her hands down his body to his expectant groin. She cupped his balls and stoked his cock with her thumbs. "What's that?" she said.

Grinning inanely he said "That's Mister Lurve Machine".

"No, that smell" she shrieked, letting go of his balls and throwing her hands up to her nose and mouth. Jeff stood there dumbfounded, unable to take in the sudden turn of events. He wanted her hands back round his balls and he wanted them now. Then it hit him. He couldn't think what the smell reminded him of

but he knew it was the most repulsive odour he had ever encountered. He put one hand round his nose and bent to peer down the plug hole to see if some rotting monster from hell or something was making an appearance. Seeing nothing untoward he threw back the curtain. His watering eyes wildly took in the whole small bathroom in one fell swoop and through the mists of shower fog he could make out a figure in the corner crouched low on the toilet. He reached over and turned off the shower in an attempt to stop the steam from worsening and gazed into the fog. Both he and the girl stood there, naked and exposed, unashamedly holding both hands up to their faces as the smell showed no sign of going away.

"Danny?" he said into the mists.

"Sorry" was the muffled response.

"What the fuck are you doing" demanded Jeff.

"I've got the shits. It must have been that kebab" was the miserable answer. As the steam started to clear through the open door, Jeff could see his fat friend sat, head hunched into his body in a pathetic attempt to hide his shame, with his skid marked pants round his chubby ankles.

He gamely looked up and tried a weak smile as if to placate them. Even in his tortured state he couldn't help but admire the graceful lines of the girls body and he felt a little twinge down below. Unfortunately, for all concerned, he felt a bigger twinge round the back and he deposited some more of his insides into the Spanish sewage system. The air visibly thickened around him and two seconds later the girl coughed uncontrollably as the smell reached them.

"Sorry" Danny offered but it was never going to be enough.

"Not as fuckin' sorry as I am" challenged Jeff as he climbed out of the bath in an effort to get away, ungallantly leaving the girl to climb out herself and make her own escape. Five seconds later they were safely ensconced on the balcony with the glass door holding back the awful smell and gulping in deep mouthfuls of fresh air. For a full five minutes they breathed in deeply, never noticing their wet skin or their exposed nakedness. Eventually they gained control of themselves and removed their hands from their faces. They looked at each other and realised the absurdity of the situation and cuddled up for warmth.

Eventually, of course, mother nature took it's course, as it has a habit of doing and they made love on the balcony in the open air.

Ten minutes later Danny decided it was safe to leave his haven and gingerly stood up and even more gingerly wiped his incredibly sore arse. Flushing the lav he walked out of the bathroom, looking for all the world like a man who has just completed a two day horse ride without a saddle, on a very bony horse.

Reaching his bed he realised he was going to have to sleep on his belly so he gently lowered himself into that position and with great relief and a deep sigh tried to sink back into sleep. After a couple of minutes he moved the position of his head and opened his eyes. He stared blankly into the early morning dawn and watched two bodies writhing in energetic sexual gratification. He watched, uninterestedly for a while then carefully lifted one arm and picked up his pillow and covered his head. Three seconds later he was asleep.

CHAPTER SEVEN

By seven thirty, Linda was showered and dressed and sat on the end of her bed waiting impatiently for nine o clock to come around.

Claire was snoring softly and Linda desperately wanted to be out of the room before she woke up. She had had enough of the girls well intentioned banter the night before and now just wanted to get away with Giorgio and enjoy herself.

They had visited several bars and then a couple of clubs and, although she had enjoyed herself, she couldn't wait for last night to end and this morning to arrive. Impatiently she recalled the platitudes that had been given her all night.

"Don't go anywhere secluded", "Stay in the town centre", "If he tries anything you don't like, knee him in the balls" and so forth. She knew the girls meant well but she felt more than a little patronised and while she wouldn't dream of telling them, she wished they would pack it in.

Making a decision, she picked up her bag and purse and headed silently for the door. Once outside she felt much better although the butterflies in her stomach were fluttering away. Glancing at her watch she realised she had plenty of time to have breakfast and still be back in time to stop Giorgio in the foyer before he called up to her room. As she descended in the lift she nervously watched herself in the mirror and ran her fingers through her hair.

As soon as the lift doors opened she bounced out almost into the arms of the waiting Giorgio. He was nervously biting his fingernails and looked shocked when confronted by her.

"Linda. I…er I was coming up to see you" he spluttered.

"Already" she asked "I thought we were meeting at nine?"

"Yes I know this, it's just I thought, well perhaps, er you would have breakfast with me." He answered, obviously ruffled.

As cool as you like Linda said "I'd love to. I don't normally eat at this time, however I'll make an exception for you"

Nervously he took her arm and led her outside.

"You too were early Linda. You were not trying to escape me were you?" he asked as they walked out into the cool early morning sunshine.

She coloured up, her previous cool deserting her, and admitted "To be honest Giorgio I couldn't wait any longer. I'm so excited I'm full of nervous energy. If I'd waited any longer I would have exploded" and she giggled girlishly and rather fetchingly.

Giorgio puffed out his chest, feeling proud that this beautiful woman was so eager to meet him. He leant forward and asked, in a sexy accent "*Senora*, may I?"

Linda was unsure as to what exactly he was requesting but to be honest he could have asked her for the keys to her dad's house and she would have handed them over, smiling.

He leant closer and kissed her softly on the cheek. She could smell him. It was warm and manly, clean and lightly scented and she thought she would go giddy at the richness of it.

As he leant back he held out his hand and when she placed hers in his he said

"Come, let's eat. I know a little café where they will look after us" and they skipped down the steps and onto the main road.

Ron woke with a start and sat up. Leaning on one elbow he remembered that he had just had an erotic dream. His erection bore testament to that. He wracked his brain to remember details from the dream. It was important to him. For one thing, was he involved in the proceedings?. And who with?. That was really the key question. Had he been dreaming of a man or a woman?. He closed his eyes and tried to recall, but of course the more he concentrated the more his grasp of the details slipped away. After thirty seconds the only proof that he had just had a dream was his erection. He scratched his balls thoughtfully and got up to go to the toilet. After standing there for a couple of minutes his old man had subsided enough for him to pee so, whistling a happy tune, he got on with the job in hand and allowed his mind to wander. It wandered, almost immediately to Ros. To be truthful, he had thought a lot about Ros these last couple of days.

Maybe it was because she was good company or maybe it was because he still felt terribly guilty about hitting her in the airport. Either way he couldn't wait to get home and see her.

He suddenly realised that his dream had featured Ros but for the life of him he couldn't remember how.

It was a great shame he had decided to be gay because he thought a lot of Ros.

He wasn't too sure about this gay thing either. He looked down at his cock which still sported a "lazy lob" and thought about where he would have to put it if he were in fact gay. He didn't fancy it at all.

As his face suddenly contorted in shock his free hand involuntarily shot round to his backside, pressing the cheeks firmly together. Perhaps that meant he was the woman in any relationship. A taker, as it were, not a giver. "Fuckin' hell. I don't fancy this queer shit at all" he mumbled under his breath as he finished his pee and shook it dry. He had a wash and tried to figure things out. He decided to play it by ear. There was no use wondering which way to turn, so to speak, when he hadn't anyone to turn to, or from..

Linda was having the best day of her life. When they had left the hotel that morning she was surprised to find a gleaming brand new Puglia 125cc motor scooter parked outside with two helmets hanging from it, one of which was offered to her by a beaming Giorgio.

"You like my baby eh?" he asked as he stroked the handsome machine.

"It is beautiful Giorgio" she said having seen the pride on his face. If it was possible he smiled even more at the compliment.

From the hotel they had travelled to a little café that he knew where two of his cousins, who were waiters there, served them a full English breakfast. The two giggling waiters fussed about them and obviously worshipped Giorgio and Linda felt like royalty and couldn't believe when they were waved away at the end of the meal without having to pay. Throughout the morning he ran them around his hometown showing her churches, mosques and museums that most tourists to this area would never see.

Around lunchtime he stopped outside the beautiful byzantine church on the northern outskirts of the town and pointed out it's unique features.

"Our history is a troubled and a mixed one resulting in a very mixed race with many facets to our culture and this is perhaps best expressed in our varied architecture." And he swept his arm around indicating the small area with it's many, often jarring, differences.

This may have been Linda's first visit abroad but she loved it. The heat, the warmth of the people, the bustling town centre and the peaceful, tranquil parks and side streets. She loved the contrasts. She loved everything about it and wondered whether she would be able to return later that year and sample it all again. Who knows, maybe Giorgio would invite her. "Don't rush things" she ordered herself. "Just enjoy it while you can". But she knew she was falling in love with Giorgio and couldn't really face up to going home and not seeing him again.

They lunched at a beautiful clifftop restaurant overlooking Fanals where again they were greeted by an uncle of Giorgio's who fussed around them and promised them only the best. He was a huge man with a balding head and an enormous belly, which he tried vainly to cover with a huge white apron. He served them Gaspacho soup, followed by lobster and a creamy white sauce along with a very expensive bottle of wine.

They talked and laughed and Giorgio pointed out Common Scoters and Razorbills flitting in and out of their homes in the cliffs. Once he shouted his uncle over and pointed to a spot where he said a Velvet Scoter had just entered with food to feed it's young. His uncle clapped his hands together and spoke quickly in Spanish so Linda had no idea what he was saying Giorgio laughed and turned to her as his uncle made his way back to the kitchen.

"He says we have brought good luck to his café" he explained.

"How's that?" she asked curiously.

"The Velvet Scoter is a rare bird around these parts and is almost never spotted here on these cliffs. My uncle says it is a good omen to have one nesting so nearby, so, as we spotted it, we have brought him the good luck. They both laughed and Linda looked back to the kitchens and saw the old man carrying out two huge servings for his other customers who he greeted with a smile and a bow.

"I'm glad" she said simply and he watched her with pride in his eyes.

In the afternoon they headed inland on the C260 up to Figueras and then pulled off and took a *camino* or mountain track into the hills. They went through Olive groves, orchards and vineyards where the workers all waved to

them in a lazy laid back way. At first this embarrassed her but when she got used to it she waved back enthusiastically.

As they reached the brow of a hill Giorgio pulled his scooter to a halt and they got off and stretched their legs. He produced a bottle of water and they drank thirstily. It was hotter here on the mountain and Linda wiped her cleavage with a hanky, which she had drenched in the cold water. She looked up and caught him smiling at her and she blushed furiously which made him smile even more.

"Giorgio" she said, as if to change the subject, "How come you have so many relatives working around here?"

"Ah, that is because my family are good Catholics" he smiled.

Not being from a religious background she didn't understand what he meant and shrugged her shoulders and shook her head slightly to indicate this. He took her hair in his hand and stoked it into place behind her ear and explained.

"A lot of the younger people no longer listen to the Pope." She was still nonplussed so he went on "The Pope, he says that contraception is a bad thing and that sex is for making babies as

132

well as for love. The young people round here they don't listen because it is so easy to pick up the tourist girls but if the girl she wants contraception, then he will say okay and produce a condom from his back pocket."

Fury blazed in her eyes then changed to panic as she realised she was halfway up a mountain in a strange country with a man she had met yesterday. "Don't you think I'm an easy lay you, you Gigolo" she warned and backed away.

Suddenly realising what he had said Giorgio darted after her "No, no Linda you misunderstand. I am not like that. I was explaining my countrymen's feelings towards contraception"

She put her hands over her ears and backed off some more "Stop saying that word. It sounds awful" she shouted, and backed perilously close to the edge of the track and to the steep drop beyond. Realising how closely she was flirting with danger Giorgio made a decision and suddenly pounced on her. As her left foot retreated over the edge into thin air soon to be followed by her right foot and then by the rest of her he caught her by the wrist and pulled with all his might. She was a big girl and it took all his strength to yank her back onto terra firma. As he pulled she was whiplashed into his arms and he had to move one foot behind him and lock his knee to stop them toppling over backwards. They stood there close together, both breathing heavily, him from the exertion, her from the shock. Slowly she looked behind her and saw the sheer drop down onto the rocks below and she spun back to him and cradled her head into his neck. He stroked her hair and made soothing noises to her until she was alright.

Eventually she pulled herself together and moved her head slightly away from his so she could see into his eyes. "Thank you. You saved my life" she said simply and there was no mistaking the love and trust that was in her voice or indeed in her eyes. He looked deep into her baby blues and said "Linda I did not mean to alarm you. I was trying to explain why I have so many relatives around here. My father, he is the head of the family, yes. He is the oldest brother so he is the head of an even bigger family yes. My father is a good Catholic and he believes what the Pope he says. So my father he makes sure

that his whole family follow his example and be good Catholics. We all love and respect my father so we follow his wishes. " He smiled broadly "I have many, many cousins and many, many aunts and uncles and we are all very close. It may be days before I see them again or it may be weeks but the greeting will always be the same. I prefer our way to the more modern ways of some of my friends and their families."

She nodded her agreement and wished her own family life could be so full of love and shows of affection. While she was certain that her parents loved her she knew they had difficulty with obvious shows of affection. She too was not exempt in this. While she wouldn't hesitate giving her father a kiss in the privacy of their own home she would die rather than do it if they met up in the high street. She envied Giorgio his simplistic view on family life and wished she could be a part of it. She smiled inwardly as she came to a decision and decided to act on it before she changed her mind. They were still entwined so she lifted her head nearer his and asked throatily "This greeting, this show of affection, does it extend beyond family or is it purely for them?"

He swallowed and seemed to be considering the question before he said "It depends on who the other person is".

"What if the other person was an English tourist who welcomed the show of affection?" she asked sweetly.

Again he seemed to consider the question carefully, then he leant forward and kissed her, for the first time, on her lips. They hung together for a few seconds then he pulled away and opened his eyes, full of uncertainty, and waited for her reaction. Linda stood there, eyes closed, head back, lips still parted slightly and savoured the moment until eventually she opened her eyes and looked deeply into his and smiled with a beautiful show of love and satisfaction. He kissed her again, this time more passionately and when he stopped she looked at him and this time his eyes were still closed and his lips were still parted as he savoured the moment.

"I like this old fashioned Catholic way" she breathed and they kissed again, long and hot, full of passion and fire.

Eventually they walked back, hand in hand, to the scooter and put on their helmets. As she climbed on board he reached across and held her hand. He had a curious look on his face and she waited patiently for him to tell her what was on his mind. He suddenly blurted "Linda. I am not sure why I want to tell you this, or that I should, but I will." He stopped and took a deep breath, as if he needed it to pluck up the courage. "I am a virgin" he suddenly said and guiltily looked around him, worried that the deserted mountain top had suddenly become crowded.

She thought about this for a while, wondering why he had elected to tell her.

She decided that it was to show her that he wasn't like the others he had mentioned earlier, to put her at her ease. And then she thought what a wonderful secret to share with someone. She realised that, as it obviously meant a lot to him, that he must feel very comfortable and close to her to want to divest himself in such a way. She whipped off her helmet and leant forward and planted a big kiss on his lips. "Thank you for sharing that with me" she

whispered and then added "Giorgio, I am a virgin too". They both giggled then kissed again. He bent down and picked up her helmet and lovingly returned it to her. Two minutes later they were skirting the hill top and flanked by the clear blue of the med and the heather and maquis scrub they made their way down to the coast and rejoined the C260 and headed inland to Besalu.

She hung on tightly as they gathered speed, not through fear but through love and affection. Half an hour later he pulled off and stopped in the entrance to a huge vineyard. Turning off the engine he pulled off his helmet, then after waiting for Linda to do the same he asked "Linda would you like to meet my family?"

"What, some more of them. Are you everywhere?" she asked looking into the vastness of the vineyard".

He laughed out loud. "Along the coast and for miles inland the Dos Nascimentos name is heard everywhere. We are" and he held his arms wide like a boasting fisherman "a massive family" and he laughed infectiously.

Laughing along with him Linda said she would love to meet more of his family then her hand suddenly shot to her mouth and her eyes looked terrified. "You mean your father don't you?" she said in something approaching awe.

He nodded sagely and she looked horrified. He smiled sweetly at her and took her hands in his. "Do not be afraid" he said "My father he will love you the moment he sees you." She didn't look so sure. She tossed her hair back and felt in her small backpack for a brush. Giorgio laughed out loud and she couldn't help but smile herself as she realised how silly and panicky she must look. He took her chin between his thumb and finger and gently raised her head. He leant forward and kissed her softly and her eyes cleared of the panic she had felt and she was ready to take on the world with him there by her side.

"He will love you like I love you" he whispered and the world stood still as she savoured the moment. No one had ever said they loved her and secretly she had worried that no one ever would. She looked deep into his eyes and fell deeper and deeper in love with him. "Giorgio. Do you mean that?" she asked, needing him to say it again. He nodded. "I love you Linda" he said simply. She raised her head and kissed him and mumbled "I love you". They kissed for several minutes until they needed to stop for air. With a huge grin on his handsome face he asked boyishly "I'm sorry I didn't quite hear that young lady. Would you say it again please?"

She smiled coyishly back at him and pushed him gently in the chest "I think you heard me perfectly well" she laughed and he took her hands in his. "Still I would like to hear you say it again" he said seriously. She gazed into his dark eyes and said in a rush

"Oh Giorgio I love you so much. I can't believe this is happening to me. I never expected any of this. I feel a little overwhelmed yet deliriously happy. Oh Giorgio I am so happy" and she snuggled tightly into his chest. When she parted from him she looked up at his face and he was beaming from ear to ear. "I am very happy too" he laughed "Very happy"

In the pouring rain Sheila tried again to get her key in the front door. It had been sticking for a few weeks now and despite her nagging Danny to get it

fixed he still hadn't done it. As the wind got up it blew more rain into her face as she finally got the key in and entered the house. She furiously threw her key down on the little telephone table and kicked off her sodden high heels.

Shaking her coat to get rid of the excess wet she hung it up and went into the front room and lit the fire. She was cold, wet and tired. She hadn't slept much last night. She had waited for Danny to come home until she had finally dropped off at around three o clock. She knew he was sulking about his mates going away and was worried that he might do something stupid. She had been doing a lot of thinking, the last couple of days. Since Ros had told her a few home truths she had been forced into thinking about her lifestyle. This was something she hadn't done for a long time. She had played the crap wife for so long she did it without thinking now. She had determined to make Danny pay for his unnecessary and hurtful remarks and had continued to do so ever since.

She now had to concede, after much soul searching, that she actually enjoyed her trampy lifestyle and that, as much as she hated to admit it, she was being selfish and grossly unfair to him. Last night she had decided to have a heart to heart with him and make the effort to change. She wanted to be a proper wife to him. She was tired of living the high life with whoever took her fancy while he sat at home most nights alone. It had to be said, as much as this hurt her, that she wasn't getting any younger and there

137

comes a time when you're no longer considered to be that young girl about town and are thought of as that old slapper. Sheila had worried for a while now that she may have crossed the line but had managed to push it aside and continue her seemingly endless quest for continued excitement and new men to conquer.

The more she thought about Danny too the worse she felt. She realised that it must have cost him a lot of self respect to have to sit back and quietly watch as his wife made a fool of him time and again. Ironically, she realised that the more he had turned a blind eye to her lifestyle the more outrageous she had become. She had even flaunted her new affair with her shift supervisor in his face and he had still turned the cheek. Every time he had done that she had smacked him when he wasn't looking and hurt him when he wasn't expecting it. She had faced these harsh truths and had decided to tell him about them last night but he had never shown. She wasn't mad with him last night, just worried, as he may have done something stupid without the guiding hand of one of his friends to keep him on the right path. She loved that part of him.

That stupid bit when he did something that made her laugh out loud and go

"Oh Danny" in almost a patronising way. But it wasn't patronising it was love.

She missed that. They hadn't had that kind of love between them since they had married. She thought maybe it was a stupid marriage, a marriage based on the belief that she was expecting his child. How could a marriage built on such shaky foundations have any hope of working especially when, as it turned out she wasn't carrying his child. She wanted him to walk through the door now so she could sit him down and tell him these things. Get everything off her chest and watch his reaction to see if he still felt anything for her. If he did then she was willing to work from there to make this marriage work She would do all in

her powers to make a go of it. He deserved that. And she wanted it. She looked at her watch. Where was the fat little bleeder.

She walked round and round in the living room, trying to figure out where he could be, then with a little judder she thought about the hospital. Oh God, what if he was lying in a hospital bed unconscious or what if he had been in an accident and had lost his memory. He could be there for months and not know who he was, while she was searching all over for him. She forced herself to calm down and decided to simply ring the hospital and ask. She went over to the telephone table by the door and picked up the phone book to find the number for Rotherham General Hospital. She was flicking through the pages when she spotted, out of the corner of her eye, three letters on the floor under the letterbox. She must have stepped over them when she had come in. She could see two of the letters were bills but the third had a hand written address on it. She went back to the phone book , trying to find H for hospital and cursing when she saw "See under R for Rotherham" written in bold type. She swore softly to herself and turned the pages looking for R. Her attention was drawn again to the hand written letter. There was something about it that was nagging away at her but she couldn't think what it could be. She flicked the pages of the thick book then stopped suddenly as it dawned on her what it was about the letter that was distracting her so. It was Danny's hand writing. She allowed the book to fall closed back onto the table and stared at the letter lying on the floor. After a while she bent down and picked it up. She knew what it was, of course, there could only be one reason for Danny to write to her. He was leaving her. She turned the letter over and over in the hope that it would tell her what was inside without her having to open it. She knew that when she opened it and read the contents her life would never be the same. It was all her fault, she knew that. She should have changed years ago. Or even last week.

She was going to have this huge, clear the air, meeting with Danny and now the little fat bastard had left her before she had the chance to tell him how sorry she was and how much she loved him.

She stared for a while at the letter then, with shaking fingers, opened it and stared at the contents, afraid to go any further.

"Oh God, please let this be a letter from the hospital saying they have a badly injured man there who has lost his memory but had this envelope in his pocket when we found him after the car crash. Or something like that" she whispered.

Plucking up all the courage she could muster she dipped her hand into the envelope and pulled out a cheque made out to their joint account from Post Office Counters for One Thousand Five Hundred and Eight Pounds and Eighty Pence. She turned the cheque over but there was nothing on the back. She stared, uncomprehendingly at it for a few seconds then looked back inside the envelope. She could see there was something else there so she fished it out. It was a Post Office compliment slip and written on it in Danny's own hand it said "See you next week-love Danny".

Sheila thought about this. Why would Danny send her a big cheque and tell her he would see her next week. Where had he got the money from. Where was he going for a week. What was happening. Sheila mulled it over in her mind but

couldn't come up with an answer. Then a thought struck her. A few months earlier somebody at work, who was it, Shazza, that's it, had got five numbers on the lottery. She had gone down to the paper shop where she had bought the ticket but had been told she had to go to a main post office to cash it because of the large amount. She had collected her money in one thousand pounds cash and the rest in a cheque. She had moaned that the Post Office wouldn't give her it all in cash. She ran from the hallway and went into the room and put the telly on. She then went to teletext and got the lottery pages Impatiently she waited for it to fetch up this weeks numbers and details of the pay outs. Then, all of a sudden, it was there. Five numbers paying fifteen winners Two Thousand Five Hundred and Eight Pounds and Eighty Pence each. Minus the One Thousand Pounds he would be allowed to take away in cash and she was left with the amount written on the cheque. So the little fat bastard had won the lottery and not told her. She'd kill him when he came home. But when would that be. The note said "See you next week", so where could he be for a full week. Even as the question formed in her mind, the answer jostled for it's own space. She knew immediately where he was and who he was with and as her face changed to a very nice shade of purple she exploded with rage and indignation at his treachery. "I'll kill the little fat, useless, arsehole" she bellowed as she picked up a cushion from the settee and threw it at the wall. If she could get her hands on him she'd chop his balls off. She'd rip his head off and stick it up his arse.

She'd pull his old man off and give it to next door's cat. She'd. She'd. She ran out of things to do to him and just decided to kill him. Right she'd have to find him first so how would she do that. Kicking a cup that was stood at the side of the settee she thought that the best and fastest way would be to ask Sue's mum, who only lived down the road. Sue's mum hated her, she knew that, so she would have to devise a plan. She would need to calm down too, before she accosted the old bat. She tried deep breathing and went upstairs to check that his passport had gone. It had but the few minutes searching had given her time for her blood pressure to drop and she felt able to go out and see Nellie.

She crossed the road and went down a bit until she came to the gate leading up to Nellie's and Mick and Sue's houses. She went up the path and down the gennel and into Nellie's small garden. She straightened her blouse and knocked on the door and a few seconds later a very shocked Nellie mumbled "hello".

"Hello Mrs Thomson" Sheila gushed as if meeting an old friend. "I don't know if you know me, I'm Danny Taylor's wife Sheila, I live up the road."

Nellie stared at her. She took in the fishnet tights, stiletto's, mini skirt, see through blouse and painted face and couldn't believe her eyes that this… this tart was knocking on her door. After all she was a respected elder of the community and Sheila was the village bike. She hastily looked round to see if any of the neighbours were looking and made no attempt to hide her disgust.

Sheila, however, ploughed on regardless. She would normally have retaliated at such an obvious affront but she knew that today that would get her nowhere.

She smiled sweetly and got down to business.

"Anyway Mrs Thomson, as you know the lads have gone to Spain for the week. Of course you know, one of 'em is almost your son in law isn't he." She

smiled winningly which was totally lost on the glowering Nellie. "Anyroadup.

Danny hasn't gone, can't afford it. Well he's not working is he and he's sat at home feeling right fuc… er fed up and a bit left out so I says why not phone

'em up. Surprise 'em like. Wish 'em all the best and say 'have a drink on me'.

Cheer him up a bit I thought. Anyway, cut a long story short, he can't remember the name of the hotel where they're staying. Men eh, forget their own names if we didn't keep shouting it at 'em"

Nellie stared at her cleavage and her painted face. She knew that Sheila worked at the nut factory on shifts so this must be how she dressed for work. She had never liked Sheila, or her family for that matter and had thought it a crying shame when a nice boy like Danny got caught up with her. She was surprised that Sheila would go on an errand of mercy for Danny. She had always thought that the marriage was a bit of a sham, but she was here and seemingly in an effort to cheer Danny up so she couldn't think of one good reason not to tell her the name of the hotel. "El Maritimo" she said and the winning smile immediately disappeared from Sheila's face as she turned without another word and went back down the path leaving a bemused Nellie still holding the door.

At the gate Sheila stopped and looked up the street towards her own house. She now had all the information she needed and she had a large cheque in her pocket. Should she act on her first impulse or wait till Danny returned next week. She turned right and marched down the street to the shopping parade on the main road. She passed the mini market, the DIY shop and the fruit and veg shop and pushed open the door of the Sheffield and Rotherham Building Society. Inside there was no queue so she walked straight up to the counter and asked the bored looking cashier "I've a cheque here from the lottery. Can I cash it or do I have to put it in my account first.?"

The young girl sniffed at the cheque and then at Sheila. She knew who she was, of course, everybody round here did. "You'll have to put it in your account Mrs Taylor and it'll take four working days to clear."

"Shit" thought Sheila. This was buggering up her plan She needed the cash to fly out and kill Danny. She was taking the cheque back off the cashier when, almost as an afterthought the young girl said "Course we wouldn't bounce a cheque against it. I mean being a lottery cheque it's as good as money in the bank isn't it"

Thirty minutes later Sheila was sat in the Thomas Cook branch office in Rotherham. She had a return ticket to Alicante in her hand and she smiled as she watched the handsome young assistant counting out the pesetas in front of her. When he had finished she signed the cheque and put her cheque guarantee number on the back. She was taking One Thousand Pounds, the same as Danny so he couldn't say anything about her wasting it. As he handed over the money the young man said. "Right madam, your tickets are for ten thirty in the morning from Manchester with an open return for one month. There's your cash. That will be One Thousand Pounds please" and he took the proffered cheque from her. Sheila put the cash and the tickets in her bag and left the shop. She smiled as she thought of the look on that bastard's face when she turned up tomorrow.

CHAPTER EIGHT

That bastards face, at that exact moment, was contorted in agony as another wave of the shits racked his body. Ron had been to the Chemists and had got him some powder but it hadn't had any effect yet. He had been on the lav now for twenty minutes. They say pigs don't smell their own muck, well this proved Danny was no pig 'cos the stench was killing him. After Mick had given him the box of powders the lads had all but run from the room and he couldn't blame them. Jeff had taken his clothes out of the wardrobe and put them next door to keep the smell off them. He decided that he must have finished so he stood up and gingerly wiped his arse. He couldn't see it but he knew his ring must be red raw by now. He could feel the heat off it. He pulled up his stained pants and carefully crossed the floor to find his bed. He inched himself down and tenderly laid back, pulling up the sheets to his chin. He smiled beatifically and closed his eyes to rest. Then he jumped up and ran for the bog as another wave of stomach pains took over his entire body. He made it. Only just but he made it.

Mick was by the pool, drying himself off. He was laughing at the others as Jeff was showing off doing a handstand underwater. Ron swam up to him and held his legs until Jeff's head appeared spluttering and shouting. Jeff cursed and coughed as the others laughed at him. Mick picked up his suntan oil and started to rub some on his arms when his attention was caught by something at the bar.

He turned to look more closely and his heart leapt as he saw the most beautiful girl he had ever laid eyes on. Her perfect body was barely covered by a luminous lime green bikini and as she turned he saw brilliant white teeth set in the most kissable lips he could imagine. She was one of those marvellous creatures that always look at home wherever they were. If he had seen her on top of a snow capped mountain he knew she would still have seemed the most beautiful girl in the world.

He heard voices around him but couldn't tell a word of what was being said and he could smell ice cream for some reason and it smelled strong and fresh and full of vanilla. He dropped his sun cream on the bed and walked round the pool. He didn't know why he was doing this and he had no idea what he would do when he got over there but he knew that he had to go over to the girl and meet her.

Subconsciously he breathed in giving him a flat stomach and he tested his breath on the back of his hand as he neared her. He was amazed to discover that he had butterflies in his stomach, something he had never experienced

before and his mouth felt dry. He didn't have a clue what he would say or do when he reached her but he didn't care, he just had to meet her.

The barman turned to a little transistor radio and switched it on and a weak voiced Spanish version of Celine Dion belted out *My heart will go on* from Titanic. He circled the pool in slow motion and little kids playing in the warm shallow end splashed their arms and legs sending little jets of water into his face and hair. Slowly he shook his head, nearing her all the time, and sent silver droplets spinning back to their home. It was an amazing effect that most film makers would have been proud of ruined only by the fact that as she turned slowly around and caught sight of him, his rugged body shining with the sun oil, his muscles rippling with the tension he was putting them under, he accidentally tripped over a little girl who chose that moment to run and jump into the arms of her waiting mother in the pool. Mick didn't see the child until it was too late. He grabbed ineffectually at the little girl but only succeeded in knocking her head first into the water about three feet away from her screaming mother. As he realised what he had done he lost his footing on the wet tiles and slipped sideways into the pool. He reached out with both hands and tried desperately to grab something, anything to steady his balance and felt his left hand come into contact, first with something soft and round then with what felt like material of some kind. Whatever it was it was enough to support his weight and stop him going headlong into the pool. He pushed hard and felt the material give way and heard screams from the area around the end of his arm.

He steadied himself with his other hand and looked up to see a half naked woman frantically trying to pull her little daughter out of the water with one hand while trying to cover her enormous floating bosoms with the other. Mick saw her grab the unfortunate girls arm and pull her, coughing, back into the sunshine then hold her to her breast as she sobbed hysterically. Mick knelt there staring the furious woman in the face and attempted a wan smile, but received a tirade of abuse that he expected and deserved but thought was a little strong considering the infant that was clutched tightly to the woman's heaving chest. He wondered whether he ought to apologise or go for the casual, witty response, in an effort to make light of the situation. "Nice tits love" might do it but he back heeled the idea when he realised that there was a good chance the woman might have a husband round here somewhere and he didn't want any more trouble while he was still on this mission to meet the most beautiful girl in the world. The thought of this vision of loveliness spurred him on and he spun round to see her staring open mouthed at his clumsy antics. Inwardly he cursed but he turned again to face the family he had so recently wronged and determined to make it alright. He jumped into the water and, apologising profusely, offered to take the little girl while the lady dressed herself. He tactfully managed not to stare too much at her nakedness and as she passed the struggling infant to him, he made soothing noises to her until the little girl stopped crying. He nursed her with as much affection as he could muster until he heard the woman say "I'll have her back now" and he turned to see that she now had her costume back in place and apart from a red face seemed none the worse for wear. He handed the little girl back to her and smiled broadly. "I'm

really sorry" he repeated "It was a complete accident and I just grabbed at anything to regain my balance". He watched her blush furiously and he smiled back easily knowing that the crisis was over. "Very nice" he added and saw her colour up again, unused to such attention from such a good looking young man." The little girl" he said pointing to the child in her arms and saw her disappointment as she realised what he had meant.

He turned and climbed out of the pool and shook the water off his body. He looked around and saw that the girl was still with her friends and was still watching him, now with a smile playing on her beautiful lips.

"Please, it was nothing" he said raising his hand as if to ward off unwarranted thanks from the people at poolside. "Anybody would have done the same" he added and looked around him, nodding in a self deprecating way. Some people who hadn't seen the incident but just caught this bit looked on in something approaching awe and respect at this man who had obviously just done some good deed and was now insisting on receiving no credit or thanks. An old lady who had been reading the paper when she heard the scream had seen him jump in the water and then seen him nursing a little girl while her mother stood by uselessly fiddling with her clothing obviously unable to save the girl herself.

She applauded, much to Mick's genuine embarrassment and as others joined in he raised both hands to silence them. "Honestly, it was nothing really" and he turned round to see the woman still clutching the child to her arms, but now with a smile on her face. He smiled back and shrugged his shoulders and they both laughed easily at their little secret. Ten seconds later he was face to face with the beautiful young girl of his dreams. Unsure what to do next he stood there and took in her beauty until she stepped closer to him and raised her hand up to his neck. He wasn't sure what she was going to do and he shivered slightly as she touched him. He had a little blob of sun tan lotion on his neck that he must have missed and with two long elegant fingers she rubbed it in, slowly working it round in a little circle. He half closed his eyes and wanted to purr like a cat having it's ear stroked, but fought the desire. Instead he lifted his arm and touched her on the neck and curled her dark hair around his fingers. I don't know if you believe in love at first sight, but if this wasn't it, then it was as close as any two people have a right to expect. The electricity was almost visible and both seemed loath to release their hold from the other.

Eventually he spoke, softly and throatily. "Hello. I'm Mick". It wasn't much but it was all his mind could come up with at the moment and his dry throat may have struggled with any more.

"Hola. Mi lamo Julia" she replied in a voice that thrilled him.

"Do you speak English?" he asked and he wasn't sure whether he wanted her to say yes or no.

"Si. I speak the good English" she replied proudly and he smiled at the softness of her voice.

"Would you like a drink or something?" he asked and watched her nod her head and turn and say something to her friends. The girl nearest her turned and looked at him, giving him the once over and said something back to Julia whereupon they both giggled. Embarrassed, he held his arm out indicating they

should adjourn to the bar and Julia peeled away from her friends and fell in along side him. They ordered two cokes and looked inquisitively at each other until the barman broke the spell.

"What?" asked Mick.

"Four hundred pesetas *por favor* he repeated.

Mick stared at the barman as it dawned on him that he was wearing his trunks and hadn't any cash on him. He looked, hopefully, at Julia who raised both palms upwards then touched her bikini to show him she too had no cash on her.

She giggled again and he smiled back.

"Won't be a sec" he announced and indicated to the waiting barman that he was going for some cash. He turned and set off at a pace round the pool but pulled up after ten yards and spun round to face her.

"Don't go away" he said with just a hint of pleading in his voice and she shook her head and laughed. Smiling broadly he turned again and ran round the pool to his sunlounger.

When he got there he searched for his shorts. He threw a couple of towels about and needlessly moved trainers to see if they were hiding behind them.

Jeff and Ron were laid on their beds now, drying off in the sun, watching him intently.

"Looking for something?" asked Jeff after a while.

"Yeah, my shorts" answered Mick, scratching his head. He got down on his hands and knees and peered again under the lounger.

Ron sat up, genuinely worried for his friend. "You sure you know what you are doing?" It had never occurred to Ron that Mick might be after the opposite sex during the holiday. He had known Mick all his life, and Sue, and he knew how much they had always loved each other and he didn't want to see his best friend spoil it.

Mick looked up and saw Ron watching him. He thought for a few seconds then said "No. But I'm doing it anyway." He had a defiant look in his eyes as if daring Ron to make something of it. Ron decided to bide his time and not butt in just yet.

"Give him the shorts Jeff" he ordered.

"Yeah but you said.." but Ron turned and stared at him so he capitulated and grudgingly pulled the shorts from behind his back and handed them over. Mick quickly put them on and reached into the pocket and pulled out a wad of pesetas. He looked up and saw Jeff smiling at him.

"What?" he asked him.

"Nothing" Jeff continued to smile and cast his eyes over to the bar where Julia sat patiently waiting.

"Nice bird" he continued "Fair body on her, give her that. Bet she goes a bit eh"

Mick smiled back at him then looked at Ron. His face turned serious.

"If you've got something to say, say it" he demanded. Ron stood up so they were eyeball to eyeball.

"When I've got something to say, you'll be the first to hear it" he said softly.

Mick swallowed, surprised at the venom in his friend's voice. For a split second he thought about not going back over to Julia but he quickly brushed it aside. He knew Ron was only being concerned about him, and looking out for him to make sure he didn't do anything stupid but, to be honest, he didn't care.

He had to go back to her. He felt compelled in some way to take this thing further and see how it would develop. He suddenly smiled a big friendly smile at Ron and moved away.

"Okay pal. Okay. Gotta go now. I'll see you later" and he was off, hurrying back round the pool.

Ron watched him go and his heart sank because he had seen the look of determination on Mick's face. He knew there was going to be trouble but he wasn't sure what to do about it. There was something else though behind that sadness that Ron was feeling. He was more than a little jealous. He wanted someone to love too. Someone to come home to, to hold, to cuddle up to.

Someone to talk to, to laugh with.

He lay back down and watched his friend pay for the drinks and tenderly lead the young woman to a table. He watched them sit down and saw them tentatively touch each other, and laugh at each other, at some witty remark or something silly. A tear formed in the corner of his eye at the sadness of it all and he brusquely

151

brushed it away. He turned to see if Jeff had seen him but Jeff was asleep already, softly snoring.

Ron suddenly felt very alone and scared, frightened that he would always be this way, alone without someone to share his fears or his hopes.

He saw Mick reach across and stroke the woman's hair and saw her slowly move forward in her seat until their faces were almost touching, then they inched agonisingly slowly into a kiss. He could feel the electricity from across the pool and he envied them that feeling and he forced himself to look away before he cried again.

"You're just a big soft sentimental old puff" he muttered under his breath and smiled ruefully. This reminded him that he had intended to sort out his sexuality during this holiday. He didn't know how yet, but he was more determined than ever to do it.

Danny woke up but didn't move. He had learned form bitter experience that moving was bad. Sleeping was good, moving was bad. They were the two rules that had begun to govern his life. He hadn't moved for a couple of hours now and he hadn't had the shits during that time. "If I just lay here for ever" he thought "I might never shit again."

After about twenty minutes and still no churning of the stomach he felt confident enough to risk moving his head. Carefully he inched it to one side then the other. Nothing. He lifted both his arms slowly out of the bed and laid them carefully on the white linen sheet. Nothing. Gently he forced himself into a sitting position. Nothing. He eased one hand under the bed sheets and pulled the boxer shorts from the crack of his bum where they were sticking. They were Jeff's shorts and they needed changing. He had only brought the one pair of pants that he had worn to travel in, reasoning that as he was only there for

one week he could get away with just the one. He hadn't banked on losing three stone of shit in a two day period though. He had made it to the lav on every occasion but the inevitable build up on the old ringpiece had made his own pants too whiffy even for him. He had borrowed a pair of Jeff's boxers knowing his friend wouldn't mind, but now these too were beginning to stick so maybe he would need another pair soon.

Slowly he lowered his legs out of the bed and stood up. His stomach didn't lurch or do the usual somersaults but it felt empty.

He walked round the room and felt okay. A little shaky perhaps but that was only to be expected.

Right, the final test. He walked to the bathroom and opened the door. The smell hit him almost immediately but his stomach didn't move so that was a good sign. Pulling down his boxers, to reveal a faint skid mark, he sat down gingerly on the toilet which had become like a second home to him and waited. He waited two whole minutes and not a thing. He pushed downwards and couldn't even manage a fart. He was totally empty.

"I am totally devoid of shit" he said to himself and he happily jumped up from his throne and had a quick wash. Two minutes later he was dressed in a clean T

shirt and his football shorts. On his feet he had on the old flip flops he had found in the cupboard.

"Right" he shouted, clapping his hands together "The holiday starts here" and he picked up the set of room keys that Jeff had obtained for him and went out of the room to search for the others. At the end of the corridor he pressed the button for the lift which appeared almost immediately and got in. It was full although it contained only four people and two of them were little kids. The rest of the room was taken up by a giant inflatable crocodile and four carrier bags of poolside essentials.

"Going for the week?" he asked jovially and the mother smiled back although the father looked a bit pissed off.

153

The doors closed and he pressed the button for the ground floor. However the lift only descended one floor before the doors opened again to reveal a tall blonde Germanic looking youth standing in the corridor. The youth turned and yelled something to an older couple, obviously his parents, who were stood in a doorway halfway along the corridor. The couple were staring into the room and shouting something to someone inside and gesticulating wildly in the direction of the lift. The German boy turned and stepped into the lift, determined that it would not leave without him. He purposely kept his foot on the threshold so the door wouldn't close and waved wildly at his parents.

Danny watched this with an amused grin on his face which changed when he realised that the already cramped space was now going to be worse. Inching forward he gently nudged the boy, who although he was only about fourteen, was almost as tall as Danny but obviously more wiry. The boy hadn't been expecting it and suddenly shot forward and out onto the corridor. Danny pressed the button and the doors closed leaving a shocked boy and an irate father running towards him shouting *"schnell, schnell"* at the top of his voice.

Satisfied, Danny waited for the lift to drop the other four floors. He looked

round to see the couple in the lift with him watching him with a shocked expression on their faces.

"Oops" he said and they both nodded as if to say "That's alright then"

As the doors opened on the ground floor two workmen immediately tried to shove in, dragging behind them a large bed. They were followed by a very attractive receptionist who was wildly gesticulating and pointing to the other end of the foyer. Danny squeezed past this melee and set off across the foyer and outside into freedom. He had a spring in his step, happy to be starting his holiday at last. He felt the emptiness in his stomach and wondered whether it was too early for a kebab. He thought of his sore rutter and decided to give it a miss today.

The receptionist helped the English family and their crocodile out of the lift and decided to give in to the two workmen and allow them to use the passenger lift as they obviously didn't want to walk the extra thirty yards to the bigger service lift. She waved her arms at them and ushered them into the lift. They muttered ungracious "*Gracias*" and proceeded to inch the bed inside the lift where it immediately became jammed. The receptionist saw this and turned her back and, with a smug expression on her face, walked back to her desk. It had been a long day and her shift wasn't due to end for another three hours. As soon as she had arrived this morning she had discovered that the downstairs toilets were blocked and despite repeated phone threats the plumbers had only turned up half an hour ago and locked themselves in the toilet after putting up a sign in three different languages informing people that the toilets were out of order. This, at least, put a stop to the constant stream of enquiries from the holidaymakers as to when the toilets would be open again. She had smiled her reply all day but she knew that smile was wearing thin now and was ready for a nice sit down. She thought she might scream if anything else happened out of the ordinary today.

As Danny walked out into the sunshine a wave of nausea hit him. His hand shot to his stomach as he felt it lurch in that all too familiar way. He held his breath, hoping and praying that it would go away. He doubled over in agony as another wave hit him and he realised that he had better get to a toilet quick if he wasn't going to ruin his only shorts.

He looked round him and saw with relief the universal fat stick man on a door at the end of the foyer signifying that the toilets were inside. Clutching his heaving gut he raced across and shoved hard against the door. It didn't open and he crumpled into it. He looked down at the door handle and pushed again.

No response. He rattled the door and kicked it but still it didn't budge. That was when he noticed the sign on the floor propped up against the wall. It was in three different languages, Spanish, English and German. The middle line said

"Out of Order" and Danny's heart sank at the sight of it.

Behind the locked door three plumbers were fast asleep having unblocked the offending toilet within the first five minutes of arriving. They had a minimum call out fee of two hours and had every intention of honouring it.

Danny kicked the door again and turned, wild eyed, to look for another lav. His eyes darted around the busy foyer and his stomach groaned audibly so he flip

flopped around a bit in the hope that this would make a toilet suddenly appear.

He spotted the lift and realised he still had the room key on him so he hurried over. To his utter amazement there was a bed stuck halfway in the lift and a noisy workman vainly pushing it. He looked beyond the bed and saw what could have been the workman's twin brother attempting to push the bed back out.

"What the fuck?" he thought and looked round to see if there were hidden cameras around. His arse puckered and he swore that if Jeremy Beadle or that fat bird from Emmerdale jumped out from behind the bed he'd nut 'em.

"To me. To you" "To me. To you" the two brothers called to each other and Danny almost lost his rag as he decided this was definitely a joke.

"Can I help you Sir?" a beautiful sexy voice asked from behind him and he spun round, still with one hand clasped tightly to his bum cheeks, to see the pretty receptionist smiling at him.

He wondered how she knew he was English, not realising that the old flip flops, football shorts and T shirt bearing the legend "Don't fuck with me, I'm having a bad day" were a bit of a give away.

"I need a toilet" he whispered urgently.

"*Que*" she said, straining to hear him.

"Toilet" he whispered again, looking round embarrassedly. No one had actually heard because of the general hubbub in the foyer.

"I'm sorry Sir I can't hear you" the young woman apologised waving her arms around indicating the background noise.

Exasperated and in dire need of a toilet immediately Danny lost his temper. His fingers had almost disappeared up his arse in his attempt to hold back the inevitable. As he writhed and grimaced he shouted "I need a toilet now before I shit myself".

Amazingly, as Danny reached the word 'need', the whole room for one reason or another suddenly stopped talking and as his voice sailed out across the open space every head turned to see who was in such dire straits, or diarrhoea to be more precise.

Trying to stifle a laugh the receptionist began to point to the toilets at the other end of the foyer then realised that they were out of order.

"You will have to use your room *senor*" she offered brightly.

"Yes. Good idea" Danny said, red faced. "If you'll get the Chuckle Brothers out of the lift I'll do that eh".

She saw the problem straight away of course and was just about to suggest that he use the service lift when Danny decided that as he could feel his fingers were now getting warm he had better make a move. Looking over the girl's shoulder he spotted the staircase and made a run for it. His flip flops flipped and flopped noisily across the marble floor and everyone watched the mad Englishman with an amused expression on their face. In a desperate attempt to stem the flow he crouched almost doubled over and dipped his left shoulder so as to ease the pressure on his stomach. He looked for all the world like The Hunchback of Notre Dame on holiday as he disappeared up the stairs.

He reached a landing and turned up another flight of stairs where he saw a door with a number one on it. Shit. That means another seven flights to go before he reached sanctuary. Please God just let the stairs be empty. Don't let me meet anyone on the stairs.

As he rounded the next two flights of stairs he suddenly became aware of voices above him and he metaphorically raised his fist in anger at God who obviously wasn't paying too much attention. He looked up the stairwell but couldn't see anyone so he just kept going. Flip flop flip flop he went up another couple of flights. Maybe it would be alright. Maybe the voices would disappear and he would go straight to his room undetected and undisturbed.

Above him the family of Germans were marching down to reception to complain about the lift being out of order. The head of the family, Otto Von Rupp, was loudly berating his long suffering spouse about her tardiness. It appeared that everything was her fault. Hers and that stupid woman in reception. Lunch had been late by a full ten minutes and Otto had every intention of making a complaint about that. Then, when he had reached reception, he had discovered that the downstairs toilets were out of order.

Unforgivable. He had informed the ridiculously young girl behind the desk of this and had been advised to use the toilets in his room. Totally disregarding the fact that they did in fact need to go to their room to change for the beach, Otto decided this was an affront to his dignity and demanded a complaint form.

His browbeaten spouse had watched disinterestedly as she was used to her husbands ways but her children writhed around with embarrassment.

When Otto had finally led his family up to their room to change he had discovered his teenage daughter was wearing what could only be described as dental floss to hide her shame, he had thrown a wobbly and demanded she change into something more dignified. He had been waiting in the corridor for his errant offspring to change, all the time berating her mother for her daughter's waywardness when his son had attempted to hold the lift for them only to be pushed out by an English family with a giant crocodile. He would complain loudly about this when he reached reception. Now however he was mid rant on the fact that the lift had now seemed to have stopped altogether.

This too was going on a complaint form. They turned the corner and went down the next flight of stairs. That's when Otto first heard it. Flip flop it went.

Flip flop. Otto stopped suddenly and his long suffering wife barged into him.

Otto almost went over the handrail but managed to steady himself while giving his wife a dirty look. He would speak to her later about that but for now he held his hand in the air indicating he required silence. They all stood still and held their breath. They all could hear it now. Flip flop, flip flop. Otto gave his wife a puzzled look which she returned in spades. The youth turned to his attractive older sister and she shrugged her shoulders and continued to listen. Flip flop.

Flip flop. Then, just as Otto was about to declare that he believed it was a message, morse code, maybe from someone stuck in the lift, it changed.

Flip flop, flip squelch, aarghhh, flip, squelch, ohno, flip, squelch, it now went.

Otto decided it wasn't a morse code message after all, but he hadn't got the foggiest what it was, although he soon found out.

Danny screamed as the first spurts escaped his fingers. He dug in deeper but couldn't stem the rapidly increasing flow. He felt the hot smelly liquid escape from his boxers (well Jeff's boxers) and his football shorts and dribble down his left leg. He wondered, even mid shit, why it had only gone down one leg, but couldn't come up with a logical explanation. Tears welled up in his eyes at the indignity of it all and he marvelled at the amount of liquid the human body could expunge in a few seconds. Or at least he would have if he had the time.

159

As it was Danny kept on running. Round and round. Up and up. All the time the greeny brown goo shot down his left leg where it came into contact with the left flip flop (which I suppose is called a flip) and was sent squelching behind him leaving a trail of devastation in his wake.

He looked up again and to his great relief realised that the voices above him had disappeared. Whoever they had belonged to must have reached their floor and gone through the door. Thank God.

Otto decided that, as the noise was getting nearer and showed no sign of stopping he had better lead his family off the stairs. He was just about to issue his orders to that effect when Danny, still doubled up with his left shoulder leading, suddenly came into view round the staircase just below him.

Danny saw the Germans as he turned and decided that his best option, possibly his only option, was to keep going, so he dropped his shoulder even lower, closed his eyes and flopped and squelched right up to them.

Otto's wife grabbed her offspring and pulled them into the wall. It was as if it had been carved out in their exact image, so neatly did they disappear into it.

Otto, on the other hand, didn't react so quickly and as the mad English Humpback approached him, he had to throw himself up against the railing.

That was when the smell hit him. It was a smell that Otto had never experienced before. If you imagine rotting cabbage mixed with old sprouts kept in a runners trainer and wrapped in a pair of lepers knickers you still wouldn't have been close. Otto didn't have time to imagine anything. As the hunchback passed him and the smell first hit him hard in the face, something else happened that totally took Otto's mind off the smell. Flip, squelch, flip, squelch, it went. Straight into Otto's face. Nay, straight into Otto's mouth.

"Aaarrrghhhh" he screamed as the awful liquid shot past his lips and hit the back of the throat. That was when he was sick. Well the first time anyway. Otto screamed again, then retched again, then screamed then retched a couple more times.

Danny heard the screams, but wasn't sure if they were his own. He kept on running anyway just to be on the safe side. A couple of turns later and he saw the door with a number five on it and with deep gratitude he pushed it open. He stopped as he opened the door and looked around but couldn't see anybody.

Then a thought struck him. He pulled off his shirt, then his flip flops and wrapped the shirt round his left foot and lower leg. He knew it wouldn't stem the flow for long but as long as it got him back to his room without leaving a greeny brown trail he would be happy.

Back on the stairwell, Otto was still screaming, watched by his bemused and totally shit free family. Otto had tears streaming down his face such was his

shock and utter distaste of the situation which perhaps was just as well because if he had been able to see clearly he may have made out his wife, still clutching her children to her bosom, laughing uncontrollably.

CHAPTER NINE

That evening, in the Hotel Rosemary Park bar, three very worried girls sat nursing three untouched drinks. They were, of course, waiting the arrival of Linda. Not for the first time Sue looked at her watch.

"What time is it now?" asked Ros, even though she had on a watch of her own.

"Half eight" Sue answered with a sigh. "Where is she?"

Claire turned her drink round and round on the polished table. "I told her to be careful. I said don't go anywhere where it wasn't crowded. I told her."

Ros reached over and held her hand." She'll be alright" she assured her.

"Do you really think so Ros?" asked Claire.

With much more conviction than she felt Ros nodded "Yes. I'm certain." Claire nodded and smiled and took a little sip from her glass.

"I'm sure you're right" she said, but she put the glass down and started to turn it round and round again.

Sue looked at her watch again.

"What time is it?" asked Ros.

"Still half past" she answered and they half smiled at each other.

"You ladies. You are ready for another drink, yes" came a voice from behind Sue, who half turned to see Manuel, the snidy waiter, sidling up to them.

"No thanks" Claire said and indicated their full glasses on the table.

Manuel saw the full glasses and tutted. "Come on ladies. You are on holiday yes, so let your hair down a little yes"

"Go away" said Sue in as nice a voice as she could muster.

"Ladies, ladies please. I am only doing my job. My job is to serve you drinks, yes, but also it is to make sure you have a good time while you are in my country." He puffed his chest out self importantly as a thought struck him. "I am like an Ambassador for my country, yes" he looked at the girls to see if this news had sent them bandy legged at his importance but was disappointed to see them glance at each other and giggle, mocking him.

Sulkily he changed tack and went on the attack. "How come you girls are not out clubbing or meeting some nice drunken English yob who will slaver all over you until he falls asleep in his own vomit."

Sue and Ros looked at each other and pulled a face. "Who on earth did he think he was talking to them like that?" Sue thought but she felt a little intimidated so she kept her mouth shut.

"Look just fuck off" Claire said, as she felt no intimidation at all.

Manuel moved closer to Claire and bent down slightly to see into her eyes better. It also gave him a much better view of her cleavage, which was a bonus.

He whispered softly, yet loud enough for the others to hear, "Or maybe it is to see me, eh. Maybe you can't resist Manuel's charms, eh."

Claire laughed in his face, and said, loudly enough for not only Sue and Ros to hear, but also, half the room "Who the fuck do you think you are, eh, talking to us like that. You arrogant fuckin' ugly, smelly, oily, smarmy, fuckin' dago"

Manuel stepped back in amazement at this foul mouthed tirade of abuse. This wasn't what he had in mind at all. He looked around him, nervously searching out his supervisor, who he knew would sack him if he found him bothering the guests. He knew this for a fact because the supervisor had told him so three weeks earlier after a similar incident involving another English girl who hadn't taken kindly to his heavy handed advances. He had never learned the art of subtlety because to be honest he hadn't needed to. Most of the girls he met were drunk for the whole holiday and subtlety would be wasted on them. He was a good looking lad and that was usually enough to get into their pants. That and persistence. On occasion he had also turned a deaf ear to any mention of the word 'no', especially if the girl was really drunk. It didn't matter to him then if the girl kept saying no. He knew she wanted it really so he just got on with it and forced his attentions on her anyway. They were always so drunk that in the morning they couldn't remember anyway. Not everything.

Sometimes though things went wrong, and this seemed to be one of them. He had already stated his intention of having Claire but unless she turned up one night completely wasted, and then it would have to be alone, he couldn't see how he was going to do it. He backed off now and decided his best bet was to get out of there as soon as he could.

"So sorry" he offered and then made a dash for it as Claire got out of her chair and moved toward him. He dashed behind the bar and disappeared into the store room at the back where he stayed until he thought things would have died down and then he avoided eye contact with Claire for the rest of the night.

Almost everyone had heard the outburst though and he knew people were mocking him as he went about his work, for the rest of the night. He would have his revenge though. He never doubted that.

On a dusty mountain road, travelling at around forty miles an hour in the gathering dusk, Linda clung onto Giorgio for all her worth. She felt no fear however, it was just a marvellous excuse to hold him close for as long as she possibly could. She could willingly have carried on that bike ride forever but she knew it would end soon as she could now smell the sea very strongly, and

true enough, as they topped a steep incline, she saw the Med glistening in all it's glory beckoning them on. On a nearby clifftop she saw a Night Heron take flight, no doubt due to their approach, backed by the silver sea and she caught her breath at the beauty of it. She hugged Giorgio even tighter and felt his muscles relax at her touch. A voice inside her nagged away, telling her to be careful. Saying this was just a holiday romance. Don't get hurt. She brushed it away with ease and concentrated on the beauty of her surroundings.

They had been riding non stop now for over an hour from the vineyard entrance where he had first asked her if she would like to meet his family. They had travelled first back on the main C260 towards Figueras then turned off on a smaller road heading north of Tossa De Mar but again turning off before reaching S'Agaro. They had then circumnavigated several orchards and vineyards before crossing Maquis scrub filled sandy fields, which reminded her of old cowboy films. For the last ten minutes they had been travelling uphill into the mountains and now they seemed to have crested these and were going down towards the rugged coastline.

Suddenly, opening up before her, was a beautiful cove, backed by the beach and surrounded on two sides by two steep purple cliffs. On one sat a beautiful medieval castle which was lit on the outside by uplights in the manicured gardens. It looked magical. The cove was lit by a huge fire on the beach and, as Giorgio killed the engine, Linda removed her helmet, and immediately heard singing and flamenco guitars. She almost clapped her hands at the unadulterated joy of the scene in front of her.

Giorgio, too removed his helmet, and surveyed the joyous tableaux before him. He took a deep breath and she couldn't help but notice a catch in his voice, he proudly announced "Mi Familia"

He turned to Linda and kissed her . He looked deeply into her eyes and reassured her that all would be well.

"Come" he said gently, climbing off his precious machine. "The *camino* here is dangerous. It would be safer if we walked."

He kicked the scooter rest down and leant it to one side and fastened his helmet to the handle. He took Linda's and did the same, then reached to the back of the machine and pulled out a torch which he used to light their way down the steep sandy incline.

Linda held tightly to his hand and refused to look over the edge, even when he held her tightly and teased her. They stopped twice and kissed and as their descent began to flatten out they sat on the soft warm sand and cuddled.

Giorgio waved the torch around lighting up the surrounding gloom. Linda spotted a small building built into the cliffs off to the right and pointed it out to Giorgio. He smiled broadly and stood up over her. "Come" he said softly "I will show you" and pulled her to her feet. They walked hand in hand the thirty or so yards to the building which Linda could now see by it's stained glass windows was a small church or chantry of some sort.

Giorgio shone the torch at it and the windows seemed to sparkle into life, the glass mosaics winking at them as they approached. Giorgio stopped about three yards short of the nearest window and moved the torch around, highlighting

various architectural designs that were soon lost again in the darkness that followed.

167

"It's beautiful" Linda suddenly announced. She felt really at ease, for some reason, as though the building was calming her down, steadying her nerves ready for the imminent visit to Giorgio's parents.

She tore her eyes away from the path of the light and looked at Giorgio. "What is it?" she asked.

"My family's *Santiaro*" he said simply and quietly, as if in awe of the building.

"Our church" he added by way of an explanation.

Linda watched him and was impressed by the obvious way he treated such an old religious building with such respect.

"I was baptised here" he told her, "and my mother and father were married here" he smiled self consciously and glanced at her "as I will be too one day"

he added.

She smiled back at him and looked back at the beautiful small building in the middle of nowhere. With such a history here, there was no wonder he referred to it as 'his family's church'.

He suddenly took her by the hand and led her off towards the beach. "Come"

he said "It is time to meet my family"

They made their way back to the big fire and as they neared it Linda could smell cooking. Upon closer inspection she could make out an enormous barbecue to one side of the fire. It seemed to be packed full with meats and peppers. She could also make out three chickens on a huge spit turning slowly.

Everyone on the beach seemed to be involved in some activity. No one was still for a minute. They were either dancing, playing music, cooking, fetching or carrying. Everything seemed chaotic, yet everyone seemed to be moving with a purpose so maybe they all knew exactly what they were doing.

Linda took everything in in one big sweep and reckoned there must be about fifty people, young and old on the beach. Obviously his family also had some friends with them.

Suddenly someone screamed and Linda turned to realise that an old lady had spotted them and was pointing in their direction. To her amazement everyone stopped doing what they were doing and rushed towards them.

Cheering and clapping and shouting in sing song voices the happy throng engulfed them. Linda lost her grip on Giorgio's hand and was quickly separated from him as he shook hands and kissed the women. Linda watched, in fascination as he was almost overwhelmed by the love that was on display.

She couldn't help but feel a sense of pride in him, and giggled to herself nervously as everyone continued their greetings and totally ignored her.

He seemed totally at ease with them all, whether it was the young girls, giggling at his handsome looks or the old men who continually slapped him on the back. Giorgio seemed to grow in confidence too, she noticed. He had about him an air of authority and respect that she hadn't noticed before. She had fallen in love with his honesty, openness and innocence but here was a different side to him and she loved this just as much.

Then a gap appeared in the crowd and all the chattering and backslapping stopped. Even the children who were there stopped their jabbering and dancing and watched in a respectful silence. Out of the gap emerged a huge bear of a man, clad in rough workman's clothes and wearing a black waistcoat which it looked as though he would struggle to fasten across his ample belly. He was holding hands with a small ample woman in a check pinafore dress who seemed to ooze kindness. Linda could feel the love that this woman's aura emitted.

The two walked through the gap until they were face to face with Giorgio. The giant bear man stared fixedly at his son for several seconds until it looked as though, instead of a wonderful family gathering, this was, in fact, the start of a terrible fight. Linda suddenly worried that perhaps Giorgio was in bother for something and perhaps this huge man was going to give him a good hiding.

The bear growled something low and unintelligible and Giorgio shrugged his shoulders and answered back in Spanish. The crowd oohed and aahed and suddenly the big bear man burst into tears and flung his arms round Giorgio who responded by patting his father on the back and making sure he wasn't suffocated by this monster love.

Giorgio's mother then came forward and roughly pushed her husband out of the way and took her son into her arms, berating and consoling him in a flowery manner all at once. When Giorgio eventually freed himself from her heaving bosoms he held her at arms length and spoke for some time in Spanish.

Linda, of course, didn't understand a word of it but knew that he was telling them about her as every head turned in her direction. Giorgio smiled proudly at her and she smiled embarrasedly back.

After, what seemed an eternity, the big bear man pushed his way past the others and walked towards her. He brushed away his tears that he had just shed for his son and wiped his massive hands clean on his trousers as he neared her. She had seen that he was big, but as he reached her she was surprised at just how enormous he actually was.

The big bear stopped just in front of her and held out his hand. Linda lifted her arm and immediately her tiny hand was enveloped in his. He lifted it gently and kissed it. "Don Edson Arantes Dos Nascemento at your service Senora" he announced in a low rumbling voice. Linda recognised the name as one her dad had spoken of many times. "Ah like the footballer" she replied. "No" he said

170

"I'm taller than him". Then he roared something in Spanish and pulled her towards him and hugged her tightly. Everyone immediately started laughing and singing and clapping and then Giorgio's mother forced herself between them and loudly berated her husband for something. He pretended to be stung by her words and retreated back to Giorgio leaving his wife to hug and kiss his son's new girlfriend. It could easily have been too much and Linda could have been overwhelmed by the whole experience but she took it all in her stride and the shy, overweight girl from Brinsmarsh who had never had a boyfriend and who would have died rather than have her own family and friends embarrass her with such an overt show of affection, was the brightest star of the evening

and even though she didn't understand a lot of what was going on they all accepted her for her simple loveliness and inner beauty.

Later, after they had eaten their fill from the magnificent barbecue they sat together by the fire and watched as one by one the members of this enormous family entertained each other with songs and dances. Giorgio explained to her that they were all family, not as she had thought family and friends.

"I can't imagine all of my family getting together just for a barbecue. They don't even manage that for a wedding" she laughed.

"Oh this is not my entire family" he corrected "this is only about a third of it.

These people all work or live on the farms and vineyards around here with my father"

"Is your father really this well liked and respected?" she asked then added quickly in case she had offended "I mean he's lovely and everything but back home we wouldn't revere someone like this. Maybe it's just a cultural thing"

Giorgio thought about it for a while then nodded. "Maybe you are right.

Perhaps it is just a cultural difference, but here my father is treated with deference and respect and in return he treats everyone else in the sane manner.

He is very important to most people in these parts and has a very profound effect on many lives. Most of the farms and businesses around here wouldn't survive without help from my father"

Now it was Linda's turn to mull this over for a while. In the end she asked him the most obvious question. "What is it that your father does Giorgio.?"

Giorgio turned to look at his father and she could see the love and respect in his eyes. "He is a manager" he said then thought about it for a while then added

"An advisor. Yes, and a partner. And anything else you want him to be. He is a good friend to have in business as he is in life and no one would ever cross him." He looked again at his father who was up now, dancing with Giorgio's mother in the firelight as the others watched and clapped in time to the music.

"And do you know what I love most about him?" he asked. She shook her head dutifully and he smiled again at his parents dancing "He hasn't an enemy in the world" he said and Linda followed his gaze and saw the old couple dancing in the moonlight to some flamenco tune and she understood what he meant.

"I think your family is wonderful" she said wistfully and leant back on the sand and closed her eyes. She could feel him beside her and felt his hand touch her belly. She opened her eyes slowly and he was there, close to her. He leant forward and kissed her softly. She could feel his hot, warm breath and she responded immediately. His arms entwined her and she melted into them, kissing him back, hard and strong. Her own hands stroked his back and hooked under his shirt. She could feel his skin, soft and cool, and could feel his arousal against her body. She thought her ears would explode, the quietness around them was so deafening. She couldn't hear the music any more, couldn't detect any chattering or laughing. It was as if the world had stopped and they were the only two people moving. She sucked hungrily on Giorgio's mouth and thought she would die if he didn't take her soon. Beside her she heard a gentle cough and immediately they both stopped kissing. She opened her eyes and there beside her was Giorgio's father smiling adoringly at them.

"Excuse me Senora. I did not mean to disturb you, but the children they are blushing" he said in a gentle teasing voice which, despite her embarrassment, she noticed reminded her so much of Giorgio's. She smiled back at the big man and blushed herself. She buried her face into the arm of the smiling Giorgio as His mother stepped forward and playfully punched her husbands arm and berated him again in Spanish. Linda looked up again to see the old man apologising profusely to his wife and then lift her effortlessly up and kiss her full on the lips. This brought a huge cheer from the watching crowd and the old lady punched him on the arm again in an effort to make him put her down. He laughed easily and placed her on the ground. She took a couple of ineffectual swipes at him then reached up and pulled his head down until he was near enough for her to plant a big kiss on him which also brought a huge cheer. The old lady then stepped aside and moved closer to the prone couple. Linda blushed furiously but made no attempt to move. The old woman bent down and stroked her long hair and whispered "You look beautiful when you blush so, *Senora*. The colour, it suits you. As does my son I think"

Linda looked carefully at the old lady's face. If those words had been spoken, in these circumstances, back home she would have expected a hint of sarcasm in them and would have stood up and brushed herself down and considered it a warning, but here, with these people, it seemed natural and good and she took it in the spirit it was intended. She stroked Giorgio's hair softly and answered

"Yes. This man suits me very much"

The old lady's face burst into a beautiful smile, as did her husbands and suddenly everyone seemed to be laughing and cheering and kissing each other.

The younger ones started to dance as the music struck up again and the older couples just held each other closely in the darkness with the flames from the roaring fire lighting up their faces. Linda watched everything, afraid to miss a second of it, and thought this must be the most beautiful and romantic place on earth.

Later they sat together and watched the fire die down. Giorgio had fetched her a rug from somewhere and draped it around their shoulders to ward off the cold of the night. They talked forever, Giorgio telling her stories of how his parents had met, of Castro and the civil war, which had been quite bloody in these parts. His father had been known as an activist and had been on Castro's death lists for many years. He had hidden in barns and outbuildings and up in the hills until Castro had given up and he had been allowed to return to his farm and live in peace. He was something of a hero to the people of these parts and Linda could feel the pride in Giorgio's voice.

She also discovered that the language these people spoke wasn't strictly Spanish. It was a dialect, Catalan, and had been the official language of these parts for centuries.

Linda thought it all so romantic and dreamy. The scenery, music, ambience and the friendly nature of the locals combined with their heroic history all added up to a powerful aphrodisiac and Linda cuddled up even closer to her loved one.

Eventually though it was time to leave. Giorgio mentioned it first and Linda was amazed to discover that it was after midnight and realised the girls would

be worried about her. She desperately wanted to stay and keep this evening going forever but she knew she had to return to the hotel and put everyone's mind at ease.

Giorgio announced their departure and there followed thirty minutes of backslapping and hugging and farewell kisses. Everyone there kissed her on both cheeks and solicited promises of her return to them shortly. Finally Giorgio's parents walked them up the hillside to his scooter. As they reached the little church his father stopped and stared at it misty eyed. He said something in Spanish to Giorgio who smiled and looked across at Linda before returning his gaze to his father and nodding. He said something back to him and they both hugged and slapped each other on the back while his mother clapped her hands and watched them proudly.

Once at the scooter, they all hugged and kissed and Linda thanked them formally for their hospitality.

"Please" Giorgio's father said, raising his hand to quieten her " *Mi Casa et su Casa.* Besides, you are almost family eh" and he squeezed her hands tightly and laughed infectiously. They all joined in and hugged each other again until Giorgio insisted they must go as it was a one hour drive back down the motorway and Linda's friends would be worried. He climbed on the scooter and gunned the little engine into life and she climbed on and hugged him tightly as they made their way over the small mountain pass and rejoined the C260 which would take them straight back to Lloret.

Sue, Ros and Claire were sat at a small pavement café down the road from the hotel, debating whether to go to the police now or wait until morning when they heard the soft put-put of an engine pulling up beside them. They turned to see Linda taking off her helmet and climbing off the back. She was laughing as she shook her hair and there was no mistaking the love in her eyes as Giorgio removed his helmet and they immediately embraced and kissed passionately. In fact she was still giggling as she came up for air and hung on to his neck and stroked the back of his head.

Sue glanced at Ros, then Claire, who in turn exchanged glances with each other. The mixture of fear and anxiety was replaced by relief and happiness at their friend's sudden arrival and they couldn't help but join in the giggling that Giorgio and Linda were enjoying. They jumped up from their table and ran to the road and hugged Linda and all talked at once and Giorgio watched the scene slightly taken aback.

Eventually calmness was resumed and Linda announced that she was alright and they had been on a wonderful day out and she would tell them all about it later.

Giorgio nodded and said that as he was working very early in the morning he would leave her here with her friends and that he would see her in the morning.

Linda tried to keep the disappointment from her face and obviously failed miserably because Sue stoked her hair and Claire and Ros put a hand on her shoulder. Giorgio leant over and kissed her tenderly and said softly

"Tomorrow" and replaced his helmet and drove away.

They watched him disappear round the corner then sat down and ordered more drinks as they waited for Linda to spill the beans on the days events.

They twitched around in their seats as they waited for her to begin until Claire couldn't stand it any more and snapped "For God's sake, what the bleedin'

hell happened?"

Linda told them the full story and they watched, goggle eyed, as she recounted the tale from start to finish.

"Meeting the folks eh" Claire said "That'd be after at least three months back home"

"And then only as a last desperate measure to get in your knickers if all else failed" added Ros and Claire looked at her askance and thought "Yeah, like I've held out for three month. Three days more like" but she didn't actually say anything.

Then Claire asked the question that the others wanted to ask but daren't.

"Did he get anything then?" she said bluntly. Linda blushed furiously.

"No of course not. He's a gentleman. He didn't even try" but there was a definite hint of regret in her voice as she said it.

CHAPTER TEN

Danny stayed in bed the rest of the day. When he had safely made it back to his room after his disastrous attempt at leaving earlier, he had quickly showered and changed. He had cleaned his flip flops and washed his shorts and shirt out as best he could in the sink. Then he wiped the floor in his room until there were no more marks. Eventually he had opened the door and looked in the corridor but couldn't see any sign of a greeny brown trail so he had shut it up again and gone to bed where he had fallen immediately into a deep sleep. He didn't even hear Jeff come in and shower and change for his evening out on the pull. He woke much later when Mick and Ron came in to see how he was, but was so tired that they left him after a while and went downstairs to meet Jeff for their dinner. He forgot to mention his little escapade.

The lads had quite an eventful night all things considered. After they had eaten in the hotel restaurant they had gone out on the town. At the second bar they went in, a delightful pseudo English Bar called El Paloma Blanca or Mucky Duck as it was commonly known, Jeff pulled a busty bottle blonde from Birmingham and her mate. He had his arms round them both and was squeezing the giggling blondes left boob as he led them outside. Mick shook his head in wonderment and announced, in mock sincerity "Jeff the Studmuffin has left the building". They both raised their bottles and toasted their departing friend.

After a while they moved on to another bar where a definite atmosphere descended on them. They hadn't mentioned the afternoons events and Ron was mulling it over now as to whether or not to fetch it up. Mick saved him the worry however when he suddenly said "I know what I'm doing".

Ron considered this for a moment then answered "I'm sure you think you do".

Mick spun round, ready to argue his corner, "Look Ron" he said "I know you mean well but you don't know her like I do"

"You met her this afternoon. You've known her about three hours" Ron countered.

"I know but it was…. Oh you wouldn't understand" he trailed off.

"Try me" offered Ron.

Mick thought for a second, took a deep breath and tried to explain.

"Back home" he said "everything is geared to the wedding. My life is being mapped out for me"

"You asked her, you daft twat" Ron interrupted.

"Yeah I know that. Fuckin' hell. But I didn't know it was going to be like this.

We were alright before, you know, but now it's all too organised, too….

formal, clinical I suppose." He ran his fingers through his hair "I wish I'd never asked her now" he said lamely.

"Tell her. She might feel the same way" advised Ron.

Mick considered it. "No. She'd go fuckin' barmy. She's up for it. I couldn't do that to Sue, it'd devastate her" he considered it again to see if there was a flaw in his argument and there might just be the slightest chance that he could get out of it. His shoulders sank as he realised that the upset would be too much for Sue and they couldn't just go back to how they were. "Nah" he shook his head throwing the thought away "she'd be devastated"

"And this girl?" asked Ron.

Mick's face suddenly lit up. "Julia, with a soft J" he grinned.

"She should go to the doctors for that" butted in Ron. Mick didn't laugh, just ignored him. "Yeah, then today I met Julia and bang" he smashed his fist into his palm "It was love at first sight".

179

"Lust. It was lust at first sight" corrected Ron.

"No honestly it wasn't. I don't know how to describe it really. It's never happened to me before. I just saw her and thought, 'wow. I've got to have her'"

"See. Lust" shouted Ron. "Told you. Everything's getting on top of you at home so you want a fresh challenge. A different bird, who's not going to talk about churches and limo's and flowers and seating arrangements and just wants to lie down in front of a warm fire and screw and then at the end when you've done the dirty will get up and fetch you a beer and cuddle up to you while you slowly drink it, basking in her adoration." Ron gazed off into the distance somewhere, lost in his beautiful vision. He could clearly do with a bit of that himself. Mick too gazed into the middle distance, but his cheeks had flushed a little, as he was embarrassed to discover that Ron had got it exactly right. That was exactly what he wanted, and the maddening thing was, that was exactly what he had had before all this wedding shit had taken over. He looked at Ron

and wondered how he had guessed it so precisely. "What a load of bollocks" he said. Ron shrugged his shoulders and drank his beer.

"What happens now?" he asked.

"Now I'm going to meet Julia tonight and just see what happens. I'm not going to think about Sue or back home or the wedding or the fuckin' flowers. I'm just going to go with the flow and enjoy myself for a change, alright" and he looked Ron directly in the eyes, challenging him to take it further. Ron shrugged again.

"It's your funeral" he said and drained his beer. "Come on" he added and they left the bar and went out into the warm night air. They turned right and immediately went into the next bar without looking to see what it was like.

They ordered two more beers and leant on the bar, each lost in his own thoughts. After five minutes Mick glanced at his watch and with more than a little embarrassment said "I've got to go now Ron, alright"

"Yeah whatever" Ron shrugged and took another swig.

Mick hesitated and then a thought struck him "Why don't you come with me.

Julia's got a roommate, right little piece, we could double date" he blurted out.

Ron stood up straight and moved closer to Mick. He took a deep breath and then told him what he thought of him. "Look Mick, you're my best mate right, always have been, but Sue's a friend too. We've been friends just as long as you and me have. You might want to throw that away so you can shag your bit of Spanish rumpty but I think Sue deserves a bit more than that."

Mick bristled visibly at this affront and stood toe to toe with Ron. He thought about taking a swing at him but not for long. Not only was Ron the best fighter Mick had ever seen but he was also right and that took the edge off Mick's anger. "Does that mean you don't fancy a foursome then?" he grinned sheepishly. Ron glared at him.

"Right. Gotta go" Mick announced and drained his bottle. He slapped Ron on the back and left the bar quickly before Ron said anything else that may lie heavy on his conscience later.

Ron sighed and finished off his own bottle and nodded to the barman indicating he wanted another. The barman, a tall swarthy looking Spanish type smiled at him showing dazzling white teeth. Ron smiled back pleasantly and waited for his drink. He turned round and had his first proper look at the bar. It was darker than the ones they had been in earlier and more seedy. It was also less crowded.

In the far corner, on a little dance floor, he could see a couple smooching to some Spanish love song, which he hadn't noticed before. There were only about half a dozen other patrons in the place. He was thinking that it was a bit of a dive when the barman placed the opened bottle on the bar next to him. Ron reached into his pocket for some money when the barman raised a hand and softly, in a very strange effeminate voice lisped "No need Thenor. The gentleman at the end of the bar hath bought your drink" and he nodded towards the end of the bar which was even darker than the rest of the room. Ron slitted his eyes and peered into the gloom and could just make out a figure in a white suit. He turned back to the barman "How much for the beer?" he asked throwing some pesetas onto the bar. The barman giggled and rolled his eyes.

"No thilly" he lisped again and slapped Ron's hand in a very girly way. He was

in fact English and had stayed in Spain when he had first come here on holiday and met up with a very nice Spanish man who had promised him the earth but had failed to deliver. He pointed to the white suited shadow in the corner.

"Jothe hath paid. You don't have to pay" he leant closer which caused Ron to lean back to keep some distance between them "If you play your cardth right, you will not have to pay for another drink all night" he giggled like a schoolgirl

"All week or all year". He leant even closer and looked suddenly very serious

"Jothe ith very rich. And very generouth" and he winked at Ron which unnerved him slightly.

From out of the shadows the white suited Jose appeared and seemed to drift towards Ron, rather than walk. Ron almost looked down to see if he was on castors but managed to fight the inclination and locked eyes with the mysterious stranger. He couldn't help but notice however, the mans white suit complemented by a white shirt cut open to the chest revealing a mass of dark springy hairs which acted as a cushion for the large gold medallion which hung from an enormous gold chain. His hair was swept back into a quiff and he looked for all the world like John Trevolta's stand – in, in Saturday night fever.

Ron fought back his urge to laugh out loud and instead smiled amiably and looked away. He took in the rest of the room. He was sure now that he was being hit on but he wasn't sure what he should do about it. This was his first time and although he had set off on holiday with the intention of sorting out his exact sexuality, now that the chance had arisen he was strangely noncommittal and even a little embarrassed. He scanned the room and saw again the couple dancing on the small dancefloor, then he noticed a couple kissing at the table just in front of the dancefloor. As the man pulled away from his partner he playfully bit her lip and then let go and smiled. It was a nice scene until Ron suddenly realised that it wasn't a she but a he that had just had their lip bitten.

He looked round to the other end of the bar and almost gasped out in shock as he realised that the two couples sat at that side were also all male. One man had his hand on his partners leg and was stroking it vigourously while the other two watched with a smiling satisfaction.

Ron looked back to the dancefloor. At least he was sure that there was a woman there. He saw the high heels and short skirt and low cut top revealing a large cleavage and was almost grateful for the normality of it when he saw her dance partner kiss her on the neck and chest. She threw her head back and Ron had a perfect view of her Adams Apple. "Fuck me" he thought and as if reading his mind the Spanish Travolta brushed up along side him. "Hi I'm Jose" he purred in a butch kind of way. "Hi. Ron" answered Ron and he was surprised to notice that his own voice had gone deep and manly. He held out his hand and Jose took it in his and turned it over and looked at it.

"Fuckin' hell, he's going to kiss it" thought Ron but he was wrong. Jose just looked at it then stroked it a few times. "You have very manly hands" he said

"You must work with your hands. That is very good for one so beautiful as you" and he stroked Ron's face with his free hand.

Ron was transfixed like a rabbit in a car headlights, he just stood there not knowing what to do next. Jose nodded to the bar. "Why don't you finish your drink Ron eh, maybe we have a little champagne later eh. To celebrate no."

Ron pulled his hand away and picking up his bottle took a big long swallow.

He wasn't at all sure about this now.

"You want to dance?" Jose asked and Ron spat some of his beer back into the bottle as the absurdity of the situation hit him. "Did he want to dance. With Travolta. Did he fuck!" he thought.

Jose saw him choke on his drink and shivered slightly as Ron wiped the beer from his chin and knocked away a few damp specks from his chest.

"Don't rush" he said as he moved nearer "There is plenty more. You can have anything you want tonight." He stroked Ron's face again. "If you're a good girl"

"What?" thought Ron "I'm the girl then. Fuckin' hell. This is my sugar daddy.

He's going to buy me nice things if I treat him right in bed tonight" A sudden thought raced into his mind from nowhere "Shit. I've turned into my cousin Denise. She married that older man for his money and the whole family turned against her and said she was no better than a common whore. Bleedin' hell I'm a trophy wife"

Other thoughts tried to vie for his attention and kept racing to the front of his mind. One was "If he tickles me on the chin again I'm going to lamp him" but the main one was "What am I doing?"

Jose nuzzled up closer to him and leant forward as if to whisper to him. Ron braced himself but wasn't ready for the hot wet tongue which circled his ear. A thousand volts raced through his body as the tongue repeatedly flicked into his lobe. He was still recovering from this when Jose suddenly placed a hand behind his head and roughly pulled him forward and kissed him, long and hot, on the lips. For a second Ron thought he was going to be sick and he struggled to move his mouth away from the assault. Against his thigh he felt something long and hard and to his utter shock he realised that Jose was aroused and ready for action.

Ron decided there and then that he wasn't gay and there was no way he was having that thing anywhere near his arse. He forced his mouth free and almost shouted "I'm sorry"

Immediately Jose forced himself on him again and covered his mouth with his own, working it backwards and forwards for all he was worth. He was grinding his groin into Ron and Ron worried that Jose would get too excited and have a nasty premature accident over them. That awful thought galvanised Ron into action and he roughly tried to push Jose away, however with his arms locked around him Jose was clinging on tightly. Even in his frenzy Ron was pleased to note that his own penis hadn't responded to anything that had happened. If anything it had shrunk back into his body in protest at any call to action. His anus too seemed to be shrivelling up and he doubted whether he would ever be able to shit again.

He suddenly realised that Jose's tongue was trying to find his tonsils, and he almost laughed as he had had them removed when he was four. He pushed

again but Jose was hanging on for dear life so, without giving it a second thought, he bit down hard on the probing snake in his mouth. With their faces so close together Ron had a close up view of Jose's eyes suddenly opening very wide and tears pour out of the corners. He felt blood fill his own mouth and he jerked his head back and spit before he choked and had to swallow. As well as the blood, a half inch piece of flesh shot out of his mouth and landed on the grubby floor. Jose shot backwards and both his hands went up to his face only to be covered in the bright red blood within seconds.

Now he was free, Ron felt much better and thought he had better explain himself. "I'm terribly sorry" he said with an apologetic smile "There's been a terrible mistake"

Jose stared at him, then at the blood oozing from his hands. "Mithtake" he spat and a stream of blood shot from between his lips. "You've bitten off my tongue and you thay thereth been a mithtake."

Ron smiled in spite of himself and put his hands up in mock surrender. "Yes.

My fault, alright. I thought, and you'll laugh at this, I thought I was gay. Yeah, even though I've never actually had a gay experience I thought that maybe, well I haven't had much luck with women, you know, in the bedroom department, that, well it might be that I was gay. Anyway. I'm not. Hated it, every minute of it when you were slobbering all over me. Old man. Gone. No interest whatsoever. Sorry about the tongue thing though. Couldn't get you off me see." He leant forward and could clearly see the blood spurting between Jose's fingers. "Looks nasty that, better get that seen to".

Jose's eyes were wild with rage and excitement. He spun round to his friends in the room looking for some support. Ron also looked round and was mildly surprised to see that everyone in the room was now stood in a little semi circle about ten feet away.

"Did you hear what he thaid" spat Jose "He thaid thorry" blood spattered onto his friends and to a man they stepped back out of range. "Thorry. That'th alright then ithn't it." The man dressed in high heels and a dress giggled until Jose stared at her/him and he/she looked to the floor and kicked her/his shoe distractedly.

Jose turned to the barman who had found a baseball bat from under the bar and was now holding it menacingly in Ron's direction..

"Did you hear him Thteven, he thaid thorry" and he showed the barman the blood flowing into his upturned hands.

Steven, the barman, nodded but didn't take his eyes from Ron. "I heard" he said in a much deeper voice than he used before. Then he spun round to Jose and giggled "But I mutht thay that the lithp thuitth you" and he smiled affectionately before returning his hard man stare back to Ron who couldn't help but laugh out loud.

Ron thought Jose was going to explode with rage. His face was purple and he seemed to be holding his breath for some reason. Just when Ron thought that Norris Mcwhirter might pop out from behind the bar and announce that Jose had broken the record for holding his breath accompanied by Roy Castle singing the theme from Record Breakers, Jose screamed out in Spanish.

Immediately the other patrons of the bar moved forward, closing in on Ron, their intentions obvious. Ron smiled to himself, happy at the knowledge that he was going to be in a ruck. He had been unsure of so many things lately that it was a relief to be presented with something that he felt comfortable with.

Fighting he knew. Fighting happened to be something he was very good at.

Ron glanced round and decided to take the weapon out of the action first. He shot his left arm forward, catching Steven unaware, and took the bat easily from his hands. In almost the same movement he lifted and pushed the bat back in the barman's direction, hitting him squarely in the nose, breaking it. The barman, who minutes earlier had looked very threatening, screamed and shot both hands to his nose. "My nothe" he spluttered as blood oozed through his fingers. He noticed the blood dripping on his expensive silk shirt. "My thirt" he cried and reached under the bar and pulled out a bar towel, which he held alternatively to his nose and shirt.

Ron turned to see the man/woman dancer running at him so he kicked out and caught him in the groin. Judging by the soft bulge that met his foot, the dancer was more man than woman. This was confirmed when tears sprang to his eyes and he collapsed in a heap on the floor. His dancing partner cried out in sympathetic agony and knelt down to administer first aid. He rubbed the injured area gingerly but was warned off by a series of screams and Spanish oaths. Another attacker moved in but Ron feinted to his left drawing the man in that direction. This enabled Ron to move up right alongside him and hit him in the solar plexus. As he doubled up Ron dropped down slightly and gave him a neat uppercut to the jaw which knocked him out cleanly. Ron then leant forward and grabbed his partner whose gaze was directed down to the floor. He pulled him forward and nutted him between the eyes. He lowered him gently to the ground where he joined his lover in an unconscious heap.

Ron looked up and stepped aside, away from the mountain of bodies building up at his feet. The two remaining attackers glanced at each other and thought better of it. They turned on their heels and minced away through a concealed exit door at the back of the dancefloor.

He looked round for any other sign of attack but no one seemed interested.

Jose was the only one standing and he was still holding his blood stained face.

The barman had pulled out a mirror from under the bar and was crying onto it, holding his bent nose tenderly.

Jose suddenly spat out blood and called angrily to him. "Hey, *bathstado* you have finished eh. You have your fun eh. You fight these pretty boys eh. How about me having my fun now eh" he rubbed his groin with a blood stained hand which ruined his trousers. "Thee Jose ith thtill hard for you pretty one. Ith now Jothe'th turn for fun, yeth"

Ron looked at him curiously. "The little puffs only turned on by it all" he thought. He suddenly shot out his right leg which connected swiftly with Jose's groin. He collapsed with hardly a sound, save a sharp intake of breath, and Ron smiled down at him.

"I hope that helps keep the swelling up" he said and turned and walked out of the bar.

The warm breezy night air hit him and he took a deep breath. It felt good to be alive. It felt good to be straight. He wished he had someone there to share it with. He wished Ros was there. He thought about Ros and felt himself getting aroused. He looked up to the night sky and whispered "Thank you God" and went back to the hotel to have a good think about Ros.

Early next morning Bill was driving his sister to Manchester Airport. Sheila had told him the purpose of his visit and he was in something of a bad mood.

He had worked out, which was very bright for him, that Sheila was going to half kill Danny when she found him in Spain and he was a bit pissed off that he couldn't be there to finish the job off. More than once during the journey over the Pennines he had offered to go with her but each time she had declined. Ben sat in the back of the van amidst life's flotsam and jetsam dreaming of flying in an aeroplane. He imagined being so high and looking out through the window and seeing all the world underneath him. He suddenly came over all dizzy and fell forward hitting his head on a lawnmower, which they used to cut old peoples gardens, badly, for an extortionate fee. The grassbox, which was resting on top of the mower fell off and landed on his head. Unfortunately it was still full of grass from a job they had done for a soft old lady in Clifton.

She had been almost blind and said she could only see about fifteen feet so couldn't keep on top of things. Bill had offered to tidy it all up for a very reasonable fifty quid which was all she had, and then had cut the first fifteen feet of grass, before retiring with a cuppa and a sarnie, until he felt it was time to go back in and collect the money. By standing in the middle of the doorway he kept the old lady from having a detailed examination of his work.

189

Her Englishness came to the fore, as he knew it would, and anxious to avoid a scene, she had paid up and complimented him on his work.

Ben laid where he had fallen, unconscious, his head covered by the grass box and slept the rest of the journey.

"Look" Bill was saying, trying again to get in on the action. "All I'm saying is, if you need a hand just give us a shout and we'll come and give him a good kicking."

Sheila was getting annoyed now. He hadn't let up all through the journey.

"Why couldn't he be the strong silent type like our Ben" she thought and turned to see her youngest brother asleep in the back. From where she sat it looked as though he had his head in a grassbox. She laughed softly to herself and turned round again in her seat.

Eventually they reached the airport and she jumped out when Bill pulled up at the departure point. She reached back in the van and picked up her small travel bag. She only had a couple of changes of clothes as she didn't intend to be there long. Just long enough to find Danny and give him the biggest pasting of his life. Then she'd drag him home and give him to the boys. She banged the door of the van closed and checked in her handbag for her passport and tickets.

Bill joined her and decided to have one last go at changing her mind. "Let me go. I'll do him, then bring him back so you can finish him off. I'll not cut him

or anything, I'll leave that to you" He smiled winningly and prayed silently that she would relent and say yes.

"You don't touch him till I say so right" she ordered and his face fell to the floor. The back door of the van opened and Ben came out, blinking in the sunlight. Sheila looked at the grass covering his head and shoulders and smiled. Bill turned to see what his sister was looking at and did a double take when he saw his green headed brother. He was going to ask him how he had got grass all over him but decided against it. Sheila leant forward and kissed her youngest brother on the cheek. She picked up some grass from his ear and handed it to him. He looked at it in astonishment. "How did that get there?" he asked incredulously and was amazed as a shower of grass fell from his head past his eyes. He looked up, squinting in the sunlight, to see where it could have come from. A plane went past and he decided someone must have dropped it from there.

Bill gave him a disgusted look and turned back to Sheila to try one more time, However she was too fast for him and raised her hand to stop him in his tracks.

She leant forward and kissed him on the cheek. "Now fuck off" she said

"before you get a ticket" and turned on her high heels and clomped into the airport. She was wearing a low cut blouse that left nothing to the imagination and a pair of hot pants that emphasised her shapely bum. Her high heels made her legs look as though they went on forever and many a male head turned as she walked by. However only one thought occupied Sheila's mind. She would kill that fat bastard when she laid her hands on him.

With the bright morning sun trying to blaze it's way through the blinds, Sue woke and stretched luxuriously in the crisp cotton sheets. She glanced over to see if Ros was up yet and smiled at her sleeping friend. She climbed out of bed and went to the bathroom and five minutes later poked her head round the door to see Ros still fast asleep. She ran her fingers through her hair and stepped on to the balcony, immediately noticing that , although it was sunny, the morning air was still on the chilly side. She felt her nipples harden and looked down the top of her frilly white nightie and giggled to herself at the naughtiness of it. She pulled at the thin cotton material and held it tight against her breast, producing a perfect impression of her erect nipples against the soft cotton.

"Very nice" she thought to herself and then from nowhere a memory of her Aunt Irene came to her. She had developed breast cancer at an early age and had died after an awful time of it. Ever since, Nellie had drummed into Sue, the importance of regular checks. She tucked her hand up the bottom of her nightie and examined the left breast. Satisfied all was well she reversed the procedure and tried the right. She was just about to issue a little sigh of relief, when a voice said. "If you need any help in there, just ask"

She spun round to see a young man on the next balcony watching her with a huge grin on his face. In his hand he held a glass of milk and he was wearing just a small pair of shorts. Sue's face turned a darker shade of beetroot and she hurriedly removed her hand from inside her nightie.

Embarrassment was quickly replaced by anger at his forwardness and she huffily crossed her arms and tapped her foot on the tiled floor.

"That is very rude" she said indignantly.

"What is?" he asked.

"That. You know, saying that to me when I didn't know you were there.

Butting in like that" she trailed off lamely knowing that she was more angry with herself for being caught like that rather than with him for just looking.

"Well actually I was here first" he said, defending himself. He took a drink of his milk and wiped his mouth with the back of his hand. "I was quietly drinking my milk and enjoying the view when you appeared and started playing with yourself". His eyes lowered from hers and he took in her breasts, which were being cradled by her arms. The nightie, pulled tight, revealed her pert orbs, which were still adorned by erect nipples.

"Actually I still am" he added and smiled mischievously.

Sue looked down at herself and immediately removed her arms, releasing the material. She thought that she had better explain what she had been doing. "I wasn't just playing with 'em you know. I was actually checking"

"And are they still there?" he asked.

"What? Oh right. No I mean I was checking for lumps"

He leant forward and raised a hand. He pointed at her. "There's a big pointy one on the end of each boob" he grinned.

Sue coloured up and was at a total loss for words. Why was this man's outrageous flirting embarrassing her so much. He suddenly stood up and she couldn't help but be impressed by his well toned physique. "I'm sorry" he said.

"I was only teasing. I know what you were checking for and I sincerely hope that you found everything was alright" and he looked her earnestly in the eyes.

Sue melted and was a little shocked as she caught her heart fluttering a little, and her eyes roving his tanned muscles.

He offered his hand. "Dave" he said simply.

She placed her own hand in his and was thrilled when he squeezed slightly, showing a hint of power.

"Sue" she replied.

He made no effort to let go of her hand and she was mildly surprised that she didn't mind. He looked down at their hands locked together and said "It's still warm" and she blushed again at the thought of where her hand had just been and where it was now. She felt a little tingle down her spine and shivered slightly.

"Sue."

The voice behind her made her jump, guiltily, as she turned to see Ros. She quickly removed her hand from Dave's and crossed her arms, then thought better of it and quickly uncrossed them.

"Ros" she said and forced a smile to her face. "This is Dave, he lives next door.

So to speak. For a week. You know" she babbled on and had to force herself to stop rambling. Ros stared at her, then turned and said hello to the semi naked man stood on the next balcony. She turned back to Sue and nodded in the

direction of the bedroom. She shivered a little and said "Come on, let's go and get some breakfast till it warms up" and went back inside.

Sue followed her but stopped short of the door. She turned to Dave, who was watching her intently. "I'll see you around. I suppose." She said with a little uncertainty in her voice.

"I hope so" he replied and she burst into a glorious smile and slipped back into the bedroom.

Ron woke up and idly looked around the room. He stretched luxuriously until he spotted the empty bed next to him and his heart sank a little.

Mick had been his best friend since, well forever, and he knew that Mick wasn't the sort to just have a one night stand so his empty bed could only mean one thing. Mick was getting involved.

194

He lay on his back and looked up at the ceiling. There was also Danny to worry about. He had had the shits for about twenty four hours now and last night he had looked bloody awful. He decided that if Danny was still the same this morning he would go and get him a doctor.

He closed his eyes and thought of Ros. He couldn't wait now for the holiday to be over. He wanted to get back home and see Ros. He would wait until they all went into the Maggies and then would make his move. He reasoned it would be easier with all the lads around. Wouldn't it.

His thoughts were interrupted by the door opening. In walked Mick. Well danced in more like with a very dreamy far away look in his eyes. He groaned and lay back as his worst fears were realised. Mick had fallen head over heels in love.

He leant up on one elbow and coughed to gain his pirouetting friends attention.

"You look very pleased with yourself" he stated dryly.

Mick smiled in what he thought was an enigmatic way but was actually closer to leering.

"So would you if you'd been doing what I've been doing all night" he replied.

"I've a pretty good idea what you've been doing all night and I don't particularly want to hear about it" Ron said, laying back down and closing his eyes.

"Ah don't be like that Ron" Mick said, contritely and he sat down on the edge of the bed.

"Ron I don't know what to do" he said after a few seconds.

"Well keep practising with Julia and I'm sure Sue will be more than grateful for the improvement when you get back" Ron answered and climbed out of bed and loped off to the bathroom, determined not to get into a serious conversation about Mick's problems.

"You know what I mean"

Ron stopped at the bathroom door and turned to see his mate sat stone faced on his bed. He softened a little and went back over to him "Look" he said and sat down next to him. "You've shagged the Spanish bird all night so now you kiss her goodbye and go back to Sue and feel like a shitty twat for a couple of

weeks and hope and pray that one of your best mates doesn't drop you in it otherwise she'll have your balls on a plate and to be honest my old mucker I don't blame her"

"It wasn't like that" Mick said quietly. "I wasn't shagging all night. We walked and talked up and down the sea front and sat on the sands and watched the sun come up. It was beautiful. And then we made love. It was just so .. so.. right"

He gazed off into the distance, lost in the memory of it and then he pulled a face and shivered slightly. "Except for the cold" he added, and shuddered involuntarily "My arse was freezing"

Despite himself Ron had to smile.

Mick looked down at his feet and seemed to be thinking things over. Ron waited patiently, although he dreaded hearing what he felt was sure to come next. Mick eventually made up his mind and sat up straight. He looked Ron in the eye and stated clearly "I love her".

Ron's heart sank. He had been expecting it but it still made him angry and upset. "You don't love her, you soft bastard, you're just trying to justify your actions." He was shouting now, clearly angry. "You're trying to make it OK

that you've been out shaggin' all night. It would normally be morally repulsive to you to just have a one night shagfest so you turn it into something it's not so your little Jiminy Cricket on your shoulder can say "It's love. It's OK. Carry on. You can worry about the consequences later""

Ron stormed off to the bathroom, he was that close to hitting Mick and he didn't want to do that. He was losing control, he was so angry and he was annoyed with himself for getting into such a state. The thing was, besides from his annoyance at his friends behaviour, he was feeling pretty jealous of Mick's closeness to this girl. He wanted somebody to hold, to walk in the moonlight with, and make love to in the early morning dawn light. He wanted someone to come home to, to miss when she wasn't there. He stared into the mirror and saw his sad reflection staring back. "Get a life" he thought and snorted into the mirror. Old reliable Ron, that was him. Why couldn't he be wild carefree Ron, the free spirit who had women climbing over each other for his affections. Or even better, Old happily married Ron who came home each evening to a happy house of laughter and children's voices.

He thought of home and his mum who would be cleaning up now ready for a hard days sewing and cooking and cleaning and knitting. His head dropped to his chest. God he couldn't wait to get back and see Ros and start off the next chapter in his life.

Mick appeared in the mirror and Ron looked up to see his sad face.

"I do love her Ron. And I do love Sue" It looked and sounded like he was going to cry.

Ron softened visibly at his friends discomfort and sighed deeply "I don't know what you're going to do Mick. I know you can't keep 'em both, so sooner or later you're going to have to make a decision, and I'll tell you what. I don't envy you that one bit"

Mick stared at the floor and wondered how he could feel so miserable and happy at the same time.

Sue and the girls flip flopped their way across the foyer carrying their bags filled to the brim with all the accoutrements required for a hard days ligging on the beach.

"Hang on a sec'" called Linda as she peeled off towards the little shop off to one side "I need some film for my camera. I used all mine yesterday."

They waited patiently, watching the other holidaymakers carrying their own overflowing bags and struggling with inflatable crocodiles and sharks and other survival essentials for pool or beach. Sue spotted a child who was wearing an enormous swan life ring and was about to comment on it to the others, when from behind it appeared Dave. He was with a friend and they carried a single towel each and were both wearing polo shirts, baggy football shorts and flip flops, the bare essentials for holiday survival.

Involuntarily she sucked in her breath. He looked a handsome figure but the intensity of her emotions surprised her. Ros looked round to see what had startled her friend and Sue coloured up as she realised she had actually made a sound when she had set eyes on him. Ros spotted him coming their way and tut tutted and turned away. Sue though couldn't drag her eyes away from him. He was laughing at something his friend had said. He seemed to turn towards her and she saw him look her up and down, admiration clearly showing as he lingered on various parts of her body. She breathed in and tilted her head slightly. She was wearing her bikini covered only by a fetching pink sarong tied loosely on one hip. She had on dark sunglasses and a big floppy straw hat.

The light pink colour of her skin from her sunbathing sessions made her skin look soft and healthy and Sue was confident that there had been few times in her life when she had looked lovelier. She knew by the look in his eyes that he was hooked and she almost preened as he came closer. His eyes still enjoyed their sweeping traverse of her body and he was smiling broadly as he came up to a level with her. Their eyes almost met, although obviously he couldn't see hers behind the sunglasses, and then right at the last moment, just as a witty greeting thrust itself into the forefront of Sue's brain he dropped his gaze and swept past. He said something to his mate as they passed and they both laughed heartily. Sue was devastated and visibly crestfallen. She spun round to watch his retreating back and couldn't hide the disappointment on her face.

"Hi" she suddenly blurted, then shot her hand to her mouth as she realised she had shouted it much louder than she had intended. It seemed as though everyone in the room turned round to see who was shouting, including Ros and Claire who were staring at her with puzzled expressions. Linda stuck her head round the door of the shop to see if Sue had been shouting at her and an old lady who had been putting on her sunglasses at the door poked herself in the eye and cried out in pain.

Dave and his friend turned slowly to see who was making all the noise and he was surprised to see the beautiful girl he had just been admiring, staring directly at him. Surely she couldn't have been shouting at him, could she. He had fancied her the moment he had taken in her full body and it was only the

early morning hour that had stopped him from making a play for her. She smiled invitingly at him and his mate nudged him as if to say "You're in there"

He smiled back, but the surprise on his face was plain to see. Sue said "Hi"

again, softer this time and more in control, but she was acutely aware of Ros and Claire watching her.

"Hi" he ventured back, but it was clear by the way he said it that he didn't understand what was going on or who she was.

"Remember me?" she asked and was rather annoyed when he clearly didn't.

Now if she had been thinking straight and more clearly or even had more time, or even had more experience in this sort of thing, she would now slowly have removed her sunglasses, then her straw hat, shook her hair loose and smiled winningly and softly purred "This morning on the balcony" and then smiled demurely as the penny dropped and he came rushing over to her all apologetic.

The trouble was, she wasn't thinking clearly because the girls were staring at her, and she didn't have more time because he would turn on his heels and leave at any moment, and she didn't have any experience because she had been with Mick since she could remember so she lifted her left hand and cradled her right boob and kneaded it around. "Lumps" she said simply and was relieved when a big grin appeared on his face. She ignored the gasps of astonishment from Ros and Claire and concentrated on the handsome young man moving towards her.

"Sorry" he said with a cheeky grin "Didn't recognise you with the disguise on"

and he indicated the hat and glasses.She giggled nervously and couldn't think of another thing to say. Now she had him here she was totally lost for words.

She became aware of his friend moving over to Claire and chatting easily with her but knew that Ros was still staring at her. She coloured up slightly and giggled again.

"Going to the beach?" he asked unnecessarily and she gushed like a smitten school girl "Yes. Where are you going?" a little too eagerly and she heard Ros tut.

"We're off to meet up with some lads we've met over here." She tried but couldn't hide the disappointment from her face and he stepped closer and said softly "If you like though we could meet up later and have a drink, or something"

She blushed again despite herself and nodded. She just stopped herself saying

"Yes please" but only just. Instead she settled for "That would be nice" and smiled a little easier. He smiled back then glanced over to his friend. "Steve, come on pal, we're going to be late" then turned back to Sue "See you later then" and turned and went out of the door closely followed by his friend who waved easily to Claire as he went.

"Mmmm" purred Sue under her breath even though she knew Ros was still watching her.

"Small world innit" Claire said as she stepped up to them.

"Why" asked Ros although she was still staring directly at Sue.

"That was Steve from back home and his mate ..er Dave I think. I had a bit of a fling with him a couple of years ago. Nice lad. Can't remember why I dumped

him" Sue's eyes flashed with anger until she realised that Claire was referring to Steve not Dave, then she was embarrassed at her sudden emotions. She knew Ros had seen it and she knew she didn't approve but sod it, it was her life.

"From Whiston I think" Claire was still saying. "They both play football for Whiston, I've seen their picture in the paper."

Sue wasn't sure whether she was happy or sad at this news. Whiston was only a few miles from her home and that was a bit too close for comfort. Still, if anything came of this brief affair. She smiled wickedly to herself. That was the first time she had actually thought of it as an affair. If anything came of it maybe, just maybe, she could carry it on back home. She immediately brushed the thought aside. It was ridiculous to even consider such a thing, absolutely stupid. She could no sooner cheat on Mick than he could on her. Anyway she had only spoken to the man twice so how could she even think of calling it an affair. She laughed awkwardly and noticed Ros still watching her. "Come on"

she said, hoisting her bag back onto her shoulder "Let's get Linda and hit that beach"

CHAPTER ELEVEN

Ron sat on the balcony of Jeff and Danny's room watching the heat rise from the road in front of the hotel. It was going to be a scorcher and he was ready for it. He needed a good long relaxing day in the sun to think things over. He had some plans to make and he needed the time to mull them over.

Behind him Danny hopped around like a madman. He was pulling on his shorts but kept getting the foot stuck in one of the legs. Although he was puffing and panting he felt happy inside. He had fallen over twice and his stomach hadn't lurched at all. He had tried two bottles of water this morning and hadn't visited the toilet. He hadn't actually been to the lav since late last night and he was pretty confident that his shits had gone. He stood up straight and completely naked and sorted out the twisted legs of his shorts.

Ron turned round and couldn't resist a smile at his fat little friend. "It's true then that Sheila married you for your money" he said and smiled broadly at the big V sign that his friend gave him. When he sorted the legs out and actually managed to get the shorts on, he ran round the room looking for his flip flops.

Amidst much cursing and muttering he eventually found one but couldn't locate the other. He searched under the bed for the third time to no avail. Ron glanced down and spotted the errant footwear on the balcony but instead of handing it over he covered it with his foot.

"Have you tried the bathroom?" he asked innocently and watched Danny flip flip flipping off into the bathroom. "

"Come on Danny" he called after him "I want to catch some rays today"

Danny rushed out of the bathroom searching the floor as he went. At one point he even checked the ceiling, presumably on the off chance that it might be floating just above his head. "Sorry" he muttered "Cant find my other flip flop"

and he checked under the bed again.

"Hey" he suddenly called out. "Maybe we can find Jeff and Mick and convince

'em to tear themsens away from whichever bird they're slavering over today"

Ron curled the right corner of his lip and said softly "I wouldn't count on it"

He bent down and picked up the lost flip flop and threw it to Danny. "Look" he said, smiling, "it was here all the time".

Danny caught it and happily put it on his foot. "Right" he said clapping his hands and picking up a hotel towel and a bottle of Jeff's Ambre Solair "Let's hit the beach. Me and you Ron are going to have the best holiday ever. I'm telling you I can feel it in my water" He looked round the room which resembled a students flat a full week before his mum was due to come round and give the place a good tidy. "I've had enough of this shit hole" he said disgustedly. He rubbed his arse tenderly "And this one" he groaned. Then he suddenly sprang back to life. "Come on Ron. You and me. We'll show 'em how to have fun. We'll show 'em how to party." He marched to the door and grabbed the handle and turned it. "I've had enough of sitting in here. I came here to party and party I will. Nothing can stop us now Ron. Nothing"

He pulled open the door and head high marched forward. That was when he actually saw her although his momentum carried him forward another two steps. He saw the bleached hair, the sunglasses, the skimpy top, hot pants, long legs and white stilettos. All this he saw in one fleeting instant. What he didn't see, and he would never understand why, was the big black leather handbag crashing towards his face. Now big black leather handbags,

204

especially those with hairdryers in them can be quite heavy, and this one turned out to be quite a good example of one of those. It hit him square in the face and the only two things he was able to do in any effort to defend himself were a) fall to the floor, and b) emit a little girly scream which embarrassed him even as it left his lips.

He felt his head hit the floor hard and for a second his senses reeled as he fought for control. His hands released the towel and sun cream and shot up to his head as if that would ease the pain. They soon left his head alone though as a Stiletto drove easily past his thin Bermudas on their way to his groin. His head shot forward and air escaped from his lips in a kind of death rattle. At the same time his feet shot up in the air so he looked as though he was doing some high speed aerobics. He vaguely heard shouting above him but his ears seemed to be filled with the sound of the sea and he couldn't make out any words. He felt disoriented and tried to wipe the tears from his eyes. He rolled over and felt a pointy shoe in his side and sunk to the floor again. He heard the voices again but the sea still drowned them out. He got up on all fours and crawled. He hadn't a clue where he was going but he reasoned that being somewhere else was better than being here right now. After a few feet he sunk to the floor. A few agonising seconds later he realised no one was kicking him any more. He opened his eyes and focused. He was in the corridor, alone and that seemed to

him to be the ideal place just now. His hands probed his tender balls. He even counted them as he rubbed. What had happened, he thought. He shook his head and gingerly got to his feet. He looked up and down the empty corridor and decided to risk going back into the room, dreading what he would find inside.

He stopped and haltingly poked his head through the open door. Each poke took him a little further inside until he could just make out Ron's legs off to one side. It looked like Ron was sat on the bed. He poked his head in a bit further and suddenly screamed like a girly mouse. (Right, that was the last time he would ever do that, he promised himself). Ron was sat on the back of a snarling, spitting, tigerish Sheila. He had his hand on the back of her head, shoving it into the mattress. She kicked out but couldn't reach him and he smiled at Danny easily.

"Is she alright" asked Danny, concernedly as he watched his friend push her face deeper into the bed.

"It depends what you mean by alright" he answered' looking down at the woman underneath him. "Personally I think she's fuckin' mental but who am I to judge"

Danny moved a bit closer. He could see her cheeks turning blue. "Do you think you ought to let her go?" he asked nervously.

"Dunno. 'sup to you" shrugged Ron.

Danny rubbed his balls, which felt sore and were probably turning black. God he'd look like next doors cat by the morning.

" No better not eh". Ron shrugged and sat tight.

Danny thought things over for a while then asked Ron "What do you think she wants"

"Let's ask her eh" Ron said and released her head from his grasp. Immediately a stream of filth filled the air ending with the phrase "up your arse" and was only halted when Ron grabbed the back of her head again and shoved it firmly back into the bed.

Danny grinned sheepishly. Ron tutted and looked down at her "You want your mouth washing out with soap young lady." He looked back at Danny and smiled.

"Do you think she meant you or me?" Danny asked innocently and swallowed hard.

"Look Danny, just a wild guess here" went on Ron "but, and correct me if I'm wrong here. Did you or did you not bugger off to Spain, taking half your lottery winnings without telling your wife?"

Danny jumped from foot to foot and put a finger over his lips "Sshhh you gobby twat, she might not know about the money yet. It might be a coincidence she's here" he trailed off lamely as even as even he knew he was clutching at straws here.

"Yeah, course it might" Ron grinned. He turned to look at Sheila and she started kicking again. He waited for her fury to subside a while then leant forward and spoke softly as close to her ear as he could get. "Listen" he said " I will let you go if you promise not to kill fat boy here, or hurt him too much. If he starts with that girly screaming again, you're going straight back here,

understood." Sheila kicked out again but her heart wasn't in it now. She breathed fast and heavily and she waited until she had it under control. "Yes"

she finally said in a rasping cough.

Ron was about to get up when she added. "I promise not to kill him, but after what he's done to me I can't promise not to hurt him some more".

Ron looked up at Danny who was vigorously shaking his head. He considered it for a few seconds then said "Fair enough" and much to Danny's disgust got up.

When she had recovered her composure Sheila climbed off the bed and straightened her skimpy clothing. Then she faced Danny squarely and looked him, challengingly, in the eye. "Well" she demanded "what have you got to say for yourself.

"About what?" he replied hoping that if he played for time God might take pity on him and strike him down with lightning or something.

"About drawing out a thousand pounds of our lottery winnings and flying to Spain without telling me, you twat"

"I never" he said aghast at the very thought.

Sheila slapped him hard across the face and turned to face Ron, daring him to intervene. Ron raised his hands indicating he was keeping out of it.

"I'm going to hit you every time you deny it" she said directly to Danny.

"I don't know what you…." Smack.

"Where do you get these ideas fr…" Smack.

"Look. If I had won that kind of…." Smack.

"I'm sorry, alright. I'm sorry. I couldn't help it. Just stop hitting me alright"

and he covered his face with one arm so she couldn't hit him again.

Sheila put her hand down by her side and breathed deeply.

Ron glanced away, embarrassed, and then decided to get out of there, save Danny any more embarrassment, and let them sort it out themselves.

"Listen" he said "I'm going down to the pool. I'll be there if you need me. You two sort it out. Just remember, this is Spain. It's hot, it's cheap and to be honest it hasn't been a bundle of fun up to now. We've got a few days left so let's make the most of it. I think we deserve a bit of fun, you two can make up your own minds." And he grabbed his bag up from the dresser and made his way out. He quietly shut the door behind him and listened a few seconds but couldn't hear anything so he went downstairs.

Inside the room Danny stared at his wife for a while until a lazy grin appeared on his face. "I can explain" he offered and then she hit him again.

Ron went straight to the pool bar and was just about to order a drink when he spotted Mick on one of the sunloungers holding hands and gazing dreamily into the eyes of the beautiful Julia. Ron turned from the bar and walked over to them.

"Hiya" he said.

Mick looked up and pulled his sunglasses off his forehead and over his eyes to shield them from the burning mid day sun. He was a little surprised, but glad, to see his old friend. He wasn't sure how Ron was taking the recent turn of

events and felt pretty bad at how he had just left him to fend for himself the whole holiday. He smiled at him now and returned the "Hiya" and asked him what was up.

Ron grinned back. "Just thought you'd like to know. We've got a visitor"

Mick sat up quickly and let go of Julia's hand. "Who?" he asked warily.

"Sheila" he replied and glanced up at the hotel "she's up in the room now"

"Fuckin' hell" Mick exclaimed loudly then lowered his head as he realised people had heard him and were turning round now. Looking back up at Ron he asked in all seriousness "Has she killed him yet?"

"Not yet" Ron laughed and continued "although it's not for the want of trying"

"I'll bet" laughed Mick.

"I'll give 'em an hour then go back up and see if he needs the kiss of life" and they both grinned. Then Ron's face turned solemn and he coughed a little as he said "'course Danny's isn't the only holiday that will be affected is it. Anybody who doesn't want certain things to get back home had better be careful, know what I mean" and he turned to the lovely Julia and nodded and then turned and left.

Mick's face, which had been turning a very nice shade of red thanks to the sun, suddenly lost all its colour and he looked just as pale as the day he arrived.

He had been quietly confident that the lads wouldn't say anything about this holiday fling but he knew that Sheila would break her neck in an attempt to tell Sue the whole sordid tale. Besides which, he still hadn't made up his mind that he was just going to go back home and forget Julia. He still had half a mind to take his chances in Spain and spend the rest of his natural life with her.

Beside him, Julia stirred and held out her hand for his. "What is the matter Miguel?. What did your friend want?. I only catch parts of it, who has come?"

"Nothing luv, nobody" he said absent mindedly and patted her hand but his face said otherwise.

Danny sat on the edge of the bed tenderly stroking his aching groin. He had taken a sneaky peek inside his shorts when Sheila hadn't been looking and had been relieved to see that although his tackle looked a bit red and chafed there appeared to be no cuts and no trace of blood.

"Right then. Let's get this sorted eh" she suddenly said coming in from the balcony where she had been having a look at the view.

"OK luv, what to do you want to do" he said brightly. He had quickly devised a strategy while she had been on the balcony. Act Dumb. That was it.

Sheila strode towards him and raised her hand as if to strike him on the face.

Danny grabbed her wrist and decided on Plan B. Don't act dumb.

"Alright. We'll talk. Calm down" he shouted and was relieved when she stopped struggling and relaxed. He released his hold and sat down on the bed.

She stood there a moment looking at him then shrugged her shoulders and sat down next to him. Danny took a deep breath and let it all out. All his frustrations at a very disappointing holiday and an even more disappointing life came out.

"OK I took the money, you know that. I sent you the cheque for the rest of it, you know that. I came away to be with the lads for a week, you know that.

You've found out now where I am staying so you know everything. As always Sheila you know fuckin' everything" His voice was raised now as his anger and resentment tumbled over each other. What a shitty holiday. What a shitty life seemed to be his mantra. It was his and he was sticking manfully to it.

"But there are some things you don't know about Sheila" he went on, warming to his theme. "There are plenty of things you don't know about actually and I'm going to tell you what they are. Yeah how about that then eh". He was on his feet now pacing the room and taking little darting runs in her direction and pointing a finger at her accusingly.

"One" and he jabbed a digit in her direction to help her understand that this was the first in a long list of things he wanted to get off his chest.

"You don't know that I know about your shaggin' right, left and centre with every bloke that you can lay your hands on. Two" and he jabbed two digits at her. "You don't know how that used to tear me apart. Really fuckin' kill me inside. Yeah. Then, but not now. Not for a long time. Three" and he added a third digit and stuck them right in front of her face.

You don't know that I know all about your sordid little affair with your supervisor from work. Eh. Fuck me Sheila, everybody knows about that" he snorted as he laughed and wiped away spittle from

211

his lips. He shot his hand forward but he had lost his count now that he had used his hand for something else. He desperately tried to recap on what he had said but couldn't remember a single thing. He suddenly shot out four fingers and a thumb.

"F" he shouted in triumph as he thought he remembered where he was up to.

Sheila smiled slightly at his stupidity. Danny spotted it and decided he had got the count spot on and had impressed her no end. He waggled his hand in front of her face to emphasise his cleverness.

"F" he repeated. "You could shag one of your fancy blokes here, right now and it wouldn't bother me. Eh. You didn't know that did you. Eh. It wouldn't bother me 'cos I'm dead inside see" He put his hand on where he thought his heart should be and tears sprang to his eyes. This was the crux of the matter, wasn't it. This was the point that he really wanted to convey. This was the whole point of the message that he needed Sheila to understand. "I'm dead inside and you killed me." He stared at her expressionless, over made up face and looked for some feelings of remorse. He blinked tears away from his own eyes but resolved not to wipe them away. Sheila spat in his face and he just carried on staring. The spit mingled with his tears and he felt his lips tremble.

They were inches from each other, each one determined not to break the spell that bound their eyes together.

"I love you" he suddenly conceded and the spell was broken.

She spat again in his face but he just blinked and continued to stare. He felt confused and angry with himself, and not a little surprised. I love you. Where had that come from. He hadn't intended saying it, it just sort of appeared from nowhere. Now he watched her closely for her reaction.

Her face seemed contorted with pain. Every emotion, every thought was written clearly for all to see. She realised that her control of the situation was running away from her. She had come here, of course, to give him a good kicking but what next. She could have waited till he had got back home and given him a right pasting and then handed him over to her brothers. She could have blown the rest of the money on herself and just said "Fuck him" after all half of it was his. Had she really come all this way just to confront him. Or had she really come to show him that she still cared what he did. Or didn't care. Or, or.... She wasn't sure any more. Maybe she never had been. She stared at her spit running down his face, faster at the points where it met his tears. She wiped his face with her hand and he stared at her, unsure what to do next. She was sure of one thing though. She still loved him.

She inched forward and almost touched him. Her fingers slowly, nervously searched for his until they engaged and locked together. She gently squeezed.

They were only inches apart now. He could feel her hot breath on her face. Her mouth inched nearer until their lips touched. They kissed, softly and slowly. It was a long time since they had kissed like that. Danny felt himself getting aroused and then a thought stuck him. He was in a very vulnerable position if she decided to knee him in the groin. She kissed him again and this time he kept his eyes open. He returned the kiss fully but a tiny part of him held back, ready for an attack. Sheila's eyes were closed and all dreamy and she was obviously putting everything into this kiss. He felt his inhibitions disappear as he kissed her back. Everything was going to be alright. That was when she kneed him in the groin.

He went down faster than a ten bob whore and tears filled his eyes. He gasped for air and as he landed on his knees he made a small gagging noise.

"You bastard" she shrieked and metaphorically rolled up her sleeves to lay into him. "You self centred supercilious, holier than thou bastard." She breathed deeply and walked slowly round him, taunting and teasing him.

"You fuckin' love it that everyone feels sorry for you 'cos I'm shaggin' around.

Poor Danny…." and she put on a mocking voice for this bit "…married to that slag. It must be a nightmare for him. I feel sooooo.. sorry for him. I don't know why he puts up with it." She was round in front of him now and she stuck her face in front of his. "Eh" she shouted and he winced visibly.

"Well they've no fuckin' idea." She was fuming now. All her hatred and fury at those petty minded fools back home was bubbling to the fore and she determined to take it all out on Danny. After all that was what she had come here for. Wasn't it?".

"They have no idea what goes on in here" and she touched her head for emphasis, "and they certainly don't know what's happening in here" and she put her hand on her heart. She took a big drag on her fag and purposely blew it in his face.

"They don't know what you did to me either, do they? They don't know what you said on our honeymoon that broke my bleedin' heart."

Danny had regained his breath now and as she had moved away from him slightly he decided to risk life and limb and crawled to the bed where he sat

down heavily. He picked up the cigs and lit one. After a few seconds he ventured "What did I do?" in a soft voice.

She glared at him and he was sure she was going to hit him again but instead she curled her lip in disgust and spat out "You really haven't a bleedin' clue have you" He shook his head and took another drag.

She in turn shook her head and said "You sad bastard". She sat down next to him on the bed and in a voice you would normally use when explaining something tricky to a small child she explained to him how he had hurt her all that time ago.

"I know what I was like before we were married but I thought I could change. I thought I had found someone special. Someone who loved me, who saw deeper than just the tart. I also thought I

214

was pregnant" Danny harumphed and was about to say something but she shot him a stare that made him stop in his tracks. "I thought I was pregnant" she continued "and I thought it was yours.

You don't seriously think I would fake that just to snare you do you?. You must have a very high opinion of yourself". He harumphed again but couldn't think of anything to say so he snorted down his nose, a sort of mini harumph.

"There were a lot better catches out there I can tell you and I could have pretty much had my pick" she went on and then with a tap of her finger she flicked her ash on the tiled floor and added "Within reason" She thought about it a while and smiled laconically to herself "Somebody richer" He nodded, just a little as he knew it was true. They hadn't had much money since he had lost his job. "Someone with better prospects" Again he knew this was true as his prospects appeared to be nil at the moment. He had been in a rut for a while and he just couldn't gather the energy to pull himself out of it. He nodded again. "Taller". Another nod. "Thinner". Nod. "Bigger cock". "Hang on. Hang on. We're getting a bit personal now don't you think" he shouted as he jumped to his feet.. She was smiling so he could see she was teasing him so he grinned sheepishly and sat back down. He crossed and uncrossed his feet a few times until he was sure he wanted to ask the question.

"Why me then?"

She turned to him but seemed to be staring straight through him, as if she was trying to recall something that had happened to her in another life time.

"Because I loved you" she said simply.

Maybe it was the simplicity of it or perhaps it just felt right but Danny leant towards her and kissed her, slowly and sensually. At first she seemed to stiffen and hold back but after a few seconds she responded and held onto him tightly.

Gradually things started to heat up and clothing began to be discarded and eventually nature took its course until they lay sweaty and spent in each other's arms. Danny couldn't wipe the big daft grin off his face and Sheila had never looked so happy and content.

The sound of a key in the door disturbed them and Danny was pleasantly surprised when Sheila made a grab for a blanket and hurriedly covered herself up.

Ron appeared in the doorway and coughed. "Er, just making sure you were both alright" he muttered, a little embarrassed. He saw them laid naked and

entwined on the bed and broke into a big grin. He stepped inside and closed the door behind him. "Well you seem to be doing fine" he smiled.

Sheila stroked Danny's arm. "Hmm not bad" she breathed and Danny blushed slightly, although he was rather proud.

"Not killed him yet then?" he asked Sheila and Danny butted in "Almost" and blew out his cheeks and drooped his eyelids, indicating he was shattered. Sheila drew the thin cotton sheet around her and nuzzled up to Danny who put his arm lovingly and protectively around her.

Danny looked lovingly at her and then turned to Ron "Yeah I think we're going to give things another go. A proper go this time" He looked again at Sheila and asked "Yeah?" a little concerned that he may have jumped the gun. She snuggled up tighter to him and breathed "Yeah" and kissed his chest. Danny beamed.

"I'm glad" said Ron "It's about time".

Danny glanced down at Sheila and asked "How long are you here for?"

"I go back the same day as you " she said. "But I've nowhere to stay yet. I came straight here from the airport"

"Well we can't stay here with Jeff" answered Danny. "Although he hasn't actually slept here yet it is still his room. We'd best go and get somewhere this afternoon."

Ron was thinking. "Tell you what" he suddenly shouted "You two stay here in this room. Jeff can kip down in Mick's room. Like you say he's not actually likely to need it. It's just somewhere to hang his clothes. He'll not mind"

"Yeah but what about you?" asked Danny.

"Me? Said Ron, suddenly looking all mysterious "I've got other plans"

CHAPTER TWELVE

About an hour later Ron was parking his newly rented hire car in the hotel car park and was just running up the steps to the foyer when Mick suddenly appeared from nowhere.

"Where are you off to?" he asked, nodding towards the car. Ron explained about Sheila and Danny and that Jeff would be moving in with Mick. Mick smiled broadly at the suggestion that Sheila and Danny were playing happy families but felt it necessary to voice his opinion that Sheila's presence might spoil his own plans.

"Look Mick" said Ron who was getting more than a little annoyed with his friends selfishness. "If you're so bothered about what Sheila might say when we get back, it just means that really you know that at the end of this holiday

you are going to go back to Sue. You're not going to stay here with Juanita or whatever her name is"

"Julia" corrected Mick "and I do know that you know. I'm not stupid. But I love her Ron, I really do. I can't just walk away."

Ron nodded, his anger gone now. "I know pal. I know" he said sympathetically.

Mick looked round him and spotted the car. "So what are you going to do.

You're not thinking of sleeping in the car are you?"

"Of course not" Ron laughed and weighed up the best way to tell him. "You've got somebody to be with. Danny has now. And Jeff always has. I want somebody now. I want somebody I can be with." He paused, wondering how best to phrase it, knowing his friends likely response. He decided to just come out with it. "I'm going to see Ros" he stated as if daring Mick to question his right.

"Ros. You and Ros. I didn't know you had a thing going with Ros." Mick blurted out, genuinely surprised.

"I haven't got a thing going with Ros. She's my friend and I'd rather be up there with her than down here on my own."

Mick looked at him as if he'd gone mad.

"Have you gone mad?" he asked incredulously. Ron waited for what he knew would follow.

"What will Sue say when you turn up halfway through their holiday. She'll wonder what's up. She'll badger you into telling her everything. She'll grind you down until you can't help yourself. You'll talk. She'll make you. You have no idea how ruthless she is when she gets going" He was panicking now. He could see his whole world coming crashing down around his ears. He knew he shouldn't be having this affair with Julia but he couldn't help it. It all felt so right it had to be Ok. Well apart from the guilt he felt over his two timing Sue.

He had managed to shove that to the back of his mind. It was something he would have to deal with at some point but not now. Not here.

Ron snapped. He had had enough of his friends selfishness. He darted forward so they were eyeball to eyeball and spat out "I don't believe you, you selfish bastard. What do you expect me to do eh, sit here on my own all week while you shag Miss Spain. You're unreal."

Mick was on his high horse though and had no intention of backing down. He could see his steamy affair with the beautiful Julia coming to an end and he was desperate to drag it out for as long as he could. "I'm fuckin' warning you"

he said in his most menacing voice "Say owt to Sue and I'll fuckin' kill ya"

Ron stared back, confident in his knowledge that he could handle anything his mate threw at him, but upset and angry that he had made the threat. His voice oozed menace when he replied, as softly and succinctly as he could.

"Don't go there Mick. Don't even think about it. I don't want to hurt you but if you threaten me again I will. It's up to you"

The tense atmosphere could be cut by a knife. At one stage Mick thought of nutting him and running away before he had the chance to recover. He fully considered it as a legitimate option for about half a second but hurriedly

reconsidered and went for the only other option available to him. Don't fuck with Ron.

He smiled weakly and the tension lifted a little. He stepped back creating a more amiable space between them. Ron though had other ideas. He stepped forward, closing the gap again and Mick's heart sank. He was certain now he had pushed Ron too far and he was going to get a good hiding. Ron leant forward into his face and in a sort of terrifying stage whisper spelt it out for Mick.

"I am going to see Ros. I want to see Ros and it's got fuck all to do with you or anybody else. I've no intention of telling Sue about your great affair, that's something between you and your conscience. If you've got one. One day Mick you're going to get caught out and I hope and pray that I'm there to see you get exactly what you deserve. But you don't give a fuck about that though eh, all you're bothered about is you, you fuckin' shit, and making sure you get your end away for a bit while you're on holiday." He backed away to leave and then remembered something else he wanted to say and returned to his position directly in front of Mick's face. Mick, as soon as Ron backed off, opened his mouth to say something back in his own defence but stopped as soon as Ron appeared once again in front of him.

"And something else for you to think about over the next few days" Ron continued, in the same harsh whisper. "Just remember who'll get hurt at the end of this. You? Doubt it. Julia and Sue? Definitely" He shook his head in disgust "You don't know what love is you twat." And he gave Mick a withering look and shoved roughly past him.

Mick turned and watched him go into the hotel. He knew Ron had been right.

He knew he was in the wrong. He knew he should stop the affair now before it got out of hand. He thought of Sue, alone and faithful. She would never in a million years do what he had done. He felt disgusted with himself for the way he had behaved. He thought about Julia. She was the most beautiful woman he had ever seen. She oozed sex appeal and he became turned on every time he thought of her. How could that be wrong he thought for the millionth time. It's just nature. It's out of my control. He thought of Julia lying by the pool, as she now was, in the smallest of bikinis hiding hardly any of the most beautiful body he could wish for. He headed off in the direction of the pool, shooting a quick glance at the disappearing back of Ron.

"Yeah, well you'd better not say owt anyway" he mumbled
CHAPTER TWELVE

Claire sat on the edge of her lounger and gazed deep into the eyes of the tall brummie man sitting cross legged on the hot sand, himself staring back at the blonde beauty who was paying him so much attention.

Claire had called him over, supposedly for a light, about fifteen minutes ago and they had immediately struck up a mutual admiration and it now looked as though he was set there for the day.

Linda watched, as they gently reached forward to caress each others long shiny limbs, amazed at such overt shows of affection after such a short time together.

She wished Giorgio was here but new she would have to wait until he had finished work. Even then she knew they wouldn't indulge in such public displays of lust. Still, you can dream. She closed her eyes and did just that.

Hidden amongst her erotic (although naïve) thoughts she couldn't help but think that Giorgio was holding something back from her. They had talked extensively about their childhood days and Linda had desperately tried to make hers sound much more interesting than they actually were. Giorgio, however seemed to go so far with his stories but then suddenly clam up or change the subject, sometimes so subtly that it wasn't until later that Linda had realised what he had done.

Of course she had her own theory on why he did this. It was the poverty that he was trying to hide from her. He was much too proud to admit that his family, although large and good humoured and full of love were poor. She had no evidence to base this on, other than a notion that his family were kind of like Gypsies, hence the barbecue on the beach and the fact that there were so many family members there. She had gently mentioned this to him yesterday but he had coloured up slightly then laughed and said he came from a large house full of aunts and uncles and cousins and he couldn't remember being "poor".

She had laughed back and said she was glad but a thought had occurred to her.

They had been for four meals so far in different restaurants or café's and so far he hadn't had to pay for a single meal. Each time his offer of payment had been flatly refused, usually brushed aside midst hugs and kisses. Surely this proved her theory. He couldn't afford to eat in nice restaurants on his wages as a waiter so his family looked out for him and made sure he didn't have to pay. They probably fiddled the receipts or overcharged somebody else so the owner would never know. She smiled now as she thought about it. She loved the way they all hugged and kissed each other when meeting or leaving. They would get up to leave and people would come out of the restaurant or even the kitchen and hug and clasp hands and talk very loudly and oh so fast in Spanish. Then they would all turn to her and repeat the procedure all over again, as though she were some special relative who they wouldn't see again for a while. She loved it. She hadn't experienced anything remotely similar before being English. The Brits aren't too good with all these shows of affection and truth be told most Englishmen would find it embarrassing to have to kiss and cuddle members of their own family when they met. She couldn't imagine her own dad, for instance, clasping to his chest her Aunty Doreen, her mum's sister, when she said she was going home. He usually just breathed a sigh of relief.

Sue and Ros lay together on the far side of the group. They were laid on their sides facing in to each other. Sue was talking and Ros was listening and they had been that way for a while now. Ros knew that although Sue had been prattling on for ages she hadn't actually got round to saying what she wanted to say. She reached into the sand and picked up a handful and let it slip out between her fingers as her friend got around to the point.

"So you see, my mum has just taken over" Sue was saying. "It's all she ever talks about. Flowers, reception, best man, bridesmaids, dresses, fittings, cars, music. It's too much. It's doing my head in."

Ros reached down for some more sand. "Perhaps she's just excited" she offered, studying the fineness of the sand and wondering idly why it didn't just form a ball like at Skegness.

"Mick's fed up with it too" Sue continued "I can tell. His mum's let my mum get on with it although his dad has offered to pay half, which was nice. Mick just nods in agreement now and seems to cut himself off"

Ros dropped the remaining sand onto the beach and looked up at her friend.

She considered for a moment then said "So your problem is that your mum is organising your wedding for you, your boyfriend is agreeing with everything and your future father in law wants to help pay for it". She looked at Sue with a sarcy smile on her lips waiting for her friend to respond, probably by correcting a few misconceptions.

"Exactly" Sue shouted triumphantly. "I knew you'd understand straight away"

and she smiled thankfully at Ros. Ros stared back and wondered whether she should tell her friend she was being sarcastic but decided against it and just smiled.

"Sometimes" Sue went on "It just gets on top of me and I just want to run away and hide. Just… oh I don't know… do something different I suppose". She sat up and tied her hair into a bun then lay back down.

Ros smiled knowingly. "So you think that as you're still single you could treat yourself to a little pre marital distraction here on holiday and no one would get hurt, eh".

Sue sat back up, a look of utter horror on her face. "What are you saying. What do you mean. Are you implying that just because I'm on holiday I would have an affair with Dave behind Mick's back?"

"Who mentioned Dave?" asked Ros, raising one eyebrow slightly. Sue stared back at her. She knew she had slipped up but there was no way she was going to admit it.

"I meant anybody, have an affair with anybody behind Mick's back I meant.

That's what I meant". Her voice trailed off unconvincingly. She stared out to sea and thoughts ran around in her head, confusing her. At last she turned to Ros, who had closed her eyes and was almost asleep so long had she waited for her friend to continue, and whispered "Do you think that's wrong of me then.?"

Danny rolled over and blew air out of his lungs. He had a satisfied look on his chubby face. He glanced across at Sheila who looked at least as equally smug.

They had just made love for the third time that afternoon and although Danny

was as happy as he had ever been he was secretly terrified that Sheila would want to go again. He was knackered and just wanted to be left alone now to sleep. He flinched as she turned into him and snuggled right up close. He held the scream that came to his throat as he felt her fingers cradling his balls, but only just and he was mightily relieved when she asked him gently "How much of the money have you actually got left?"

She held her breath as she waited for the answer. She dreaded it being "none"

as she knew that however much she loved him at this moment she would half kill him and ruin everything if he had blown it all already.

He turned to her and smiled. "Nearly all of it" he said happily. "I paid for the tickets. I've had one night out and then I've been stuck in here the rest of the time with the shits"

"Ah that explains the awful smell" she thought. She had assumed it must be the drains.

She squeezed his balls lovingly and jumped up. He didn't hold the girly scream this time and he was relieved when she ignored it and climbed out of bed.

"Come on then" she said, happily "let's spend some of that money" and she loped off to the bathroom. He wiped the tears away from his eyes and watched her go. She wasn't a bad looking bird, he had to give her that. Nice arse. The nice arse disappeared through the door and Danny got up and followed it in. He turned the shower on and climbed in. he washed thoroughly and turned it off again. As he bent to pick up a towel he was surprised to see her still sat on the closet watching him. "Not bad" she said throatily. "Nice arse". He picked up the towel and proudly wiped himself. He half turned to give her a better view of his bum and saw her smile.

"I love you" he suddenly said.

Sheila shook herself a little to get rid of any lingering droplets and stood and walked towards him. She pulled his neck down and kissed him passionately.

When they parted she stroked his hair then released him so he stood up again.

"And despite everything" she said and her face took on an almost saintly beauty "I love you too"

They dressed and like two giggling teenagers off on some illicit, secret tryst they went out kissing and touching into the corridor where they almost bumped into Ron who was just hoisting a big holdall onto his back.

"You two okay?" he asked as he swerved to avoid them.

Danny took Sheila's hand and raised it to his mouth and kissed it gently. He looked at her but spoke to both of them "Yeah I think we are"

Ron broke into a big smile, genuinely happy for them. "Good. It's about time"

Danny smiled at him then noticed for the first time the big bag. "Where are you going Ron" he asked concernedly.

Ron eased the bag off his shoulder and swapped it into his other hand.

"I'm off to see some friends, well one friend in particular. I should have done this a while ago, but … well I've had other things on my mind" He turned and set off down the corridor. Danny and Sheila looked quizzically at each other.

Ron slowed down and called over his shoulder. "I just hope she's pleased to see me"

Ros was pissed off. Claire had pulled with the brummie lad and they had gone off for some privacy when Linda kept tutting every time they fondled each other. Linda herself had gone off to meet Giorgio on his lunch break. No doubt for a free meal somewhere. From what she had heard he hadn't paid for a meal yet. Maybe he was blackmailing them. She laughed to herself at the absurdity of it. You only had to meet Giorgio once to instantly know he could never hurt anyone.

She turned to Sue who was chatting away with Dave who had turned up unexpectedly. Ros had been amazed at the transformation that Sue had undertaken. She had gone from a beach babe, coolly covering herself with Ambre Solaire and enjoying the rays to a giggling schoolgirl who was infatuated with the handsome young man paying her some attention. She had even dropped the sun cream all over herself. Ros looked down and smiled at Sue's legs, which were white, through the half gallon of factor ten on them. It would take a week of rubbing to get that lot to soak in.

Dave's mate, Steve, had arrived with him but had buggered off after an embarrassing fifteen minutes where he had tried vainly to catch Ros' attention.

She had almost succumbed at one point but to be honest she didn't fancy him and she just couldn't be bothered so she had smiled weakly and closed her eyes. After a while she had sensed that he had gone and opened one eye and had a crafty look around. She saw Sue give her an evil look for her bad manners and shut her eye quickly. Balls. It was her holiday. She could talk to whoever she wanted.

She was annoyed at Sue anyway. It was bad enough that she was going to play away, but to do it with somebody that lived locally was madness. Ros had a bad feeling about it .

Ron bounded up the stairs and knocked on the girls room. There was no answer as he had expected so he went back down to the foyer, unsure what he should do next. It had been a nice steady drive along the coastal road and he had made the journey without any delays. He looked at his watch and went into the bar for a drink. It was six o clock now so the girls could still be on the beach.

Alternatively they could be having a meal. He wondered whether they would eat early and then get ready for a night out or get ready first and then eat. He had no idea. Or maybe they were out shopping. Should he hit the shops in the hope that he might come across them. He shook his head and decided to stay in the bar for a bit and play it by ear. The bar was empty so he bought a bottle of San Miguel and took it out to the pool. Straight away he saw a familiar face.

The pool. Of course, why hadn't he thought of that. He waved to Linda who appeared to be watching him with a big grin on her face. She didn't respond so he edged past the waiter who was serving drinks to a group of sunworshippers and walked over to her. She appeared to be leaning over now to see round him and he turned to see who she was looking at. He couldn't see anybody other than the waiter so he shrugged and carried on. Linda was leaning over so far

she was almost horizontal and as he reached her he had to shoot his arm forward to catch her as she overbalanced on the flimsy plastic chair.

"Linda are you are right" he asked as he placed her upright again. She looked at him, shocked that he knew her name, then burst into a huge grin as she recognised him. She jumped up and gave him a huge hug and kissed him on the cheek. "Ron, what on earth are you doing here?" she asked as she squeezed him tightly to her.

Ron gazed down on to the top of her head as she hugged for all she was worth.

He had always liked Linda but in all the years he had known her he had never known her be so forward or affectionate. He smiled at her like a long suffering big brother and gently eased her away from him.

"Well" he laughed as he got his breath back. "Somebody's glad to see me".

"I'm always glad to see you Ron" she smiled back and then much to his surprise she suddenly leant over to one side and gazed round him. He half turned to see what she was looking at. There was just the waiter who he had passed earlier, only now he was coming towards them at speed. Linda stepped back and brushed her hair straight with her fingers and as the young man appeared by her side she grabbed hold of his arm as if fearful that he would escape. The waiter eyed Ron suspiciously for a few seconds and then turned to Linda and gave her a huge smile, which was immediately returned.

After a while Linda turned to Ron and grinned warmly. She held Giorgio close as she announced proudly "Ron I want you to meet Giorgio" she squeezed Giorgio's arm then held his hand. She looked lovingly at Giorgio. "Giorgio I want you to meet Ron, a very good friend from home."

With his free hand Giorgio reached out and shook hands cordially with Ron.

He was being civil but guarded and Ron could tell although he wasn't sure why.

"Hello Ron. How are you?" he asked haltingly.

"Fine thanks" Ron answered, amused at the man's discomfort. "You?"

"Si" responded Giorgio then he hesitated as if wondering whether to ask the next question, then decided to go for it so asked in a rush. "You are a long way from home yes? Are you travelling all this way to see Linda or are you just passing through. A coincidence eh perhaps."

Ron smiled easily. The man was jealous. He thought Ron was here to see Linda and he didn't like it.

"Actually I've not come from England, well at least not today. I've travelled up from Benidorm and" and he nodded to Linda "as nice as it is to see Linda again after what, three, four days it's actually Ros I've come to see." He smiled again at Giorgio and watched amusedly as he suddenly broke into a huge smile.

"Ros" he beamed. "Linda's friend Ros" he laughed. "You have come up to see Linda's friend Ros" he giggled. He leant forward and hugged Ron who was slightly taken aback and had a sudden flashback to the other night and Jose squeezing him tightly. He could almost taste the blood in his mouth and he wondered idly if Jose had been to the hospital and seen to his tongue.

"Linda's friend Ros she is on the beach, yes" he turned to Linda for confirmation and she nodded loyally. They gazed lovingly at each other and Ron couldn't help but envy them their obvious new found love".

"Right" he smiled as he stepped back "I'll leave you two to it then and have a walk down to the beach and see if I can find Ros"

They all but ignored him as they looked into each others eyes so he turned and headed round the pool and set off for the beach, eager now to see Ros. He stopped at the shallow end and turned back to see Linda and Giorgio embracing. He smiled to himself and headed off now to the beach.

Mick strolled down the prom from Levante beach heading off towards Poniente. He held tightly on to Julia's hand and almost danced as he heard a snatch of music from one of the open air cafes. It was Sammy Davis Junior belting out Mr Bojangles and Mick couldn't resist adding a little skip to his walk.

"I love Sinatra" he informed Julia who looked at him adoringly and marvelled at his vast knowledge. Mick basked in her adoration and skipped again but unfortunately caught his toe on a kerbstone and shouted out in pain. He pulled his leg up and shot his flip flop forward into the café where it hid under a table.

Limping, he entered the café and searched for his errant footwear. The lady who was seated at the table where the shoe was hiding took it mainly in good spirit, as he crawled on all fours through her legs, and only hit him because of the initial shock. When he produced the flip flop from beneath her she apologised profusely, as did he, until he sat on the floor and looked up to see the most beautiful girl in the world wearing the most beautiful pink bikini and the most beautiful pale blue sarong laughing the most beautiful laugh he had ever seen. He sat there and watched her in awe and knew that he couldn't just leave her. He stood up and walked towards her and as he reached her he held out his hand, which she took, still laughing, and pulled her gently towards him.

He felt no resistance at all and held her tight as he kissed her. There can't have been another couple in Benidorm as much in love as these two at that exact moment.

Except maybe Danny and Sheila who were walking slowly towards Mick and Julia, happy and content in their new found togetherness. Danny carried two shopping bags and wore a very smug expression and Sheila had on a very smart Spanish style dress that they had just bought from an expensive boutique in the old town. Every few steps Sheila squeezed Danny's hand and Danny responded with a kiss. Sometimes they were long and passionate and caused passers by to wink and nudge each other.

Others were merely pecks on the cheek or lips, given as a love token, a sort of affirmation of their love or maybe they were promises of things to come. Whatever. Danny enjoyed them and Sheila seemed to blossom in their presence.

It was at the end of one such peck when Sheila was still looking adoringly at her husband that Danny turned his head forward and spotted Mick and Julia snogging about ten yards ahead in the entry to a small café. Danny squealed his little girly, squeal that he seemed to have taken to as a habit, which shocked

Sheila who immediately asked him if he was alright. He panicked and tried desperately to think of something to say. Obviously the more he concentrated the more his mind became a blank.

"Danny are you alright?" asked Sheila, more urgently now. Danny fought gallantly for words to issue forth from his lips but couldn't think of a single thing. Suddenly, just as they reached Mick and Julia, it came to him in a blinding flash of inspiration. "Shark" he proudly announced.

"Shark?" repeated Sheila, staring at him as though he had gone mad, which she clearly though he had.

"Yes shark" he confirmed with a firm nod. "I thought I saw a shark".

Sheila stared at him in amazement, worried for his sanity. As they passed Mick and Julia Sheila waved her arms round, catching Mick on the shoulder as she did so and said loudly "Danny, look round you. Shops, bars and café's. She squinted forward and craned her neck. I can't even see the fuckin' sea."

They were clear of the kissing couple now and quickly leaving them behind and the sudden sense of adrenaline left Danny as he realised they were safe. As much as he loved Sheila and as much as she seemed to have changed and improved he wasn't going to risk her finding out about Mick and blabbing it all over Brinsmarsh when they got back. He felt relief that he had successfully avoided such a calamitous encounter and thought that perhaps he should clarify things with Sheila now. He looked at her concerned face and offered "It's okay it wasn't a shark after all"

"No" she said in mock surprise. "What was it?"

Danny looked around him for inspiration but as he was in a street full of shops, bars and café's found none. "It was…". Still nothing. "….a…" Even more nothing. A dog suddenly ran past and Danny pointed at it excitedly and shouted

"…A dog. It was a dog, see, it was a dog all the time." Several people stared at him as they passed and Sheila looked curiously. "When was the last time you ate?" she asked. Danny thought for a second and was surprised at his answer.

"Two days ago" he said.

"Come on then fat boy. That blubber'll not keep you going forever, let's get you fed, I think you're getting delirious." She grabbed his hand and pulled him back, past the over amorous couple stood in the doorway of the nearest café.

Danny almost screamed again but managed to hold it in as he allowed himself to be ushered into the café past Mick and Julia.

"Excuse us" called Sheila but the couple ignored her so she pulled Danny past.

They found a table in the corner and went towards it. Danny followed, all the time glancing over his shoulder. He was relieved to see that the table Sheila had picked did not afford them a good view of the doorway and even more relieved when Sheila sat down with her back to the door. He relaxed visibly as he sat down heavily opposite his wife.

"You must eat" she said solicitously, when they were comfy.

"I've been ill" he offered by way of explanation and she stroked his hand lovingly. A shark?. She could see that she hadn't been taking proper care of him and he obviously couldn't cope on his own. She vowed to take better care in future.

Outside Mick nibbled on Julia's lip as their long passionate kiss ended. She gazed adoringly at him and he looked, equally as lovingly back. Then he slowly looked round to see if the coast was clear. He hadn't seen Danny and Sheila approaching, as he was locked in a loving embrace with the beautiful Julia but he had heard their voices. Never being the bravest of men he had decided to continue the kiss, metaphorically burying his head in the sand, hoping they would go away and indeed they had. He heard Danny mention the shark and the dog and it was all he could do not to turn round and slap him, but he had kissed on until eventually the voices had disappeared and he deemed it safe to come up for air. He spun Julia round a little and she laughed delightedly, as did he, but his was through relief at his escape. He wouldn't allow anything to spoil what he and Julia had and if he rode his luck a little he could get away with this. He looked adoringly into her eyes.

"Hungry?" he asked. She nodded. "Come on then, let's eat" and he took her hand and led her into the café.

Ron walked hurriedly down the beach. He was thinking of giving up and going back to the bar. He had covered the same area three times now and hadn't caught a glimpse of the girls.

There were plenty of girls here of course, girls of all shapes and sizes. There was the couple of chubby ones at the waters edge who were hanging around two fit looking lads who were splashing about and generally showing off in the foam. There were two slim looking girls laid side by side on sun loungers but one was coloured so he had gazed on past them. There was a very attractive brunette, laid alone amongst a cluster of loungers, sunbathing topless. She was wearing just a small pair of bikini bottoms and sunglasses and even on his urgent mission Ron couldn't help but admire her shapely body. Eventually he turned away from her and carried on his search. There was a group of girls further down the beach who were being preyed upon by a gang of noisy youths.

He headed off in their direction but halfway there got a better look at the girls and knew it wasn't them.

Placing his hands on his hips he stopped and determined to make a decision.

Sod it, he would go back to the car and collect his things then find somewhere to stay and then later he would return to the hotel and look for Ros. He turned to go back up the beach and surprised himself when he realised he was looking forward to passing the gorgeous near naked brunette again. As he neared her he subconsciously held his stomach in even though the girl was asleep. Or at least he assumed she was asleep, he couldn't be sure as she was wearing sunglasses.

As he drew level with her he blatantly stared down at her boobs, so sure was he that she was asleep. What did it matter anyway. She didn't know him so why should he feel embarrassed. It wasn't as if she was going to shout out his name or anything, just for staring.

"Ron?" the girl suddenly called out and he almost let out one of those Danny squeals. In any event he dropped his bag off his shoulder. He bent down to pick it up, mainly to afford him some time to gather his thoughts. Who knew him

here? Why had she called out in such shock horror? Had she spotted him staring blatantly at her knockers?

"Ron?" she repeated so he looked up as though he had just seen her for the first time and smiled. It occurred to him that he recognised the voice but he couldn't place it. Then she smiled at him and there was something about the smile, something about the inner beauty hidden behind something so simple as a smile that made his heart skip a beat. "Ros" he said simply and walked toward her.

She sat up, completely unaware of her near nakedness and held out her hand indicating he should sit down.

He sat down on the bed that had been Sue's and placed his bag on the warm sand.

"Well fancy seeing you here" he began and then looked down at the sand moving under his toes aware that it was a poor start to a conversation.

Ros tried to see through his dark shades but couldn't but she could detect his unease and decided to tease him just a little. "Ron I'm on holiday here all week so it's no big shock" She reached behind her and tied her hair back in place.

She couldn't help but notice his head move slightly in her direction and she suddenly realised that she had no top on. She almost reached across for it but a delicious little tingle shot up and down her spine so instead she arched her back and pressed her breasts forward a little. "My only surprise is that you're here"

she seemed to purr.

He laughed self consciously "Yeah well, to be honest I wasn't really having a good time in Benidorm and I thought, well you know, I thought perhaps like, if you were all bored as well like, I thought, well maybe, all of you I mean perhaps …." He trailed off pathetically, aware that he was making a total balls up of this. He had looked forward to it for so long and now because he was such a useless jerk he was ruining it. He glanced up at Ros and couldn't believe how beautiful she was. The sun had given her a glow that really suited her and he suddenly realised that she was totally gorgeous and totally out of his league.

"You came all this way just to see us?" she asked innocently.

He looked round to his left, then over to his right, then down, then up. Then, as if he had just regained control of his neck, he steadied himself and stared her in the face.

"No Ros, just you," he almost whispered. "I've come to see you."

Ros raised one eyebrow slightly, surprised, and then realised that it was the best answer she could have possibly hoped for. She looked hard and long into his face, desperately trying to seek out his eyes behind his shades. Ron gazed longingly into her beautiful face. He too was trying to search out her eyes, those beautiful.. God what colour were her eyes, he had no idea. It didn't matter. She was beautiful, even more beautiful than he had imagined. She had a beautiful open face that showed her honesty and innocence. Her shoulders were white, now with a hint of bronze, and were perfect in shape and size. Her breasts. Oh those gorgeous orbs. Despite himself, his eyes wandered down her body, taking in all the perfection.

At last Ros spotted some movement behind the sunglasses. It was a downward movement, indicating that he was no longer staring intently into her eyes.

Without smiling she said "I can't see them but your eyeballs had better be staring straight ahead."

Through the darkness of his sunglasses she saw his eyes flicker upwards although his head never actually moved. "Of course" he said and a grin appeared on his face. Ros noticed how handsome he looked, how open and honest his face was. And something else. What was it? Innocence, that was it.

He had an innocent quality about him that was very attractive.

He casually removed his sunglasses and smiled at her. She in turn removed hers and smiled back. "Brown" he thought. He knew her eyes would be big and brown. He then told her about meeting Linda and she laughed out loud "Loves great young things" she said. "they're never apart and so desperate for it, it hurts but unless they get a push in the right direction they're never actually going to get round to having sex before it's time to go home". Her face dropped a little "Either way, Linda's going to be very hurt when it's time to leave him"

237

She thought for a while and suddenly laughed again. "Although, no more than poor Giorgio I think". Ron laughed too then thought about it and stopped, suddenly saddened at the thought of their parting. Ros saw it and leant forward and touched his shoulder. "At least they have each other for now. That's important isn't it?"

He looked at her for what seemed like ages then leant forward and kissed her softly on the lips. She responded warmly so he kissed her again. His hand came up and stroked her hair and hers did likewise. They kissed until they had to come up for air then smiled lovingly at each other.

"For now or forever Ros?" he asked and the sadness in his voice brought a lump to her throat. She kissed him again and swapped positions so that she could be even closer to him. He put his arm round her and she sat on his knee.

He could feel her nakedness and something stirred. She clung to him and kissed his neck and could feel his arousal.

"That's up to you Ron" she sighed contentedly.

Otto Von Ruppe complained long and hard to the girl in reception. He couldn't understand why she couldn't get it into her thick head why he was so unhappy.

It wasn't as if he was bad at complaining, he was very good. He had had a lot of practise.

He was moaning now about the tennis balls on the local tennis courts. They were too soft. They didn't have enough bouncyness he told her in his best English.

In the beginning the girl had been most helpful but now Otto detected a definite slip in her attention. It seemed the more he complained the less helpful she became. He couldn't figure it out.

Oh it wasn't the first time he had encountered such behaviour, it was getting to be more the norm, but for the life of him Otto couldn't work out why people hated his attitude. Surely if you work in the service industry your only wish must be to provide a service that was perfect in every way. Surely. Otto could never work out that some people treated their job as just that, a job. He also had never fully understood how

people could not do their best to make that service particularly good for him.

Even in Germany he noted that people weren't as helpful and subservient to him as they used to be, especially, and this bit really confused him, after they had dealt with him on more than one occasion. He would have thought that after understanding his needs through past experience people would do their utmost to ensure that things were even more perfect in future, but for some reason it didn't work like that. Everybody seemed to be worse the second or third time he had dealings with them until he decided enough was enough and moved on to pastures new where he could start the whole unsatisfactory cycle again.

However there was something else, a benefit even, that he had discovered over the years. The more you moan and complain about a service you receive the bigger the discount that will be offered at the end. Otto had hit on a sure fire way to avoid paying in full for almost every service received or purchase made.

It had made a big difference to his life and gave him a much better lifestyle than he could actually afford.

In fact this holiday was actually paid in full by the travel company who had provided his last holiday to Africa. He had religiously followed all their instructions regarding jabs and medication as had the rest of his family. He had been amazed however, when they had reached the end of his holiday without contracting even the mildest of bugs. He had counted on catching at least one small disease to enable him to claim some money back, but nothing. The second week of his holiday he had slept without the mosquito net over his bed but didn't get even one bite. Bloody mossies. Never there when you need them.

On the last day he had decided to risk it and go for broke. He drank the water.

He returned home none the worse for his trip and went back to work on the following Monday morning depressed that he couldn't get a mark back from his insurance. That afternoon however he began burning up and by tea time was feverish and dizzy. A colleague had noticed this and called for an ambulance. The last thing he heard as they loaded him onto the trolley and wheeled him outside was someone saying how brave he had been.

"Yes" someone else said. "I could swear that he had a smile on his face as he left"

Three weeks later and one kidney removed and Otto had his free holiday.

Unfortunately for Otto he had allowed his family to talk him into going to the more hospitable Spain instead of the back of beyond as he would have preferred. Otto had intended to keep this free holiday thing rolling and was aware that he was less likely to catch any tropical diseases in Europe. He had altered his plans, therefore, to cover every single thing that was wrong, in his opinion, with his holiday.

He had thought he was building up a pretty good dossier the first week, but then he had met the shitty Englishman on the stairs and he was convinced he was on the way to a free trip to Egypt once he got back home. He had chosen Egypt because he had always wanted to go down the Nile on a steamer like Poirot did in that book. He also wanted to see the pyramids. He had also heard

that Dysentery was rife. Another free holiday. He metaphorically rubbed his hands together.

Bella, the beautiful young lady behind the counter, sighed as she wrote down his complaint in her little complaints book. It was a small black leather notebook sized pad and before last week she had entered only three complaints in it in the two years she had been working here. She now had thirteen entries and this was the fourteenth. "Tennis balls not bouncy enough" she wrote in a beautiful hand. Otto watched her carefully, making sure she didn't miss anything out. A sudden thought came to him and he suddenly blurted "And the strings on the rackets were not tight enough."

Bella glanced up from her book. She noticed the fat Germans wife tug at his sleeve. He pulled his arm away and ignored her.

"The strings were loose. You should look after your equipment better" he informed her and glanced down at the book to see if she was writing it all down. Bella saw the young son nudge his father and whisper "Farter" but the man roughly pushed him away without even looking at him. He looked up at Bella, puzzled as to why she hadn't written down his new complaint.

"The strings of your rackets were too loose" she repeated and he nodded enthusiastically. "Ya. They should be maintained better. It is disgraceful that such shoddy equipment is offered. Disgraceful"

"We do not hire out tennis rackets Sir" she informed him demurely.

Otto stared blankly at her. What was the woman talking about? He turned to his family for support and was surprised to see them sheepishly holding out the offending tennis rackets.

"These are our rackets farter" his son quietly informed him.

Otto coloured up as he realised that the rackets were indeed his own. He stammered for a while unable to come up with an explanation.

"Balls" he said as he backed away, pushing his family behind him. "they were not my balls." He turned to his wife who was ushering the kids along, as if pleading for help. He didn't get any.

"I never use my own balls on holiday" Otto informed Bella as he left the reception area. His wife looked back at the young Spanish woman behind the counter. Their eyes met and without speaking a word Bella knew that it was true.

Danny held Sheila's hand tightly as they strolled up the little hill back to the hotel. Most of the shops and bars were behind them, just the odd gift shop and bar remained as they sauntered languidly home.

Danny was content, very content. And full. They had just eaten a lovely light meal of a variety of fish with a very nice sauce and after the initial shock of seeing Mick walk in with his Spanish bird he had thoroughly enjoyed himself.

As it turned out, Mick had seen them sat in the corner and made some excuses to Julia and left. As he ushered her through the door he had turned to Danny and waved. Danny smiled back, which Sheila noticed causing her to turn and see what her husband had been looking at, but she had just missed Mick exiting

through the door. She had asked Danny what he was smiling at but he had lied convincingly and said he was just thinking of the afternoon's bedroom activities. She had smiled demurely back, which he thought might be pushing it a bit, and promised that those activities would be repeated on a regular basis.

He had gulped loudly at the fearsome prospect and wondered whether he could cope with his wife's demands. He smiled to himself. "Oh well" he thought.

"I'll give it my best shot and either I'll wear her down or die in the attempt."

So Danny was very content, very full, very tired and moderately horny as they meandered their way back to the hotel. There were a few people brushing past them on their way down to the beach to catch the last of the hot afternoon sun, but most of the foot traffic was people making their way back to their hotels for a rest or to change for the evening. He glanced up, as he came parallel with a gift shop with a wide variety of inflatables hung up, and to his utter dismay spotted the family of Germans marching down towards him. He held back the little girly scream that rose in his throat and silently congratulated himself on his new found willpower. He had wondered what he would do the next time he came face to face with the Germans. I mean what do you actually say to a man that you have covered in shit. Worse still when you have shot it into his mouth via a running flip-flop.

He had decided that the only honourable thing and the only thing that could possibly repair Anglo German relations was to meet the problem head on, offer abject apologies, blame the Spanish for their poor hygiene whilst preparing food, and offer to pay all cleaning bills. If this didn't have the desired effect he would then offer to take all the family out for a slap up meal on him.

Danny stood transfixed, as the Teutonic tyrant closed the gap between them.

Danny noticed the determined expression on his face. The face even looked red as though he was about to explode. The fifty yards or so that lay between them seemed to disappear so Danny could suddenly see the mad bulging eyeballs close up and almost smell his hot fetid breath. Of course Danny had no idea of Otto's recent encounter with the lovely Bella, but he was witnessing the after effects. Otto had marched his family out of the foyer, furious that he had ballsed up his latest whinge. He had of course realised that he was actually en route from the tennis courts to his room when he had stopped to berate the receptionist but he had been so mad when he left her that he had decided to march around the streets for a while until his temper cooled. His long suffering family followed, like a reluctant shadow, behind him, knowing that eventually he would either tire or calm down and they could go home and put their feet up for a bit.

Danny saw the look in those eyes and abandoned all thoughts of apologies. He released Sheila's hand and flung himself sideways into the row of inflatables.

Sheila turned, wondering where her husband had suddenly disappeared. She looked on in shock as he got himself entangled in a big green crocodile and almost swore at him as he tripped over a large swan managing to pull down two dolphins as he did. She lost him for a second behind a big black tyre and was shocked when he reappeared wearing goggles and a snorkel.

"Danny, what the fuck are you doing?" she asked solicitously. He was temporarily hidden from view then suddenly appeared with a large sombrero to compliment his sub aqua gear.

"Danny" she said again and stamped her feet. She thought he was just messing about but the mad demonic grin on his face belied it. She didn't know what to say so stood with her hands on her hips and tapped her feet. A small round man pushed past her without any apology, closely followed by a woman rushing to keep up. Then a young gangly teenager ran past and finally an attractive girl of around eighteen with a bored expression on her face. Sheila watched them pass her by then turned her attention back to her mad husband. He was watching the family too and as soon as he thought they were far enough away he removed the sombrero and goggles and snorkel. He watched for a few seconds longer then came out of the shop and stood in front of Sheila with a sheepish grin on his face.

"Danny, what was that all about?" she asked again.

He took her by the arm and led her back to the hotel. On the way he told her his embarrassing, shame filled story. As they reached the doors to the foyer he had finished. He was making the squelching noise of his flip- flops fading into the distance when she suddenly burst into floods of laughter. Tears ran down her cheeks and she slapped her thighs enthusiastically as families turned to see who was making all the noise. Danny shrugged his shoulders and eyed everybody up shyly wishing a hole would appear and swallow him up. Sheila suddenly grabbed hold of him and pulled him to her. She kissed him hard on the lips. At least it stopped her laughter.

When she finally released him she held him close and laughed again.

"My God I love you, you little daft bastard" she shouted endearingly into his ear.

CHAPTER THIRTEEN

Mick stood in the doorway of the bedroom wearing just his bermudas, T shirt and a very smug grin on his face. He lolled against the door frame with his back to the corridor, grinning inanely back into the room at the near naked, half asleep Spanish temptress that had stolen his heart. She lay on the bed gracefully with just a white cotton sheet barely covering her and he all but drooled at the sight of her. They had been there all afternoon after he had made his excuses about the café and half dragged her outside. It had been a close shave and he knew he owed Danny one. He blew Julia a kiss and told her he would call for her in a couple of hours. She blew one back and like some sickly love struck teenager he pretended to catch it. Even he realised how sickly this was so he

looked guiltily up and down the corridor then waved to her and closed the door.

He hummed a tune, which he couldn't place. He guessed it to be "It must be love" by Labi Sifre (or Madness depending on your age), so he sang those words, although it wasn't.

At the end of the corridor he pressed the button for the lift and leant back against the wall, looking longingly back down towards Julia's room.

"Nothing more, nothing less. Love is the best" he informed the empty corridor, tunelessly.

"Ping" announced the lift.

Mick turned and did a little dance that for some reason he imagined Suggs would do. He looked like an old man wanting the loo. Without looking up he danced into the lift.

"Mick!" squealed Sheila in a high pitched voice.

"Sheila!" squealed Mick one pitch higher.

"Aahh!" squealed Danny in a high soprano.

Mick and Sheila turned and stared at him.

Danny decided there and then that if he ever did a girly scream again he would rip out his own vocal chords.

"Well" said Sheila, turning back to face Mick, who was stood frozen in the doorway.

"Yes. Well" he repeated.

The door attempted to close, caught his foot and opened up again.

"Aren't you getting in?" Sheila asked with mock concern in her voice.

Mick and Sheila had known each other since they were kids but had never got on. As they grew up they hung around with different crowds and to be honest Sheila's growing reputation as a bike terrified Mick. He had been with Sue all that time and the thought of getting off with someone like Sheila really put the willies up him. You know what I mean.

After Sheila and Danny married she had made a big play for Mick, which sent him scurrying home. He would never have done anything to hurt Danny anyway but he certainly wouldn't have done it with Sheila.

Sheila, of course, had made the play just to get at Danny. She had made the same play at Ron but he had taken her by the scuff of the neck and carried her out of the club they were in and threatened her within an inch of her life if she ever tried that again. She had more success with Jeff. She hadn't really tried he was so easy. However she had found the sex a bit unsatisfactory. He had been quite a selfish lover and when she thought about it she could have been anybody that night. Jeff didn't care. For that reason she had never mentioned it to Danny as had been her original intention.

"Er yes, sure" he mumbled and moved inside the lift.

"Got a new friend then?" she asked as he turned to face the door.

"What do you mean, new friend. Why? What friend?" he stuttered and stammered. He spun round and glared at Danny, convinced he had told her about Julia. Danny gave him a weak smile back. He tried with all his might to convey, through one single smile, that he hadn't said a word to Sheila, indeed he had done his best to keep the news from her all day, and that it was unfair

for Mick to glare at him like that as if he was a snitch and he couldn't explain further because Sheila was now watching him with a curious look on her face and that meant she was bound to ask questions later and it wasn't his fault if she then managed to wheedle it out of him and, if he was so concerned, he should take greater care when moving around the hotel and then he, Danny, wouldn't be in bother.

Mick thought "What's he fuckin' smiling at?"

"I just mean you're four floors away from your room so unless you can't count you must be visiting a friend" she stated clearly but her eyes were shining as she realised with absolute clarity that Mick was up to no good. She couldn't wait to get back to the room to quiz Danny.

Mick quickly pressed the button for the lift to ascend to the eighth floor.

"Got confused" he said with a nervous giggle. "Pressed four instead of eight with them being so..." he pointed at the panel next to the door. He was going to say "...close together" but saw to his horror that they were nowhere near each other so he trailed off lamely "....similar in design"

He thought he heard Danny tut and blow in disgust but he daren't look up to confirm it.

Sheila almost wet herself at the sheer joy of it. He might as well have said

"Okay, I'm up to no good and now you've caught me and you've got me over a barrel. I' m not going to confirm or deny anything but I hope you manage to pump my little fat friend here for all the juicy gossip."

Instead he said "Nearly there" with a nervous inflection and almost fell through the doors as they opened on their floor. He bounced back slightly and Sheila grabbed his arm. She wasn't letting him off the hook that easily. She deftly positioned herself between the two men and walked slowly down the corridor to their rooms arm in arm.

She could feel the tension running down their bodies into hers.

"Tell you what" she suddenly said. The men eyed her warily.

"Me and Danny'll take you out for a big slap up tonight. How about that? Our treat eh"

Mick's face fell to the floor with a thud. "No honestly. Thanks very much but honest it doesn't matter. You two want to be alone don't you? Yeah course you do. Don't you two go whittling about me." he prattled on, horrified at the thought of missing out on a night out with Julia

"We don't want to be on our own silly. We want a bit of company don't we Danny?" Danny was just about to say he would rather they were alone when she butted in "Anyway we wouldn't dream of leaving you on your own. I know Jeff's been off flying his kite and now Ron's buggered off you'll be all on your own what with me turning up and pinching Danny off you an' all so tell you what. We'll call round for you in about an hour and we'll go for a slap up meal and then on to a club. Our treat"

Mick started to protest but Sheila raised her hand as they reached their door.

"That's it, settled We'll pick you up in an hour and that's final"

She edged past them and stood at the doorway. Danny took the hint and joined her, producing his key as he did. Mick allowed them to go past with a desolate

frown on his face and almost whimpered as they went inside and shut the door but for the life of him he couldn't think of an excuse to get him out of it.

Disconsolately he trudged off towards his room. Inside their room Sheila put her shopping bags down on the little table and kicked off her shoes. Danny watched her from the doorway as she stretched luxuriously like the cat with the cream. His heart fell as she turned to him and with a big grin on her face asked

"Okay fatboy who's he knocking off?"

Ron showered slowly and luxuriously. He was taking his time as he wanted to be just perfect for his first date with Ros. He had managed to get a room in the girl's hotel right at the other end. In the corner of the room there were a beach ball and a football that some previous occupant had left. Ron had spent the first fifteen minutes after dropping his bag on the bed, playing keepy up with the football. There was no view as such but the room was nice and airy and he could smell the mountain air in the distance.

He had been thinking of Ros since the moment she had left to get ready for their night out. He imagined her telling the others and smiled when he thought of the shocked look on their faces.

He couldn't believe his luck that Ros felt much the same about him as he did about her. He felt himself becoming aroused at the thought and smiled to himself. A knock at the door interrupted him and he irritatedly stepped out of the shower and pulled the biggest towel he could find round his large frame. He stepped gingerly to the door and opened it a few inches, peering round to see who was there.

"Hiya" Ros greeted him happily and he pulled the door open a bit more and waved her in.

"You're early" he said as she brushed past him. She gave him a little peck on the cheek as he closed the door behind her. He smelled lovely and clean and she couldn't resist touching his wet shoulder as she crossed to the middle of the room and put her bag down on the little table.

"Or am I late?" he enquired earnestly.

She smiled a big smile and fought to keep her eyes centred on his. She was aware that he was wearing only a towel and that he seemed to have a tent or something underneath it and she resolved not to look in that direction.

"No I'm early" she laughed, then added "couldn't wait" and giggled self consciously.

Despite herself her eyes dropped to his towel and Ron self consciously crossed his hands in front of him.

"Er I'd best get ready" he said and set off for the bathroom.

He tried not to think of anything in general and Ros in particular, so his embarrassment wouldn't increase, so to speak, but he took a sly little glance at her as he passed and couldn't help but notice the sheer silk dress she was wearing or the erect nipples that protruded almost through it.

He began sweating a bit as he picked up his trousers and shirt from the bed and looked around for his shoes, painfully aware of the growing tent pole down

below. He decided to give up on the shoes and just go and get dressed. He turned to face her praying that she would be looking directly into his eyes and wouldn't notice anything else.

251

Ros was staring at the straining towel. She had told herself not to but she couldn't drag her eyes away. She fought for control and decided to speak to break the spell. That was it, say something witty and clever to put them both at ease and lessen the tension. She looked round for inspiration and spotted the football and beachball in the corner.

"Nice balls" she said smiling at him.

"What?" he gasped and looked down at his towel.

"No, I meant…." She squeeked and pointed to the corner of the room.

He turned and saw the balls lying where he had left them and laughed loudly.

He held his rolled up jeans in front of himself and nodded to the door.

"I think maybe I should take this away and get changed" and he set off for the bathroom.

"Yes before you have somebody's eye out" she offered and was cringing with embarrassment as she said it. God what was she doing, she was in her mid twenties and was acting like a giddy schoolgirl just because a man had an erection in the same room as her.

Ron rushed over to the door and had his hand on the doorhandle when she said, nervously "Ron are you hungry?"

He thought for a few seconds to see if it was a trick question seeing as they were going out for a meal.

"Not particularly" he ventured as he turned back to face into the room.

"Me neither" she said throatily and he could have sworn he saw her licking her lips.

She pointed down at his towel and he thought he would explode as she said

"There are other ways to get rid of that you know"

Ron turned that over in his mind a bit. It wasn't that he was particularly thick it was just that he was very inexperienced in this sort of thing. No he couldn't think of any other way to get rid of the stiffness other than…. Wait a minute, did she mean…

Ros stepped forward until they were touching and she slowly undid the towel from round his waist and let it fall to the floor. With exquisite apprehension she slowly looked down and he heard her gasp audibly.

"I knew you were pleased to see me this afternoon but I didn't realise how pleased" she giggled dirtily and he had to laugh himself.

Well they never did get out for that meal.

Mick banged the door behind him and raced into the room looking for the whisky bottle. He needed a stiff drink and a sit down. He needed to think this through. There was no way he could get out of this evening with Sheila and Danny without arousing Sheila's suspicion and he had no intention of missing out on an evening, and hopefully a night, with Julia.

He found the bottle and poured himself a large glass. It occurred to him that he ought to have something to eat first as he hadn't had anything since that

morning. He glanced round the room and shrugged his shoulders as there was nothing available. Sod it, just a couple wouldn't hurt, so he drained his glass and poured himself another.

He heard a noise from the bathroom and was surprised when Jeff came into the room.

"Hiya" Jeff called when he saw him on the bed. "Didn't hear you come in, just been for a tom tit. You okay?"

Mick nodded unconvincingly and offered the bottle.

"No thanks" Jeff declined, waving his hand. "Bit early for me." He watched Mick who was pouring himself another. "Bit early for you as well isn't it?"

Mick snorted loudly and wiped his T shirt with his free hand. "Yeah, s'pose so"

He lay back on the bed and closed his eyes. "Got a major problem though pal, and I aint got a fuckin' clue what to do? he said, resting his glass on his forehead.

"If it's to do wi' a woman, Uncle Jeff's yer man. Anything else see Ron" Jeff offered.

Mick thought about it a while then sat up. "OK pal you're up" and he proceeded to tell Jeff his problem.

When he had finished Jeff broke into a big smile. He didn't really see the problem, what with him having virtually no conscience to speak of, and with his come a day go a day attitude he didn't really envisage any repercussions later on. If Jeff was in Mick's boots he would do the dirty with Julia and if word got back to Sue he would simply deny it. Problem solved.

"Right, your problem is, you want to go and give Julia one tonight but Sheila and Danny have invited you out and you think if you don't go Sheila will realise you're up to no good and make Danny, if he hasn't already done so, tell her what's going on, yeah?"

Mick pulled a face. "Well I wouldn't put it quite as crudely as that but yes, that's the general gist of it"

"Right. Simple really. Do both" and he held his arms out like a magician showing there was nothing up his sleeves. "Easy"

Mick rolled his eyes and laid back down heavily. "Thanks a fuckin' bunch" he said through gritted teeth. Jeff shrugged and walked to the door. "Anyway I'm off out. Don't wait up" and with that he was off out into the night.

Mick lay there a bit longer then sat up and poured another large drink. He was feeling a bit of a buzz now. He took a large swallow and was about to refill it when a sudden thought struck him. He mulled it over for a few seconds then burst into laughter. "Jeff you're a genius" he shouted to the closed door and raised his glass in salute. He drank the rest of his drink and jumped off the bed, swaying slightly as he did. "Better get something to eat before I have any more" he thought as he headed off to the bathroom.

Of course, what Jeff had actually meant, when he offered his words of wisdom, was that Mick should go for his meal with Sheila and Danny and then make up some excuse and slope off to meet Julia for the rest of the night.

What Mick thought he meant…. Well let's just say Mick, thanks partly to the whisky, misjudged it slightly.

He quickly showered and shaved and found some clean clothes. He checked his watch and realised he would have to get a move on. He had a plan firmly in place and if he stuck to it rigidly and kept his thoughts concentrated he was pretty confident that he could pull it off. He reached for the whisky bottle for a little Scotch courage and poured himself a large one.

Five minutes later he was pounding on Julia's door. She opened it wearing only a towel around her wet glistening body and another in her hand which she was using to dry her hair.

"Ready?" he asked with a big smile.

She laughed and leant forward and kissed him. He breathed in her cleanliness and felt dizzy. Or maybe that was the drink. He really should have had something to eat first.

"Of course I am not ready, silly. Come" and she took him by the arm and led him into the room.

Rosetta, her room mate, quickly wrapped a towel round herself and smiled at him from the chair in front of the little mirror on the wall. She spoke little English, so went back to applying her make up.

Julia led him to the bed and urged him to sit down. "I wont be long" and disappeared into the bathroom.

"Don't be long" he called after her, unnecessarily but she had already gone.

He sat on the bed and looked round him. The room was almost identical to his but somehow it seemed much more homely, inviting even, but he didn't know why.

Perhaps it was the smell. There could be no denying that this room smelt of rich aromatic fragrances instead of farts and lager. Maybe it was the presence of two near naked ladies that did it. That would help. Or maybe it was the fact that they had simply tidied up. His room was now awash with three days worth of dirty clothes and even he had noticed the mess whereas this room was clean to the point of perfection. Yeah maybe that was it.

He thought over his plan for tonight and smiled to himself at the cleverness of it.

He spotted a bottle on the dresser and reached over for it. He turned it over and read the label. Grand Marnier. He opened the bottle and took a sniff. Very nice.

Looking round he spotted a glass so he reached over and retrieved it and filled it with the dark liquid. He took a sip and felt it burn his throat. Drink it faster, he thought, so he did and it tasted much better. He giggled a little but stopped when he spotted Rosetta watching him. He thought he should leave the drink alone tonight, at least until he had sorted everybody out and had a meal. He poured himself another one and drank it straight down. Popping the lid back on the bottle he replaced it on the dresser and sat impatiently for Julia's return.

Five minutes later he was asleep on the bed as she emerged through the door looking beautiful in a light cotton dress.

"Miguel" she called in surprise and he jumped up quickly and stared round him, trying to get his bearings. "Sorry, I… I must have dropped off" he grinned sheepishly. He looked at his watch and realised he had only been asleep five

minutes. Still, if he was going to keep this plan going with military precision he had better get things moving.

"You look beautiful" he said as she picked up her brush and started coming her long, damp hair.

"Muchas Gracias senor" she smiled back and curtsied a little. "I shall not be long Miguel. I have just to dry my hair"

His heart sank a little. That would take forever and as he glanced again at his watch he realised he didn't have the time.

"I wouldn't bother. It won't make any difference" he suggested and she looked at him quizzically. "Thank you. I think" she smiled weakly.

"No, no I meant. I like it like that. It looks beautiful and natural and…" he searched for the right word, the one that would really swing it and make her leave the room now.

"…wet"

She smiled again and looked into the mirror and carried on brushing.

"Wet" he berated himself. "It looks wet. Brilliant, just fuckin' brilliant" and he metaphorically smashed himself in the face.

As she brushed it straight, he watched her intently, and was amazed when she suddenly stopped and tilted her head and stared at her reflection. "You know Miguel, I think you are right. I think I will leave it damp and let it dry naturally" She placed the brush down and stood up facing him, as if for inspection. "Ready" she said happily and he rushed across and kissed her. She closed her eyes and raised her arms to place them round his neck., but he was gone. She felt him catch her hand and whisk her to the door. "Come on then"

he said as he grabbed her bag and gave it to her. He opened the door and almost shoved her through it. She looked at him uncertainly. "I'm starving" he offered by way of explanation.

Arm in arm they rushed down the corridor. A couple of times Julia glanced up at him to see what the urgency was. He smiled back brightly and surged on. At the end of the corridor was the lift and Mick pressed the button enthusiastically, then another couple of times to make sure. He watched the panel, and noticed the numbers light up from eight downwards. Eight, that was his floor. A sudden, horrible thought flashed into his mind. What if it was Danny and Sheila in the lift. He couldn't think of any reason they would be in the lift at this time, after all they should be getting ready now, but what if they wanted fags, or a drink, or to stretch their legs. Or what if Sheila was suspicious and had decided to investigate further.

Seven.

Mick broke out into a cold sweat.

Six.

Mick inched sideways, releasing Julia's hand so gently she didn't even notice.

Five.

Mick was away from the door now, off to the right. If the doors opened now to reveal Danny and Sheila they wouldn't instantly see him. He hadn't a clue what he would do next, but the main thing was not to be seen.

Four.

Ping.

The door opened and Mick pressed himself into the wall.

"Hola" Julia said softly to someone inside. She entered the lift with a light step.

Mick pressed further into the wall, actually raising one leg in an effort to climb inside the plaster.

"It's them. I know it's them." He screamed inside his head.

To his left Julia's head reappeared from the lift doorway. She peered round and was amazed to discover her lover apparently trying to climb up the wall.

"Miguel?" she said in a worried voice.

Mick stared at the wall a few millimetres from his nose and knew he was lost.

"Come on man" he ordered himself. Slowly he edged towards the lift, until he was near enough to peep round. Julia watched horrified as he leant his head over and peered inside. The elderly couple almost jumped out of their skin as his head appeared in view.

He smiled a huge smile of relief at them and they grinned back nervously. He thought he should explain his strange behaviour, not only to them but also to Julia who was still watching him curiously.

He decided to give them a bit of the old Mick wit, that never fails sense of humour and quick repartee that he knew he used to such devastating effect on Sue and her mum and many others. He broke into a cheeky, disarming grin and opened his mouth, but…. nothing. Not a sausage. Bugger all. He couldn't think of a single thing to say that might explain his actions. As the doors closed he jumped in the lift and smiled again at the rapidly retreating old fogeys.

Julia held out her hand and he gratefully took it. "Miguel, what happened?" she asked nervously. Mick decided to say the first thing that came into his head. "I missed" he announced sincerely and decided to never again say the first thing that came into his head. Julia frowned but held onto his hand and the old couple leant further back to keep clear of him.

Two minutes later they were out in the warm night air and Mick felt much better. Quite light headed actually. They walked down to the sea front and chatted inanely and gradually Julia relaxed again and held his arm tightly as they strolled into the dusk. As they reached the promenade they came across several restaurants together in a row and Mick picked out the second one, "Le Jardin", an intimate little restaurant with a little patio at the front, as had the others on this stretch.

"Le Jardin" he read and decided to impress her with his knowledge of the local language. "That means "the noisy jar".

She hugged him close. "Oh Miguel, you make me laugh you are so funny" she informed him and she reached up and pulled his neck down so she could kiss him.

He grinned back but hadn't a clue why she thought that was funny. He decided to take the compliment anyway and ushered her into the restaurant happily.

He picked out a nice table right in the centre and held her chair for her as she sat down. He had purposely held this particular chair out as it afforded her no view of the back of the restaurant and that was very important for his plan to

work. He glanced at his watch and realised he would have to get moving soon if the next part of his plan was to fall into place.

He sat down himself and took the proffered menu from the smiling waiter. He looked at it hungrily, almost licking his lips, but realised that he would have to wait until he could actually have something to eat. Some things were more important than food and he looked up and smiled at one of them. She smiled back and reached over and held his hand. The waiter coughed a little and Mick grinned, a little embarrassed and ordered the drinks.

"Er wine" he said and looked to Julia for confirmation. She nodded.

"House white please and a bottle of beer" he said and closed the menu. Julia cocked her head a little to one side questioningly.

"We'll order in a little while" he smiled. As the waiter left the table Mick had a sudden thought. "And a Grand Marnier" he called out and the waiter nodded and went off round the bar.

Julia looked a little surprised.

"Got the taste for it, I guess" he said and grinned sheepishly. Two minutes later the waiter deposited the drinks and left. Mick poured the wine, then knocked back the Grand Marnier and took a slug from the bottle. He felt the now familiar warmth flow through him and decided he really liked this drink. His cheeks looked a bit red and flushed now. He hadn't eaten since that morning and that had only been rolls and butter with a coffee so the drink was starting to have an effect on him. He grinned at Julia who seemed more than a little concerned.

"Miguel are you alright". she asked.

"Fine. Fine" he assured her and carried on grinning.

He surreptitiously glanced at his watch and realised he would have to start moving now. He fumbled in his pocket and tutted noisily.

"Would you believe it. Well I never. Tut. You're never going to believe this.

Tcchh."

Julia put her glass of wine down and held out her hand to him. He took it and stroked it.

"What is wrong Miguel?" she asked.

"Well I've only gone and left my wallet back at the hotel" he said in a stage whisper and added a few tuts.

"That is okay Miguel I have money here" she offered and reached round for her handbag.

"No" he almost shouted and she jumped back slightly. He realised he had overdone it and reached for her hand again and stroked it which brought the smile back to her worried face.

"Sorry. Didn't mean to shout. I meant I couldn't let you pay. It wouldn't be proper"

She smiled brightly. "Miguel you are such a gentleman"

He coloured visibly which she took for modesty, but was actually a bit of guilt.

He would have no qualms whatsoever about Sue paying for the meal.

"Yes, well. Tell you what. You wait here and I'll run back to the hotel and fetch my wallet. Shan't be more than a couple of minutes."

He quickly drained his beer bottle and was almost gone when he suddenly picked up her wine and downed it in one.

"You order some more drinks. Wont be long" and he was off before she could say anything.

He raced back along the prom and up the little hill to the hotel. In the foyer, to his great relief, he saw the lift doors opening and a family of four got out. He ran across and jumped in, pressing the eight button before he stopped. The doors shut and he travelled up to his floor, impatiently checking his watch.

When the doors opened he nervously scanned the corridor for signs of life.

Seeing none he raced down it and was pulling the key from his pocket as he heard Danny's door open. Quickly he unlocked his door and jumped inside his room. He spun round and quietly closed the door. Less than two seconds later there was a knock on the door and he pulled it open again and smiled brightly at the two faces in the corridor.

"Ready" he called cheerily and walked out, pulling the door behind him.

"Sheila, you look lovely" he smiled, overdoing it a bit. He saw she was wearing a nice pink pinafore, her hair was in plaits and she had a big straw bag over her shoulder. She was wearing hardly any makeup and seemed strangely young and innocent. He stopped in his tracks and seemed to look her up and down. "No really" he felt compelled to add, "You look lovely"

She blushed slightly and Danny puffed out his chest proudly. Then Mick remembered he was on a strict timetable and ushered them down the corridor.

"Come on, I'm starving" he ordered as they went. To speed things up a bit he took Sheila by the arm and forced the pace.

"Hang on Mick" she protested "we've got all night"

"Hungry" he said as he jabbed the lift button. Danny tried to attract his attention but Mick either didn't see him or studiously ignored him.

Once they were in the foyer, Mick forced the pace again and hurried them along to the sea front, where the sea air went straight to Mick's head and he felt a little woosy.

"You alright Mick" Sheila asked noticing his green complexion.

"Fine" he lied and tried to clear his head. He must really get something to eat soon to settle his stomach, he thought.

Danny tried to catch his eye but he just smiled greenly and turned his attention back to Sheila. She looked worried at his silly grin but didn't say anything.

Soon they arrived at the little row of café's and restaurants that he had deposited Julia in. He stopped outside the first one, which proclaimed proudly

"Le Grand Palazio", which was neither grand nor a palace but was exactly the same shape and size as the others on this stretch. He glanced across at the next restaurant and smiled because he had seated Julia in such a position that she couldn't be seen from outside, which meant of course that she couldn't see him out here.

He happily decided to tell his friends his brilliant joke that had floored Julia a few minutes earlier. He pointed up at the sign next door and proclaimed loudly

"That means the noisy jar". He guffawed and had to wipe his nose and mouth but when he looked up, to his surprise they were just staring at him.

"Philippine's" he thought but decided not to pursue it. "Come on, let's go in here" he said and set off through the tables and chairs on the patio and went inside. Sheila and Danny shrugged and followed.

Mick had already chosen a table and held out the chair for Sheila. Once seated she smiled easily at him and he gave her a big grin back. As if by magic a waiter appeared from nowhere and gave them a menu each. Sheila perused hers intently but Danny tried to get Mick's attention by waving his in his direction.

"Three beers and three Grand Marniere's please" Mick said to the waiter and waved him away. He turned to Danny and informed him "You've got to try this drink, it's brilliant. Burns your throat. Brilliant."

Danny nodded then glanced at Sheila who was still studying the menu intently.

He looked back to Mick and nodded towards Sheila. Mick grinned. He nodded again in a manner that clearly said "Mick, I've told her everything so tread very carefully. I'm really sorry but she made me tell her. I am a failure as a person and as a friend" Mick grinned back in a manner that clearly said "You're my mate you are"

Danny thought "fuck it" and searched his menu for something appetising.

The drinks appeared and Mick downed his Grand Marnier in one. "Brilliant" he gasped. Sheila and Danny smiled indulgently and had a drink of lager.

"Don't you want yours then" Mick asked aghast that someone didn't share his enthusiasm for the fiery liquid. "I'll have it" and before they could react he had picked up their glasses and emptied them both. He placed them, upside down, on his head and shouted "I won" and laughed uproariously.

They looked a bit worried now but he didn't notice.

"Gotta go to the lav" he suddenly announced and shoved himself up from the table. He made his way, unsteadily, through the tables to the back of the building to the toilets. There was an open door that led to the outside. He glanced over his shoulder and seeing that no one was watching him, raced through the open door. Turning left, he spotted an identical door into Le Jardin.

He raced through that and ran into the restaurant.

He could see Julia sat patiently at the table with fresh drinks in front of her. She was toying with a wine glass and watching the door at the front for his arrival.

He silently made his way through the tables and placed his hands over her eyes.

"Boo" he said and he felt her jump a little.

"Miguel, where have you been.?" She asked as he sat down.

"Sorry. I couldn't find my wallet" he lied and tapped his back pocket to show he had eventually located it. He smiled earnestly and she was shocked to discover that he looked quite drunk.

"Miguel, are you alright?" she asked concernedly.

"Never better" he said, and to prove it grinned alarmingly at her.

She smiled back, unsure what to do. He raised a glass and made a toast.

"To us" he said too loudly. "To Julia and Miguel"

She raised her glass and sipped her wine. He downed his in one and wiped his mouth with the back of his hand. He noticed the room spinning round slightly,

"I have got to have something to eat" he told her.

She smiled brightly "I have ordered. I hope that is okay" He nodded.

"I remembered you say you have not tried the squid, so I order squid for starter and Paella for the main course, yes"

"Brilliant" he slurred and put two thumbs up to emphasise the point. He wasn't sure about the squid but he liked paella. He imagined the squid would come in batter like onion rings so he would just wolf them down. He was quietly confident that once he got something substantial inside him he would feel a bit better and the room would stop spinning round. He knew there was something important to do tonight but for the life of him he couldn't remember what it was.

Julia was watching him intently. He hadn't drunk all that much but he was acting strangely. Maybe he had been drinking while she hadn't been there. It was a possibility but she dismissed it out of hand. Not her Miguel. She had grown to love this kind, genuine man. She was dreading the end of the holiday and was praying that he would say something to indicate that he wanted it to be more than just a holiday romance. She watched him now as he fought to control his head as it kept trying to fall on his chin. So what if he had had too much to drink. She loved him and would forgive him anything.

The object of her adoration suddenly stood up, his chair screeching backwards.

The other few diners all spun round. He tottered a bit but regained control of the situation. He breathed in deeply and announced grandly "I am going to the toilet."

It was as much as he could muster for now so as the air left his lungs to be replaced by alcohol fumes he staggered past Julia and went round the back to the toilet, which he went straight past and out of the back door into the darkening night. He took another deep breath, which didn't help one bit, and crashed into a dustbin. Looking round him he put his finger to his lips and went

"Sshhh" to the night sky. He giggled to himself and repeated the sshhh.

"There's nobody there" he whispered and laughed again. Eventually he gathered himself and went inside the restaurant next door.

"Where the fuck have you been?" Danny asked as soon as he sat down.

"Toilet" Mick replied and laughed to himself.

"Are you pissed?" Sheila asked.

"Moi?" he said in mock surprise.

They watched him with raised eyebrows and furtive glances to each other but to be honest they could have held a conversation and Mick wouldn't have noticed. The stress of the occasion and the drink on top of an empty stomach was just too much. Mick was now pissed.

He picked up a bottle of beer and drank it, spilling most of it down his shirt.

Sheila smiled at him and then Danny. "He's going to regret this in the morning" she laughed. Danny nodded sagely and watched his friend attempt to wear the condiment set as a hat.

"Mick are you alright?" Danny asked.

"I'm marvellous, me, I am" Mick informed him whilst hiding behind a menu.

He closed his eyes and almost fell asleep but suddenly remembered Julia and jumped up. From somewhere deep in the hidden recesses of his mind he dragged up a memory that he had to keep Julia a secret from Danny and Sheila

or was it just Sheila or was it Danny. He couldn't remember, but he knew it was important.

"Gottago" he mumbled and fell backwards. Danny jumped up and caught him before he landed on some fellow diners.

"Where are you going now" asked Sheila who was also on her feet trying to get him to sit down. He straightened himself up and regained his composure. He looked at Sheila who seemed to be swaying alarmingly. Then he turned to Danny who also was swaying back and forth. They also seemed to go in and out of focus at a remarkable rate. What was the matter with them. He was genuinely worried for their safety. He blinked slowly and gradually they returned to focus and managed to stand still. Thank God. Now, which one did he have to keep in the dark about Julia. He looked from Sheila to Danny and then back to Sheila. Of course, how could he have forgotten. He leant forward and put his arm round Sheila and pulled her towards him. In a loud stage whisper he told her "I've got to go and see Julia next door but don't tell Danny.

It's a secret" and he put his lip to his finger and went sshhh.

Sheila's face lit up like a Christmas tree. She had wondered where tonight would finish up. She would have settled for Mick's admission that he was having an affair but this was even better. She now expected to be able to confront the philandering pair next door and very soon.

Danny heard it all of course and sat down heavily, burying his head in his hands.

Mick winked at Sheila in a conspiratorial fashion and Sheila winked back with a huge grin on her face. Mick glanced down at Danny and back to Sheila and returned his finger to his lips. "Sshhh" he said loudly. He backed out from his chair and made his way through the restaurant to the back door and outside where the fresh air hit him like a ton of bricks. He stopped and leant against the wall trying to recapture his balance. After a couple of minutes he felt in control.

He stood up and immediately fell over. He lay there a while, surprised at how comfortable the floor was and contemplated staying there for the night. A vision of the lovely Julia, naked in his arms roused him from his slumbers and he knew he had to get the night back on track. He rose ungraciously to his feet and gathered his wits about him. Right, he decided, the most important thing now was to get back to Julia and pretend nothing had happened.

Stumbling he managed to negotiate the door and hauled himself through the restaurant to the waiting Julia.

"Daddy's home" he sang, out of key, and Julia spun round. She gave a little gasp and held her hand up to her mouth she was so shocked at his appearance.

"Miguel" she almost screamed, "what is wrong?"

He managed to work his way round the table and sat down heavily on his chair.

Looking up he smiled a big smile and rolled his eyes. "S'nothing wrong" he slurred. He looked down at the table and tried to focus. He could see a beer bottle so he reached out for it but missed. On his second attempt he caught it and downed it in one. As he pulled it away from his lips he dribbled beer over his already wet shirt. He stared at the drips and tried, ineffectually, to wipe them away. Julia watched in horror at his drunken behaviour. Behind her a

waiter suddenly appeared with two steaming plates. "Scusi senora" he said as he passed her and deposited the plates on the table. He said something else very quickly in Spanish, which Mick hadn't a hope of understanding even if he had been interested. As it was Mick was staring goggle eyed at the plate in front of him. He couldn't work out why the waiter had brought him a big plate of sick.

The waiter finished talking fast at Julia and they both turned their attention to Mick. Julia then began talking fast back to the waiter until eventually they both shrugged. He went back to his duties, she sat down and watched her drunken boyfriend.

Mick stared and stared at the offering in front of him. He couldn't quite work out what it was supposed to be. It looked like a lump of sick in a sick sauce.

Surely there had been a mistake. He decided to call the waiter back and explain to him that in fact he had ordered Squid and by mistake the waiter had fetched him sick lump in sick sauce when Julia leant forward and asked, in a very soft voice, "Miguel, you are ok, no?"

Mick pointed to his plate and tried to explain the mix up over the meal. "Sick, lumps, sauce" was all he managed which thankfully was not enough for Julia, even with her good English vocabulary, to understand what he was trying to say.

"Miguel. I think, maybe you should leave your Squid. You do not look well"

she offered and was surprised when he suddenly seemed to cheer up.

"Squid?" he said, pointing to the plate. She nodded. "Squid" he repeated, obviously relieved. "Not sick, Squid.". He thought about it for a while and then burst out laughing. She sat back a little. The waiter popped his head round from the kitchen and said something to someone behind him. Two more waiters heads appeared and they watched, fascinated, at the drunken Englishmen.

"How much did this cost?" Mick asked, in between fits of laughter. "Six quid?"

He laughed loudly again and Julia decided she should take the plate away and perhaps get him home to bed. She went to get the plate but Mick's hand shot forward and he grabbed it before she reached it. "No, wait. That's mine." He said defensively. He pointed to her plate. "That's yours" he said and cradled his lovingly.

"Miguel, I think we should go now. I take you home now and put you to bed.

Yes."

"S'good idea" he slurred. He winked at her and sort of nudged his elbow forward. "Can't wait. Let's go to bed" he stared again at his plate, then felt on the table for a fork. "First though I'm going to eat my sick squid" He cut himself a piece with the side of his fork and gingerly put it to his mouth. "Or squid sick" he mumbled and thrust the piece in. He chewed for a while and, without altering the quizzical expression on his face, swallowed. Julia watched, waiting for some sort of reaction. It surprised her when it eventually came.

Mick's face suddenly broke into a big smile. "That is brilliant" he shouted and immediately broke off another piece and eagerly shovelled it into his mouth. It was soon followed by another, then another. He couldn't talk for a few minutes as his mouth was never empty. As soon as he swallowed one piece he forked in another. Despite herself, Julia had to smile at his child like enthusiasm. This

man was certainly a contradiction. When he had finished his plate he sat back and licked his lips. He rubbed his stomach and kissed his fingers and pointed at the kitchen. "My compliments to the chef" he informed no one in particular.

"Let's have another drink" he slurred and motioned to the waiter. Julia however turned and shook her head and the waiter agreed and disappeared out of the way. Mick ignored it or didn't notice and waited patiently for his drink.

He leant precariously to one side but miraculously didn't fall over. He eyed Julia's plate for a few seconds, and then with great difficulty pointed at it.

"Don't you want that?" he asked softly. Julia looked down at her forgotten meal. She had been too concerned over Mick's behaviour to eat. It sat there, going cold, congealing, and looked most unappetising.

"I think not" she smiled back at him, uneasily. He had gone quiet and she was watching him carefully now.

He suddenly sprang forward and grabbed her plate.

"Right then. I'll have it" he announced and proceeded to devour it before she could complain too loudly.

In the entrance to the café a small fat German was reading the menu board and complaining long and loud to his long suffering family who were waiting behind him. He was berating them on the extortionate prices that all the café's in the resort were charging. It seemed to him that a monopoly was at work and that most of these restaurants should lower their prices to create more competition. He said it with thorough conviction and inferred in the process that it was in fact a vendetta to ruin his holiday.

This was in fact the sixth restaurant that they had entered tonight and although they were careful not to show it, especially when he was watching, the whole family was now thoroughly pissed off and starving. They knew from bitter experience, however, that if they voiced their opinions it would just make matters worse and prolong the ordeal because without fail he would then repeat the process in at least six other restaurants before he found one to be satisfactory. Eventually though, Otto spotted items on the menu that were in his price range and ushered his obviously relieved family into the restaurant. They sat near the door, Otto with his back to the entrance, and as soon as the waiter appeared he ordered water for them all while he perused the proffered menu.

His wife and children didn't bother to look at theirs as there was little point.

Otto would choose for them and that was that.

At the doorway of the entrance stood Sheila. She was holding something at arms length just out of view, that appeared to be

273

struggling to get away. She fought with it for a few seconds then turned and snapped "Danny" in a sharp evil hiss. Her arm relaxed as Danny sulked into view. He was dreading what he would find and resisted the urge to look through the big open door. He heard Sheila's mutter of approval, as soon as she saw Julia, and then heard her tut of disgust when she took in Mick. Danny decided to ignore both and instead concentrated on admiring the large green and white parasol on the table next to him. He felt Sheila tug at his hand again and resisted just enough for her to give a second tug of increased power which pulled him into the restaurant. Sheila

purposefully marched over to Mick's table dragging Danny behind like a reluctant child on a shopping trip.

Otto's face was inches from the menu as he scanned it for bargains. He had found three meals that were cheaper here than the other places he had tried.

Just one more for the boy and he would definitely stay here for his evening meal. He didn't notice Danny being dragged past him, but his family did.

Danny looked as though he wanted to go back and examine the parasol again, his attention was so drawn to the outside world, so he didn't see Otto or his family who were sat watching him with great big smirks on their faces.

Mick finished off his second helping of squid and wiped his hand across his mouth and patted his belly.

"Brilliant" he exclaimed as he sat back in his chair and undid his top trouser button. He looked round the table for his drink but couldn't find it. He reached over for Julia's wine and asked "D'ya mind?" as he drained it in one. He smiled drunkenly at her and announced "I love you" for the whole room to hear. He waved his arms round to add emphasis and caught Sheila on the arm.

He looked up and squinted at the couple stood over him. He thought for a second and then pointed a finger at her.

"I know you" he said and tapped his nose for confirmation. "I do. Don't tell me" he closed his eyes to aid thought but opened them sharply as his head jerked backwards uncontrollably.

"You're Sheila" he announced and Sheila nodded in agreement. He put his finger to his lips and whispered "ssshhhh, don't tell Danny. It's a big secret"

Danny raised his head heavenwards and sidled behind Sheila for cover.

Julia looked puzzled and asked "Miguel, who is this?"

"This" slurred Mick, waving his arm in Sheila's general direction "is the tart with a heart, the village bike"

Julia looked even more confused. Sheila looked as though she would explode.

Behind her, Danny looked for the exit.

Mick smiled drunkenly. "This is Sheila" he said. "She's had more men than the Grand Old Duke of York" He laughed out loud then added for the benefit of Julia who obviously hadn't a clue what he was talking about "and he had ten thousand" and he laughed again uproariously.

He belched a little and had a taste of Squid in his mouth. It didn't taste nearly as good as the first time. He swallowed hard to get rid of the taste and looked round him. Someone was shouting and it was giving him a headache.

That someone was Sheila who had taken umbrage at his name calling. He heard something about 'the pot calling the kettle grimy arse' and his 'little bit of Spanish fluff' and wondered what all the commotion was about. "Sshhh" he advised her as he stood up and attempted to placate her. "Be quiet or Danny will hear and found out my little secret" he whispered loudly. He belched again and recoiled at the taste in his mouth. He looked down at the table for a drink to take the taste away but couldn't find one. Julia asked him what was happening and he shrugged his shoulders and pointed to Sheila. "She's mad" he said circling his finger round his ear. He needed a drink and he searched the area for one to no avail. He could hear raised voices again, only more of them now. He

focused his attention on the voices and heard Julia ask "Who is Sue?" in an extremely angry voice. He stared at her for a while, then turned his attention to Sheila. They stared back, both waiting for his answer, but for different reasons.

He thought 'How does she know about Sue?' and then spotted Danny cowering behind Sheila. Slowly reality crowded in on him and with a sickening thud he realised that it was Danny who could know his secret and not Sheila. He thought about the last half hour or so and realised that he had been telling his secret to the wrong person. How could he be so stupid. He pointed, open mouthed, at Sheila and blurted out accusingly "You tricked me".

Sheila crossed her arms and smiled back defiantly. She wasn't going to let him get away with this and was quite willing to wait for his comeuppance. She looked over to Julia who was also stood, arms folded, waiting for an answer.

"Come on Mick" she urged "The lady's waiting"

Mick turned to face Julia, who indeed was sat waiting for an answer.

Mick dredged his befuddled mind for something to say. He was gloriously drunk, he knew that, but he still knew that if Julia knew about Sue it would be the end of everything. She wasn't the type of girl to be the bit on the side for anybody, even him. He desperately rallied his thoughts to come up with the one answer that would get him out of this mess. It didn't come. He looked wildly round him for an avenue of escape. The other diners were all watching him intently now. The arguing and shouting had alerted everyone to the fact that there was a bit of a domestic going on and being nosey buggers they were all watching. Otto and his family were among the watchers. He had been overjoyed to find a cheap meal for his son and was in a good mood as he placed his order with the waiter. He heard the commotion behind him and turned to see what was going on. The smile was immediately wiped from his face when he spotted Danny and he suddenly jumped to his feet to confront his tormentor.

He crossed the floor at lightning speed for such a fat man and grabbed a startled Danny by the shoulder. Danny turned and did his girly scream. He was so shocked to see Otto that he didn't even berate himself for doing the scream that hc had promised himself he would never utter again.

"Dumkoft" shouted Otto followed by a stream of invectives that would have cut any normal man down as soon as they hit home. But Danny was no normal man. He had developed thick skin over the years through Sheila's antics so it would take more than this to really get to him. Of course it helped that he didn't speak a word of German.

The others all turned to watch, bewildered at this turn of events. Mick was relieved at his escape from answering the big question and sighed deeply at his good fortune. He belched and the horrible taste of second hand squid came back to his moth. It seemed that the longer it stayed down the worse it tasted when it came back up.

He shouldn't have thought about it coming back up because he immediately felt sick. He held his hand up to his mouth and held his breath. He knew he couldn't stop it but he tried valiantly anyway. He searched the area for something to be sick in but couldn't see one. He noticed, through the gap

between the noisy fat man and Danny, that the front door was open. He decided to go for it. He was going to 'say excuse me' but decided against it so he shoved roughly past Sheila and hit Danny on the arm to clear a space. He was almost through the gap on his one chance to reach safety when he felt an arm tugging him back. He turned to see Otto pulling him furiously. He could just make out voices but they were extremely muffled as he seemed to have a raging tidal wave in his ears crashing over some beach. He felt his

277

guts rise and knew instinctively that this was the exact moment that he would hurl. He pushed his fingers deep into his lips to stem the tide that was to follow but only managed to create a perfect spout from which his hot fishy vomit would pour.

His eyes were huge which enabled him to have a fantastic view of the plume of spew emitting from just under his nose as it shot forward at a speed of around eighty miles per hour. Of course at that speed what chance would Otto have to throw himself out of the way? None. So he stood like a rock as the relentless stream of second hand squid hit him fully in the face. It seemed to last at least twenty minutes but was actually only twenty seconds but it was indeed a fantastic sight to behold. At the end of it Otto was still stood in the same spot only now he was covered from head to foot in vomit. It was also in a pool around him. Miraculously not one other person in the restaurant was touched by the sick, although obviously it had put one or two off their supper.

Sheila was gobsmacked. She stood with her mouth open at the awesome spectacle of it all. Julia too was suitably awed at the volume of it. Danny almost applauded at the sheer scale and majesty of it all, but didn't out of deference to Otto who seemed to be in a trance of some sort.

Mick was hugely relieved. Not only did he feel much better but he had realised that everyone had forgotten the big question. This would buy him valuable time to think up a suitable lie. He also felt a lot more sober now so that would help too.

He grabbed Julia's hand and led her past the statuesque Otto who seemed incapable of even blinking. She slipped a little as she passed him and he steadied her and she took his arm easily. He smiled to himself, sure now that he would be able to talk his way out of this. He put his hand in his pocket and pulled out some pesetas and threw them on the table and with a little wave to the waiters who were watching in shocked amazement he took Julia by the hand and led her out into the moonlit night.

A few seconds later Sheila roused herself from her stupor and grabbed Danny by the hand and pulled him roughly outside. She looked round but could see no sign of Mick and Julia so she smiled ruefully to herself and kissed a bemused Danny.

"Gotta hand it to him" she laughed "That's a hell of a way of getting out of a tricky situation"

Inside, Otto was still frozen. The congealed vomit hanging from his lips and nose had more or less all dropped off now and his face looked quite angelic in it's stillness. His clothes, however, were a different story. There was nothing poetic about them. He was simply a man covered in sick.

There was complete stillness in the restaurant, save for the occasional drop of squid from his trousers onto the floor and then slowly a sound could be heard from somewhere behind Otto. Slowly the sound seemed to seep through the fog that was clouding his brain and to bring him back from whatever place his sub conscious had taken him. He turned slowly to face the sound. His clothes dripped squid a little faster and he almost slipped but managed to steady himself as he turned to see what the strange sound was. There in front of him, not twenty feet away was his wife as he had never seen her before. Twenty years of frustration, loathing, fear, hatred and most other emotions known to man bubbled up and out in one long continuous fit of laughter. Her legs were off the ground and she hugged herself at the sheer pleasure of it. As Otto watched she had to hold her jaw she was laughing so loud it hurt. He moved toward her and slipped in the pool around his feet and she screamed out loud again and rolled backwards and forwards pointing at him and trying to speak but being unable. This just served to make her laugh even more. Otto looked at his two children who were watching their mother in shock. They turned as one and stared at their father sat in a pool of another mans sick and sighed deeply.

Otto felt love and affection for them as he saw the horror on their faces at his humiliation. That was when theytoo burst into floods of laughter.

CHAPTER FOURTEEN

In the early morning light Ros and Ronlay in each other's arms, totally exhausted but unable to sleep, neither wanting this night to stop or to miss a single minute of it.

They talked quietly but relentlessly of their plans and their lives, their families and their friends.

Ros made the decision that she couldn't keep any secrets from him so she told him about Sue's affair with a local lad and her fears that she may do something stupid like carrying on when they got married. She held her breath as she waited for his response as she knew how close he was to Mick. She was almost relieved when, with a deep sigh he told her about Mick's own torrid affair with the beautiful Julia and of his own fears that Mick might not even go back.

"I ought to be there for him now really" he said and turned to face her. He looked long into her trusting eyes and smiled "But I'm glad I'm here" and she smiled back and held him tight.

Later, totally spent, she kissed him goodbye explaining that she must go back now before the girls left for the beach as they would be worried sick by her absence. They kissed sad goodbyes and agreed to meet at lunchtime. They both laughed when they realised they hadn't managed to get out of the room last night so hadn't had anything to eat since yesterday lunchtime. The funny thing was that even after all that exercise during the night neither felt hungry in the slightest.

As she closed the door softly behind her, Ron leant on one elbow and thought about the previous night. It had been everything he had thought it would, only more often, and he smiled smugly to himself. As he lay back, a thought popped into his brain and he laughed out loud at the absurdity of it.

"Me a puff"

As the laughter subsided it was replaced by sheer exhaustion and, still with a stupid grin on his face, he fell fast asleep.

Ros glided along the corridor and into the lift. She hummed happily to herself as she waited for it to ascend to her floor. Once there she dreamily floated down the corridor and round the corner to her room. She almost tripped over the policeman before she saw him. She stopped suddenly and didn't know what to say, so just smiled nervously and moved round him. Without seeming to shift his position he watched her go past and heard her gasp as she realised he was guarding Linda and Claire's room.

The colour drained from her face as she pushed past and tried to gain entry to the room. The burly constable just put his hand out to bar the way and gave her a stern look. She backed off, unsure what to do next when the door suddenly burst open and a man in a suit appeared in the doorway and spoke quickly in Spanish to the policeman. When he had finished he looked across to Ros, taking in her whole body in one fell swoop. He nodded as if to ask what she wanted and without thinking she hysterically asked for Linda or Claire. He obviously didn't understand her as he just shrugged his shoulders and stared at her. Quickly losing any semblance of calm she may have possessed she frantically called out the girls names and pushed forward in an effort to get into the room. The young swarthy man easily held her at arms length and spoke quietly to her which had no effect whatsoever as she grew more and more hysterical.

"Ros" shouted a voice from the doorway and Ros turned to see Sue peering round the gap in the door. She looked ashen.

"Sue, what's going on, what's happened?" she nodded in the direction of the two interlopers and Sue forced open the door and tapped the young man on the shoulder to get his attention. He held on to Ros but turned to see what Sue was telling him.

"I -t -' s o- k -a -y" she mouthed slowly as if talking to some particularly stupid child. "T-h-I-s I-s R-o-s, m-y r-o-o-m m-a-t-e"

She smiled brightly to reassure him that everything was alright and he looked at her solemnly.

"Senora" he said with a heavy accent. "I do speaka da very good English you may know." And gave her a filthy look.

Sue threw him a disgusted look and reached over for Ros' arm. "Yeah, course you do" she said as she pulled her friend past the men and into the room.

Ros coughed as she entered as there was a thick fog hovering around the ceiling. She covered her mouth and stared in disbelief at the sight before her.

There were about six policemen searching the room while two men in grey suits stood on the balcony smoking. They were looking at a sheet of paper that one of them was holding up. Ros could see writing on it but had no idea what it could be about. As her eyes became used to the smoke and cleared a little she noticed the beds at the other wall. Linda was in bed and Claire was sat on it stroking her hand. It didn't take a detective to work out that Linda was upset and that all this melee had something to do with her.

Ros ran over to the bed, dropping her handbag on the way, and sat down on the edge. Claire smiled at her and she sort of nodded back. Claire just shrugged and looked down at Linda.

Ros followed suit and was shocked to find the pale drawn tired face with the bloodshot eyes that stared back but didn't seem to see her.

She held her hand and whispered "Linda, are you alright?" but got no response.

She edged forward and tried again, quieter, gentler, "Linda, it's Ros. Are you alright luv"

The eyes stared back but there was nothing behind them. No one was home.

Ros glanced up at Claire, who was still stroking her pale, clammy hand. Claire sighed and spat out, almost venomously "She was raped last night by that bastard Giorgio. Sue found her this morning". Ros gasped and shot her hand to her mouth. She looked back down to Linda, instantly full of pity and sympathy, love and affection. She also felt utter hatred for that bastard Giorgio because she knew that what he had done to Linda was more than just a physical thing, it would damage her mentally for a long, long time. Linda absolutely adored him, worshipped the very ground he stood on. She knew Linda had been a virgin and she knew that Linda wanted to change that with Giorgio and now the bastard had treated her like this. How could he?. And how could they have been so wrong about him. They had all trusted him, all felt that there was something pure and innocent about him. It was hard to believe that Giorgio could do something like this. She suddenly realised that if it were hard for her to understand how Giorgio could behave like this, then how many more times harder must it be for Linda who loved him dearly. She took Linda's hand and stroked it. She saw Linda's eyes focus on her for a second then drift off into the distance somewhere, somewhere safe. Then one huge solitary tear appeared at the corner of her eye and rolled unchecked down her cheek. Ros' tears however flowed free and easy.

CHAPTER FIFTEEN

Over the next hour or so, several more policemen, some in uniforms, some in plain clothes, and two in white paper overalls came and went about their business in the small room. For the most part they ignored the girls who were all sat close together on the bed. It was as if the girls had closed ranks and were protecting the weakest member, Linda. Unfortunately, as they were all too aware, it was much too late.

As the policemen busied themselves with checking forensics, filling in forms and ordering each other around in loud voices, The girls quietly pieced together last night's sequence of events.

Sue said that Ros had been the first out and she had left five minutes later. Ros wasn't too happy at this news as she realised that Sue had just been waiting for her to leave so she could go and meet Dave. She said nothing though as this was neither the time nor place.

Linda herself had then left some thirty minutes later to meet Giorgio downstairs in the bar. He had swapped his shift and was due to finish in a short while and had promised to take her out somewhere special. Linda stared into the distance as though this had all happened a long time ago and the details were somewhat sketchy. She screwed her eyes up in thought and suddenly turned to face Ros.

"How did your date with Ron go?" she asked with what enthusiasm she could muster. Ros nodded without smiling "Fine love" was all she said, overcome with guilt for her own happiness while Linda had been going through…. She couldn't bear to think about it. "Good" said Linda "I'm happy for you both"

and attempted a smile. Ros' tears flowed again and she reached out and held her hand. "Oh Linda. I am so sorry…" was all she could get out before tears choked her. She rubbed her eyes and Linda leant forward and hugged her. Ros was amazed at her strength and wondered if she could behave with such dignity in similar circumstances.

As they parted Linda stroked her hair and wiped her tears away. "I hope you stay together always" she half smiled "You and Ron look good together" and now they both smiled.

Linda lay back, as if exhausted, and sighed deeply. She then continued her story. "Claire had never even come back to the room. She had gone off with somebody in the afternoon and stayed out." She shook her head in wonderment and looked round at Claire "Didn't even come home to change her clothes or have a wash". Claire coloured up a little but shrugged her shoulders. "I didn't need any clothes where I was" she offered and then, noticing their scowls of disapproval, added "Hey I'm young, free and single. I can go with whoever I want." The others looked away, avoiding her eyes, so as not to show their disgust at her behaviour. "Unlike some" Claire suddenly blurted out, obviously

riled by their contempt. Sue's head spun round "Do you mean me?" she snapped.

"Well if the cap fits" answered Claire.

"You tart" Sue screamed and several of the police officers turned to watch them. "You must have slept with half a dozen men since you got here so don't start on me"

"But I'm allowed" Claire shot back. "I'm here for just that reason. You're supposed to be getting married next month to a man you've supposedly loved since you were a baby or something. So you tell me, clever arse. Why are you shaggin' that bloke next door if everything's so bleeding perfect at home.?

Eh?"

Sue started to say something. It was something witty and effective. It was something that would shut Claire up and win her the argument. Unfortunately it disappeared from her head as it reached her lips and she was left mouthing empty nothings. She knew Claire was right and she was as much of a tart as Claire was. She had managed to hide that fact from herself up till now, but in the cold light of day when someone actually came out and said the words they hit home and no amount of fooling yourself was going to cover up what she had done.

Ros came to her rescue, although it was more for Linda's sake than for hers.

"Come on" she said. "Arguing between ourselves isn't going to help Linda, is it" She looked down at Linda who was staring dreamily at the ceiling.

"She needs our help now, so we've got to stay together for her. We owe her that. God knows we weren't there for her last night".

The young policeman who Ros had met at the door later came in and tried to take a statement from each of the girls but didn't get much joy. They all seemed ill at ease talking about their activities the previous night. He listened to their hesitant answers then sat down heavily on the bed and sighed deeply.

He closed up his notebook and put it away in his pocket. He placed his hands on his knees and perused the girls carefully.

"Senora's" he said softly and despite their lack of any desire to share anything with him they all leant forward to hear him. "My name is Pablo Montoya, and I am Detective in this case. I want you to know that is my job to catch rapist, yes.

Is not my job to judge you on your …er morals, yes. As long as you no break the law then is okay but I need to know where everyone is last night for my enquiries, yes. Is good now, yes? Now you tell please where you were and what time you left apartment" and he nodded to Sue who immediately coloured up. Her eyes never left the floor as she told him of her whereabouts.

287

"I left next door two minutes after Ros left. I went down to the bar and had a drink. I saw Giorgio working and asked him why he wasn't meeting Linda. He said he had to work but was waiting for her to come down so he could tell her.

He was hoping to meet her later after he had finished his shift" She curled her lip slightly at the thought of Giorgio lying to her, sighed, then continued.

" Anyway at the bar I met a man I know, Dave, he's staying next door but one, and we went out on the town. We came back about three this morning and went

straight back to his room. I went back to mine at eightish and went to bed. I was just going to sleep when I heard crying. I put my ear to the wall and realised it was Linda or Claire. I banged on the door but no one answered so I went back into my room and climbed over the balcony. I let myself in through the open window and found Linda here sobbing. I phoned down to reception and they sent for you. Claire came in just before you got here and Ros arrived, what, twenty minutes ago."

She kept her eyes to the floor as Detective Montoya wrote everything down.

When he had finished he smiled broadly at Sue and said "Thank you very much. Is not so hard, no" and he turned to Claire "Please" he said and held his pen ready.

Claire, with no embarrassment whatsoever told how she had gone back, with the big coloured lad she had met on the beach, to his flat. His mate had later turned up with another girl and they had all stayed the night. She had returned that morning to find Sue and Linda sat on the bed crying. Then the police had turned up. The young man blushed slightly at her candour but before he could ask any questions Claire added "And I don't know any of their names or what hotel we were in, only that it was on the sea front at the other end of the beach." The policeman nodded and turned to Ros. "Senora. You next please"

288

She smiled weakly. It had been a long time since she had been with a man, a long time. And now she had only gone to bed with Ron because of the strong mutual attraction and affection they had for each other. She wanted to scream that this wasn't just a holiday fling, that they were going to continue this at home. They had plans, God damn it. She wanted to but she knew it would just sound like she was trying to make excuses, to cover up for her own errant behaviour. She felt like an old slapper and told her story shamefaced. When she had finished she haltingly looked up. Sue seemed a little shocked, Claire had a big grin on her face and winked, and Linda leant forward and hugged her.

"I'm so happy for you" she gushed.

The policeman smiled at the little show of affection then straightened his face seriously. " Now Senora McCarthy your story if you please"

Linda released Ros from her grip and sat back. She grabbed at the blanket and pulled her legs up to her. She looked reluctant to share her story but the policeman sat there patiently and waited. Eventually, with her eyes locked on some distant object, she told them what had happened.

" I heard Ros go out first, then Sue. She tapped on the door and shouted 'see ya later'. I wasn't ready. I couldn't get my hair to dry so it must have been half an hour later when I left. I was rushing around like mad 'cos I couldn't wait to meet Giorgio. I must have left the window open then, what with rushing and that. Anyway I went down to the bar and Giorgio was there working. He apologised like mad and said he had arranged to swap somebody but they had changed their mind at the last minute so he had to work. He said he would be through about ten so if I waited he would take me out after work. I said yes and decided that, as it was very busy I would go back and wait in my room. When I got back I opened the door and reached for the light switch. Something hit me on the side of the head and I almost fell to the floor. I grabbed the wall and stopped myself falling. A hand grabbed me roughly by the hair and shoved me face first into the wall. I could taste blood and almost screamed but something, tights or something, was pushed into my mouth and it came out in a mumble.

His hands were all over me now, ripping at my clothes and touching me everywhere. Then they stopped and everything was deathly quiet. It was almost peaceful. I could just hear my own short sharp breathing and his, deeper and strange. Then he swore, or at least it sounded like swearing. It was in Spanish and was so low and guttural that I only just heard it. It was almost as though he realised he was making a mistake, that he shouldn't be doing it and had stopped, ashamed of himself.

"Then he suddenly hit me. First it was a punch to the kidneys, which winded me and dropped me to my knees, then he came round to the side of me and hit me in the face." Linda stopped, ashen faced, and stared into the distance. She was clearly mulling something over, unsure whether to tell anybody what happened next. Then as if the decision had suddenly been made she continued.

" As I fell to the floor I saw his feet, well his shoes. They were black loafers.

They were Giorgio's shoes. I had once mentioned them to Giorgio, that they looked comfy, he had said that was why he wore them. When he was on his feet all day he needed a comfy pair of shoes.

"I looked up, shocked, and could see the crisp white shirt that Giorgio wore. I tried to get the gag out of my mouth and talk to him. Ask him why he was doing this to me. He grabbed my hair and dragged me to the bed. It hurt so much. I put both hands to my head trying to ease the pain but it didn't work. He shoved me roughly onto the bed and tore at my clothes. He bit me on the back of my head and I wanted to scream but couldn't. He pushed my head into the bed with one hand and pulled my legs apart with the other. Then, then…." She couldn't bring herself to say it and burst into tears as the girls all leant forward and held her tightly until her sobbing slowed. The policeman waited patiently for them all to calm down then gently encouraged her to continue.

With a big sigh she said "After he had finished I just laid there, shocked I suppose, I didn't move a muscle. I could hear him though, behind me, getting dressed. I wanted to turn round and confront him. To scream and rip at him with my fingernails. But I didn't. I couldn't. I was frozen stiff with fear and shame. I lay here trembling without a thought in my head. Then he spoke, in English, in a voice that sounded more animal like than human. It was like a whisper but carried menace and threat. He said 'It doesn't matter who you are, you English get what you deserve. Always'. He came close to my head and I almost wet myself with fear. I was sure he was going to do it again, but he didn't, he just said 'keep quiet' and hit me in the kidneys again to make sure I understood. Then he was gone. I heard the door open and close and I could tell I was on my own but I didn't move. I daren't.

" I stayed there for ages until, much later, I heard a noise at the door. I climbed further up the bed and wrapped the blankets round me and waited in the dark for the noise to go away. It was him. He was shouting that he was sorry and he could explain if I would open the door. He kept apologising over and over and asking me to open the door. I sat here cocooned in my blankets and listened to

him saying sorry and all I wanted was for him to go away. To die and leave me alone.

"Eventually he went and it was peaceful again. I sat here all night just staring at the door, waiting for the sun to come up. For morning, hoping it would all be over. Maybe it would be a dream. It felt like a dream. A bad dream."

She suddenly laughed loudly which made them all jump.

"What am I like" she said slightly hysterically "You lot could get laid for England but me, I find the man of my dreams, the man I thought I would spend the rest of my life with and the only way he wants to have sex with me is by rape. Am I that ugly that that's the only way I'm going to get a man, to allow him to beat me first, eh, is it?" She was sat up now, clearly hysterical and the girls tried valiantly to calm and reassure her to no avail. Detective Montoya motioned to a man at the other end of the room who stepped forward with a syringe in his hand.

"To help her sleep" Montoya reassured them as the Doctor administered the drug and stepped back.

Linda immediately became calmer and laid down, halting her fight with the girls.

"Giorgio" she cried as her eyes closed and then quieter as sleep started to take hold "Why?".

When they all thought she had dropped off they eased back off the bed and left her to sleep herself better. As Detective Montoya ushered everyone out of the room he heard her whisper before sleep finally won "There was no need Giorgio. No need"

CHAPTER SIXTEEN

Around lunchtime, after Linda had slept peacefully for four hours Detective Montoya rounded up the girls and their companions from the night before and shipped everyone down to the police station. Ros explained everything to a confused Ron on the way there and cried when she realised how genuinely upset he was. At the station which was nice and modern and seemed clean enough everyone was questioned individually and statements where signed.

Much to her shock and utter embarrassment Linda was given a medical and swabs and samples were taken from her for checking. She gritted her teeth and clung onto Sue who had accompanied her into the small medical centre. Ros and Claire waited outside the room and Ron was left upstairs in a waiting area.

He had given his statement and had been told he could leave but had decided to

wait for Ros. He was surprised to find someone there who he vaguely knew.

The tall good looking lad was also hanging around the waiting room looking ill at ease. Ron nodded and tried to work out where he knew him from. It suddenly dawned on him that this must be the one that Ros had mentioned. The one who was knocking off Sue. Ros had said that he was from back home but it hadn't occurred to Ron that they might know him.

"Football" he suddenly thought. "He plays football for….. think, think…..

Whiston. That's it, he plays for Whiston Warriors"

"Alright" he offered by way of breaking the ice.

"Alright" returned the man without looking up.

"Ron" continued Ron.

"Well done" the surly little bleeder countered.

Ron stood up and crossed the small room until he was toe to toe with his new adversary.

"I told you my name, I didn't ask for any lip" he said clearly and succinctly.

Dave stared deep into his eyes and didn't like what he saw there. He knew instinctively that this man was hard and he shouldn't cross him without very good reason.

He took a step back and Ron followed keeping his nose as close as possible to his.

Dave smiled disarmingly and slowly raised his hands in a gesture of defeat.

"Hey back off pal. Sorry alright. I meant no offence, did I." He took another step back and Ron allowed him to go. He stepped round a small table and felt a little safer. He offered his hand.

"Dave" he smiled. Ron thought for a moment then shook the proffered mit and relaxed a bit.

"You here for the business with Linda?" Ron asked as he sat back down.

"The fat bird? Sue's mate? Yeah. It's a right arse this innit. I mean on yer fuckin' holidays an' all. I mean yer really wanna be here in this hovel on yer fuckin' hols don't yer"

Ron's blood boiled but he stayed in his seat although his grip on the chair arm increased.

"I mean" Dave carried on, oblivious to any effect his words might be having on the stranger. He leant forward slightly in his seat as if sharing a confidence. "I mean, have you seen her" he opened his arms wide and puffed his cheeks out indicating she was a bit on the large size. "You'd think she'd be grateful" and he laughed loudly and sat back in his chair.

Ron would never know how he kept his temper under control but somehow he managed it, but only just.

He had taken an instant dislike to the man but he decided not to show it yet as there were certain things he would like to know from him.

" Well there's nothing stopping you from leaving now is there? I mean if you've done your statement, can't you just go.?"

"Not done it yet. They did everybody else's then told me to fuckin' wait.

They'll probably be all asleep or something. Fuckin' fiesta" he snapped back.

Ron wanted to just hit him. Only once, he reasoned. That would be enough, but he forced himself to wait.

"Still. Get you in the good books eh with Sue" he said in a nudge, nudge voice.

Dave leered. "Too fuckin' right, she'll be all over me like a rash after this." He leered again. "Like she was last night eh"

Ron decided he didn't want to know any more so he got up from the chair and moved swiftly forward and hit him. Just the once.

When Dave recovered consciousness, Ron had already sat him on one of the chairs. He looked around him, bleary eyed and confused. Ron sat on the little table in front of him, patiently waiting for him to come round.

Dave started a bit when he focused on Ron.

"It's alright" Ron said, holding both hand up to show he wasn't going to hit him again. "I just wanted a word before I went". He leant forward and despite himself Jeff leant backward.

"I just wanted to say that, if I were you, I would be thinking about the implications of me seeing Sue when I got back. I mean I wouldn't want to be accidentally bumping into her fiancee when I got home. He's a big lad and I wouldn't want to meet him some dark night all alone."

Dave started to speak but Ron lifted one hand and he stopped short and waited for Ron to continue. Ron smiled easily.

"That's a good boy. Now you think over what I've just said eh" and he looked at him questioningly.

Dave nodded.

Ron smiled again and patted him on the head making him wince.

"Good lad" he said as he turned and left.

When they returned to the hotel the girls went straight up their rooms. Ron kissed Ros and said he would see her later. She smiled weakly and said she'd call round for him when Linda was settled.

As it was she didn't get away until tea time. She rushed into the room and threw herself into his arms and wept uncontrollably.

He realised she needed to get this off her chest so he kept quiet and just held her until her sobs slowed down.

When she had cried herself out she leant back a little and looked up into his eyes.

"Thank you" she snuffled. "I needed that" and she attempted a smile. He kissed her and smiled back.

"I know what you need" he said and turned away from her. He picked up a bottle of cheap Spanish Brandy from the bedside table and went into the bathroom before returning with two glasses. He poured two large drinks and offered one to Ros.

"Drink" he ordered gently so she did. She coughed a little as the harsh liquid bit at her throat but she downed it in one and smiled through watery eyes. He refilled her glass and she took a little sip.

"Thanks. You're right. I needed that as well" she said and he leant forward and kissed her lingeringly.

"Mmmm" she almost purred "and that".

They lay on the bed happy in each others company and without feeling the need to clutter the ambience with chit chat, or to invade each others thoughts with speech.

They were very content to be in each others company and felt that it was enough.

Eventually though Ros turned to him and apologetically announced that they were leaving the next day.

"Inspector Montoya called round and said that they had everything they needed and that if we wanted we were free to go home. Linda jumped at it and none of us felt we should argue with her. She then fell into a deep sleep as if a weight had been lifted from her shoulders. I'm sorry"

"Don't be silly." he said, hugging her just a little closer. "It's only right that you stay with Linda and take her home. She'll want her mum and dad now so it's only fair."

She looked lovingly into his eyes, thankful that he was so understanding. She kissed him softly and then again more urgently. They hugged and caressed and stroked each other until they could hold it no longer and pulled each others clothes off and made passionate love for the remainder of the afternoon until, breathless from the pleasure of it all, Ros announced she would have to go. She had promised she would only be an hour and it had long passed.

When she returned to the room she knocked for several seconds before a sleepy eyed Claire opened the door.

"Sorry, I was sparko there for a bit" she yawned as she ushered Ros through to the room. Ros quietly checked on Linda who was still fast asleep then turned and whispered "Where's Sue?" to Claire who was stretching by the little dresser.

"She went out straight after you" she yawned. "Linda woke up and had a drink not long after. She seems pretty keen to be getting back. Wouldn't shut up about it. Then she fell asleep about…" she looked at her watch "….about an hour ago. I must have joined her not long after"

Ros was fuming about Sue sneaking off as soon as she thought the coast was clear. She must have thought that she could have the afternoon with lover boy and get back before Ros knew she had been missing.

Even as these thoughts were forming in Ros' head she heard a scuffling on the balcony and both girls turned to see Sue climbing over the railings onto one of the plastic chairs. She was wearing a short skirt, which she had hitched up and gave a full view of her crisp white cotton knickers. In the distance they heard a muffled cheer from the lads in the hotel opposite and saw Sue look up and give them the finger. The cheer was repeated and then Sue pulled back the curtain and entered the room. She jumped guiltily when she saw Ros and Claire stood in the middle of the room obviously watching her.

She smiled uneasily and they smiled back, although Ros' was a little frosty, then she turned to Claire and asked how Linda was.

Claire nodded and said "Asleep most of the time. Woke up once and rattled on about how she couldn't wait to go home."

Sue nodded back "I know what she means" and turned to the window and stared through it.

Ros softened a little and asked "What's with the back door entrance?"

Sue attempted a weak smile and said "I didn't want to wake anybody up so I climbed over the balcony instead of using the front door"

"But how did you know they would be asleep?" persisted Ros.

Sue shrugged. "Just a guess" and went into the bathroom leaving Ros and Claire to shrug their shoulders and leave it alone.

Sue sat on the lav and thought about the last hour or so. She had decided to risk the wrath of Ros and go and visit Dave who she had seen from the balcony, which of course was only two doors away. When she had knocked on the door his mate had answered and had given her a dirty look up and down her body, which had taken her by surprise. He had turned back into the room and shouted

"Guess who" into it before picking up his cigs from a little table and pushing past her into the corridor. He indicated she should go in, which she did somewhat uncomfortably, and pulled the door closed behind her leaving them alone. She hadn't liked his attitude, which showed little respect, and it served to steel her resolve for what she knew must be done.

She had gone into the gloomy room and saw that it was empty. The drawn curtains were blowing slightly and she caught a glimpse of him sat on the balcony still.

In the dark she edged forward and made her way round the two beds. She pulled the curtain to one side and squinted in the sudden sunshine.

He didn't turn round or acknowledge her presence in any way but she knew he knew she was there. He was sat facing the sun with his feet up and a bottle of San Miguel dangling from his hand and she watched him breathe slowly, seemingly without a care in the world.

What she didn't know was that it was all a front. After Ron's little chat earlier he had thought long and hard about what he should do. He hadn't really though about the future before. He had sort of half thought it through, well he had thought about the good bits. He knew one thing for certain and that was that Sue was fantastic in bed. He had decided that once back in Rotherham he would try to strike up the affair again. Nothing permanent of course, he knew Sue was getting married, she had told him herself, but he knew he didn't want to just walk away from the sex.

He had sort of half decided all this prior to the fat bird getting raped but after his meeting with Ron he had changed his mind slightly in that he had now decided to never see her again.

He had also decided that he should part with her on good terms. Dave was not into long term commitment and he was against being beat up by angry husbands, or their mates come to that, but he did realise that the best way to leave this affair was cleanly with no animosity felt by Sue. He knew this because he had no intention of his scorned lover spilling the beans at some

point in the future in some misguided attempt to wreak some sort of revenge on him for being such a bastard now.

Dave was a coward but he wasn't stupid. He didn't relish the thought of breaking it off with Sue because it wasn't his style. He had always been pretty ruthless with women in the past but after much thought, and in fact, discussion with his mate he had realised he would have to play his cards differently this time if this wasn't going to bounce back on him in some distant future.

In fact he had been sat on the balcony discussing it when Sue suddenly appeared two rooms away and waved to him. His mate had advised caution and said if she came round now he ought to end it cleanly and with as much dignity for both of them as he could muster. He had added that if Dave got the chance to give her one before she went he should jump at the offer. They had been laughing about it when the doorbell rang and his mate jumped up to answer it.

"Tell you what" he had called over his shoulder as he strode through the room

"You can give her one for me too" and he laughed dirtily. He heard Dave laugh on the balcony as he opened the door and couldn't help but give her a good eyeball as he let her in.

Sue pulled apart the curtains and stood framed in the sunlight. He turned and gasped as if in shock at her beauty. He jumped up and moved towards her and kissed her on the cheek. She looked longingly into his baby blues and couldn't help herself. She kissed him on the lips and stroked his hair. He of course responded and they stood there framed in the doorway for quite some time until they were forced to part through their mutual need of oxygen.

Sue wasn't sure what to do next so she pulled at his hand and led him into the room and over to the bed. They sat on the edge and held hands. Dave decided to tell her straight away and get it over with. Sue made up her mind to come out in the open with everything and tell him that it was all over as she had to return home the next day to Mick and she couldn't see him again.

"I've something to…" they both said together then immediately stopped.

"It's just that…." They chorused.

"I'm…." they echoed.

They stared at each other then both laughed out loud.

Dave put his finger up to his lips indicating she should be quiet.

"One of us had better shut up or we're never going to finish this conversation" he said and smiled brightly.

She returned it and put her finger on his lips. Her face was serious as she said

"I need to tell you something. I don't want to but I have to"

He listened, first out of politeness, waiting for the right moment when he could break his own bad news to her, then with a sense of amazement as he realised what she was telling him. She was splitting up with him. Dumping him. And it was for the best for both of them. This way they weren't going to get hurt as much. They couldn't go on seeing each other. They had to get on with their lives and try to forget each other although she would never forget what they had together and how much he had meant to her these last few days.

Dave was gobsmacked. These were almost the exact same words he had decided to use on her. Perhaps he wouldn't have phrased them in as beautiful a

way but the general feeling was the same. He had decided on this approach as he though it let her down gently while making him seem like a mature and thoughtful person. He also thought that it left the door open for one last bit of how's your father before they parted.

Sue watched him carefully. She didn't want to hurt him and she knew he was madly in love with her. He had told her often enough. She had thought at first that she might like to see him again when they got back home but had decided against it. She had reasoned that it was asking for trouble and, although she hated this bit, she knew that it wasn't fair on Mick. She had convinced herself that a holiday fling was alright but to take it home with her was a no no.

So she had decided to keep the confrontation out of the split up and leave it in as dignified a way as possible.

She also hoped against hope that if he took it well she might get her end away one last time before they went home.

As it was it ended up being probably the most amicable and certainly the most energetic break up for many years. They both exceeded their expectations in that they made love twice that afternoon. Eventually, exhausted, Dave fell asleep with Sue curled up in his arms. Later she lay there watching him, full of mixed emotions until, she gently eased herself out of bed and dressed quietly.

She moved to the door but decided not to use it. She passed back through the room and onto the balcony. She stopped silhouetted by the bright sunlight and looked back at her sleeping beauty. She blew him a kiss and stepped out and climbed over the railings to her own room and then again to Linda and Claire's.

Unbeknown to her, behind her in the dark of his room, the exhausted Dave lay with his eyes open and a huge grin on his face. He was congratulating himself on a job well done. He wasn't sure how he had managed it exactly but he had extricated himself from a tricky situation and got his leg over to boot. Twice.

He couldn't wait for his mate to come back so he could brag. He jumped up from his bed and rushed into the shower. He had a few days of his holidays left so he wasn't going to waste any time moping around here. He was off out on the pull.

The next morning Ron drove Ros to the airport, followed by the others in a taxi that the hotel had laid on for them free of charge.

Everyone had been extremely kind to them since the rape and the hotel management couldn't do enough to help. Even Inspector Montoya had called round and offered his sympathy for what had happened and hoped that it had not spoilt their holiday (of course it had) or put them off ever returning to his country (it hadn't). He had shaken their hands and said he would keep in touch with them at home should he need to. He explained that even though they had

303

Giorgio in custody he hadn't actually been charged yet as he was protesting his innocence and they were still awaiting the results of the samples they had taken to come back from the lab. He explained that these things take time but assured them that everything would be sorted out soon.

Ron kissed them all goodbye and promised to see Ros as soon as he got back.

She smiled winningly but there were tears in her eyes as she walked into the

departure lounge. In fact all the girls were crying with the exception of Claire and they all attempted to hide their tears from each other. Claire watched them all and shook her head sadly. She couldn't wait to get home. She felt desperately sorry for Linda but there was a part of her which kept nagging away at her which said that it was all a lot of fuss over nothing. I mean it was her boyfriend wasn't it. And she did really want it didn't she. I mean, didn't she?

She hitched her bag on her shoulder and walked through to the bar. She needed a couple of stiff ones. Steady. She had every intention of dumping her bags when she got home and going out on the pull, whatever the time. Felling a little cheerier she hurried along to the bar. The other girls followed, each lost in their own misery.

Ron drove back to the hotel and collected his bag from his room. He went down into the foyer and settled his bill. He thanked the pretty receptionist and went back into the early morning sunshine and threw his bag into the back seat of his hire car. Alongside him drew up a smart black limousine and a chauffeur jumped out and opened the back door, standing to attention as he did so. A huge bear of a man, looking decidedly uncomfortable in an in immaculate black suit climbed out of the back seat and growled something to the chauffeur as he strode purposefully into the hotel. Such was the huge man's overpowering presence that even Ron had to admit he wouldn't like to be on the wrong end of that mans anger. He jumped into his car and manouvered around the shiny black limo and set off back down the motorway. He drove for three hours without noticing anything. It was only when he saw a sign for Benidorm that he returned to full consciousness and concentrated on the road.

His mind had wandered, as his did, at parallels and now he was concentrating on the traffic he couldn't remember much of what he had been thinking. He knew though that a large part of it had been about Ros and he smiled at the recollection. He had made a decision. When Mick and Sue's wedding was all over he would ask her to marry him.

As Ron passed through the foyer he glanced over to the bar but didn't really expect to see any of the lads in there. He thought they would all be out with the woman in their life. He was surprised to see Jeff hunched over the bar with a bottle of San Miguel gripped fiercely in his right hand. He walked over to him, unseen, and placed his hand firmly on his shoulder.

"What have you been doing with my daughter?" he growled and saw the bottle fall from Jeff's hand and splash along the bar. Jeff's shocked ashen face spun round and his shoulders hunched up in a "who me?" kind of way.

"I..." he began and then recognition dawned in his eyes.

"Fuck off" he said as he turned round and picked up his bottle. It was almost empty now so he drained it and indicated to the barman that he wanted more.

Ron sat on the stool next to him. He looked across and saw the glazed expression in his friend's eyes.

"What's up?" he asked. The barman delivered the bottle and Jeff pushed a pile of coins in his direction. The Spaniard selected two and took them away. Ron watched, as he drank half the contents of the fresh bottle in one go and then just stared straight ahead.

"Well!" he said.

Jeff pretended he hadn't heard him.

Ron thought he'd try a new tack.

"Where's Mick?" he asked softly.

"Hmph" Jeff snorted and wiped some stray snot onto his arm. He looked down at the smear on his suntanned muscle and contemplated rubbing it off but decided against it.

"Where's Mick?" Jeff repeated.

"Where's Mick?" he said again and rolled his head and put on a silly voice that Ron took to be an impersonation of Mick but was actually nothing like him.

"Haven't got time for your problems. I've got to shag my beautiful girlfriend.

Again. Oooh she's all over me she is, she won't leave me alone. Oooh isn't she beautiful. Oh don't you wish you could pull a beautiful bird like that eh. Well you can't. 'Cos you're a fuckin' loser that can't get a bird so fuck off out of my sight while I sit here and drool over my gorgeous Spanish bit of stuff"

He finished off the bottle and waved it at the patient waiter who returned and replaced it without asking. He took more coins from the pile and went back to the other end of the bar.

Ron watched his friend with curious amusement. He was obviously pissed and that was most unlike Jeff. He was also feeling very sorry for himself which, again was unlike him.

"Where's Danny?" Ron asked, not sure what else he should say for the moment.

"Hmph" Jeff snorted again and again removed the stray snot from his upper lip but this time didn't wipe it on his arm. He held his hand out and flicked the offending mucus onto the floor. For the first time since Ron had arrived, Jeff smiled, happy at his forethought. But then his brow furrowed as dark thoughts invaded his mind.

"He's with Sheila" he mumbled and then added. "He's too busy for me now"

His shoulders sagged and he seemed to age ten years. Ron was amazed at the way Jeff had let things get to him. It wasn't like him at all. He would usually be so aloof and off into a world of his own making, or sometimes, imagination, but he never let things get to him. Actually it was usually the opposite. He didn't take things seriously. Ron had always thought it was a fault of his.

"Come on Jeff. It's not like you to let things get you down." He looked around him. "Where's all the women. Don't tell me you've not got a bird lined up for this afternoon" he slapped him lightly on the back and tried to jolly him out of his depression. Jeff ignored him and drained his bottle in one go. Some stray lager dribbled down his chin and he wobbled as he tried to stand. Uneasily he turned to face Ron. Ron backed off at the first whiff of his breath. He could detect whisky so he must have been on chasers earlier.

Jeff shook his head but didn't enjoy the sensation of spinning around that it induced so he stopped that. He focused, very slowly, on Ron. Unsteadily he lifted his hand and pointed a finger.

"I've gone off women" he slurred and stumbled forward slightly. Ron reached out and grabbed him. He felt the full weight as his legs gave way and he fell forward into Ron's arms. Ron gently lowered him to the ground and knelt over him as the barman tactfully turned his back in case he was required to help the drunken Brit.

Ron slapped him lightly on the face and called his name but to no avail. He stopped and thought a moment. Suddenly he stood up and reached over the bar.

Sure enough he found a huge ice bucket which contained just as much melted ice water as it did the solid stuff. He lifted it up and emptied the contents over his sleeping, drunken friend. The cold did the trick and with a gasp Jeff lifted his head off the floor and opened his eyes. He spit out the cold liquid and caught his breath. He looked around him wildly and spotted Ron sat on a stool grinning at him. He collected his thoughts for a while and stared back at his mate, then an unmistakable tear fell from his eye and his whole face clouded over as the reality of his situation returned and the warm beer buzz wore off.

"Why is love such an arsehole?" he asked simply and clearly as more tears ran down his cheeks.

CHAPTER SEVENTEEN

"Aaarrghhh" screamed Jeff as the cold water gushed down on him. He tried to climb out of the bath but Ron shoved him back down.

"It's fuckin' freezin'" he shouted and tried again to climb out. Ron reached forward and dunked his head back under the shower head. Cold water streamed down Ron's arm.

"You're not wrong there" he said in a sympathetic voice which, it occurred to him, might lure Jeff into a false sense of security and lead him to think that Ron would release him from his watery nightmare.

"Let us out then pal eh" pleaded Jeff who had indeed been led into a false sense of security by his friend's sympathetic manner.

"No fuckin' chance" Ron said as he shoved his head back under the freezing jets.

"Aaarrghhh" repeated Jeff.

Ron kept him there for a further ten minutes until he was sure Jeff was completely sober.

He had carried him up to the room from the bar and placed him on the bed to sleep before he had thought of throwing him in the shower. This way he had sobered up much quicker, and it had been much more fun for Ron than just sitting there waiting for him to wake up.

"Yyy..ooo…uuu fffuckkkkinnnn' bbbbastarddd" Jeff stammered at him through chattering teeth.

"Pppppardon" mimicked Ron.

"Fffffuckkk offfffff" answered Jeff.

He stripped off his wet clothes and wrapped a towel round himself in a vain attempt to get dry and warm. He rubbed between his legs and half screamed.

"Mmmmy bbbbballs have disappppeared"

Despite himself Ron had to laugh. "Just as well there are no lady friends about.

You'd be no good to 'em with that" he guffawed, pointing at his icicle dick and his two blue marble balls.

Jeff frantically tried to rub some life back into them.

Ron smiled again. "Do you want me to leave the room?" he asked.

"Fuck off" was the answer.

"Ah the chattering teeth have warmed up anyway. Perhaps the human body warms up from the top down." Ron offered helpfully.

Two minute later and Jeff was warming up all over now. He stopped rubbing his wedding tackle and peered down at it.

"That's better. Everything's back to normal" and he sighed out loud with relief.

"Are you sure?" Ron asked jumping up and stepping closer. He made goggle shapes with his hands and held them up to his face. He peered down at his friend's manhood.

"It looks awfully small" he said in a very concerned voice.

Jeff looked down and stared at it for a bit. Eventually he looked up and cheerfully declared "No, everything's fine now"

"Well if you're sure" said Ron who removed his hands from his eyes and sat back down on the bed while Jeff hunted round for some clothes. He eventually settled for a pair of shorts and a big woolly jumper. He hurriedly dressed and climbed into bed. He felt the warmth flooding back into his body and felt much better.

Ron watched him until he saw the colour returning to his cheeks then he asked him "D'ya wanna talk about it".

Jeff told him all about it.

Ron listened in amazement at Jeff's story. It wasn't that the story itself was so amazing. I mean it didn't involve alien abduction, animals talking or Rotherham winning the Premiership (ha ha ha) or anything like that. No it was much more far-fetched than that. It was about Jeff falling in love.

To be exact it was about Jeff falling in love with Maria Von Trappe the lovely daughter of Otto Von Trappe, the small fat German who had spent half the holiday covered in Danny and Mick's bodily fluids.

Ron held back the laughter which gathered around his mouth and forced it back inside as he could see that Jeff was in no mood for having the piss taken.

Instead he listened, straight faced, to his tale of woe.

It appeared that Jeff had gone out on the prowl, as usual, on the night of Ron's trip up to Lloret but hadn't had much joy. He had double backed towards the hotel in the hope of finding Mick or Danny but hadn't seen either. He had then decided to get something to eat and wait until the clubs filled up later on before he went back on the pull. He was in search of a decent restaurant when he had spotted a nice open air Chinese. He quite fancied a nice Chicken Chow Mein, but on closer inspection he saw that it was pretty full and he didn't want to wait all night for a meal, so he had passed by the two fighting Dragons archway and gone into the Burger King next door. Ah well, when in Rome.

He hadn't noticed her at first. She was sat in the corner reading a book, the half eaten remains of a Double Whopper Big Bopper Meal with extra large fries and Giant Coke left unwanted on the table in front of her. He nonchalantly joined the queue for his supper while surreptitiously looking round the bright room for a woman.

He didn't spot anything that took his fancy so he ordered his King Size Heart Attack Burger with extra fries and a large milkshake (20pesetas extra) and waited patiently for the spotty Spanish youth to deliver his fast food. Ten minutes later and his patience was wearing thinner than Prince Charles' hair.

He scoured the gaudy room but was amazed at the number of spotty youths, girls and boys, who were noisily enjoying their Fries and Freedom. "This must be the place where they hang out when their parents have had enough of them for the day and are desperate for some peace and quiet," and was promptly saddened by it. What on earth was he, a grown up, doing here midst all these kids. He spotted one spotty berk who was apparently trying to free a rogue fry from his equally spotty girlfriend's throat. Jeff almost threw up.

He had just made up his mind to leave his order unclaimed and go and find a decent restaurant when he felt a tug on his sleeve and realised that the spotty kid behind the counter was trying to attract his attention.

"Senor. Is ready" he beamed holding out a tray with a brown bag, a sleeve of french fries and a large milkshake on it as though they were the crown jewels.

Jeff thought again about just walking out but thought "fuck it" and reached out and took the tray unsmilingly.

"Have a nice day" beamed the youth in an unexpected American accent.

Ungraciously Jeff ignored him and turned to find a seat. He looked round doing his best to ignore the snogging couple of fifteen year olds at the table in front of him. He noticed an alcove and could see two empty tables through it so headed off in that direction.

As he cleared the alcove he realised that there was actually four tables in this little section three of which were empty. It was the person at the fourth table that made him catch his breath. It was a young girl, certainly younger than he

would normally be interested in, sat reading a book. That in itself would normally be enough to finish off any passing interest he may have shown but for some inexplicable reason this time he found it particularly attractive.

He thought about just plonking himself down at her table but decided this would be too gauche for one so young. Instead he sat down at the table next to her. He fiddled about with his meal not really hungry now. He watched her easily reading her book without noticing him and coughed lightly but she ignored him. He took a sip from his milkshake but nothing came up the straw.

He sucked up a bit harder and crossed his eyes in an attempt to watch the strawberry coloured liquid (if it could be called that) rise halfway up the straw.

Undeterred he took a deep breath and sucked with all his might. He reasoned that there must be a knack to it and his head shook slightly with the power of his suck. With a triumphant sigh he felt the cold thick goo slide slowly over his tongue and hit the back of his throat. He realised that the effort was well worth it and smacked his lips happily. He reached for his burger bag and glanced up to make sure the pretty blonde girl was still there when, to his utter horror, he saw that she was watching him. He coloured up immediately and he saw her smile at his embarrassment displaying beautiful white even teeth.

He smiled back and to his delight she smiled even more broadly. He felt a little flutter in his stomach, which surprised him but he decided to press home his advantage while he had the chance.

"Hello" he said softly.

"Hello" she said back shyly. She coloured slightly and Jeff felt his pulse quicken.

"Jeff" he smiled, offering his hand.

"Maria" she replied, returning the gesture. He leant forward and shook her hand. He held it longer than necessary and looked into her baby blues. She smiled again and he let go of her hand reluctantly.

He wasn't sure what to do now. Him, the great lover, not sure of his next move.

That confused him a little but he tried to shove that thought to the back of his mind so he could concentrate on the job in hand.

His mind raced as he desperately tried to think of something witty to say. To his horror he saw her sigh slightly and return to her book. Shit, he had lost her.

He cursed his stupidity and decided to just go for it and say the first thing to come into his head.

"I've read a book" he announced grandly and immediately wished someone would run into the room and shoot him.

"Good" she answered, obviously confused as to why he should have told her that and unsure whether she was supposed to be impressed or not. She returned her gaze to her book, more for sanctuary now than anything else.

Jeff decided never to use the 'say the first thing that comes into your head' ploy again.

"No I meant I've just read a good book. Just finished it actually. This afternoon. Brilliant it was. Really good. Quite intellectual too. Y' know, big words and that."

What on earth was he blathering on about. 'Big words'. For fuck's sake Danny could do better than this.

"What was it called?" she asked politely, putting her book back down on the table.

A little bead of perspiration ran down his forehead. It was two years since he had read a book and that had been a cheap porn novel so he couldn't tell her that one. He didn't think 'Lady Chatterleys lovers' would impress her too much. He racked his brains to think of another book. Any book. To his everlasting shame he realised that he had never actually read a book. He had started a few but had never finished one.

Then a brilliant thought struck him. Most films came from books so he could just name a film and pretend that he had actually read the book. Genius.

"Saving Private Ryan" he said with a little shrug as if it had been on the tip of his tongue all along.

"Like in the film?" she asked.

"Yeah I believe so. I've not seen it though. I prefer the books see. A good book is always better than a bad film I say" He shook his head, exasperated at the way his brain was playing tricks on him.

"Ya I think maybe you are right." She nodded her agreement and seemed suitably impressed. Result.

He rattled on for a few minutes about the story of 'Saving Private Ryan' and it's moral ramifications and by the end she was suitably in awe. The old Jeff magic had come to the fore and saved the day. She didn't even notice that twice he had used Tom Hanks real name even though he had said he hadn't seen the film.

Eventually he asked her why she was sat here all alone.

"My family they are next door in the Chinese restaurant, but I cannot eat the Chinese, it makes me with the spots ya!"

"Allergic" he said smiling at her broken English which he thought sexy.

"Ya allergic. I am allergic to something in the food so I don't go. My father though he loves the Chinese food so every holiday he takes my mother and brother into a Chinese restaurant and I am made to sit in the nearest café."

"What do you mean 'made' to sit in the nearest café, you're old enough to do whatever you want aren't you?" he said.

"Nein. I am not eighteen until next week and my father is very strict. We all do what he orders, even my mother. To be honest I do not think reaching eighteen will be sufficient to stop my father from ordering me about." She sighed and lowered her eyes.

That was it. Just then when she lowered her eyes. It was like….. Jeff searched for something to compare her to but struggled, possibly because he was falling in love and the giddyness was overwhelming him but possibly because he was pretty ignorant. Love. Shit. Was he really falling in love. Is this what it was like. Is this….

"My father is something of a tyrant I think" she was saying which broke the spell he had found himself caught in. He half listened to her, his head spinning.

"Sometimes I think he is almost like…"

"Princess Diana" he butted in.

"Sorry" she said aghast. No one had ever compared her father to Princess Diana. She was amazed.

He stared at her, wondering why she was sorry. Had he missed something, had she said something stupid and he hadn't heard her? He played the conversation back in his head as she watched him.

He suddenly realised what he had said. Berk.

"Sorry" he smiled awkwardly. "I didn't mean your father was like Princess Di, I …" he blushed shyly. "…I was wondering who you reminded me of when you looked down at the table and it just popped into my head"

She smiled broadly at the thought that she looked like one of the most beautiful women in the world. She was extremely flattered, and from such a good looking young man too.

From there on in he was back to his old self and fully in control. He made her laugh and he made her sad, he made her happy and within thirty minutes he made her feel like the most wanted, needed, loved woman on the planet.

For his part Jeff was in heaven. He had never felt like this before, never even close. He desperately wanted to be with her, for this night to never end but he was afraid to mention it for fear of ruining everything. He wanted to say 'look let's bugger off before your old man comes back, let's just disappear into the night, anywhere. This is Spain, let's go somewhere romantic and just look at each other and not sit here in a bloody burger bar until it's time for you to go and then never see each other again because your father won't allow it'.

He wanted to say that but he daren't.

She said "Look Jeff I know this is forward of me but would you mind taking me from this awful place and walking me in the moonlight, somewhere romantic, before my father turns up and ruins everything by creating a scene and banning me from ever seeing you again."

"Fuckin' hell" he thought and reached out for her hand. Seconds later they were out in the balmy night air which just seemed to heighten their sensations.

Jeff could clearly smell Jasmin although he had never seen or smelled it before and couldn't possibly know what it smelled like. They walked along the prom, alone amongst thousands of others. They talked, they stopped and stared lovingly into each others eyes, they walked on. They sat at a picturesque café and drank strong black coffee from a tiny cup and Anisette which burnt his

318

throat although he didn't even notice until he spoke and sounded like Lee Marvin singing Wandering Star.

They laughed and walked on into the beautiful night totally oblivious of time.

Eventually they came to an area where the promenade lowered itself onto the beach and they followed it's gentle decline onto the soft sand. They walked on, arm in arm until they came to a row of sun loungers ready and waiting for tomorrows trade. They sat down on the nearest and cuddled up as a chill blew from the sea. They edged closer together and made themselves more comfortable and eventually laid down side by side arms entwined and then legs. He realised that after all they had been through together tonight, all that she meant to him, he still hadn't kissed her and then to his utter shock he

realised he didn't mind. It didn't matter. All he wanted, all he would ever want was to be laid next to this beautiful woman forever.

Then he thought 'sod that' and leant forward and kissed her gently. She responded and kissed back more passionately so he increased his force and kissed her back with greater urgency. Almost like the last five minutes of an England, Germany football match they tried everything they knew to beat the opposition. They threw everything into their kisses, cuddles and strokes of various body parts. They grabbed at each other's clothes and would have ripped them off had it not been for a sudden surge of willpower on Jeff's part.

He suddenly stopped his frantic love making and sat back exhausted. Maria breathed short raspy breaths and stared wildly about her. "What is wrong?" she asked "Why did you stop.?"

Jeff sat up on the edge of the bed and kicked sand with his feet. He looked lost and forlorn. He had made a massive decision and for the life of him he couldn't remember why.

"I'm sorry" he eventually offered, turning to look at her. He held out his hands and to his immense relief she took them in hers. He tried to formulate his thoughts and get them into some sort of running order so he could explain but his fevered brain was working overtime and he struggled to turn his thoughts into cohesive speech.

Eventually though he calmed down and rallied his thoughts. He held her hands tightly and looked deeply into her shining eyes.

"I'm sorry. It's just that… well I don't…" he took a deep breath and held it.

Then all his words came tumbling out as if he were unable to contain them any longer.

"It's just that I have done this every night since I arrived here on holiday, either here on the beach or back at somebody's apartment, and I didn't want to just go through the motions with you because ultimately it will just cheapen it, and I don't want that to happen. I think what we have is something special and I want it to stay that way and having sex on the first night although obviously very enjoyable, for me it's not out of the ordinary so it can't be special can it. I don't want to ruin it, I want this to be something that goes on and on, something that will last for ever".

He stopped now, worn out by the emotion of it all. He watched her, suddenly afraid that she might not understand, might laugh at him or mock him. What if he had misread the signs and she had just wanted a quick shag after all.

Maria turned everything over in her mind. Her English was excellent but he had spoken so quickly and with such emotion that she had not taken in every word so she played it back in her head. Slowly it dawned on her what he had said. He had gone the long way round in saying it but it was crystal clear what he had meant. Her heart leapt at the thought. When he had walked in the burger bar and sat at the next table she had felt it skip a little then and wondered what it had meant. She had listened to his chat and gone into a kind of dreamworld although she could still clearly hear everything he had said. She had stayed in this heightened state as they walked through the night and even as they sat on the beach. She was even willing to give up her virginity for him, such was her

overwhelming feeling for this man. She hadn't given a second thought as to why she felt like this but now as he unburdened himself to her and she snapped out of her dream state thanks to his sudden change of heart she realised two things with sudden clarity. One, he loved her, pure and simple. And two....

"I love you too" she breathed sexily.

"Bleedin' hell" Ron said and blew his cheeks out. He was shocked. Not just at Jeff's obvious infatuation for this young girl but also for her reciprocation.

"Yeah I know" agreed Jeff. "It was a bit of a shocker for me too."

"What did you say then?" Ron asked, keen to hear the rest of the story. "I mean did you try to get out of it, I mean, you know, 'loves' a bit heavy innit"

Jeff stared at him blankly.

"Haven't you listened to a word I've said? Do you really think I wanted to get out of it? Jesus, this is the best thing that's ever happened to me" he shouted indignantly.

"Yeah that's why you were sat pissed at the bar crying that nobody understood you" responded Ron reasonably.

"Yeah but that's nowt to do wi' Maria" Jeff shouted back "That's 'cos of what happened next"

Ron smiled and shook his head. He held up both hands. "Okay I've jumped the gun a bit. Go on what happened next.?"

Jeff bristled a bit and wrapped his blanket round him for comfort.

"Her dad happened, that's what. Adolf fuckin' Hitler"

Jeff was taken aback by her sudden declaration of love, but only for a short while. He burst into a huge grin and she threw her arms around him. They kissed and laughed at the same time, which was ridiculous and made them laugh all the more.

They were locked together in a lovers embrace, certain in their love for each other, sure in the knowledge that nothing could come between them.

"Gott in Himmel" someone screamed from behind them.

They jumped up, nervously and parted. Maria suddenly turned white, even in the darkness, and she wrung her hands desperately. Jeff felt at his flies, making sure they were fastened, and glanced round for a means of escape. They had both recognised the voice immediately. Maria because she had dreaded hearing the gut wrenching scream all her young life, Jeff because he knew an irate fathers shout when he heard one.

Running down the slope from the street, which appeared bathed in sunlight from where they stood, they watched Otto plunge into the darkness of the beach. As he disappeared in the shadow of the big wall they lost him for a moment but heard the soft 'pfutt' sound as he fell over. They listened to the moans and gutteral cursing, in some bemusement as he obviously charged aimlessly about in an attempt to get into the light.

After a few moments he reappeared looking a little dishevelled and hot and bothered, and continued on his endless journey. He fell over twice more before he reached them and he had to wait until he got his breath back before he could

rent his full anger on them. He sat down heavily on the sun lounger and produced a handkerchief from his pocket, which he dabbed vigorously around his brow and neck. He appeared to be sweating profusely and Jeff decided that he must have been running all the way from the burger bar right at the other end of the beach. This was a false assumption on Jeff's part because Otto had merely run the twenty or so yards from the sea front to where he now sat.

Eventually he did recover his breath and stood up sharply to face Jeff man to man. Unfortunately he only reached Jeff's shoulders which he decided was a bit intimidating so he spun round to berate his cowering daughter.

He laid into her with a vengeance in the harsh East European dialect and Jeff couldn't make head nor tail of it. He watched as Otto wrung his hands for emphasis, then indicated a small child with his hand held so high flatly by his waist. He pointed back to the street and Jeff looked round and noticed for the first time Maria's mother leaning over the railings craning her head to see what was happening in the relative darkness of the beach. Beside her was the young boy that he assumed must be Maria's brother. He was sucking on a lollipop and watching disinterestedly at the events in front of him. Jeff gasped at what he saw next. Standing next to the boy, wearing a brilliant white uniform, was a policeman. He was resting his white gloves on the railing and craning forward for a better view. Jeff realised that if the cops were involved he could end up in trouble here. If that copper came down onto the beach now with Otto waving his arms about and screaming like a mad man it wouldn't look too good for Jeff and there was a fair chance of him being arrested. He decided he had better calm things down here as quickly as possible before they got out of hand. He needn't have worried too much as Constable Albert Perraiso of the Benidorm Beach Patrol had no intention of going on the beach unless it was strictly necessary. He had had his uniform cleaned that very day and as it was easily his most prized possession he had no intention of getting sand on it. He even held the railing by the fingertips so as not to dirty his immaculate gloves. He peered into the blackness and watched the fat sweaty German and prayed that he wouldn't be called upon to make an arrest. What if the young man was dangerous, what if he resisted.

There could be blood everywhere. Worse, it could be his blood everywhere. He fought the sudden urge to run away, and manfully stood behind the small German woman and her lolly sucking son, offering moral support should it be required.

Jeff turned back to the melee beside him and realised that Maria was arguing back. He saw her point to him and her father turn his head, disgustedly in his direction, so he realised she must be talking about him. He smiled weakly.

Otto suddenly turned on his heels and faced Jeff squarely in the chest. He rose to his full five feet and six inches and shoved out his own sweat stained chest as far as he could.

"So you are English" he blurted out in a comic book German accent.

"Yes" answered Jeff logically.

Otto seemed to mull this over for a while as if it wasn't the answer he had expected. He screwed his face up in concentration until a lightbulb went off in his head. He turned a deep purple colour as though he was going to explode

unless he could get some words out quickly. He stammered, unable to speak, until, with a torrent, he spewed forth his pent up frustration.

"You... you... you... are one of them" he declared.

"I'm not" Jeff immediately denied it.

"You... you... you... are one of the English dirty bastards" continued Otto, warming to his theme.

"Hey, there's no call for that" Jeff interjected. "I mean I know you're mad and that but..."

"English Dirty Bastards" he repeated but this time managing to include capital letters.

"Now look here, I…"

"English"

"Look.."

"Dirty"

"I'm warning you…."

"Bastards"

"Right, call me that again an' I'm gonna chin yer, yer fat German twat"

"Jeff" shouted Maria, and Jeff suddenly realised what he had said and dropped his clenched fists to his waist, nonplussed.

"That is my father" she chastised.

"Sorry" he offered under his breath, suitably chastened.

They all went quiet for a while, allowing tempers to cool.

Otto looked from one to the other. His only daughter, not yet eighteen, and here she was, on the beach, alone, with this English man. The shame. He turned to Jeff and saw his sorry face gazing down miserably to the sand at his feet.

"Dirty English Bastard" he spat out.

"Right, I'm gonna fuckin' do you" Jeff shouted back.

They closed on each other, murder in their eyes. It was never going to be a contest. Otto, the fat, overweight, old man against the young, fit, toned, athletic Jeff.

Otto swung first, reactions surprisingly quick for one so old. Jeff easily dodged the blow and countered with a round house punch to end it immediately, clean and quick.

Otto was still in mid swing as he overbalanced on the uneven sand. If Jeff had timed this right he would catch the old man on the side of the head and knock him to the ground, with the minimum of injury and end it then and there. This would no doubt earn him the undying gratitude of his beloved Maria.

"Go on then" Ron encouraged, sat on the edge of the bed now, eager for the conclusion of this epic duel.

Jeff rolled over in the bed burying his face in the pillow. He groaned loudly.

"Come on, what happened" Ron chivvied him along.

Jeff eventually removed his face from the pillow and stared, unseeing at his friend.

"Come on" said Ron softly, but firmly.

Jeff sighed and sat up with all the cares of the world on his shoulders.

"From somewhere behind me" he began slowly "I heard a scream. A fearsome, blood curdling scream. It sent a chill down my spine I can tell you." He shivered at the thought of it and swallowed hard.

"Anyway, it put me off my aim a bit, I must have looked round, mid swing like, to see what was happening on the street". He paused, unable to continue and hung his head in shame.

"You missed him, didn't you?" offered Ron.

He nodded wearily. "Worse than that" he almost cried.

"You hit Maria didn't you"

Jeff rolled over into his pillow again, unable to face his friend. "Yes" he cried, full of shame.

Ron bit his lip and just about managed to hold back the tears of laughter that welled up in his eyes.

From his pillow hideaway, Jeff asked plaintively, "You're laughing now, aren't you"

"No" mumbled Ron, unable to actually speak for fear of releasing the laughter for ever.

"Well they did, them bastards. Mick and Danny. They pissed themselves.

Really. Actually pissed themselves. Thought it was bleedin' hilarious".

Ron put his fist into his mouth and bit down hard.

"I know you're laughing" said a miserable muffled voice from behind the pillow.

"I'm not" denied Ron with tears streaming down his face.

Eventually he won control and asked the question he was dreading.

"Is she.." he laughed and only just managed to regain control. "Is ....er.... is she alright?"

Jeff sat up and stared at the ceiling. He knew Ron was laughing at him but he didn't care. Nothing could be as humiliating as that night. It would stay with him forever and haunt his every waking moment.

"I broke her jaw." he said simply.

Ron screamed. That was it. He couldn't hold it any longer. The floodgates opened and an ocean of guffaws, a sea of hee hees burst forth. And then it happened. In the finest tradition of mates sticking together and being there for each other when tragedy strikes he almost did exactly what Mick and Danny had done. He almost wet himself. He curled into a ball and clutched at his groin and screamed even louder. There was a bang on the wall and this set him off again. He tried to regain his feet and get to the bathroom but he spotted Jeff's disconsolate face in the mirror and fresh paroxysms of hilarity descended on him.

He knew he shouldn't laugh. He knew he should place an arm round Jeff's shoulder and tell him everything would work out but he couldn't help himself.

Here was the Great Lover, God's gift to women and he had managed to break the jaw of the first woman he had ever loved on their first date. Jesus, he was even worse than Ron was.

That thought slowed him down some. It wasn't all that long ago that he himself had accidentally punched Ros in the stomach. He remembered how gut

wrenchingly awful he had felt at the time. He thought he would never live it down. It seemed like the end of the world at the time and could well have been if Ros hadn't been so understanding. And what had Jeff done. He had put an arm round him and taken him for a drink. Ron felt like a right bastard as he wiped the tears from his eyes. He focused on the lonely figure on the bed and wished the earth would swallow him up. He felt like shit.

"Sorry" he mumbled. "I… I…er I didn't mean to laugh, you know, it's just that, well, you know"

Jeff sighed and turned to face him. There were tears on his cheeks. Real tears.

"Yeah I know" he said sadly.

Ron wished someone would run in the room now and pluck out both his eyes and one of his balls so ashamed was he. For the merest millisecond he decided against losing one of his testicles. Surely both eyes were sufficient, but guilt overcame him and he gave up his right to be a bi testicular person and wallowed in his shame.

"So how is she now" he asked kindly and he hoped, with great sincerity.

"I don't know" Jeff sighed. He climbed out of his bed and went to the little dresser and opened a cheap bottle of Brandy. He poured two glasses and passed one to Ron. He took a big swig and wiped the tears from his eyes.

"When all the commotion died down, and boy was there some commotion, they took her to the hospital. I waited outside all night. In the morning I plucked up the courage to go in. She was gone. They had released her during the night.

They must have gone through a different exit. Anyway I came running back here. They'd left. Just like that. Adolf must have rushed her away from me. Or maybe she just wanted to go. Who knows. Either way, I'm up shit creek."

He finished his drink and poured another. He offered the bottle to Ron but he refused it.

"So I've had my head in a bottle ever since. I thought it might make the pain go away but it didn't"

Ron mulled things over for a bit. He wasn't sure about something but he also wasn't sure if he should bring it up. He decided to ask anyway.

"Jeff, what was it?. You know, the scream, that made you miss the bloke and hit Maria"

Jeff took another drink. "It was the copper" he said, wiping his lips and pouring another. "It seems Maria's little brother stuck his lollipop where the sun don't shine and made a mess of his best white suit. He was pretty proud of that suit apparently."

Ron, who was having a swallow of his Brandy at the time, spit out the dark liquid and ran to the lavs screaming hysterically and holding his groin. A little tell tale patch told the truth that this time he hadn't held it. This time he had actually pissed himself.

CHAPTER EIGHTEEN

Linda woke with a start, tears running down her cheeks. She had been dreaming but for the life of her she couldn't remember what about.

It had been the same all night. She had continuously woken up crying but her subconscious had immediately blocked out the bad bits.

Her mum leant across the bed and stroked her hair and cooed soothing 'there there's' to her. She had been there all night, sitting by her bed, ready to help as soon as the nightmares became too bad and she had jumped up crying.

Her dad was sat downstairs in his big armchair, his pipe clenched firmly between teeth. He had the paper on his knee and occasionally he glanced at it, but the words and pictures kept going out of focus, so he had to wipe his eyes, clearing the little tears that formed, as he looked guiltily to the door, fearful someone should come in and see him crying.

He was heartbroken. His little girl had been ….. He couldn't even bring himself to put a name to it …. 'Abused' was the best he could come up with. Abused and he hadn't been there to help her, to stop it. And worse, now she was home and safely tucked up in bed and here he was again helpless. Unable to do anything, unable to say anything and unable to show anything. Whenever he was with her he just clammed up and the thousand things he wanted to say, to make it all better, to put the past behind her and help his beloved daughter regain her life disappeared from his brain to be replaced by utter sorrow, shame (her shame, not his) and abject pity. Another thousand emotions fought for space in his foggy grey matter and he ended up sucking disconsolately on his pipe and staring through the window into the distance.

Sue was washing the pots when her mum stuck her head round the door.

"It's only me" she shrilled as she entered and went straight over to the table and rearranged it before sitting down to await her customary cup of tea. Sue winced at the intrusion and then pulled herself up as she guiltily realised that it was nothing to do with her mum, it was her. She only felt that her mum's visits were an intrusion because she felt guilty in her presence. She would have to get a grip on her emotions if she were to stand any chance of keeping her dark secret. Why on earth had she had an affair? She had asked herself the same question a thousand times since she had got back. It all seemed like it had happened to someone else a million years ago in another life. So why did she feel so bloody guilty?

Claire opened her eyes and rubbed her throbbing head. There was an awful taste in her mouth and she rolled her furry tongue around it to try and remove it. It didn't work.

She stared at the ceiling and tried to remember what she had been up to the previous night. Her head throbbed again so she decided to let it go. It couldn't have been that important, or indeed that good if she couldn't remember. She remembered going out. She hadn't even bothered to unpack her bags when the taxi had dropped her off. A quick shower and changed (something white to show the tan off) and out on the town.

She remembered that she had needed to get out and enjoy herself. As sorry as she felt for Linda, the oppressive atmosphere coming home had got to her and it had taken all the willpower she possessed not to flip and shout out something that she would certainly have regretted later. She wanted to be free again, not tied down with other people's expectations. She couldn't be involved in other people's problems, it wasn't her style.

All this thinking made her head throb even more and she turned on her side and closed her eyes. A movement next to her made her eyes open rather quickly as she hadn't a clue that anyone was there. A tousled head lay on the pillow and she heard soft breathing. A fleeting memory came to her and she remembered she had fetched someone back with her. A smile played on her lips as she recalled pulling the tall good looking lad with the wavy hair. Hadn't he been with someone too. She vaguely remembered a good looking dark haired girl dancing with him when she had made her move. She had sidled up and done her provocative little shimmy and wiggle and seen his eyes open wide and a big grin appear on his handsome face. The dark girl didn't seem too worried at the time and just stood to one side watching with fascination. Claire smiled to herself. She was obviously too much competition for the dark haired girl so she must have just decided to throw the towel in and watch and learn.

'Another victory' she almost purred to herself.

The bedroom door opened and Claire spun her head round to see who on earth it could be. To her utter amazement it was the dark haired girl carrying a tray with three tea cups. Claire stared at her. The dark haired girl saw her and smiled brightly. "Hope you don't mind" she said cheerily, putting the tray down on the bedside table "But I was gagging for a drink". She smiled again and lifted one of the cups to her lips and sipped greedily. She was stark naked.

Memories suddenly flooded back to Claire as she stared at the naked body climbing back into bed next to her.

The dark haired girl looked across at the sleeping man on the other side of the bed. "Still asleep eh, bless. Still he ought to be knackered after what we made him do eh"

Claire actually blushed as she remembered some of the things they had made him do. God, how drunk had she actually been last night.

The dark haired girl leant closer and stroked Claire's inner thigh, which made her jump. "My name's Susan by the way. I don't think we actually introduced ourselves last night" She giggled dirtily. "I don't think we had the time"

Claire stared at the ceiling as it all flooded back. Susan leant on one elbow and kissed her full on the lips. Claire stared at her.

"You must be pretty tired yourself, after what we made you do" Susan observed brightly.

Well that answered that question then. She had been absolutely smashed.

Ros lay in the steaming hot water and stretched luxuriously. She held her breath for what seemed an eternity and then slowly let it out with a little moaning sound, stretching even more.

She was thinking of Ron and remembering the good times, the intimate times, together on holiday and looking forward to more of the same when he got back.

She put her arms down by her side and searched for the soap. A guilty feeling crossed her mind as she thought of Linda and what she had been through. Did she have the right to be so happy when Linda was suffering so much. Even more guiltily she realised her answer was 'yes'. She couldn't help it. She was deliriously happy with the way things had turned out for her and Ron. She couldn't wait for him to get back home. As sad and unhappy as she may be for Linda her own happiness overshadowed everything else. If that made her a bad person then so be it.

As she soaped her body her face seemed to become covered with dark clouds.

She thought of Linda again and the guilt overwhelmed her. Even her own happiness, which she knew in her heart would go on forever, was overshadowed by Linda's intense pain.

Ros burst into tears.

Mick closed the door softly behind him and leant heavily against it. Behind him he could hear her soft deep sobs and it broke his heart. He almost turned round and knocked on the door shouting that it was all a mistake and that he wanted to stay with her forever. But he couldn't.

As much as he hated himself for it he knew that he had no choice but to break Julia's heart. He knew that he couldn't just up sticks and leave Sue like that. He had been desperate to take the easy way out, just phone Sue, or better still send back a message, then bugger off with Julia and live at her place. He had wanted that so much but when he had sat down and thought it through he had to admit that the main reason he had wanted that was so as to avoid a confrontation with Sue. He had examined the other alternative and that was to tell Julia it was all over because he had to go back to England to marry his childhood sweetheart, who he had to admit he still loved, and that he could never see her again.

He knew she would be devastated and he didn't fancy telling her one bit.

In the end he had decided to forget about the actual telling people bit and have a good think about what he actually wanted out of the rest of his life.

After a long time and much soul searching he had plumped for going home to Sue and ending it with Julia.

It had taken a lot of guts to go into that bedroom last night, especially when she had worn such a beautiful sexy outfit for him, and tell her that he was leaving her for someone else. A lot of guts. In fact more guts than he possessed so he had lied to her.

'Only a small white lie' he had convinced himself. 'And it's for her own good, not mine' he had continued. 'Bring her down gently like'.

So he had concocted a story that he hoped would convince her that although he was going home and leaving her, alone and upset, that he was really a marvellous guy after all.

The first part of his story, that his mother was suffering from a rare bone disease that made her bones all soft and brittle so that no one could touch her

without breaking her, was plausible. He had panicked a bit when, full of concern, she had asked the name of the terrible disease.

"Brittleboneyitis" he had said unconvincingly but she had nodded knowingly as if she had heard of it before so he carried on happily.

"I have to take care of her, you know, lift her up and that. I wrap cotton wool round my arms and wear boxing gloves to cushion the effect".

She held his hand and patted his leg in sympathy.

"Cannot your father, he help you?" she asked matter of factly.

He thought a second. "He would." His face dropped to his knees and he sighed deeply full of shame, "were it not for the drinking".

She held his hand tighter and stroked his leg again. He was enjoying it now. He had no guilt about his little white lie as it was used only to protect the innocent like those films on the telly where they change the names. Yeah.

She asked about his fathers drinking but he explained how since his accident at work where he had lost a leg in a freak kettle explosion in the canteen he had become steadily worse. Added to that the deep love he felt for his wife had sent him on an ever-spiralling downward journey into the bottom of a whisky bottle.

"Is there no one else to help you. Does she not have a nurse?" Julia asked.

"Well there is a nurse available sometimes. She does what she can" he lied. He was getting into the swing of it now.

"Sue, yes" she almost shouted.

"What?" he choked. Everything seemed to crash down on his head. She knew all along and was stringing him along.

"I hear your friend Ron, he mention Sue, I wonder who she was. I thought perhaps she was your girlfriend"

Mick breathed a huge sigh of relief. Game on again.

"Girlfriend, huh, time would be a fine thing. I never seem to have a minute to myself. I think she wouldn't mind though. I think the nurse, Old Sue, she fancies me but there's no time for anything like that. No I don't think a girlfriend is on the cards for a while yet" he shook his head sadly.

"Miguel I am so sorry" she declared and almost with a trace of guilt he believed her.

She pulled him to her and kissed him passionately on the lips and stroked his body all over. She squeezed him so tight he thought she was trying to get inside him. In truth she did feel so close and so in love with him at that moment that she wanted to be as near to him as humanly possible. As she stroked and caressed him she felt herself becoming aroused and decided that she wanted him right now. She started to pull at his shirt which surprised him a little.

"Er... you do understand what I am saying" he breathed as he allowed his shirt to be lifted over his head.

She nodded.

She pulled at his shorts.

He stood up to allow his shorts to be pulled down to his ankles.

"Er… you understand that I'm saying I will have to go home and look after my parents and that you and me will not be able to see each other again" he asked nervously as he stepped out of his shorts.

She nodded again.

She stepped back and lifted the sexy little dress over her head and dropped it on the floor. She was naked and beautiful underneath.

Mick couldn't believe his luck. Good and bad. Good because here he was telling this beautiful girl that he was dumping her and she was clothing off and obviously wanting a goodbye shag, and bad, well for much the same reason.

"OK then" he smiled as he bent down and pulled off his pants. "As long as that's understood. No problems".

Sheila laughed like a drain when Ron explained about Jeff. She thought it was one of the funniest things she had heard for a long time. She only stopped when she saw Danny and Ron staring at her, their faces like thunder.

"Well" she said into her handkerchief as she wiped her eyes.

"So as I was saying" Ron continued, still staring at her".

"Bollocks Ron" she spat at him. "I bet you fuckin' laughed your balls off when he told you, eh".

Ron shook his head sadly as if the mere idea that he could find Jeff's plight funny was abhorrent to him.

"Anyway" he decided to carry on as if she wasn't there. "What I was thinking was that we should all go out together tonight, you know with it being our last night and all. Try and cheer him up a bit".

"Good idea" Danny answered, looking at Sheila for confirmation.

She nodded and looked away with a wry expression on her face.

Danny and Ron looked at each other, each one sure that she was going to say something to embarrass Jeff.

"What about Mick?" she suddenly turned back to them and asked. "Do you think he will tear himself away from J-Lo".

This time the lads smiled at her. Ron nodded.

"Don't worry about Mick. I'll make sure he's there." he said. He knew he might have a fight on his hands but one way or another he would make sure Mick turned out to support his mate in his hour of need.

"No problem" Mick said.

Ron waited for the excuse to come. It didn't.

"You understand we'll be out all night. Probably get rat arsed."

"Yeah. Can't wait. What time are we meeting?"

Ron watched him. He seemed alright, not uptight or anything, just lounging round the pool, a bottle of San Miguel by his bed.

"So what about the lovely Julia?" he asked "Not meeting her tonight?"

Mick lowered his sunglasses and leant on one elbow so he could see his mate clearly.

"You'll be pleased to know that I've dumped her. Alright" he said in a low voice.

339

Ron was gobsmacked. Happy but gobsmacked.

"When did this all come about?" he asked.

"This morning" Mick said, rolling back onto his bed and replacing his shades.

"You were right all along it was just a holiday fling. When I really sat down and thought about it I was just getting my jollies. It never was the real thing and it was never going to be. Let's just put it down to the wedding jitters eh."

"Yeah but…" began Ron.

"Yeah but nothing" Mick butted in. "You were right, I was wrong."

"And you're alright about it?" Ron asked after a while.

Mick spun round and with the most venom Ron could remember his best mate ever spitting out he hissed "I'll handle it alright. Look you've got what you want, Julia's okay with it, I'm alright. Everybody's happy so just fuckin' leave it yeah!"

Ron was going to have a go back at him but decided to let it go so he just shrugged his shoulders and got up from the seat. He turned and left the pool area to go for a walk.

Mick turned and saw his friend going. He thought about shouting him back but a vision of Julia laying in bed… alone… gave him a little catch in his throat so he closed his eyes and lay back on the lounger. He couldn't wait to get back home now.

The night was a disaster as Ron told them all about Linda's ordeal and the mood was sombre as they picked at their food.Sheila tried cheering them all up but her heart wasn't really in it and she eventually gave up and suggested they had an early night. They all agreed.

As they arrived back at the hotel they made their way to the lifts. Ron pressed the button and they all watched as the numbers on the wall lit up from sixteen down to the ground floor. Danny Looked at Jeff and wondered if he was going to burst into tears. He felt tremendously sorry for him and wished there were something he could do to help. The lift arrived and they all walked in. Danny was last so when he turned round he was nearest the door. He reached across to press the button when a movement across the foyer caught his eye. He looked up and saw Bella moving around the desk. That's when the idea hit him. He turned round and saw Jeff staring at the floor. Right.

He pressed eight on the panel and as the doors closed he shot forward and out of the lift.

"I won't be a minute he shouted as he turned to see Sheila and his mates disappearing in the gap of the doors. They closed between them and he saw the numbers lighting up. He turned and crossed the hall to the reception desk. Bella looked up as he was halfway across the floor and smiled. He smiled back, positive now his plan would work.

"Right where the fuck have you been?" Sheila demanded as soon as he entered the bedroom. She had changed into the little nightie and silk bathrobe he had bought her in the little market the other day. He had thought it would suit her and he hadn't been wrong. It rode up in all the right places and stayed where it was everywhere else. He smiled at her but she didn't return it. He held his hands up in mock surrender and crossed the room to the bottle of brandy on the

bedside table. He picked up two glasses and filled them. He passed one to Sheila and smiled again.

It was a sign of their new relationship that she didn't just smack him in the gob.

Instead she took the glass and took a large swig. As the hot fiery liquid hit her throat she decided that if he didn't have a good excuse in the next five seconds she would just smack him in the gob. So some progress there then.

He explained to her, as he sat her on the bed, that he had spotted Bella as he had walked into the lift.

She was just going to scream "Who the fuck's Bella?" when he continued

"Now you're probably wondering who Bella is".

She shrugged so he went on "Bella is the pretty little receptionist who I asked for a toilet that day I... er... you know... had my accident on the stairs" He coloured a little, still embarrassed at his shameful race on the staircase. She smiled at his embarrassment.

"Anyroadup I've wondered a few times why the fat man never came calling on me here in the room. I mean surely he reported it, and surely Bella would have put two and two together and realised it was me who had just shit all over him, seeing as I had just begged for a lav with my fingers stuck up my arse".

Sheila nodded and then looked puzzled "So" she said.

Danny smiled at her. "Well I thought maybe she was a nice person who didn't want to get me in trouble. Or maybe she didn't like the German. Or maybe she fancied me."

Sheila harumphed. "Ooh I wonder if she fancied the little fat English bloke with the dodgy shorts, flip-flops and his fingers stuck up his arse".

Danny looked crestfallen. He knew he should have stuck with just the first two options.

"Yeah well anyway. It turns out that it was a bit of the first two put together".

Sheila took another swig from her glass. "This story had better be going somewhere" she threatened.

Danny sighed. He could see he wasn't going to get any credit for his brilliant plan so he thought he may as well tell her and get it over with.

At the end of it she turned and kissed him full on the lips.

"You, my little fat genius" she breathed when she came up for air "are fuckin'

lovely".

'I know' he thought as he watched her slowly undress for bed with a big silly grin on his face.

CHAPTER NINETEEN

Manchester Airport was packed as they walked across the tarmac as the season got fully underway. They saw hundreds of youths, boys and girls, all heading

off to the sun to let their hair down. They felt old and weary as they set off to look for their luggage. The end of an holiday, no matter how bad or good, always seems to bring out the worst in people. I'm not sure when it happens but there must be a split second when people go from reasonably happy, if not a little tired, to sod it I just can't wait to get home. Our heroes had crossed that line.

They waited by carousel number three as indicated on the flashing board and took mental bets on their bags being the last off. Danny knew his would be the last because they always were. He hadn't been abroad a lot but each time he had some difficulty with his luggage. The worst time was, when he was about eleven and he had gone to Majorca with his mum and dad. His case had somehow ended up in Italy for the first week. He had been a big lad so he had had to wear his dad's clothes for the whole seven nightmare days. Can you imagine trying to make mates on the beach wearing a twenty year old pair of army shorts with thirty inch bottoms that flapped about in the breeze.

He had also tried his first actual chatting up of a girl in a bar one night. He had thought it was going quite well. She kept giggling at him through her steel brace. He was beginning to think it was love at first sight until he heard her telling her brother about the strange boy in the cord trousers and fairisle sweater who kept sweating all over her.

Danny shivered at the thought as he watched the empty carousel turning endlessly. To his amazement and then his utter horror he saw his bag appear from behind the plastic strips. Amazement because his bag was first. Utter horror because he immediately realised that the bag had burst open. Under the heavy handled handling of the Manchester baggage handlers his zip on the old sports bag had burst.

Now back in his hotel room Danny had had a quandary. What to do with his dirty washing. Now I don't mean sweaty T shirts or twice worn socks. I'm talking about the pants and shorts he had worn when he had got the shits on the staircase. Also there were the several pairs of pants he had 'borrowed' off Jeff.

Most of these had severe skid marks in them. Some were worse. He had thought about just sticking them back in Jeff's drawer and hoping he wouldn't notice but had decided to do the decent thing and put them in his bag until he got home. If Sheila had known they were there she would have thrown them out and bought new ones but Danny was a tight arse and didn't like to see money just thrown away so he had hid them until he could get them back to a washing machine.

Well now those very same soiled undies were doing the rounds on Carousel number three in Manchester Airport. Danny spotted them first although he was way over the other side of the carousel and couldn't get to them. Then a young boy burst out laughing as they spun round to him, followed by his dad, mum, sister, old man stood next to them, young girl with a lolly etc etc.

Each one burst out laughing as the mucky pants made their way towards Danny. To make it worse no other baggage followed so they were alone in their moment of glory. The smell came next. Even as they all laughed and pointed at the hypnotic sight they held their noses and pulled faces. As the pants made

their way to Danny he looked round and saw his friends all laughing and pointing and nudging each other. It certainly seemed to have broken the spell of doom and gloom that had seemed to descend. He realised that they hadn't sussed that the pants were his yet so he quickly hatched a plan. It was genius in it's simplicity and he couldn't find a fault in it. He would simply leave the pants, grab his bag when everyone had got theirs and march off as quickly as he could without looking back. He might get a few looks from these strangers but it was his friends and Sheila that he was desperate to fool. Flawless.

"They look like mine" Jeff said softly at the side of him.

'Bollocks'.

"In fact if it weren't for the shit all over them, I've got…" Jeff counted the stained undies as they reached him "…those five". He pointed to a big pair of boxers which looked like something George Foreman had to wear at the end of his career, except these were crusted with dried shit. "Except those, they're like the ones Danny wears at football. They all laughed as indeed they always did at Danny's enormous boxer shorts. Then the penny dropped. Their mouths fell open and as one they all turned to Danny.

"You haven't" Ron mouthed.

"You've never just brought them all back" breathed Mick.

"You dirty bastard" shouted Jeff. "You've shit in my pants".

Twenty minutes later they were walking through the nothing to declare gate and out into the wonderful cold of Manchester. They shivered as one as they all reached into their bags for assorted jumpers and jackets. Except Danny, of course, who had scooped up his soiled belongings along with the broken bag and dumped the whole lot in the nearest bin to a resounding cheer from the watching hoards. He stood there now with just what he had on his back, which was baggy shorts, flip-flops, T shirt and denim jacket.

He looked longingly into Jeff's bag where he could clearly see a pair of tracksuit bottoms.

"Jeff…" he began.

"Fuck off" answered Jeff.

"You don't know what I want yet" Danny countered.

"And I don't give a flying fuck. Whatever it is you can't have it"

Sheila laughed and grabbed Danny by the neck and pulled his head to her. She planted a big smacker on his cheek, which brought a big smile to his face.

"God knows why, you dirty bastard but I do love you" she finished which wiped the smile off again.

Ron grinned and turned to Mick who had been extremely quiet all the way home.

"You alright yet?" he asked quietly so no one else could hear.

Mick turned away from Danny and Sheila and looked at Ron. "Yeah I will be. I suppose" he mumbled. He shuffled his feet a bit and looked at them, embarrassed at something.

"Look" he eventually said, looking back up at his mate. "I was a bit of an arsehole back there, more than a few times, so…." He shuffled again.

"…I'm sorry. Alright".

Ron beamed at him but Mick thought he seemed to be looking over his shoulder.

"It's not me you need to apologise to" he said "It's Sue."

Mick wondered why Ron was looking over his shoulder but the mention of Sue sent his mind racing off at different angles. "Oh don't mention Sue to me" he sniffed. "I'm dreading seeing her for the first time. I haven't made my mind up what to say to her yet"

Ron was still looking over Mick's shoulder and his face was set in a huge grin.

"Well you had better make it up quick, 'cos she's here" he laughed and brushed past Mick. Mick turned and saw Sue and Ros walking towards them. Ron rushed up to Ros and swept her off her feet. He spun her round and round laughing all the while. She laughed back, giddily, until he lowered her into his arms and kissed her passionately. Danny, Sheila and Jeff cheered and Ron and Ros parted red faced. Ron looked her in the eyes and with a pleading look on his face asked "Is this alright?". He waited, nervously, for the answer.

"Perfect" she beamed at him and he returned the smile and kissed her again.

Mick walked up to Sue and they both looked suitably embarrassed and ill at ease but as neither knew why the other should feel that way they just kissed awkwardly and guiltily.

"Missed you" said Mick.

"Missed you" said Sue.

They both opened their mouths to say something else but nothing came out so they shut them again and grinned sheepishly. If they hadn't been so consumed with their own guilt they would surely have been able to see the others, but they didn't. Oh well, a missed opportunity to come clean. The first but it wouldn't be the last.

On the way out to the mini bus Sue asked Mick what was wrong with Jeff who was hanging back and being very quiet. Mick said it was a long story and he would explain it later.

When they arrived at the pick up point Ron turned and offered Danny and Sheila a lift which Danny accepted immediately but to his dismay Sheila said no as her brothers would be picking them up. The last people Danny wanted to meet were "Babe Ruth and Edward Scissorhands" but he just smiled a lopsided grin and waved them off.

Two minutes later the old van banged and clattered its way up to them and Bill and Ben jumped out fussing over Sheila who took it in surprisingly good spirits. Danny watched on knowing it would soon be his turn to receive some unwanted attention. Sure enough they eventually quit fawning over Sheila and turned to Danny who was now both inwardly and outwardly cowering away.

Sheila however went on the attack. She grabbed both brothers by the ear and twisted. They both bent over and groaned but neither tried to get away.

"Right" she said slowly as if speaking to two children, which I suppose in a way she was. "Let's get something straight yeah. Me and Danny are back together,right, we're together and that means while we are together you don't touch him ok."

The brothers nodded their understanding and squealed a little as she squeezed a little harder.

"Good" she said and released her grip so they could have a good rub on their sore lobes.

"However if he ever runs off again you have my permission to chop his balls off" she finished.

Danny rolled his eyes. It was good to be home.

With the wedding only four weeks away everything now moved up a gear and Mick and Sue were kept busy by Sues mum, Nellie. Due mainly to the guilt he felt Mick didn't complain once and stoically dealt with every drama and crisis that came their way. When they had arrived home from the airport they had gone straight to bed and had stayed there until Nellie called round with some food and a list of jobs for Mick to do for the wedding. Even though they had made love both Mick and Sue seemed, to the other one, distant but neither said anything and as that was the easiest option it seemed that things would definitely remain unsaid.

After tea they had gone round to Linda's and although he didn't know what to say Mick gave her a big hug and she cried softly into his shoulder. Her mum fussed around her but her Dad was sort of crumpled up in front of the fire unsure what to do or how to do it.

Ron and Ros were practically inseperable. He had virtually moved in with her and he would have if it weren't for his mum. He had introduced her to Ros a couple of days after they got back and they had got on like a house on fire and they chatted away easily , ignoring Ron in the process. He had smiled to himself and thought how happy his mum looked and how upset she would be when he moved out and left her all alone. He didn't like the thought and decided there was no rush, he would just take his time. His mum thought Ros was lovely and more to the point she thought now he might, at last, move out and give her a bit of peace and quiet. Families eh.

All the boys went round to Lindas over the next couple of days. Ron went with Ros, of course, Jeff took flowers, which made Linda's mum cry, and Danny brought Sheila which surprised everybody. Through it all though Linda just smiled absently and seemed to be drifting off into another world, one less harrowing than this one.

CHAPTER TWENTY

And so the wedding preparations continued. Mick dutifully did as he was told, he ordered what he was told to order, he bought what he was told to buy, he carried what he was ordered to carry and he chose what he was cajoled to choose. Sue dutifully did as she was told, she .....well she did much the same as

Mick all at the behest of her mum who had turned into the ultimate wedding planner or as Sue called her a "right pain in the arse."

Nellie loved it, she was in her elements. She took on all the responsibilities with ease and try as they might Mick and Sue couldn't fault her commitment to the cause.

After a couple of weeks and more than a couple of tentative requests Linda managed to force herself out of bed, out of the house and join the other girls to have the final fittings for the bridesmaids dresses. It wasn't a fun day for Linda but she put a brave face on it and laughed along with the others. Her dress had to be taken in quite a bit and the shop lady commented on how much weight Linda had lost in the run up to the wedding.

"You must be dieting like mad" she said and Linda looked mortified and didn't know what to say.

"She's put us to shame" piped up Ros and Linda smiled at her gratefully."

At around the same time as this Danny and Sheila were sat on their settee having a cuppa and a sarnie when the back door burst open and an excited Mick burst in. Danny jumped up

"What the fu..." he began but Mick cut him off.

"Freds dead" he said

"Who's Fred"

"Fred from work"

"I don't know him"

"I know and you never will now 'cos he's dead"

"So you've rushed over here to tell me somebody I don't know is dead"

"Yes"

"OK. Thanks. Shall I start grieving now or wait till you've gone"

"Don't be a clever arse or i'll not tell you the rest of the good news"

"Oh there's more good news is there. Has his cat been given a week to live or maybe his mum's gone missing feared kidnapped by the local branch of the Columbian drug cartel"

"You're gonna get a clip round the ear in a minute" Mick snapped back

"Sorry but I haven't got a clue what you're talking about"

Mick thought about that for a bit. "Fair enough. I'll start again. Freds dead"

"Who's Fred"

"Fred from work"

"I don't know him"

"Im gonna fucking hit you if you don't behave"

"Please tell me what's going on." begged Danny.

"Will you two get a grip and get on with this ...whatever it is or i'll clock the pair of you" interjected Sheila.

Danny looked admiringly at his strog competent wife and Mick stared at her wondering what his chances were in a straight fight. Not vey good he wisely decided.

"Right" he sighed "I'll start again"

After a pause he said "Fred's dead"

Danny opened his mouth but Mick put his hand up in warning.

"Don't you fucking dare" he said

"Fred from work has passed away rather unexpectedly and his jobs going"

Danny thought about it but shrugged his shoulders "OK i'll apply for it but so will a hundred other blokes so why the excitement"

"Because, my little fat friend, because we're coming up to the holiday season and because we've got people off sick we have something of a crisis in that we haven't got enough electricians to cover normal time never mind overtime and weekends. You have exactly the same qualifications as we do at work so you could walk straight into it no problem. Ive had a word with my gaffer and he's found your CV on file from the last time you applied. He's checked it out and you're in if you can get your fat arse down to the office in the next.." Mick looked at his watch "...forty minutes so chop chop, washed and changed and we'll go straight down there."

Danny pumped his fist in the air. He had been out of work a while now, getting by on odds and sods, cash in hand jobs and what have you and it was eating him away. This wasn't a good time to be unemployed and chances of good jobs coming along like this were slim so this was a godsend. "Thanks Mick. He said simply and Mick smiled and said "No probs."

Then Danny ran from the room whooping as he went leaving Mick with a big grin on his face.

Sheila stood up and walked across to face Mick who tensed as she approached.

Her and Danny might be back together and all lovey dovey but this was still Sheila and he knew what she was capable of.

Sheila came closer and closer and put her hands on Mick's cheeks . She pulled him gently towards her and planted a big kiss on his forehead. Mick just stood there, frozen with shock.

"You're a good friend Mick" she stopped and thought for a second. "A shit boyfriend but a good friend"

At that moment Danny ran down the stairs. "Come on" he gasped "Put my woman down and lets be off. Lets get to work" and he ran to the door and held it open for Mick. He smiled back at Sheila and she smiled at him,

"See you in a bit then"

"I'll be here" she smiled back at him.

Danny smiled a while longer then shut the door and raced after his friend.

CHAPTER TWENTY TWO

Meanwhile back in Spain a big beast of a man was emerging from the police station and climbing into his waiting limousine. The chauffer closed the door behind him and climbed into the front seat. He waited patiently for instructions.

"To the hotel" the big bear said.

The massive man was deep in thought. He had just visited his son Giorgio and it greatly troubled him. Giorgio was sruggling with incarceration and he wasn't at all sure he could take much more of it. And it wasn't just being locked up that was eating at him. The penalty for rape was very heavy and Giorgio was looking at a lengthy sentence if convicted. Now of course, his father was a very wealthy man and he had engaged very expensive lawyers but the justice system was slow and while that was often a good thing, in this instance it meant Giorgio was languishing in a cell quickly losing the will to live. The main problems were the lack of witnesses and that the samples that the forensics had taken were in a system that was struggling with under funding and was creaking along slowly.

But that wasn't the only problem that Giorgio had, and this intrigued and interested the giant bear more than anything else. Giorgio was more concerned for Linda than he was for himself. He had begged his father to get in touch with her to check up on her and to explain that he, Giorgio was thinking of her.

Now he never for one second thought that Giorgio had committed such a heinous act but this just confirmed it to him. It also showed how much the boy loved the girl that his only thought was for her welfare.

He had been prepared to contact the girls family and asked his lawyers to sort it out but they had strongly advised him that that would be dangerous and may seem to be pressuring the victim. They said there should be no contact with the family under any circumstance at least until after the trial and then only depending on how things went. So he did nothing and waited.

Jeff fretted. He sulked. He sighed. He threw anguished looks around the room all to no avail. He couldn't get this ache from his stomach that seemed to be gnawing away at him. They had left the hotel without him seeing Maria again and besides the guilt he obviously felt at breaking her jaw ... oh God it sounded worse every time he thought about it... he also had this void in the pit of his stomach, an emptiness that wouldn't go away. He knew what it was even though he hadn't experienced it before. It was love. He had fallen hook line and sinker for the beautiful young fraulein and he was desperate to see her again but had no way of finding her and even if he did he was pretty sure she wouldn't want anything more to do with him. One thing he knew for certain was that her Father wouldn't allow her to have anthing more to do with the idiot Englishman who had knocked her out and who could blame him.

It was rubbish living alone when you needed someone to unload to. Someone to share your pain. Someone to confide in about all the things that were missing from your life. How can you tell someone you're lonely when you're all alone.

Of course he could have gone round to one of the lads houses and had a little tete a tete or even gone round to his parents and asked for a bit of advice but no, he wasn't ready for that yet, he was a man and as a man it was his God given right to have a good sulk. If only there was somebody there to notice.

Now by an amazing coincidence the following Sunday there was to be a football match and not just any football match this was the long awaited fight fest that masqueraded as a football match. This was Athletico Brinsmarsh versus Whiston Warriors. Every year they played each other twice in the league and it was always a battle. This year was no exception.

The morning started normally enough. Mick and Sue had a little lie in then came down for a full English. Well Mick did, after all he was playing in a bit.

Sue had Muesli and a bit of toast.

"You coming to the game today" he asked.

"Yeah, course I am. Got a bit of ironing to do first so I might miss the kick off but i'll be there" she smiled.

"OK love, no rush" he smiled back. "Should be a good game"

"Yeah" she said absently. She wasn't that interested in football and didn't go to every game but she was going to this one because she knew Ros would be there watching Ron. She had no idea who the opposition was and was oblivious of the events that would unfold or the consequences she would have to face. Mick got up from the table, put his plate and cutlery in the sink and went to get ready.

Ron was down at the changing rooms at the Recreation ground early and he stowed his bag away and went out to help put the nets up.

Jeff walked over with a long face. "Hiya" he muttered

"Cheer up you miserable sod. Its the biggest game of the season." Answered Dougie Stone their top goalscorer and youngest player on the team.

"Is it" moped Jeff "Is it really"

Ron finished tying his corner of the netting up and came over to his mate.

"Still got the grumps on then"

"Sod off"

"Now now don't take it out on me 'cos theres no gorgeous German Frauleins around for you to hit on...... or just hit for that matter" he smiled back.

"Dont" Jeff raised his voice then lowered it and looked around conspiratorially

"I don't want it getting around, you know, what happened in Spain. This lot would never let me forget it and I dearly need to forget it"

"Your secrets safe with me" Ron winked back.

Big Ron walked up to them and quickly inspected the nets. He nodded to all the lads there and smiled when he spotted Jeff.

"Congratulations" he said "Well done"

Jeff looked at him curiously "What for?"

"I heard you won the under eighteens womens boxing championship while you were in Spain. Knockout in the first round."

Jeff stared back at Big Rons smiling face then realised the others were smiling too including Ron who was desperately trying to hold his laugh in.

"Don't look at me I've not said a word" he spluttered clearly losing the battle to control it

"Do you know" Jeff sighed as he turned and walked away

"You break the jaw of ONE German fraulein and nobody ever lets you forget it."

A few minutes later they were all changed and ready and waiting for Big Ron to come in and do his big speech. Excitement filled the air. Well half filled it.

The other half was a mixture of linement and last nights beer farts.

Ron walked in screwed his face up. "Fuck me who's died" he cried while trying to wipe his eyes and hold his nose at the same time.

"It'll be me if we don't get outside soon" shouted Mick frantically waving his arms around.

Big Ron agreed "Fuck the team talk. Murder the bastards. Now lets go. Come on" and he was almost trampled underfoot as everybody rushed past him. He wiped his eyes again and lifted his bobble hat and fanned himself.

Unfortunately he lifted his wig off with his hat and when he put it back on it had twisted round and his fringe was now on the side of his head.

Outside the teams were warming up and going through their drills Mick was the furthest forward and was doing one twos with Danny.

"Alright Mick" a voice said from just beyond the halfway line. Mick turned and saw one of the opposition stretching out. He knew him vaguely "Dave" he replied "Alright".

"Yeah. Looking forward to this. Should be a good game."

"Yeah, usually is"

"Hear you're getting married next week"

"Yeah"

"Well don't go getting injured or anything. Don't want anything to ruin the big day now do we. Or the night" and he laughed dirtily.

Mick just looked at him. He knew he was just trying to wind him up but was there something else there. He thought maybe there was but couldn't think what it could be so he thought better of it and turned to carry on his warm up.

Dave turned also but before he ran back to his teammates he shouted "Give my love to Sue" and he was off.

"What was that about" asked Danny.

"Don't know" mused Mick "just trying to wind me up" but he was watching Dave as he said it and when Dave reached his mates he pointed at Mick and they all laughed. Was there more to it than mere gamesmanship. We'll see.

Big Ron called everbody in to give them their instructions. Nobody listened but they did stare. They all wondered why Big Ron had a fringe on the side of his head.

"Ron" ventured Danny

"Big Ron" corrected Big Ron.

"Big Ron" repeated Danny "....er"

"Come on son. We haven't got all day"

Danny wasn't sure whether he should tell him or not. Big Ron had a short fuse and he might just lose it.

"Come on. What's up" said Big Ron now getting annoyed.

"Well....."

"Spit it out then."

"Well...."

"Is this about you being sub again. I've told you, when you lose some of that blubber you'll be considered for a starting place"

Danny took the easy way out. "OK. Sorry" he said . "I'll er .... I'll not mention it again"

"Thank fuck for that" replied Big Ron and he lifted his hat and scratched his bald dome. "I've got enough on my mind without you blathering on" and with that he pulled his hat back on oblivious to the fact he now had a fringe on the other side of his head.

As one the whole team saw it at the same time and all ran on to the pitch laughing and smiling at each other.

That good mood at the beginning may have accounted for the cordial atmosphere that accompanied the first half as for the most part it was an even game played out in good spirits.

However during the half time break Sue arrived. She approached Ros who seemed surprised to see her.

"Didn't think you'd be here today" she said

"Well I've done my ironing, mum's got a joint on so I thought it's this or wedding planning with "Mother of the bridezilla" so here I am"

"Yes but you know who we are playing don't you"

"No"

"Whiston Warriors"

"So"

"With a certain holiday romance playing for them" Ros whispered.

Sue's face darkened . she had no idea.

"Oh no. Has anything happened yet" she asked with dread.

"No it all seems very civil up to now"

"Lets hope it stays that way"

It was never going to stay that way was it.

Two minutes into the second half a loose ball in Brinsmarsh's own half resulted in Mick and Dave both racing each other. As it happens it was very close to where Ros and Sue were stood. Dave just had the edge and was first to the ball but Mick was there a split second later and clattered into him sending them both sprawling and the ball out of play landing at Sues feet. Both players got up and Dave walked to retrieve the ball. He had a smirk on his face as he picked it up.

"Hello Sue. Didn't recognise you with your clothes on"

Sue went white.

Ros went white.

Mick went mad.

Five minutes later two ambulances were on the scene. Each contained two Whiston Warriors.

None of them knew the full story of why they ended up in A and E with various broken bones and fractures.

Later that day Danny was telling Sheila all about it.

"It appears that Sue had a holiday fling with that arsehole Dave from Whiston.

He said something to Mick during the game and Mick lost it. He gave him a right pasting. Half a dozen of their players ran over with fists flying but by this time Ron was there guarding Mick. He covered him by laying out all six of them. Three ended up in hospital along with the arsehole. You should have seen it it was like something from a film. The rest of their team stepped back and just shouted at the referee to stop it. He watched horrified as the first four went down and decided he was thirsty and sloped off to get a drink. Two ambulances. No coppers though. They're not daft. Mick stormed off. Sue chased after him. Don't know if she caught him. Hope not for her sake. He was in a foul mood. Well who can blame him her doing the dirty on him and that"

"You must be joking. He did the dirty on her too you know. He was shagging the lovely Julia in Benidorm all week." She replied haughtily.

"Yeah but that was different" Danny said defensively.

"How"

Danny thought for a second "Well Sue doesn't know about that does she"

"Ah well that's alright then isn't it, you moron" she snapped back.

"No suppose not" he sighed. "Wonder if he'll tell her now that this has happened"

"I doubt it very much" She said "He'll take the cowards way out and keep his mouth shut until he has no other choice but to admit it."

Danny thought about it. "Yeah I suppose so. Anyway, what's for tea?"

Sue rushed home and was pleased to find her mum there putting the ironing away. She ran over to her and buried her head in her shoulder and cried and wailed and snotted and got mascara everywhere and... well you know, we've all been there.

Nellie held her tight and tried to ignore her wet shoulder and the snot and tears running down her back.

"Sue" she said "Whatever's the matter, what's happened. Is Mick alright. Calm down, calm down and tell me what's up"

She tried to push Sue backwards so she could see her face but Sue just gripped as if for dear life and continued her wailing.

"I've ruined everything" she suddenly blurted out.

"You" queried Nellie. "I doubt that very much. If anybody's ruined everything it'll be him. You mark my words. I know his sort, don't you go blaming yourself young lady, don't go covering for him and taking the blame when it's him what's been up to no good."

Sue broke her grasp on her mum, leant back and looked at her. "No mum this is definitely me. I've done something awful. I really have ruined everything."

"Sweetheart you've had a tiff that's all. It'll all come out in the wash. I promise you it'll be fine" she said soothingly but Sue looked wildly at her. She wasn't at all sure that it would ever be fine again.

BANG

They both jumped as Mick rushed into the room having slammed the back door as he hurtled through the kitchen,

He was purple with rage and Nellie surprised Sue by grabbing her and shoving her behind her. Nellie gathered herself up to her full height (and width, which was even fuller) and pointed at Mick.

"Stop right there Michael Mathews don't you come another inch nearer to my daughter or you'll have me to deal with" and she stared him down to show she wasn't messing around. However, on this occasion, Mick was having none of it.

"No good trying to protect her Nellie. It's too late for that. You should have gone to Lloret with her and then you could have done a proper job of protecting your sweet innocent little daughter shouldn't you" and he stared at Sue's back who was steadfastly refusing to turn around and look at him.

Nellie had a confused look on her face. "What's he talking about sweetheart, what happened in Spain?"

Sue went into another wailing fit and stuck her head back into her mother's shoulder. She had decided to stay there until this all blew over.

"That's the million dollar question isn't it, what did go on in Spain. Come on, you...you". He wanted to say tart or whore but held back. There was still a chance he was wrong and had blown this out of proportion. A very slim chance. "just tell us".

Nellie held her daughter away and looked into her eyes. "Sue" she said simply.

Sue looked at her mum. She still couldn't bring herself to look at Mick. She saw a look of concern but there was something else there, not suspicion, not exactly, maybe curiosity but also something else. Then she had it Disappointment. She could see her mum had twigged that she had done something really bad and she was disappointed with her.

She hurriedly and shame facedly turned away only to be confronted by a stern faced Mick who's eyes were redder now than his face was when he had first burst in. She let go of her mum and turned to hold Mick but he roughly shoved her hands away. "Tell me" he exploded and so she told him.

She said it quietly and without dressing it up or trying to justify it, she just said it bluntly just to get it over with because she knew everything was turned to shit now anyway,

"I had an affair with Dave from Whiston while we were in Spain" she said and the room fell into silence.

Nellie held her breath. She didn't know what to do or what to say.

Mick just stared at Sue, disappointment and hurt etched on his face. In his worst nightmare he wouldn't have thought that Sue would cheat on him. Sue hadn't moved a muscle. She didn't know what to do or if she could actually do anything if she did know what to do.

"Nellie will you leave us alone" Mick asked quietly.

"If you think I'm leaving her here with....." Nellie began but Sue interrupted

"It's alright mum"

"But "Sue he..."

"No he won't mum. It's ok. Just go."

Nellie looked at them both and sighed. She slowly walked past them and left the house.

Sue and Mick stared at each other for a long time Now in every life there comes a time when you get the chance to do the right thing. It might be the hardest decision you will ever have to make or it might be putting yourself in harm's way for the greater good. There are lots of ways it could come about but in almost all of the different ways there is usually one sure thing. Nobody knows what the consequences will be. It's something you have to take on trust. You have to say hang the consequences and do it anyway.

Roll the dice and see how they fall.

This was Mick's chance. His biggest ever chance to do the right thing. To admit to his own disastrous failing and see what's left standing in this relationship at the end of it.

Mick chickened out.

He just couldn't bring himself to do it.

Why should I. If I tell her I'm no better than she is. If I don't tell her I've still got the moral high ground.

I don't think Mick quite got it.

"Besides" he reasoned with himself. "I'm still bloody furious with her for two timing me. How could she. No really how could she"

"I'm going for a shower" he sighed and walked past her and she turned and watched him go, tears silently falling down her cheeks.

Ros and Ron had finished their Sunday dinner. They had had a lovely Pizza from the local Italian, you know, a traditional Sunday dinner. They were now laid on the settee with the TV on but the sound way down.

For possibly the eighth time in the last thirty minutes Ros said "But do you think they're alright"

Ron answered as he answered seven other times "Leave 'em to it. It's their problem to sort out"

"Yes I know but..." she tried a different tack. "Do you think he'll kill her?"

Ron snorted "Mick. No he'll sulk. He could sulk for England Mick"

"Do you think he's fessed about him and Julia" she asked.

Ron thought a while "Mmmm.. tricky one that. It would have been the perfect time to do it but , who knows, he might have bottled it in the hope that she never finds out."

Ros sat thoughtful for a bit. "What about the wedding, it's less than a week away"

"That, my little sugar lump, is the million dollar question" he answered Ros creased her face up. "Little sugar lump?" she asked.

"I'm trying it out, What do you think?"

"Not sure. It might grow on me. What else have you got?"

"Sugar tits" he said straight away.

"Classy" she said and hit him with a cushion.

In a hospital waiting room in Munchen, Bavaria, Germany sat a young lady with a lot on her mind. Apart from awaiting the results of the scan she had just had on what could be a broken jaw, she was also nursing a broken heart. She had fallen for the strange young man she had met in Spain the week before and although she was young and inexperienced in these things she felt inside that he had fallen for her. They had talked and talked into the night with the sound and smell of the sea as a backdrop. They had so much in common, they had so many differences too. She had been fascinated by his tales of home and he seemed mesmerised by hers. Everything had seemed perfect until her interfering oaf of a father had waded in. As he always did he had taken in everything in in one glance and jumped to a thousand conclusions all of them wrong.

Her father had begun the fight that had ruined her night, her holiday and not to be too dramatic about it, her life. For his part Jeff had tried his best not to join in but had become overwhelmed by the intensity of the flailing fists and the superior weight load of his now rapidly tiring opponent. Jeff had first tried to fend off the irate German, then to push him away and when that failed he swung out. Unfortunately it was at this exact moment that Maria had tried to get between them and she had taken a beauty right on the chin. She didn't really know what followed as she was out for the count. When she woke up she was laid on a sun lounger surrounded by bystanders (nosey people), police and her mum and dad who were both wailing loudly at the injustice of the world.

The police had talked to her, of course, and enquired after her attacker, but she had insisted that there hadn't been an attack and that it was all a misunderstanding. She had no idea where Jeff was or why he had disappeared but she had no intention of giving his details to the police, or her father for that matter.

The receptionist called her name and pointed to a door on her right, She entered, accompanied by her mother who had been by her side since the incident happened. Maybe she had been instructed to do this by her tyrant father or maybe she just wanted to be with her daughter in her time of need.

Maria hoped it was the latter but feared it was the former. Maybe both eh.

Once seated the doctor read his notes again and looking up said "Miss Von Trapp as you know the x rays you had in Spain indicated you had suffered a fractured jaw but because of the severe swelling around the area the doctors there couldn't be certain so advised complete rest and another x ray when you returned home yes."

He waited to make sure his patient was following and when she nodded he continued "Good. Well the x rays you have just had taken show there is no fracture however a little swelling is still visible" and he reached over and gently moved his fingers around the right side of Maria's jawline. He nodded to himself "Yes that's fine. You are therefore discharged. The remaining swelling will disappear over the next couple of days".

Maria was relieved and thanked the doctor. As she left his surgery she made a decision.

As they were checking out of the hotel the pretty receptionist, Bella, had taken her to one side and slipped her a piece of paper with Jeff's address on it. She then quickly told Maria that Danny,

369

the fat Englishman, had given her the address and said that Jeff was very upset and if they didn't get the chance to sort this out before they all returned home then she could write to him and give him a chance to explain things himself. She had hid the slip of paper and was unsure what to do with it but now after the good news about her face and the fact that she had had her eighteenth birthday two days before she had the courage to make big decisions. She wouldn't just write to Jeff she would visit him.

Meanwhile in the beautiful medieval town of Vic nestled deep in the foothills of the Pyrenees a young girl was exiting the local pharmacia hugging a small paper bag to her chest. Her best friend waited for her on the corner then together they hustled through the market square, up the hill and at the top turned left into a small gated villa.

The girl and her friend entered the villa and called to her mother that she was going to her room. Her mother glanced up from her duties in the kitchen and waved at the quickly receding pair.

Once upstairs the girls went straight to the bathroom and locked it behind them.

They looked at each other and nodded as if a momentous decision had been made. In actual fact the decision had been made earlier when Julia, with the help of her best friend Olivia had decided that since they had returned from their holiday in Benidorm some three weeks earlier where Julia had had unprotected sex with the crazy Englishman coupled with the fact that Julia was late with her period she ought to take a pregnancy test to put her mind at ease.

She wasn't sure if she would be able to tell at this early stage but she had found a medical journal and it assured her she would.

She lifted the toilet lid and sat down holding the stick between her legs and peed. The next couple of minutes were going to take forever.

"What will you do if it's positive" asked her friend nervously.

"I don't know" she whispered back.

"Will you keep it?"

"I don't know"

She was a good catholic girl but this was too much to take in. She couldn't be pregnant surely not after just the one time. Well not just one time, lots of times in one short period of time, she meant. She wasn't a virgin but she had only had sex one time before with a local boy and they used protection and that was six months ago so she knew she was looking at Miguel as the father if the test was positive.

She couldn't be pregnant though could she. The odds were astronomical surely. What were the chances of getting pregnant after half a dozen sexual encounters. She lifted the stick, squinted and looked at it through one eye.

Turns out the odds were pretty good.

Mick and Sue had still not spoken properly. For the last few days they had shuffled round each other each desperate not to kick things off. However the agony of not knowing where they stood was driving them mad but they were now locked into their own cycle of despair and couldn't seem to find a way out of it.

Mick couldn't get past the feeling of betrayal he felt. He had totally disregarded the betrayal he had laid at the feet of Sue as irrelevant. He had somehow managed to justify this to himself that this wasn't a betrayal because she didn't know about it. It didn't count. Sue, on the other hand, had betrayed him. He knew she had, she had admitted it, so he had every right to feel betrayed. He didn't know what to do about it but he was within his rights to feel hurt and disappointed and he fully intended to make use of those rights.

Another thing that bothered him was the knowledge that sooner or later the news of Sue's betrayal would be all round Rotherham. He had tried to convince himself that it wouldn't bother him but he couldn't. He knew that there would be times when it would be brought up by people he barely knew just to get a rise out of him. There would be snickering behind his back, People would point at him as he passed them in the street. "That's him" they would sneer "That's him that couldn't satisfy his woman so she had to go and look for it herself".

They would mock him and laugh. Women would giggle in groups and men would shun him. Some would pity him and that would be worse.

But he would know the truth. He would know that he could pull birds whenever he wanted to and had. He had pulled a right corker in Spain, a real beauty. Only he knew, and they would never know. Ah. Oh and his mates, he had forgotten about them, they knew but they would never tell, he could count on them. No he was save there, he knew that. They would take that secret to their graves. They would never tell a soul, no one would ever know. He thought about this a while. Mmmm bit of a double edged sword that.

Sue wasn't sure what to think. She knew she had buggered everything up. It was nobody's fault but hers but she was confused as to the way Mick was handling it. She had expected him to blow a fuse, to rant and rave, to storm out or kick her out, to cancel the wedding and never speak to her again. But he hadn't. He had barely spoken. He had sulked and brooded and she could see he was mulling things over in his mind but the suspense was killing her. Would he suddenly take action and everything would come to an immediate ending or would he just ignore everything and everyone including the wedding and just sulk his way through it.

Plus, of course, her reputation was ruined. She knew that. People would shun her. "Tart" they would say. "Couldn't keep her drawers on" they would say.

They would sneer at her as she was doing the shopping. They would spit on her as she walked the streets. Even her own mum would hate her for the shame she had brought on the family. Thank God her Dad was dead so he wouldn't have to share in her humiliation. What had she been thinking.

Linda was sat by the fire in her dad's comfy chair thinking about things but not really thinking about anything. She knew she would never be the same again.

She knew she had lost the one thing she wanted more than anything. Her man.

She couldn't bring herself to say his name. She still couldn't understand why he had done what he had done. Why he had felt the need to take her by force when all she wanted was for him to just take her. Why had he crept up behind her and covered her mouth. Why had he pushed her face into the bed and taken her from behind like an animal. He had growled like an animal too, his voice and words barely recognisable. And after it was over he had held her face deep into the covers and cursed her until with a final push he stood up and without looking back left the room.

She had turned and looked up just as the door closed and could see him tucking his shirt back into his smart uniform.

The phone rang. Her mum and dad were out and she sat and listened to the ring. It was the third time it had rung in the past hour and she ignored this as she did those. It kept ringing. She watched it disinterestedly and it continued.

She looked away and it still continued ringing. It was getting on her nerves now. She looked at it again and decided she couldn't stand it any longer her.

She reached out and picked up the receiver and her life changed forever.

Ros and Ron got off the bus loaded with shopping bags "Bloody hell Ros do you need all this stuff" asked Ron while juggling three bags in his right hand and two in his left.

"Yes" she said "you want me to look all beautiful and sexy don't you" she answered coquettishly.

"Not fussed" he said and shrugged

"Ah the magic's worn off already" she said.

"Yeah, you could wear an old sack and I probably wouldn't notice"

"Well you noticed last night when I put that new nightie on. The see through one."

"Yeah" he smiled "I noticed that"

"Yes and I noticed the effect it had as well"

"Ah you noticed that did you Bubbles"

"Bubbles?"

"Yeah what do you think. Its 'cos of your bubbly personality"

"Well I hoped it wasn't because I farted in the bath" she said "No keep trying.

You'll get there"

"Mum, Dad" Linda shouted as they opened the front door armed with shopping bags.

"What's up?" they asked together"

"Quick. Put the shopping down and come into the front room, I've got some news. Some great news."

Linda was beside herself with joy. Her mum and dad couldn't believe the transformation from the depressed and sad individual when they left to the

joyous giggling young girl jumping about before them now. They dropped their grocery bags and rushed into the front room.

Linda couldn't wait any longer and started to tell her story before they had sat down.

"About twenty minutes ago I had a phone call." She gushed. "From the police in Spain who were handling my case". Her mum and dad both nodded eagerly.

"They've caught the rapist" she stated matter of factly.

Her mum looked at her dad. This was the first time she had used the word

"rapist" or even referred to the actual rape. In fact she had hardly spoken of the whole holiday since she had been back. The only information she had gathered had come from Ros and Sue who had told her all about Giorgio and how he hadn't seemed the type to do this but had obviously fooled them all.

"But sweetheart they've already caught him. He's locked up. It was that Giorgio."

"No but it wasn't " she almost laughed back. "I knew it wasn't. I knew he couldn't have done that to me"

Her mum looked confused. "So what's happened then to change things."

Linda sat down next to her dad and proceeded to explain things as they had been explained to her a few minutes earlier.

It seemed that the DNA samples that the police had taken had become lost in the system somewhere and Giorgio had been languishing in jail while a search ensued. They were eventually found and the tests had been carried out, The DNA didn't match the samples taken from Giorgio at the police station so it couldn't have been him. However the police decided to double check with a B

sample they had placed in storage so Giorgio had stayed in jail until these tests had been done.

While this was going on another rape had taken place behind a night club at the other end of Lloret and the assailant had been caught fleeing the scene. The police wouldn't give his name but said he worked at the same hotel as Giorgio.

DNA samples had been taken and a match was found with the samples taken from her. This evidence was shown to the man and he admitted to both rapes.

He said that hers was case of mistaken identity and that his intended victim had been Claire in revenge for her spurning him at an earlier encounter and embarrassing him. It seemed he didn't take kindly to rejection. He had realised, of course, that he had the wrong girl but had gone too far and couldn't stop himself.

This man was now locked away and Giorgio had been freed.

"He's free dad. Free and innocent" and she hugged her dad for all she was worth.

He hugged her back overjoyed at the thought that his precious daughter had emerged from the pit of self loathing and despondency that she had been in these last few weeks. He wasn't that sure that all that much had changed. She had still been violated just by a different man but even he could see that this seemed to make a massive difference to his little girl so he said nothing and hugged her tightly.

"So what now?" asked her mum cautiously.

Linda broke away from the embrace. "First we get this wedding out of the way then I'm going back to Spain to get my man" she said confidently and both her mum and dad raised their eyebrows at the sudden change in their little princess.

Giorgio was covered in women. Aunts, cousins, his mother and friends of the family (and there were many) were smothering him in kisses and pinching his cheeks and cooing over him and patting his head and smoothing his hair down.

Occasionally one would turn to the men who were sat by the fire and curse in Spanish about what should befall the bastardo that had committed these disgusting crimes and laid the blame on their innocent sweet Giorgio.

The men, for their part, took the cursing of their women to heart. They mumbled to each other of the men they knew in various prisons who they would contact to ensure that a suitable revenge would be exacted.

The door to the kitchen opened and the owner of the villa they were in entered to a tumultuous greeting from the men and much bowing and hand kissing from the women. The giant bear of a man accepted all this attention with good grace and when it had ceased strode over to the fire to join his friends. A wine glass was placed in his big work worn hands and he turned to warm his rump.

The men started to whisper to him of the consequences that would be metered out to the villain of the piece. The big man raised one club of a hand and whispered back that it was all taken care of. Once sentenced the young man would be taken to the nearest prison to begin his sentence. Once there blind eyes would be turned by guards and certain retributions would be exacted by fellow convicts. He wouldn't be killed but he was going to have a very bad time of in prison. The big man smiled to himself.

His son walked over to him straightening his hair as he did. His father watched him affectionately. He could see he looked tired and had been under a lot of strain. He asked him one simple question but he thought he already knew the answer.

"What do you want to do now?"

Without hesitation Giorgio looked his father in the eye and said "I want to see Linda and make sure she is well"

That was the answer he had expected. Arrangements had already been made.

He knew his son.

The day before the wedding was chaos. Everything had to be done today, nothing could be left to chance on the last day. From eight in the morning onwards Nellie and Mick's mum and dad Frank and Jan were at it. They carried, built, moved, phoned, pushed and pulled the life out of anything connected to the wedding. Sue helped, of course, but her heart wasn't in it. All three parents noticed but didn't say anything, Nellie because she knew what had happened and Jan and Frank because they didn't.

Mick, on the other hand, did nothing. He slept late and then lay there. He had a big decision to make and he couldn't face it.

He weighed up all the pros and cons and there were many but couldn't tip the result in either sides favour. He was still mulling it over when he heard the

doorbell. He knew Sue was out so he reluctantly got up and went to the window. Ron was on the front path looking up at him.

"Get your arse down here" he shouted.

Mick thought about ignoring him and going back to bed b ut decided against it so went downstairs and unlocked the door.

"I'll put the kettle on" Ron said, looking at Mick's tangled hair and three days worth of beard.

"Is that your new look for the wedding?" he asked as he filled the kettle.

"Ha Ha" Mick said as he sat down.

They were both quiet for a bit but as the kettle stopped boiling Ron asked "So, what's happening then. Is it on or off"

"I don't know" Mick answered dejectedly. "I can't make my mind up"

"Well you better get a move on. It's tomorrow and you can't leave her standing at the alter, she doesn't deserve that."

"I wouldn't do that."

"So work it out then"

"She shagged somebody else behind my back"

"So did you"

"That's different"

"How"

"It just is"

"Why, because she got caught and you didn't"

"Yes.... no.... well yes actually"

Ron finished making two mugs of tea, put them on the table and sat down opposite his lifelong friend.

"You're a fucking idiot" he said.

Mick bridled at this affront "No it does make a difference. Everybody knows about her now, everybody knows what she did. All of Rotherham will be laughing behind my back. I can't stand it"

"So tell 'em what you were up to in Spain, even the score. Admit to Sue that you was as bad as she was, that you fucked it up as much as she did. Word will soon get round and then everyone will know that neither of you can be trusted equally and all's well in the wonderful world of Mick and Sue and the universe that spins round them."

"What do you mean?"

"Well this might come as a surprise, a shock even, but the universe doesn't spin round you. Nobody outside your own little circle of family and friends cares what you were up to in Benidorm or Sue was up to in Lloret De Mar. People will know of course but they won't care. In a few weeks they will have forgotten, they'll go about their own little humdrum lives and you can go about yours safe in the knowledge that no one gives a shit"

Mick thought about it. "Yeah I suppose you're right. But I'll know, I'll know what she did"

"OK. But what did she do really?"

"She shagged that dick head from Whiston" Mick barked back

"No. What she did was exactly the same as you. She took the last chance before getting married to have a fling. Look you two have been together since you were, what, eight?"

Mick nodded.

"In all that time you've never looked at another woman with the intention of doing anything and neither has Sue. On your last chance before committing you both took the opportunity to sow a few wild oats safe in the knowledge that no one would ever know.

If you think on you convinced yourself that you were in love with the lovely Julia with a soft J but you weren't really"

Mick pondered this. Ron was right, he didn't love Julia. He loved Sue, always had.

"So are you saying I should forgive her?"

"I'm not saying anything, my old mucker, you have to make these decisions yourself or it's not a decision is it."

"So should I tell her about me?"

"Again, not for me to say. I'm just laying out the facts on the table you decide what to do with 'em"

Mick was quiet for a bit. "I've been a dick haven't I?"

"Yes"

"She's not bad really, is she?"

"No she isn't"

"I ought to talk to her and sort things out"

Ron rose from his seat

"Good idea. Sort things out, clear the air. Start again"

Ron made his way through the kitchen. "So, do you think the weddings still on then, after you've fessed up. Do you think she'll forgive you?"

"What?" Mick looked horrified "I'm not telling her about Julia"

"What are you gonna talk about then?"

"I'm going to forgive her and tell her I'm willing to forget it and marry her anyway, you know, be the bigger man"

Ron reached for the door handle and pulled it open.

"Idiot" he said as he went outside.

Later that evening they were sat watching TV, Mick on the big chair, Sue sprawled on the settee.

Neither had spoken since Sue had come home. She had fetched a chippy tea (well it was Friday) and they had eaten in silence. She could tell that he was building up to say something but she was dreading finding out.

Mick was mulling things over. How to start was the problem. He had thought long and hard but couldn't come up with a good opening gambit.

"How's the preparations coming along" he suddenly asked. He was almost as surprised as she was that he had asked out of the blue.

"Good" she blurted out "All done"

"Good" he answered, unsure what else to say. "That's er... good"

"Yes" she replied "It's good"

"Right then, maybe we should have an early night then bef....."

She was on him like a rash. She kissed his face and held his head, She straddled him and squeezed him tightly. "Oh Mick" she cried "I am so sorry. I am so so sorry. I don't know what came over me. I ruined everything" she hugged him tighter and buried her face in her neck and cried even louder.

Mick stroked her hair and soothed her with "there there's " and "it'll be ok's" and "well work through it's" all the time feeling pretty good about being the better man.

She looked up with tears streaming from her eyes. "Will we Mick, will we really be alright. I couldn't stand it if you threw this back in my face every time we had an argument or disagreement, I'd rather end it now than that."

Mick wiped some of the tears from her cheeks. "I promise never to mention it again" he softly said and she looked into his eyes and saw that he meant it.

"But " he added ominously "I would like to know why you slept with ... you know ...him" he couldn't say his name. "Did you love him?"

Sue stared into his face afraid to go there, to tell him of her feelings. How would he react, what would be the best thing to say or at least the least worst thing. Then she decided to just let it all out, to clear the decks and just see what happens next.

"No I didn't love him. Well that's not true I thought I did but I didn't really.

I'm not sure what I was thinking really. My mind was all over the place. I was worried about the wedding, scared of taking that next step. We've been together forever Mick and we bought this house right next door to my mums and everything was lovely and perfect and safe and then you asked me to marry you, which I know was the next logical step but... well I was afraid, scared we'd spoil things. So there was all that. Then the drink and the sun, the near naked bodies all over the place and..... oh I don't know. It's no excuse, I know it isn't but I got a bit of attention and it went to my head. I convinced myself that it was love but it wasn't .... oh I don't know, maybe it was. Maybe it was lots of things Maybe it was love. Love, lust and some other stuff too, all mixed up. Fear of what was to come, fear of just plodding on in the time honoured tradition and a bit of wonderment. I wondered what it was like on the other side, to try something new" she stopped, looked him in the eye then looked away "someone new".

He thought about it a bit and had to ask "well then, was it better, did it meet expectations" he dreaded her next answer.

She held his stare and held his face. "I swear to you Mick. No it wasn't. It was different but not better. I risked losing everything I love for a few moments of madness. I promise you faithfully that I will do everything in my power to make you trust me again. I promise you that"

He stared at her. He knew she meant every word. He knew she would indeed do everything to reinstate that trust and love and his heart melted. Was now the time to tell her about Julia. She would surely understand why he had done what he had done, it was basically the same reasons she had just given him but he wouldn't have phrased it as nicely.

"OK" he said "Let's go to bed."

The next morning was hectic. Mick went round to Ron's place to get ready.

Ros went to Sue's to do the same. Linda and her mum came round and everybody cried when Linda told them all her news. Claire came round and couldn't see what all the fuss was about. "She's still been raped, hasn't she"

she asked. Ros tried to explain but she just shrugged. They were all surprised however when Linda said she had booked to return to Spain the next morning.

She was going to see Giorgio and see where they were at in their relationship.

She was sure it was the right thing to do but there was a little seed of doubt there that Giorgio might not feel the same as her, that he might have gone off her after ... well you know. Or maybe it was purely a holiday fling for him.

Maybe he had moved on to the next holiday romance. She didn't know but she deserved to find out, one way or another.

Outside Leeds Bradford airport a young girl was waiting in line for the bus to the train station. She had just arrived from Barcelona airport and was holding her one bag with just one change of clothes. No matter what happened here she didn't expect to be staying long. She needed to see her Mick, her Miguel and explain everything to him. She was going to be the mother to his child and although she knew that he had commitments here in England, what with his sick mother and drunken father she had to let him know that she would love and care for the child even without his help, but it was only fair to give him the chance to become a part of their life. Whatever happened she would return back to Spain and have the child there in the warm bosom of her family.

In a hanger off the little private airstrip at the back of East Midlands airport a twin engine six seater Cessna pulled up and its occupants climbed out.

"Don Edson. It is an honour" said the duty officer to the giant bear who was the first down the steps. Don Edson shook his hands warmly. "This is my son" he said turning to Giorgio. Giorgio shook the young mans hand and offered his passport as did his father. The young man took them to a table and stamped the passports.

"All is in order Sir. Your car and driver are over there" he indicated the waiting limo with its door held open by an immaculate chauffer.

"Your flight plan for your return has been filed for tonight with an alternative time booked for tomorrow morning in case of unexpected delays. Have a good stay Sir and you too Sir" and with that he was off. Giorgio took their overnight bags off the pilot and handed them to the waiting chauffer.

"Right son, lets go and see your young lady".

On a train from Birmingham airport sat a young fraulein. She gazed through the window and watched the countryside flash past. She thought of Jeff and smiled to herself. She knew there may not be a happy ending to this trip but she owed it to herself to find out. There had been a connection there and she intended to find out if it was a long term thing or a holiday fling. She was a determined girl and she was determined to sort things out.

In Jeff's flat he was almost ready. He was watching TV. His suit was hung up and his clobber all laid out on the bed. He sipped at his tea and thought of Maria. He had realised that it was all over, before it had begun really, and that it was time to move on but it had been hard. Harder than he would ever have imagined. He had never even come close to feeling like this. It had screwed him up and he didn't know what to do about it. Sometime last week, however, he had decided to stop brooding and get on with the rest of his life. He was trying to forget but couldn't so decided to just live with it and get on as best he could. Time would sort the rest out.

In a car park in front of the shops at Whiston two cars pulled up together. Dave jumped out of one and walked round to the drivers door of the other. His face was blotchy and his eyes were still dark shades of purple from the beating he had taken from Mick.

"Ready" he asked the driver. It was his roommate from holiday. He too had a black eye, given to him by Ron when he had attempted to help Dave out in the fight. Three passengers in the car nodded. "Yeah, we're ready."

"Just waiting for the others then we'll give the happy couple a wedding day they'll remember forever" Dave sneered "If they live through it".

The limousine pulled up outside Linda's house and the large bear unfurled himself onto the street. Giorgio followed and together they made their way down the path alongside the beautiful but small front garden which had come alive with summer blooms that Linda's dad had lovingly tended.

Giorgio knocked on the door which was answered almost immediately by a large chubby harassed looking middle aged man who was fiddling with his tie.

"About bloody time" he muttered without looking up "you know I always make a mess of these bloody things".

As no help was immediately offered he looked up in surprise and saw a young handsome man standing in his doorway. He had a friendly face and had his hand out in greeting. Behind him stood, what can only be described as a huge bear in an immaculate suit. He stared at the man mountain and was taken aback when the young man introduced himself .

"Sir I am honoured to meet you. I am Giorgio Arantes dos Nascimento from Catalonia in Spain.

"Er .. pleased to meet you" he answered unsure as how to handle the situation.

"May I present my father" the young man continued "Don Edson Arantes Dos Nascimento" The bear stepped forward and offered a huge paw.

"It is an honour" he growled happily. We have travelled a long way"

"Thanks Don. Same to you ....er come in, come in. I'll put the kettle on and you can tell me all about it.

Ten minutes later Linda was looking at herself in the long mirror in Nellie's bedroom. She was wearing her bridesmaids dress and even though it had been taken in to account for her recent weight loss it still hung a little around the waist and bust. Nellie had tacked it up a bit and Linda had to admit she looked

pretty good. Her face was beaming also. She couldn't wait to set off tomorrow to see Giorgio and although she was apprehensive of his reaction to her just turning up out of the blue she had convinced herself that everything would be fine.

She heard a commotion downstairs and went to the hall to investigate. She could hear voices which seemed to be getting more and more excited and thought she could hear her dad but why would he be here. There must be something wrong. She rushed downstairs and turned into the front room.

Everyone was looking through the other door into the kitchen at something or someone. Claire turned and a big smile came over her. Ros turned next and rushed to her "Linda, you won't believe who's here" she giggled.

Linda was nonplussed and made her way slowly through the small crowded room into the kitchen. Everyone went quiet and Linda seemed to take in each smiling face individually as she scanned the room until finally she alighted on Giorgio. She gasped.

"Giorgio"

"Linda" he whispered back. It looked as though he would burst into tears at any second but as luck would have it he didn't have time because Linda rushed him and dived straight into his arms.

Their lips met and they were lost in a world of their own. After a while they were vaguely aware of laughter and clapping and a general hubhub of happiness. They shyly parted and looked around them at all the smiling faces. She became aware of the giant in the doorway and threw him a beautiful smile. "Don Edson what a wonderful surprise" and rushed over and kissed him on the cheek. The bear coloured up, surprised at this wonderful show of affection and in turn kissed her on the cheek. "It is my pleasure Linda and may I say my great relief to see you in such good spirits after your... er..

your ordeal" he slowly petered off, a look of deep anguish etched on his face.

Linda's face darkened and she returned his look. Then she spun round to face Giorgio. She saw the tears forming in his eyes and felt them form in her own.

"Linda" his voice cracked and the tears rolled down his cheeks. "I would give anything, I would give my life to be able to turn back the clock, to stop this awful, disgusting, ...". he ran out of words.

Linda took his face in her hands. "It doesn't matter. It doesn't matter as long as I have you." Then a questioning look crossed her face. "I do have you don't I. I mean I would understand if you couldn't get past this. If you felt...."

"How can you think of me at a time like this eh." He asked. There was love there for all to see and there was a collective sigh from the watching women. "I love you and nothing anyone else ever did can ever change that. I want you now more than ever. You are kind, thoughtful and pure of spirit. You are everything a man could ever want. You are beautiful, inside and out any man would be honoured to be with you. Linda" and he bent down on one knee. "will you marry me".

A collective intake of breath sucked all the air out of the room as everyone waited. Linda slowly looked around her at their expectant faces, each with their mouths open. She looked back down at the waiting Giorgia and broke into the biggest smile and almost shouted "Yes" as an afterthought she added "please".

Giorgio jumped up and kissed her passionately. They embraced and everyone crowded in to congratulate them.

A sudden thought occurred to Linda's mum. "Where will you live. Here or over there"

Linda looked at Giorgio who in turn looked at her.

"I'll go wherever he is" she said.

"And I want to be wherever you are happy" he answered.

The big bear stepped forward and coughed a little into his hand.

"I don't want to be a .. er... a party pooper.. yes... but Giorgio does have certain responsibilities back home." He saw his son's face cloud over. "You know you do son. There are certain business things you must attend to, things you have been putting off for a while now but cannot put off any longer."

Giorgio sighed as he knew this to be true.

"It doesn't matter" spoke up Linda "Wherever you need to be I need to be. I can get a job over there, maybe serving in a bar or even in the same hotel as you. We'll make it work. Don't worry I'll pull my weight. I'll not be a burden.

I know it can't be easy on a waiters wage but we'll have each other and live on love.... and chips."

She laughed and he laughed too but his face soon turned serious and he softly held her hand. "No my love, you do not understand. I am not a waiter. Or should I say I'm no longer a waiter."

She looked in his eyes, his beautiful dark eyes, confused.

"My father wants me to take over the family business and has been insistent on this for a while. When I finished university I wanted to travel for a while so Papa let me. When I returned last year I wasn't ready to take on that kind of responsibility so I asked my father to give me one more year. I agreed not to go too far so I got a job in the hotel in Lloret. I just wanted to be my own man, earn my own living, just to know I can do it myself. That year is now up and I am more than ready to take my place at my fathers side."

Linda looked even more confused. "I still don't understand. I thought you were poor. Your family get together on beaches and cook on open fires. You said your father was well respected in the area, and I can see why." And she threw a big smile at the big man. He beamed from ear to ear and bowed graciously.

"but I thought, well you seemed to get free meals and drinks at restaurants and bars, I though those people were friends of yours looking after you, you know sort of quid pro quo, I'll not charge you and you return the favour and we'll both get through this together, sort of thing."

Giorgio laughed out loud. He turned to his father and laughed again and said something to him in rapid Spanish. The big bear laughed and rolled forward clasping his stomach, when he stood straight again he wiped his eyes and said something Spanish in return. Giorgio laughed and said "Si". The only bit anyone else understood.

Giorgio turned to Linda who was looking at him quizzically . "Sorry Linda. My father he says "you're definitely not after my money."

"Money?" Linda asked "what money?"

Giorgio took a step closer.

"Linda, my father is Don Edson Arantes Dos Nascimento. One of the richest men, possibly the richest, in Catalonia. He owns land and property throughout the country and Andorra and France. The beach my family were eating on belongs to my father as does the

391

surrounding hillsides, three of the closest villages and the castle sat at the top of the hill. That is our family home. I want you to come and live there as my wife. I can run most of the business from there. My father wishes to retire and spend more time with my mother and travel and see more of the world so apart from the staff we will have a big old castle to ourselves. Your parents can visit whenever they want and stay as long as they like. Mi casa es su casa. My house is your house and in your case I mean that literally . and he smiled broadly.

Linda froze. Well actually everybody froze. For ages. Slowly they started to turn to each other and mouthed various things like "wow" and "jesus" and

"fucking hell"

Linda was gobsmacked, in her wildest dreams she hadn't imagined this. She didn't know what to say. Eventually a sound reached her mouth "a castle" she whispered.

"Yes" he answered.

"A castle" she repeated a little louder.

"Yes" he repeated a little louder. "A castle. A very big castle"

Linda pondered this a while then a big grin broke across her face.

"I'll be like a Princess" she laughed.

Giorgio took her in his arms and spun her around. He was laughing wildly.

"You are a princess" he laughed. "You're my Princess" and they spun round as everyone in the tiny kitchen clapped and cheered.

Jeff arrived at the church on time and was given his instructions by the verger.

He was an usher for the day and basically he made sure everyone sat in the correct side of the church, brides family and friends on one side, grooms on the other.

He carried out his duties, well dutifully, and was mingling with a few guests who were loitering outside having a crafty ciggie, when he spotted a young women walking up the path. He recognised her instantly but it took a few seconds for it to sink in who it was. It was so out of context it just didn't register. When it hit him he almost collapsed. He excused himself from the people he was talking to and rushed to the path. They both stopped about two feet from each other and both seemed lost for words. Eventually Jeff remembered he could speak and said n "What.... I mean how... er I mean what...."

He tailed off unsure of how he should finish the question so Maria finished it for him.

"What am I doing here . I'm visiting you. How did I find you . Your friend Danny left your address with Bella the receptionist at the hotel. I have been to your flat and a neighbour said you would be here at your friend's wedding. The second what was just a repeat of the first what I think."

Jeff was stunned, he had never been so surprised in his life. He still couldn't find any words. He tried again. "But why?"

Maria smiled coyly and turned her face down "well this is where it may go wrong. I don't know but we shall see". She took a deep breath and continued."I know we only knew each other for one short evening but I felt a connection. I felt something there between us. If I am right then I am glad I came and I hope we can take this, whatever it is, further and if I am wrong, well, at least I will know and I will go and leave you in peace to carry on your life and me to continue mine."

Her German determination got her through the speech but now she looked a little nervous.

Jeff looked thoughtful

"I couldn't have put it better myself" he eventually said. "I felt the same thing but couldn't think of a way to contact you. I guess I owe Danny a drink for that.

She smiled broadly. "That's good" she giggled "I wouldn't have gone in peace if you had said no, I would have stamped my feet and made a scene,"

"Yeah I thought you might" he smiled back. "Look do you want to stay for the wedding. There's a reception after at the golf club and you can stay at mine tonight. I'll sleep on the settee."

"I would love to stay for the wedding but later there is no need for you to stay on the settee, after all, this is not our first date yah."

Jeff's smile got bigger and bigger "This day just gets better and better."

When the wedding cars arrived everybody hustled along. Linda kissed Giorgio and told him where the church was and Nellie insisted they came to the reception. In turn Don Edson offered Linda's mum and dad a lift to the church in his limo so they quickly phoned and cancelled their taxi and climbed in the back of the luxurious Mercedes.

Mick and Ron climbed out of their taxi in the square outside Talbot Lane church. The old church was on the west of the square with a couple of pubs on the east side. A road ran through the centre south to north and broke into two on the north side to take traffic either into the town centre or away from it.

Town office buildings bordered the whole square.

Straight away Ron saw Jeff with Maria. "Jesus, who'd have thought it. She's turned up. It was only yesterday he was saying he'd given up on her. He couldn't think of a way of finding her."

Danny sidled up with Sheila on his arm.

"That's down to hero here" she said. "He gave the receptionist Jeff's address and asked her to pass it on." And she gave his arm a big squeeze.

She looked lovely, all grown up and demure not at all like the brassy Sheila of old.

"You look gorgeous Sheila" Mick said and leant forward and kissed her on the cheek. Ron did the same. "And you my little fat friend did well. I'll get you a

drink in later." He turned and nodded towards Jeff and Maria. "I think somebody else might owe you a few too."

Outside the Cross Keys pub across the square three cars pulled up and twelve men climbed out. A few of them looked worse for wear, two had slings on their arm and four had the remains of black eyes still showing. They had bided their time, recovering all the while, waiting for this day to take their revenge for the beating they had taken at the football game, The Whiston Warriors were back in town.

Ron saw them straight away.

"Looks like we've got company" he said. The others turned their heads and Danny breathed out "Fuck".

"Do you think they've just stopped by for a drink?" asked Mick sarcastically.

"No" said Ron.

"Shopping maybe and they were the only parking spaces they could find?"

"No"

"Come to exact revenge and ruin mine and Sue's big day?"

"That's the one"

"Yeah, thought so"

Out of the corner of his eye Danny saw someone approaching and turned away from the invading hoard to get a better look. He let out a little scream, which he thought he had grown out of since the holiday. Everyone turned to him and then to where he was looking.

Mick almost screamed too when he saw who was approaching , for there was Julia looking beautiful and radiant and angelic and...... what the fuck was she doing here?

She smiled shyly as she approached. "Miguel they told me you would be here"

"Who told you... I mean why are you here... I mean it's lovely to see you, of course, but .... well ...." he finished lamely.

She reached out and held his hands. " I found you Miguel. I found you just in time I think"

"But how..." he blurted out. A thought came to him. "If it was Danny playing Cupid I'll fucking kill him."

"You told me you lived in Rotherham so I looked you up in the phone book when I landed in England. When I got to your house your neighbour, an old man with an old dog told me you were getting married today to Sue"

"Thanks Tom " he thought angrily "last free half you're getting.

"But why are you here?" he asked again nervously.

"Don't you see my darling you don't have to marry your mother's carer I will look after her"

As a man the others all turned their heads to Mick who was frantically trying to think of a way, any way, out of this.

"This should be good" said Ron "Go on Miguel explain to the nice lady why you are marrying your mothers carer"

Mick had a lopsided grin on his face "Yes , of course, I'm just going to do that... er would you lot give us a bit of privacy eh.."

"No" said Ron, matter of factly. "We all want to hear this"

Mick glared at him.

"Yes then ... well then... where to start. That's the thing" he mumbled as if to himself

"And your father too of course" Julia added somewhat unnecessarily he thought.

"Sorry" he asked.

"I will help you with your fathers drinking"

Eyebrows were raised by the watching pack. As far as they knew Mick's dad was tea total and never touched a drop.

"Getting worse is he?" asked Ron.

He was getting on Mick's nerves now.

"Yes he is." He answered shortly.

"How do I get out of this" he thought "God help me.

The wedding cars pulled up beside them.

"Thanks for nothing God".

The bridesmaids climbed out of the first car and smoothed down their dresses and stepped onto the path. Ros realised the crowd next to them included Mick and Ron.

"Shouldn't you two be at the altar worrying whether the brides gonna turn up or not?" she asked as she approached. She noticed the pretty girl holding Mick's hands. Mick quickly pulled his hands away.

"Who's she?" she asked Ron.

"This is the lovely Julia with a soft J" he answered and pointed to Julia as if in introduction.

"OK.... and what's she doing here?"

"Ah it would appear she has arrived in the knick of time to save our friend Miguel here from a marriage worse than death and to care for his drunken father and mother who has an undetermined illness" he was enjoying this.

"Brittlebonyitis" interjected Julia.

"Ah, of course, Brittlebonyitis" he repeated.

Ros looked from one person to another and they all seemed confused as to what was happening. Except Ron who had a big grin plastered on his face, and Mick who looked in a state of terror.

"Right" she said flatly. Shall we do this somewhere else, Sue's waiting in the car.

The last of the wedding cars was indeed waiting with a worried looking Sue watching through the window.

Next to her car the Limo pulled up and Giorgio and his father stepped out. Don Edson turned and took the hand of Linda's mum and helped her out.

"Ooh thank you Donny. Can I call you Donny I used to love the Osmonds.

He looked a little bemused but gallantly said "Yes of course and I will call you Linda's mum". She smiled at him but wasn't sure why.

Mick's mum and dad joined them and his father shook Don Edson's hand.

"Don't think we've met before, Nellie tells me you've just arrived in the country. I'm Michael, Mick's father. Hope you're staying for the nuptials."

"Don Edson at your service, Sir, and this is my son Giorgio."

Giorgio stepped forward and offered his hand. "A pleasure Sir."

"Likewise Giorgio. This is my wife, Alison.

Alison stepped forward and shook Giorgio's hand. Don Edson stepped forward to embrace her and kiss her on the cheeks when a voice called out.

"Careful of her bones".

Everyone turned to look at Julia who had her hand out in warning.

Mick sunk further into the ground. "Kill me now God, please"

Nellie pushed her way through the crowd. "What's wrong, what's the hold up.

We're waiting" she indicated the waiting car.

"Nothing to worry about Nellie jumped in Mick before anyone could say anything. "Look can everyone who should be in church go into the church.

Ron, Jeff, Danny can you stay here a minute."

People started moving away. Julia didn't know what to do so she reluctantly followed. Jeff ushered Maria towards the church and said he would be in in a minute.

"Looks like we've got a problem. My guess is they're gonna either storm the church to frighten everybody or they're gonna wait until after and then come for us." Mick said.

"No you're wrong." Ron smiled. "As usual. They're gonna come for us now.

There's not going to be a wedding today sunshine."

Mick looked crestfallen. Sue was going to kill him. All the brownie points he had built up would count for shit now.

"OK. Us four are going to have to deal with this. Whatever happens they're not going in that church"

"Five of us" growled the huge bear of a man who had been hovering in the background.

"It's not your fight" said Mick.

"You are my future daughter in law's friends. Everyone has been very kind. I would be a bad guest if I did not repay the favour in some way yes." He growled and then smiled brightly "besides, I like a good scrap."

"Six of us" interrupted Giorgio. They turned to him. He shrugged his shoulders

"What he said" he smiled.

"Seven" said a voice walking towards them. It was Bill, Sheila's brother who must have been waiting round the corner. He was accompanied by Ben obviously. Truth was they had come to see

Sheila in all her finery but had been hiding from her because she would have given them a clip round the ear."Nine"

said Ben.

"Eight" corrected Bill.

"What" asked Ben.

"Eight comes after nine. I've gone over this a hundred times bro."

"Sorry Bill. I forgot" and he stared at his feet.

"No probs" Bill said good naturedly. "We'll go through it again later" and Ben cheered up.

"OK" said Mick. "Eight it is. Against twelve, and they're all armed." He looked round his strange band. "Piece of piss."

Behind him he heard a frightened voice. It was Sue. She looked beautiful in her lacey wedding dress , hair and perfect makeup. In her clasped hands she held a tiny bouquet. Mick's heart surged and fell. He had ballsed everything up and he knew he had no choice but to come clean but he had to deal with this mess first.

"Sue please go into the church. We need to talk and I promise we will but first I've got to deal with the Whiston lot, and they aren't going to wait". He pointed to the church where he could see, in the doorway, Julia comforting his mum.

Sue nodded and dejectedly walked up the path to the front door. Julia was gently touching his mums arm and motioning something with her other hand.

His mum looked totally confused and kept shaking her head and mouthing "no". Mick's dad came to the door and Julia started telling him something. He shook his head vigorously and mouthed "never" a few times. They all turned and faced Mick.

"Problems?" asked Ron who was also watching the scene play out.

"About a thousand at the moment and they're all my fault"

"Excuse me for interfering" interrupted Don Edson. "But there is a poem which starts "I am the master of my own fate and I am the captain of my own boat.

While ups and downs are a part of everyone's journey, how you face it makes you the person you are."

They both thought about it. Mick smiled ruefully "You're right" he said. I am the captain of my own boat. Now let's deal with this one problem at a time."

And he turned to face the oncoming hoard who had obviously tired of waiting and had set off towards the church. They all took up positions and were ready.

Ron glanced behind him to make sure the women had stayed out of harm's way. Sue was talking to Julia and shaking her head frantically, Julia was adamantly telling her something. Sue was shouting "No, No.".

Julia was crying now and frantically nodding in confirmation of something.

She lowered her hands and stroked her belly lovingly and protectively and Sue's hands shot up to her horrified face.

Ron turned to face his best mate who was oblivious to this encounter and was concentrating on the Whiston Warriors who were now charging full pelt towards them now only yards away. Time seemed to stand still as Ron thought about the poem and about Mick being the captain of his own boat.

As the warriors reached them and battle commenced Ron heard above the din a lone strangled woman's voice screaming for all it was worth. "MIIIIIICK" it dragged out.

As the first blows were landed Ron turned to his lifelong best friend and said

"You're going to need a bigger boat mate".

THE END

Printed in Great Britain
by Amazon

37931357R00225